CUTTING EDGE

ROBERT W. WALKER

J

JOVE BOOKS, NEW YORK

CUTTING EDGE

A Jove Book / published by arrangement with
the author

PRINTING HISTORY
Jove edition / February 1997

The Putnam Berkley World Wide Web site address is
http://www.berkley.com/berkley

ISBN: 0-515-12012-X

A JOVE BOOK®
Jove Books are published by The Berkley Publishing Group,
200 Madison Avenue, New York, New York 10016.
JOVE and the "J" design are trademarks
belonging to Jove Publications, Inc.

PRINTED IN THE UNITED STATES OF AMERICA

10 9 8 7 6 5 4 3 2 1

This book is dedicated to my son,

STEPHEN R. WALKER,

whose love I will always cherish.

$\mathcal{P}$ROLOGUE

Arrow: protection

Helsinger tugged back on the taut wire, his face pinched and perspiring as he strained to place the bow in its locked position with the safety catch on, intent on using the high-powered, scoped, crossbow-styled weapon carefully and efficiently. From the tree line where he'd been in what now seemed an unceasingly long vigil for his prey, he stared across the expanse of ground between himself and his objective.

In his head, the steady *tap-tap-tap* of his orders persisted like an anthem, when suddenly the moment he lived for arrived at last—a slight movement at the big bay window, as the less than respectably attired Daniel O. E. Mercer himself stepped into the light from the dark of a master bedroom where he'd left the she-bitch, Marlena Nolan. Mercer had seduced her from the secretarial pool at OE's most recently opened-for-business Mercer Continental Bank of America. By now, the demonic, supernatural infusion of his blood into her veins had turned her, too, into the spawn of Satan. Mercer liked to make beautiful young women into the ugly thing that he was. Her body was now tainted, corrupted beyond redemption; her body was Mercer's to do with as he liked for as long as he walked the earth.

Tap-tap-tap . . . tap-tap-tap. . . . No doubt, no fear now. Mercer wouldn't be walking long, and his undead, unclean spirit would be cast into the bowels of Helsinger's Pit. As for the woman, she'd already become a sacrificial lamb. Nothing Helsinger might do could save her body from the evil of Mercer's touch; far worse than this, there was nothing he could do to save her lost soul from Mercer's power, or the depths of depravity into which she had sunk. She would by now be completely turned over to the corruption and malfeasance of her new master.

Yet another soul taken from the sight of God, Helsinger 2051 thought now. Mercer would now withhold her soul, as he did his own, from God's eye as long as he wished, or as long as he existed on this plane, within this realm of reality that gave to him more power than the angels, for as long as his reanimated body mocked holy life, which meant forever unless someone like Helsinger—with the staunch support of the *tap-tap-tap* commands from beyond—stopped the diabolical bastard. . . .

Now the tall, even regal man's silhouette formed a solid wall, missing only the concentric circles of a perfectly ordered black paper target here against the soft glow of candles illuminating the entire dining room alcove. A perfect target. But Helsinger feared the distance might be too much against him: too close and the animal thing he'd hunted nearly a year now might easily detect Helsinger 2051's movement, his odor, the sound of death coming on a silver shaft—*fee, fie, foe, fum,* and all that, for the creature's senses were beyond those of mortal men—too great the distance and the arrow misses its mark. Either way, a slip could be fatal for Helsinger, and Helsinger's master must begin the quest all over again.

Tap (softly now) . . . *tap* (cautiously now) . . . *tap* (confidently now). . . .

A miss and Mercer would flee like a witch, spiraling up a chimney, or worse yet, he might turn into a rabid hellhound to counterattack Helsinger—a god-awful result, disastrous for both Helsinger and so many others, for with Helsinger dead and Mercer alive, the monster's feeding frenzy, its appetite for the kill and for blood, would go undetected and unchecked. So many others would become carrion for Mercer's disgusting and filthy habits, while the work of the Helsingers the world over might be snuffed out before it'd begun, gone the way of Doom. Helsinger raised his crossbow—

"*Supper's on now, Randy Oglesby! And now means NOW!*"

"Goddamn supper," young Randy cursed, his eyes held by the scenario created for him by his 286X IBM-compatible Pionex and the Super VGA screen. He had to know if Helsinger 2051 would succeed or die in the effort of tracking the monster vampire disguised as a multimillionaire banking tycoon. "Five minutes! Be right there, Ma! Give me five minutes!"

There would be no one left to stop Mercer if Randy's carefully constructed Helsinger, armored with the coolest character traits Randy could compile, happened to fail.

Still, for Anatole Francis Helsinger, whose steady recruitment of followers meant he must put his life on the line, the moment of truth had come: Followers only follow those who are successful. He'd learn one way or another if God was on his side or the side of the smoking demon in red silk pajama bottoms just the other side of the bay window.

Got to do it now or Mercer's shadow'll disappear, he silently fretted, his finger inching along the bow for the safety catch.

But what if that's all there is on the other side of the glass—just his shadow, an image, a decoy? a voice inside him continued to worry.

"Fire, damn you, Helsinger; the likes of Satan don't have shadows. It's him!" screamed Randy at his end, now sending the message over his modem to the player who'd initiated the game an hour before, a guy with the interesting handle of Razor Oreo Teeth. Randy was known in the cyberspace world as Mr. Squeegee, a moniker he'd once felt was proudly imaginative; but now he knew he'd have to work on being far more imaginative to keep up with this guy. The game was coming to a head. "Do it. Do it now," Randy called for blood, his anticipation overwhelming.

He pulled the safety catch, and in a sudden gasp of crisp black computer Net night air, Helsinger settled his shaking hands over the weapon. A silent word of prayer for the strength and straight flight of his slim, hungry stake, and it shot away with the speed of light, splintering the window so neatly that it left only a small incision in the glass, a deadly little computer *whump* striking Randy's ear from the three-inch speakers, the deadly arrow tip, dripping with poison, striking not Mercer but the woman—one of his minions—as she stepped from nowhere.

"Damn!" groaned Randy. "Damn, damn, damn!"

Razor Oreo Teeth fired a snide, laughing message over the modem. "Dumb ass! You waited too long."

The force sent the now-dead secretary against a wall, where she slumped but did not fall, the arrow going clean through and pinning her like an insect. The instant the barbed arrow sliced through the bastard thing, blood splattered over the windowpane, the chandelier and the dining room table, setting off a musical shower of alarms and demon blood.

Randy and Helsinger simultaneously cursed their show of stupidity. Why hadn't he fired one second before? Was it Randy's fault? His mother's interruption from downstairs? And why hadn't he and Helsinger thought of the alarm?

Helsinger was in grave danger now. He raced away in a panic, crossing a black, moonless landscape that pressed in on his back, fearing some unholy, giant monster breathing fire at his neck. But he made it into the trees, his bow and additional arrows now a cumbersome problem that he dare not relieve himself of. Mercer was yet alive and no doubt prowling the Internet night for him at this very moment.

Mercer must not find him. No one must find him. The game of seek and destroy was now a game of cut and run, survive to fight another day.

Everything had gone wrong. *The best-laid plans . . . gone astray.* But they were not at all the best. Razor Oreo Teeth might mock Mr. Squeegee now, but he was foolish to think that he could do this alone as his next message suggested. ROT, as he signed off, told Randy that he'd acted incompetently, as if Randy didn't know. Next time . . . if there was a next time . . . he'd be smarter; he had to be smarter than Mercer, or the thing Mercer had become.

Exactly what Mercer, the son of Cain, *was* defied explanation, logic, nature, or science; Mercer was death itself . . . a creature of the night . . . a kind of living death stalking the holy, the good and pure, defiling all that was positive in life. Foolish, easily misled and misbegotten people, like those at Mercer's many banks, would mourn Mercer's passing; idiots that they were, they'd have no clue as to the satanic filth upon which they wasted their tears. None of them knew Mercer as Helsinger knew him.

"Randall Oglesby, get your ass down these stairs this

minute, or I'm going to shotgun that damned computer of yours myself." This time it was his dad's voice, half-kidding as usual.

And if Helsinger 2051, the single pure point of light, the only armed warrior left to defend against the darkness, were to die under Mercer's talons and fangs tonight, no one would shed a tear for him, for Randy or for ROT out there in the ether of Netland. Nor would any river of remorse flow for Helsinger if the so-called authorities who'd turned a deaf ear to him were to catch him here tonight. They would imprison him for killing the monster's bitch who'd served Mercer's contemptible and banal needs tonight. No one would come to his cell or argue against the State's right to destroy Helsinger, who would endure yet another execution.

So Helsinger ran to the beat and command of Randy's fingers.

He ran without regard to direction or circumstance, the running and the whipping of branches and cold air across his face making him feel alive and strong and in control. But soon he found himself faced with having to ford a stream—no way around it, no footbridge or stones to skip over.

The black and icy liquid instantly filled his shoes, immediately numbing his toes. He raced on for the darkness of a deeper wood, a smile of triumph curling about his lips until it became a full-blown laugh.

"Killed your whore, you son of a bitch! Killed and gone!"

Still Helsinger's exaltation was tempered with his disappointment. He'd wanted to see the beast itself killed, see Mercer squirm under the metal arrow where it should have impaled him against that wall. He'd wanted to follow up Mercer's instant demise with an assault on the vile nest where this bastard thing slept, to destroy anything that moved in the large house that Master Mercer had come to own through the foul means of his true profession.

Helsinger had also wanted to rob Mercer's lifeless body of its head, to bury the damnable, disgusting thing somewhere out here below a cross of stones so that there would be no way Mercer's reanimated body could touch it or dig it up to replace it and start over again. . . .

But everything was ruined now. Helsinger was caught and returned to his pit. Placed in chains in an asylum, thumping his head against an unforgiving, unyielding stone wall, wondering how he might escape again.

The screen erupted with the colorful game logo: a dungeon with several people of each sex chained to walls, an ancient, blood-weeping medieval rack in the center of the room, a little computer-imaged male squirming up and down under the pressure of a stake being driven into his chest. In bold red lettering blinked the words HELSINGER'S PIT. Below this came the name of its creator, copyright junk, and the software company's name and logo. Randy waved good-bye on the modem to Razor Oreo Teeth, knowing full well that ROT was long gone, signed off, and finally remembered to breathe, and that his parents were anxiously waiting for him downstairs for supper.

"Damn! All's in ruins now! Off with Mr. Squeegee's head!" the thirteen-year-old shouted as he raced from his room and down the stairs to a chorus of ignored shouts from his parents and sister. "'Stead of carvin' the ham, Dad'll carve me up, punishment for letting Helsinger down and letting the greens get cold!"

TEN YEARS LATER

764LT1:\C42119\Category 42 . . . Topic
49LOG . . . Message 388 . . . Mon.
July 8, 1996 . . . 12:10:01
Questor 1 . . . Helsinger's Pit . . .

Q1: There is a problem. Cain has risen
anew and has flown from the 13th Kingdom.
The demon must not be allowed to escape.
Take all necessary precautions and take
as much help as you require. Good luck.
Questor 1 . . . END TRANSMISSION, Category 42,
Topic 49LOG . . . 12:12:06

Category 42 . . . Topic 49LOG . . . Message 389 . . . Mon. July 8, 1996 . . .
2:51:00
Questor 2 . . . from the Pit . . .

Q2: Agreed. Taking all resources necessary. Will locate alien being in Star
Kingdom, 49th realm. The creature was
nurtured there. Will seek and destroy.
Reply this board at 0900 tomorrow. END
TRANSMISSION, Category 42, Topic 49LOG . . .
2:52:01

Category 42 . . . Topic 49LOG . . . Mon.
July 8, 1996 . . . 9:13:07
Questor 3 . . . Out of the Pit . . .

Q3: Count me in Q2. Close to your desti-
nation. Can rendezvous midnight, usual
place. Q1's communication and your message clear. In numbers we have strength.
We go now to return with the head of the
beast to place at the altar.

Q3 is your dedicated servant. Look for us
tomorrow in a new realm, sage one. END
TRANSMISSION . . . Category 42 . . . Topic
49LOG . . . Mon. July 8, 1996 . . . 9:15:02

ONE

Four ages: infant, youth, mid and old age

A reality check for most people meant a closer look at their social or economic situation, but for Lucas Stonecoat, reality was a demon god capable of inflicting great and lasting pain; for him and for most cops, reality was the prism through which violence shone. Reality also spoke to Lucas Stonecoat in her unfriendly, unsettling, judgmental tone, lecturing him, telling him what he was physically capable of and what he was physically incapable of. True to character, Lucas had chosen to ignore the bitching reality and her advice, going ahead with his life and his plans as best he could, from crutches to standing on his own two feet and learning to walk again, and now this triumph.

To some it didn't seem like much, but for him, stepping from the Houston Police Academy and into real police work for the second time in one life meant something, a rebirth of sorts. Regaining some semblance of control over his life again, getting it back on track after the high-speed chase and accident resulting from a shoot-out in downtown Dallas, might've been reward enough, but returning to active police duty? This might be considered a miracle by some, and for him it meant true accomplishment and closure. And he'd done it despite reality, despite the fact that at one time everything—including his own body—was adamantly against his ever even walking again, much less finishing the grueling training he'd endured these past months in Houston's top-flight police academy.

Still, reality just sat there atop his head, and it began to seep into his brain, to stain his mind with an ugly gray truth: Lucas "Cherokee" Stonecoat was no different from the other 999 new recruits hired by the city—just another rookie in training with the Houston Police Department, which meant a long ladder of rungs to climb to regain detective status. But at least he had a dream, even now at his age, to regain what had been his before the accident, before the mangled and brutalized body ever existed.

Still, such minor things as God Reality remained his enemy, along with God-awful Pain, and his own body, which daily conspired with the other two against him. As a result, the tiresome phrase "I am my own worst enemy" held special meaning for Lucas.

Nowadays when someone called him Redskin, it referred less to his Texas Cherokee heritage than to the burn that snaked along much of his neck and cheek on the right side of his otherwise handsome face.

The accident had even taken him down a peg or two in stature. A tall man at six feet four, he rose now to perhaps six feet two, thanks to the condition of his spine. "*Lucky to be alive; unusual, startling case; one for the books,*" the doctors had chorused.

A cursory glance at his own medical records, collected up

at the request of his lawyer when he went after the city in the ill-conceived suit that had put him on the defensive ever since, had turned his stomach. The same records had convinced at least one young medical resident to change his career path. The records showed a man near death when he was raced to the ER in the back of a police squad car that he'd bled all over. The records showed a man not expected to live, much less recover. The records also showed that he was partially to blame. The records showed in cold black Anglo lettering what had happened to a once proud and arrogant man.

The records showed:

DALLAS MEMORIAL HOSPITAL
Dallas, Texas

Date of admission: July 12, 1991
Date of discharge: June 2, 1992

Patient History: A twenty-seven-year-old American Indian male involved in automobile accident, also had alcohol in blood, admitted with multiple trauma—compound fracture of tibia and fibula, ruptured bladder, and multifocal cerebral contusions, assorted abrasions, gunshot wound to upper left quadrant of chest.

In hospital for eleven months, initially comatose and encephalopathic. At time of leaving hospital, patient was fully conscious, alert, quite full of complaints. Further, patient understood that a device was in place on his left leg, and that he must be careful in this regard to not place any undo weight on this area. He was to be given primary care by his aunt, uncle, and grandparents, all of whom seemed most concerned for his well-being, each being attentive to doctor's directives. Arrangements were made with in-home health-care providers to help with the suprapubic cystostomy as well as the pin care of the Hoffman device.

Dr. Rhymer, operating orthopedic surgeon, made plans for all follow-up care to be provided by Dallas Memorial. Arrangements were made for Mr. Stonecoat to be seen by Dr. Karl Wilkerson, urology, who performed the bladder operation and left the suprapubic cystostomy in place.

During Mr. Stonecoat's eleven-month stay, he underwent a tracheostomy as well as a hip replacement (left), a debridement of the compound infected leg, and many consultations with Dr. Sanders, on loan from the Veteran's Administration Hospital. Dr. Sanders was also involved in his rehabilitation efforts.

Final   Diagnosis: 1.   Severe chest injury—gunshot wound left upper q.
2.   Severe closed-head injury.
3.   Compound tibia-fibula fracture—left.
4.   Wound infection, tibia-fibula.
5.   Crushed hip; replacement—left.
6.   Partial paralysis, right arm, hand.
7.   Acute respiratory distress syndrome.
8.   Conjunctivitis.

Operations: 1.   Chest wound & closure.
2.   Tracheostomy.
3.   Swan-Ganz placement.
4.   Laparotomy.
5.   Hip replacement—left.
6.   Bladder repair.
7.   Suprapubic cystostomy.
8.   Arm, shoulder, and forehead lacerations.

Daniel Garvey, M.D.

TLT-219   #4314
D: 6/6/92
T: 02:07:52

Stonecoat, Lucas   Daniel Garvey, M.D.
368–58–7899   Discharge Summary

It hardly touched on the whole story. There were subsequent operations as well. Removal of this, removal of that. He had had so many needles stuck into him that soon he felt like the proverbial porcupine who was asked where it hurt the most. He didn't feel a thing.

The part of the doctors' many reports on him that'd hurt him the most in a legal sense was the part about the blood-alcohol level. He and his partner had been drinking, having just gotten off duty when the police band, at the police bar where they routinely drank, radioed the news that an armed heist was in progress at a store on Lincoln at Talmadge, a location they had been watching for days in the hope this exact guy would strike. There had been a string of armed robberies in the neighborhood and witnesses tied it all to one guy, a black man with red hair who actually called himself Malcolm and wore at one time an X cap, at another a T-shirt bearing Malcolm X's likeness. The man had grown increasingly daring, increasingly violent, and he was expected soon to graduate to murder if not stopped.

They raced out after having had two shooters apiece, and they went to work. It was the last bad idea his partner, Jackson, ever had, and for Lucas, the results became a living nightmare and continued to be so.

But no one, not even the doctors, knew of his bouts with epilepticlike seizures that came and went at unaccountable moments, coming on him as they did only after leaving the hospital for good.

He had never mentioned it to his doctors; he hadn't wanted to undergo another battery of tests, praying the new assault on his system would eventually end of its own accord, but so far, the blackouts showed no sign of abating. In fact, over the four years since the accident, the seizures had steadily claimed more and more of him, until now they might last several minutes. It was enough to disqualify him as a candidate for police duty, so he had dared not confide it to anyone.

If the force knew of such a weakness, he'd be gone in a blink.

He had spent several years recuperating out at the reservation home of his forefathers, but since his arrival in Houston and acceptance of both a rookie's status and a rookie's pay with the Houston Police Department, thirty-two-year-old former detective Lucas Stonecoat had told his lawyer to plead or bribe Dr. David L. Cass to release all his psychiatric and medical records into the care of the attorney and to destroy all remaining copies from files and computers alike. Being placed under psychiatric care after the accident was standard procedure in the Dallas Police Department, but his psychological profile was at least one area of his life which Lucas intended to keep in that rare realm called privacy.

The media coverage of the accident, his subsequent battle back from death, and the media circus surrounding both his divorce and the suit he filed against the Dallas Police Department had been enough limelight for both his lives.

Meanwhile, his body each day made war on him. Who was tougher? Who had more will, God Mind or God Pain? Often, the body seemed to be winning the struggle for control, taking delight in torturing the mind. It seemed a forced old age, the constant struggle to overcome his own physical deficiencies and turmoil, from the onset of arthritis in his hands to a near-constant bout with what could only be termed a continuous, living headache that had taken up residence inside his cranium, a pain which nothing could completely extinguish, certainly not anything found in a drugstore.

Lucas and Jackson were proven to have been under the influence while giving high-speed chase through the city streets, and Jackson was judged to have been killed in the pursuit due to his own negligence and disregard for protocol and proper procedure, so the city had little reason to do more than the minimum for Jackson's family or for Stonecoat's mounting bills. Instead, the department, via the press, stripped Lucas of his rank.

Lucas took the DPD to court, but in Texas, a lone Cherokee cop stood little chance against the circus, as the system was called. Awaiting a trial, he had little reason to stay in the city he had adopted, and he no longer felt at ease there; he had few friends to speak of on the force, fewer since his attempt to stand up for both Jackson and himself. So now he was pulling a paycheck here in Houston, working over the dust-laden files of the Cold Room. Case after piled-to-the-ceiling case of murdered men, women and children gone unsolved, cases the department had wanted badly to close out but had been unable to do so; cases that, if closed, would gain the HPD more recognition and a better statistical average on murders solved, a more sterling record, which inevitably led to more federal dollars.

Lucas Stonecoat had a simple enough job, and where better to place a deformed cop, one with half a face of scar tissue, so as not to frighten children and white women? He couldn't even pull crossing guard duty.

He suddenly pounded frustrated fists onto the desktop, and the noise reverberated about the Cold Room, sounding like a kettle drum. He stood and paced the crowded little space of his new existence like a caged bear, consciously trying not to breathe too deeply the musty, dust-laden air. He wasn't exactly Toulouse-Lautrec; he still had some height, a strong, firm body that some might call gaunt. Only the slight hunch of his back, the scar tissue along his right side, at his cheek, neck, and down to the biceps, and other telltale signs marked him as a maimed man, damaged goods.

His Indian blood served him well in one regard: The bronze-red tincture actually masked the scar tissue, at least until someone came too near.

"Fire plays freaking hell on any color skin, just the same," he'd tell the ones whose stares lingered a might too long.

His clear, dark brown eyes would then blink bright and wistful, and then he'd bring up an unfelt laugh to let the other man or woman off the hook. He had long since let go of any hope that people might show some sensitivity, and besides, in his case there was no such thing as a comforting word.

Still, he bolstered himself daily with the fact he was alive, and that he had come back from that shrouded land reserved for the dead. During his visit there, he had regained a great deal that he had once lost—most importantly, who he was in a past life, for the voice of his ancestor, the one originally named Stonecoat, spoke directly to him, telling him he must go back, that there was much for him yet to do in this reality.

Maybe that was what bothered people the most. Even those who didn't know his story seemed to sense, or judge from his scars, that he had once walked among the dead, and that he was here now as some sort of misguided spirit with wide, peeking-out eyes and what the Cherokee called "going back" characteristics associated with those who ought to've been killed in some glorious manner, such as on the battlefield, but had not fulfilled such a destiny, so in dying they go backwards and return to earth until they might find a more suitable way to die. The questionable accolade had so attached itself to one family that it had in the distant past become the family name, Goingback, his mother's side.

Lucas came from a long line of warriors, but nowadays he felt more like a mischievous ghost of himself, anxiously searching for his identity but only causing trouble for the world around him as he did so, a world in which he no longer felt at ease or to which he fully belonged. Returning to police work, he had hoped, might return him to some degree of normalcy, but such a plan had an inherent flaw. Suppose he accomplished a return to "life before the accident" only to learn that it continued to be unfulfilling and worthless?

He had recently begun to despise his own inner voice, his own musings on the subject of himself and his aims. Such self-reflection came at too high a cost. It cost in dark alleyways of hatred and anger, which led to self-indulgence, drink, and drugs. Besides, his inner voice had begun to sound too damnably much like the shrinks he'd had to contend with back in Dallas, and this thought made him explode again. "What a lot of horseshit," he said, sending a fist into one of the stuffed boxes on the shelf before him—one of the countless such boxes in the Cold Room.

The box retaliated with a nasty puff of foul gray dust mites, making him cough in turn.

What few friends he had on the force were all back in Dallas, and even their kindness hadn't always prevailed. This went tenfold for his ex-wife, who saw his disabilities more in economic terms than humane ones.

Lucas's large hands had healed well, and he had full use of them, most of the time. The occasional lockup came on him—sudden muscle spasms, like those in his back. The accident had, the doctors said, aged Lucas by fifteen, maybe twenty years. "Can I skip male menopause, then?" he'd asked one doctor, who enjoyed his dry humor.

His legs—even the left one—had, for the most part, escaped the torture of metal and fire of the inferno the squad car had become that day. The legs were now good. Sleep wasn't so good.

Since the yearlong hospital convalescence, he didn't eat well, and nowadays when he did eat, he ate sparingly, like a thin gray squirrel, putting away more than he consumed; like a camel, he went without water for days, so long as he could find some ready, pain-numbing alcohol instead—another matter not for public consumption, and certainly not for the department's bloody IAD inspectors and medical staff.

He felt both restless and weary at once, a stout weeping willow, on the one hand growing toward the sky, on the other reaching toward the earth.

Working alone, with minimal to no secretarial support, should suit the likes of Lucas Stonecoat just fine, he now thought as he once again ran his eyes over the room, a spiritless gray cavern to which he had been assigned only hours before. The heartless, unfeeling place rippled with faint light coming in at the street-level windows.

The old station house was a little younger than the Alamo, but not by much, he imagined, the exterior a pitted, boulder-strewn facade of the sort only found in old Texas towns. It had only survived so long among the sleek steel high-rise chapels of downtown Houston because it housed cops, and it belonged to the city, and so long as it remained cheap space for the city and didn't collapse, so it went. . . . There was talk of renovating a vacated city school now being broken into each night and used as a crack house in a seedy section of the city. It might do some good to turn such a damnable place into a precinct house full of the latest in crime-fighting technology, but somehow Stone-

coat didn't see it happening so long as the city fathers and
city council men and ladies gave more lip service to crime
prevention than actual dollars and cents.

So, Stonecoat imagined he was stuck here in the ancient
cavern of the Cold Room, perhaps forever, or until he broke
under the pressure of God Reality. Here the walls were as dead
and unfeeling as the cardboard boxes of the dead files stocked
here. True enough on the surface, but microscopically, the
place was a buzzing jungle of activity, mites eating away at the
paper and munching off chunks of cardboard; dust-eating
microbes carried on the wind each time the door was opened
or the fan turned on. In fact, much of the dust was created by
the walls, like an epidermal layer of skin sloughing off,
invisible to the naked eye. Dust reigned here, creating a halo
when the 9:09 sun hit the reflecting glass on the building
across the street, somehow making its curious way into this
crypt and making the walls of the Cold Room shimmer as if
alive—and it was no illusion.

Houston brass thought they'd be doing him a favor, no
doubt, putting him to clerking here amid the "lockup" of
debris. No one expected him—or anyone else, for that
matter—to actually work on cracking cases and finding
solutions where others had only found insoluble questions.
Even if there was a way to warm up a frozen-with-age case
as those surrounding Lucas, he'd have to do it in an
atmosphere filled with paper people, paper lives, and paper
events of a bygone day; he'd likely have no witnesses to the
crimes, no one alive, anyway, and no one to interview, no
one to hassle or prod or pry. Maybe the brass thought it was
a former detective's dream: Open a case, chase answers
from a safe hole in the ground, do it without the least
expense of emotion or turmoil or involvement or human
contact—which he'd had four years of as a detective in
Dallas, and the three before that as a patrol cop.

Even if he could relocate a witness or even a suspect involved in so dusty a case file as one in these, the individual would likely be of a forgetful nature or in a forgetful frame of mind, and why not? So long after the incident had gone the way of water and smoke? He didn't imagine there were people who would willingly want to dredge up an ancient, encrusted anchor to trawl about a murky paper lake of forgotten, fishtailing information that had given up nothing from its dismal depths the first time around. He wasn't sure he even wanted to dredge this lake, to raise the dead, or reenervate the tragic crimes he was supposed to somehow solve.

Of course, no one expected much. He was told that from the outset. "Do what you can, Lucas," Captain Phil Lawrence had instructed. "And keep your duty sergeant informed."

"Sure . . . sure, Captain," he had replied, while thinking, *What kind of a duty sergeant do you have on a task like this?* It was police work, but just barely . . . more like clerk duty in a necromancy file room.

He'd be dealing with the worst problem a detective faced: SCC—Stone Cold Crime. This involved more than cold, uncrackingly frigid, lower drawer, forgotten crimes; he would face here the hard fact of unending, unappealing, and unreachable time. Who gave a shit about somebody killed five, ten, fifteen, twenty or thirty years before? What good was it to dig up old bodies when the morgue was filled with fresh stiffs every day? Who in the forensics sector wanted to hear about a dead case when their medic hands were overflowing with "live" cases, as it were? Who in the Missing Persons Division wanted to hear about a ten- or twenty-year-old missing person's report they'd given up on? Who in the detective's bullpen in any precinct in the city wanted to rehash a case that had so baffled him or her that the detective on the case had pleaded for years—even in sleep—to forget?

"Life's a bitch," he muttered to the empty file room, "and then you go to the Cold Room."

The telephone rang. It was Sergeant Stanley Kelton looking for a duty report, and he wanted it pronto. "Commander Bryce is doing a walk-through today, and I'll not have our paperwork looking sloppy, Officer Stonecoat, do you understand me?"

"Yes, sir."

"Then get to it, man!" Kelton's Gaelic voice thundered through the phone.

"Yes, sir."

"I'll send Langley downstairs for your report in an hour."

"An hour? I just got here."

"An hour, officer. You think Commander Bryce has time to putter about? No, mister, he's a busy man! Now, get what you can to me within the hour."

"Aye, sir."

There wasn't much to assemble for Kelton, but he managed to bring everything up to date, putting little X's into little square boxes. It appeared there was very little activity going on with records and files here, save for what some person named Dr. Meredyth Sanger was busy with.

He noted each entry and item she'd borrowed for the past two weeks. There were occasional others who'd come down to sift through some of the ancient paperwork, but nothing quite so noticeable as Dr. Sanger's sudden interest.

He took time to examine past weeks and months. Not a sign of Dr. Sanger before two, two and half weeks before his arrival. It appeared that up to that point, his predecessor, Arnold Feldman, had documented all activity to do with the Cold Room files, so he needn't duplicate the earlier man's efforts. The whole business left Lucas feeling mildly curious about Commander Andrew Bryce's interest in the interests of others roaming about the mite-ridden stacks of dead files here, but Lucas's mild interest was alloyed with a yearning to breathe free, to inhale fresh air, to seize an opportunity to escape this dungeon. Maybe Bryce, the chief ranking officer over the division, was thinking seriously of overhauling the way things were done, perhaps loading all this paper onto a computer system somewhere. Perhaps he meant to overhaul the entire precinct, starting literally from the bottom up.

At the turn of the hour a young, towheaded officer calling himself Will Langley showed up at the door requesting the reports Kelton had so impolitely asked for. Langley seemed apologetic, saying, "Didn't give you any more time to get your feet wet than they gave me." He went on, explaining that reports were usually due at the end of the month, but that there was a push on for some unaccountable reason.

Stonecoat greeted the young officer with a handshake and said, "No problem. But there's not a hell of a lot to report. Nothing much goes on down here, from what I can see."

The kid's eyes had traveled around the room, and he glumly replied, "Damn, I thought *I* had pulled lousy duty. . . ."

"You think Kelton's going to want anything else of me today?"

He shook his head, shrugged. "Can't say, but I doubt it, sir."

"I'm no sir, son, just an officer like yourself."

"Oh, no, sir, I've heard about you."

"Heard what?"

"That you were a detective in Dallas, that you got near killed alongside your partner."

"Old water under an old bridge, Langley."

"Whatever you say, sir." The kid left and the rock-hard silence of the place was even more deafening than before.

Two

Crossing paths

Already Lucas felt claustrophobic, trapped, as if consigned to a bloody prison while fellow academy graduates were being assigned squad cars and duty on the street, out in the Texas sun. Meanwhile, time seeping like water through rock, Lucas was beginning to feel a creeping panic, a fear that he could easily lose control here, that there were, after all, only tenuous threads holding him together in the first place, and now to be boxed in like an aging wolf in a zoo? He was closing in on thirty-three, and he would have been a lieutenant detective in Dallas had he not been made a cripple. Now what was he?

Perhaps he should have listened to his aunt and uncle, and to Grandpa. Perhaps he should have remained on the reservation up in Huntsville, where a mixed bag of Indians, mostly Coushatta, Alabama and Texas Cherokees, eked out a living by supplying tourist needs, there to peacefully live out what remaining years he had coming to him. He was, even by his grandpa's standards, an old man before the accident, and now he was ancient.

He continued to pace the aisles here in the Cold Room, a stark contrast to the wide-open spaces of the reservation home below the stars of an immense sky. His father's boyhood home had been his own, and despite the reservation poverty, it was filled with the compassion of his people, the Cherokee. Looking around at the dirty little hole to which he had been consigned, the hole into which his new situation landed him, he knew he just wanted to burn the fucking place to the ground and run out screaming an ancient Indian chant that'd been running through his head: *My enemy holds invisible arrows; he is everywhere; make me invisible, too, so that I might kill him before he kills me. . . .*

Lucas dropped his weight into the chair they'd given him. The ancient chair didn't match his desk, and it made the sound of squealing, frightened pigs when he leaned back in it. "Make my arrows invisible, too . . . Make my feet silent . . . Make my hands follow my brave thoughts, otherwise there is no contest." He spoke aloud the remainder of the remembered chant, thinking of his mother, a half-breed, strong-willed woman who had been the only stable force in his life before she died of cancer. He also fondly recalled his grandfather, Two Wolves, his mother's father, who still lived at eighty-six, and a third powerful image of an ancient warrior painting his chest with clay colors and charcoal, smoking a weed that would in fact convince him of both his invisibility and his invincibility. It was no accident that Indians raced at bullets. They believed themselves invisible to the bullets fired by the marksmen of the U.S. Cavalry.

The Cold Room, this place that had been here since 1910,

had already become Stonecoat's all too visible enemy, choking him, destroying him from within.

"Make me invisible," he repeated, "so I don't have to see this place or be seen in this place."

"Ahh . . . are you . . . ahh . . . speaking to me?"

Stonecoat wheeled around at the sound of the female voice, the squeaking chair they'd given him from storage screaming in his ear, embarrassing him. He fought to regain what little composure remained and stared slightly up at a woman whose startlingly lovely smile and wide aquamarine eyes met his for a moment in the dim light.

"No, I'm sorry . . . just getting buggy down here alone," he softly apologized.

"My guess is, you didn't hear me come in. . . ."

"No, I didn't. Got to get this chair oiled."

"Well, it's no wonder," she replied prettily, a dusty file folder in her hand. "Why's the desk so far from the door? There's room for it up at the—"

"Hey, I just got here. What the other guy before me did . . . I don't know. Maybe he smoked weed back here, and I can't say as I blame him, ahh, miss."

He momentarily wondered if he'd made a mistake with her, searching for a badge, guessing she could be a lieutenant or something, in which case he ought to've referred to her as sir or madam, he supposed.

"It's Doctor, Dr. Meredyth Sanger."

"Oh, Doctor?"

"Psychiatry."

Police shrink, he thought, *just what I need. Already checking up on me, already familiar with my record, already anxious to get me on her couch, and not for the romp of it. Pretty, though . . . much better prospects of getting me on her couch than that weaselly ferret of a man back in Dallas ever had.* All these thoughts rushed in at him unbidden, in the same instant in which he suspiciously eyed the dead file she'd lifted from one of the shelves.

"What's that you're carrying out?" he asked. "You know you have to sign out anything you take from here. Here's the roster. Just sign here. Be sure to indicate the file number, date it and sign."

"I'm not taking it out, officer." He detected the sharp anger, and not even his blue serge suit could hide the fact he held only a rookie's status here. Only a rookie would get such duty, and she knew this. He wondered how long she'd been around; how much she knew about the inner workings of the department; if she could help him or hurt him, or both.

"I'm returning this." She extended the file on long, fragile fingers with lovely nails. "I think I've got all I need from it—for now, anyway."

"Sorry, I thought you'd been back there in the stacks. Call me Lucas or Luke," he corrected her, preferring it to "officer."

She smiled in response, a smile that brightened both the room and, momentarily, his spirits.

Lucas again stared at the file, which she now defensively clutched to her chest. He noticed the absence of a wedding band on her finger, although she obviously liked rings. He saw a sapphire on her right hand, a purple birthstone gem on her left hand.

"You're the Cherokee guy, aren't you? The one everybody calls"—she corrected herself before saying Redskin—"Stonecoat?"

He instinctively turned the scarred side of his face from the light and her view, realizing she'd edited her own words, that she'd almost called him Redskin. "That'd be me, yes, Redskin," he bluntly replied. "It's a nickname given me by my dead partner in Dallas, long before the flaming scar, but it's a tag that has followed me here, used liberally in the training sessions among the other rookies, who were ten years my junior. But then, you already know all about that, don't you?"

"Only what I've heard, Mr. Lucas Stonecoat."

She said it as if she'd heard many tall tales about him, but he'd already become defensive, first straightening in his chair and then standing up so he could loom over her. She was a head shorter, even if he did have a forced slouch. "Okay, Dr. Sanger, so you've found me. But don't get your hopes up."

"What?"

He stepped past her, into the shadows, which made a mosaic of his face. "I don't intend to become your guinea pig, Doctor, so—"

"What the hell're you talking about?"

"I don't intend to play twenty questions with you about my childhood or my accident or anything else that piques your curiosity, any more than I—"

"Hey, hold on there, Stonecoat!" she shouted, realizing where the conversation was going. "All I know is the Cold Room has a new guy, that Arnold Feldman's gone, thank God."

"You didn't like Feldman?"

"And where'd you learn such big words as 'piqued,' anyhow?" She still managed a smile for him, but this only made him more nervous with her.

"Then you're . . . Oh? Well . . ." Lucas began to babble, "Listen . . . listen, maybe I did jump the—"

"You're really not to worry about me head-hunting for you, officer. I have plenty of head cases upstairs to keep me busy for the rest of the year, trust me, so—"

He smiled now, almost laughed. "Is that right? Well, hey, maybe I was a little—" he attempted a lame apology, thinking how pretty her silver-blond hair and blue-fire eyes were.

"—so I didn't come slumming down here for additional patients," she forged ahead. "Don't need 'em, don't want 'em. Got a precinct full of 'em. You got that, Lucas?" She slapped down the file, sending dust bunnies flying in every direction below his desk lamp, and before storming out, added, "Maybe you ought to begin on your new duty with a can of Pledge and a dust rag."

"Hey, hey," he shouted after her, taking a few steps in her direction, bumping metal shelves with shoulders too wide for the aisle, causing her to slow at the door. Their eyes met for a moment. Masking his thoughts, which were vaulting toward a pinnacle he'd not felt in years, he simply said, "You forgot something."

"What?"

"You . . . you forgot to sign that stuff back in. Do you mind?"

She glared at him now, the pretty eyes no longer inviting or smiling, her teeth set like an angry fox terrier's. The effect was cute, pretty even, he thought, but he dared not tell her such thoughts.

She yanked the clipboard from his outstretched hand, snatched a pen from her ear, located the right line, and scrawled her name with a shaking fist. He paid no attention to either the date or the ID number attached to the file—precisely what his superior had told him he must do. He instead concentrated on her name—Meredyth Sanger—trying to determine the origin of the melodic name. French, maybe, or Cajun? he wondered as she disappeared through the door.

He could hear the pulse of the city outside the ground-level window. Houston was the largest city in the state, fourth largest in the nation, with a population of 1,657,504.

The city had experienced phenomenal growth since the days of its riverboat-landing beginnings when it was called Buffalo Bayou and a pair of brothers named Allen in August of 1836 decided to sink roots. Eventually the area was named after General Sam Houston. Today the metropolis was the financial and industrial hub of the state, with the largest seaports in all of the Southwest and the Lyndon B. Johnson Space Center. Along with nearby Galveston, all things Texas—and many an item distinctly other than Texan in origin—could be found here. But this morning's traffic report from Eyewitness News Team 2 in Houston exposed it as the cattle town it had always been when it showed film of traffic backed up for mile upon mile on the Interstate due to an overturned semi that had sent its cargo of live beef, mostly nervous longhorn steers, roaming freely about downtown Houston.

From a law enforcement perspective, Houston was to be congratulated. The largest reductions in homicide rates in the country for 1995 had been in New York and Houston, both having seen a near one-third decrease in killings in 1995, while Dallas, Texas, unfortunately, was seeing an increase in homicides.

All the same, Lucas found Houston somewhat dizzying. He had grown up in nearby Huntsville, Texas, and the changes and growth of Houston since he'd left as a young man to take academy training in Dallas was astounding. He hardly knew his way around the city anymore. But there remained a few neighborhood bars he was familiar with, places where a man could step back into the past, if only for the time it took to drink a beer. At the moment, the thought of a drink was almost too much to bear.

THREE

Lasso: captivity

Lucas had moved the desk closer to the door, and he had spent the past hour dusting off everything within reach before he announced to himself and the walls, "I gotta get outta here. . . . Talking to myself."

He had always talked to himself, just as his paternal grandfather always did, but he'd always done so with an audience of at least one other. As a detective, it was one of his most useful tools; but here, like this, it felt creepy and strange. It was one thing to talk to yourself with your partner listening in and making additions, deletions, and suggestions, or filling up your morning with a self-directed brainstorm while other detectives threw paper wads to plead for an end to what they called his Indian gibberish; but it was quite another matter altogether to talk to yourself in a closed, sealed, silent space.

He closed and locked the door and "set" the childishly florid, yellow-and-red first-grade cardboard clock on the window, indicating he'd be back at one, confident that no brass or hard-ass detective would come down here for anything within the next month.

A single flight of stone steps, more convenient to take than the elevator, led up to ground level. One doctor had told him to go easy, another to push the envelope and get all the exercise he possibly could. He wondered which was right. He also, more importantly, wondered if Meredyth Sanger had used the stairs. He imagined her storming up them, her legs pumping. Dr. Sanger—he liked the sound of it as it slipped off his mental tongue. He decided to follow in her footsteps, but on opening the stairwell door, he found the steps extremely tight and straight up. With his stiff hip, which over time was only going to get worse, he chose to wait for the dinosaur of an elevator.

He supposed it was a miracle that on the first day of his new assignment, consigned here in the bowels of the precinct, he'd actually seen a woman, and a good-looking woman at that.

When the elevator finally bellowed its way from upstairs, located him in the basement and deposited him on the first floor, Lucas Stonecoat looked out on a sergeant's desk crowded with people, all vying for attention and demanding help of the lone sergeant behind the wrought-iron cage. The bars made Sergeant Kelton look the part of the criminal. Still, Stanley Kelton, a veteran, remained unfazed by the madness around him. So far, Kelton was the only person in the building who didn't wince or pretend business around Lucas, save for Dr. Sanger, and maybe that was why he liked Kelton, and perhaps could get to like the lady shrink. But that, he told himself, was a truly stupid thought—a friendship with a head-banger named Sanger?

The melee left Kelton too occupied to notice the "rookie" slip past him. But at the door Stonecoat ran smack into Dr.

Sanger again, this time in the company of Captain Phil Lawrence, the two of them embroiled in some verbal jousting. It appeared the good doctor did not reserve her linguistic lacerations for rookies and small fry alone. She certainly appeared to have her ire up over something she felt important, but Lawrence, a mild-spoken, firm-handed manager, motioned her toward his office for privacy before going any further. Out of the corner of his eye, Lawrence regarded Stonecoat, as did Dr. Sanger, as if he were part of their confrontation. Had she informed the captain of Lucas's behavior downstairs? Had he earlier been "rude" in the least toward her? Had he been too defensive, aloof? He had a problem gauging women, especially white women.

Lucas made a 180-degree about-face, preparing to disappear, when Lawrence—who obviously didn't relish his dealings with Meredyth Sanger—suddenly called out his name. Lucas stepped up to his captain with a "Yes, sir" on his lips.

"Stonecoat, I want you to meet our resident police psychiatrist, Dr. Sanger."

Lucas put on his best stone face and said, "Very glad to meet you, Doctor."

"You needn't pretend we don't know one another, Lucas," she replied, making him bristle.

"Oh, you two know one another? That's very good, as it's my custom, Lucas, to have all new recruits meet with Dr. Sanger on a semi-weekly basis, just to stay in focus, that sort of thing."

Lucas couldn't reclaim the audible groan that welled up and out of him.

"You don't have a problem with that, do you, Officer Stonecoat?"

"Yes, sir . . . I mean, no, sir . . . no problem."

Lawrence ended the discussion with a perfunctory smile

and nod, telling Dr. Sanger, "We can continue our conversation about the Mootry case in my office." He indicated the closed door nearby.

Meredyth Sanger, looking exasperated, now frowned and found her way into the captain's office. Lawrence half whispered to Lucas, "Wish me luck with this woman. She's driving me nuts; I think it's some sort of conspiracy to get me committed." He laughed at his own joke and rushed to catch up to Dr. Sanger.

"Man, Lucas," said someone in his ear, "sorry they put you behind a desk, pal." It was Thom Finney, a friend throughout their academy training.

"Not just any desk, Thom. A real hole in the wall."

"Bitching luck."

"I don't know that luck had a damned thing to do with it; might say my past precedes me."

"That shits, man."

Thom's burly training officer partner tugged the other rookie away, saying, "No time for powwows, kid. We gotta get back out on the street."

"Later, Lucas."

Lucas followed the other two men through the door and outside the precinct walls. He breathed in deep breaths of air and squinted at the last rays of sun before they disappeared entirely in a sea of gunmetal-gray clouds, an early morning storm out over the big Gulf waters obviously brewing. Squad cars were busily pulling in and out of headquarters; Lucas watched handcuffed offenders swear and kick their way from backseats. *Frustrated dregs of humanity,* he thought.

He wasn't sure he was any different, handcuffed to the Cold Room. He wasn't sure he could go back inside and suck in dust mites all day long. He wasn't sure he could stand it without going out of his mind, at least not without a drink. Yeah, maybe a drink would help.

On the precinct steps now stood Sergeant Kelton, shouting, "Hey, Stonecoat! Where you going at this hour?"

"I need supplies. Going to requisition a few supplies."

"Well, that's done on the third floor, Mrs. Babbage's department."

"Thought I'd go the fast route, Sarge."

"And what's that?"

"Wal-Mart."

Kelton frowned. "You won't get reimbursed for any out-of-pocket expenditures, you know."

"I'm well aware, Sergeant."

"You okay, Stonecoat? I mean with the duty you pulled and all?"

"Never better," he lied.

Lucas walked away, wondering if he'd be back or not, unsure of his next move. "You know what kinda duty you can expect to get here in Houston, in that cave?" he asked himself as he went for his car. "Nada, zip, nothing . . . absolutely—"

"Then at least we know what you'll get in return," Stonecoat's other half argued back, some of the cops in the lot staring at him.

Lucas pushed past two uniformed rookies who gave him warm, unanswered salutations—boys he'd gone through his second academy training with. They took his ill temper in stride, one of them shouting, "How's that temper of yours, Redskin?"

Lucas silently, blindly pushed on for his car. Sergeant Kelton, his complexion a sickly white dotted with weak freckles, looking every bit his fifty-six years, muttered to himself, "I hope the department knows what it's doing, hiring on that one."

Lucas yanked open his car door, for some reason looking back at the precinct and up at the window where Meredyth Sanger regarded him with piercing, curious eyes. She was speaking to someone in the room with her—Captain Lawrence, no doubt—but stopped suddenly upon seeing Stonecoat staring up at her. Her sudden loss for words seemed almost as if she feared he could read her lips or hear her from this distance. A silent look passed between them. She was special. He didn't know how or why he felt so, but she was somehow special.

She pulled her eyes away and disappeared from the window. He climbed into his car and fought with the faulty ignition.

He had to escape this place, at least for now; he must search out better air, wider spaces, freedom, some substitute for, or semblance of, sanity, and some reason to go on.

Painted buses, rusted and gilded cars, limos, taxis, air traffic and Rollerbladed bodies. Houston raced around Lucas, gaudy, huge and powerfully energetic, even in the shimmering heat rising off its asphalt prairie, her network of intersecting streets the arteries by which she lived. But recently her strength had been reduced, drained like a fevered lover or an oil well gone dry. Over the past two weeks of intense, insufferable temperatures, the fiery heat had scorched the social fabric into a deep ochre, a burnt umber that seemed like a visitation from the surrounding deserts of king cactus. Competing for a record year of heat and humidity, Houston basked in 110- and 120-degree days, 101 in the shade before noon—too hot for dogs to catch flies or wag their tails, too hot for bare skin on grass, much less asphalt and tarmac and metal railings, too hot for tires, which were daily exploding; too hot for tennis or handball courts, too damned hot for sex or even love, Lucas thought.

He had burned his hand just turning the key in the ignition of his car.

Still, somehow Houston bustled with the frenetic energy of a waking giant anxious to outpace this day's harsh whiteness. If the city could move, he thought, it would take off racing into Galveston Bay, and if that did not cool her concrete and steel temples, then she might race out across fields, to spread her enormous legs and sprawl among the prairies that lay just over the horizon, out on the cooling, refreshing desert of night that had been home to Lucas's dispossessed, wandering ancestors who'd first left their ancestral homes, an area that covered most of Kentucky, Tennessee, and Georgia's Great Smoky Mountains, just ahead of the white march to Manifest Destiny. His immediate Cherokee family had avoided the Trail of Tears because they had voluntarily exiled themselves to Oklahoma long before the forced march of the remaining People. Lucas's ancestors next left the land "given" them by the U.S. government in Oklahoma when squabbling factions of the Cherokee had joined the pioneers to Oklahoma in the 1830s. Finally, the people whom Lucas claimed as his settled among the brier patches and cactus of East and Central Texas. There they knew peace only after the Texas Cherokees were massacred down to a remaining handful of women and children.

Reservation life had become the only way of life for the generations that followed, and it was the rare individual who could escape it through education and hard work. Lucas had done just that, and now he was a city-dwelling Indian who often longed for something else.

Many of the city creatures born here in Houston never went beyond the limits of their often filthy and infested neighborhoods, never got beyond the city lights to the prairie stars, dying here as they lived here, out of sight of any god worth speaking to, living their limited, tunneling, boring lives out in a grid world of narrow, confining, crisscrossing passages through which the most important business of their equally narrow lives competed for time and space.

Lucas now cruised this world, creating the necessary maps in his mind as he went. He must learn the lay of this new land. Dallas had been home for much of his life, but the new Houston—many of its skyscrapers helped to the sky by skilled Indian hands—was new to him.

According to the news, Houston's lakefront property was at an all-time premium in a quite virtual sense: Beaches had become carpets of people laid out like so many sand towels and nowhere to walk. Galveston Bay was filled with those seeking relief, swimming in the tide, bobbing like flotsam under a grueling sun that bubbled the gulf waters, melted the hearts of Houston's whores, and scorched the tile roofs of suburban homes. The air around Houston itself had become a humid, demanding and breath-stealing warrior in the most physical sense. Just like Dallas, and nothing like Dallas, except for the no-ocean option, he'd decided.

The downtown silver towers of the high-rise district stood over it all, professing to live and stand forever, if not as towering pyramids, then towering ruins below time and sand. Home base for NASA, home of major league sports teams and opera houses that surpassed anything in the East for sheer size and show, Houston now was home to Lucas Stonecoat. He wasn't ever going to be completely comfortable here, and he knew it.

"I'm still a cop," Lucas kept telling himself as he drove further and further from the precinct. "I still carry a badge and a gun, and I still have the power of arrest." He had come from a long line of warriors, beginning with the first of his line to be called Stonecoat. Other ancestors became Light-horse Guards, the 1850s counterpart of the Secret Service, but they were in the service of the Cherokee Chiefs.

Lucas had pulled loose his tie and placed a sports coat over the passenger seat removing his "medicinal" supply in the pocket. His most immediate intention was to locate the nearest safe bar. The image of the Cold Room, its four walls moving in threateningly, continued to chip away at his resolve.

"Low fucking man on the totem pole takes on a whole new meaning," he said, sipping Red Label whiskey, which he'd camouflaged in a brown medicine bottle. He took a second long pull on the "painkiller," replacing the half-pint bottle below the folds of his sports coat.

He wondered why they had bothered to issue him a uniform. Who needed a fucking uniform down in the Cold Room? No doubt it was issued for parade days and visits from dignitaries, for crowd control or if a riot were to break out in a slum neighborhood. He'd simply hung the uniform in his locker, seriously doubting if Lawrence or anyone else would call him on it if he never wore the damned thing, simply wearing plainclothes instead. What sense did it make to dirty a uniform down there on an eight-hour shift out of sight of God and everyone on the planet?

Maybe he'd test his theory tomorrow, and maybe not. If he did things by the book, if he wore the damned uniform, it would feel awkward enough, but if he did follow the letter of the precinct law, and if he impressed Captain Lawrence, it stood to reason that he'd be returned to street duty, and after that who knew? He could begin to work again toward a detective's shield, with all the privileges that followed.

"Dream on, fathead," he told himself now. As to the breaking of rules, it seemed hardly to matter; as to the whiskey, he'd have it empty and the car aired out before it was turned over to the next shift.

He was now just prowling, turning the police band up high, hopeful that he would be in the right place at the right time. In fact, he was praying for a bank robbery, a knock-over, maybe even a murder, something he could sink his teeth into. It was going to happen anyway, as inevitable as the rising temperature today, so why shouldn't it happen now while he was trawling by? Should a call come over, and he happened to be "lunching" nearby, he'd be the first to take it. Fuck the Cold Room.

Thus far, however, the radio band buzzed with cats up trees and gang graffiti calls, broken windows and stolen bikes, nothing of a serious nature or import; he hungered even for a household disturbance, something where he could rush in and bust somebody's chops. *Wrong attitude, man,* he counseled, so he simply pulled over and switched off his car, stepped out of the vehicle and into a seedy-looking bar. If he couldn't find trouble to attend to, he'd make a little of his own.

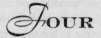

FOUR

Bear track: good omen

Dr. Meredyth Sanger watched from across the street as the man she had been following climbed from his squad car and made his way toward the bar. "Oh, shit, Stonecoat's a lush. . . ." She groaned and shook her head, disappointed at what she saw here. On the surface, she saw an on-duty police officer first sip from a questionable receptacle in his car and now step into a bar before noon. It wasn't pretty and it wasn't promising, not for Stonecoat and not for her . . . not for anyone. "Damn," she cursed.

Dr. Sanger had had it with the kind of mentality exhibited by Captain Lawrence, his wait-and-see approach, his hands-off attitude, his management-by-crisis style. She was equally tired of seeing the kind of exhibition she'd witnessed out Lawrence's window, where subordinates were treated so shabbily by ranking cops that they were denied a chance to work up to their potential; that certainly seemed to be the case with Officer Lucas Stonecoat, who must take orders from a Stan Kelton.

She had to admit, though, that Lawrence was far easier to take than some men she'd worked with in police circles. She once had had to expose a watch lieutenant who had raped a female officer and had threatened the woman's life if she should ever talk. The woman had come to Meredyth for advice, help, comfort and support. Meredyth gave her all this and more over a period of a year, while the handsome but vicious lieutenant continued a constant barrage against the young woman until finally she agreed to wear a wire. With the help of Internal Affairs, Meredyth was able to corner this man, to put him where he belonged. He was serving eight to ten for rape now, and his conviction had been upheld on appeal.

Despite the good work she was doing within the department, men like Lawrence still failed to take her seriously— partly due to the Blue Code, which labeled her a snitch, because the unspoken and inane belief held by many cops was that no matter what a fellow cop did, you never ratted on him. She sometimes wondered just who was crazy and who was sane.

How did a guy like Lawrence get ahead? He was a throwback to an earlier time, a freaking caveman without the body hair, yet he fit right into the old-boy system of the HPD. Hell, he fished and hunted with the best of the brass, told off-color and ethnic jokes so nasty they'd make Don Rickles cry and Howard Stern wince, and he talked openly in the squad room with his detectives of his many encounters and conquests of women as if some newsreel were playing relentlessly inside his self-deluded brain.

"Fatso" was Lawrence's squad room handle, but now that he was thirty pounds lighter than when he began and now that he was a captain, nobody dared call him that to his face, except perhaps the self-destructive type—maybe a guy like Lucas Stonecoat, from what she could see.

She leaned back into the cushioned car seat now; she had felt some guilt at first for having followed Lucas from the precinct, but not near so much as she had while watching him as he swilled booze a hundred yards away from her.

She had bottled up so much outrage at Phil Lawrence that her anger with Stonecoat was mild by comparison. "Damn that Lawrence," she said to the empty car. "Why can't the captain see facts in evidence when put before him?"

She had stumbled onto some interesting anomalies with regard to the recent murder and mutilation case of a man named Charles D. Mootry. The man, an appellate court judge, died under gruesome circumstances. He was first dispatched with an arrow fired from some sort of high-powered gun or crossbow, piercing the victim directly through the heart. The unusual choice of weapon used by the killer was just the beginning in this bizarre case, for the victim's head had been removed and carried off by his assailant, along with other telling body parts, such as the hands, feet and the privates. Only a torso with arms and legs remained.

She'd first learned of the case itself, minus the most heinous details, through newspaper accounts, along with everyone else. She, like the poor slob in the basement pushing dust mites about, was not on Phil Lawrence's kiss list. In fact, Phil didn't believe in either of two facts of life in 1996— that women belonged in police work, or that men who were real men ever needed psychiatric support. In effect, he didn't believe she could work effectively within the super-structure of a paramilitary organization such as the Houston Police Department, which was not only a male-dominated environment but one rooted in the history of the decidedly male Texas Rangers, another law enforcement agency under repeated siege due to sexual harassment charges that could no longer be ignored.

So what good was her mental medicine here? What possible good could she do here? Men like Lawrence hid their prejudices well for appearance' sake, allowing underlings like his detectives to do their talking for them. Perhaps no psychiatrist—male, female or neuter—could be of any damned use whatsoever to a man living out a fantasy of being Wyatt Earp or Matt Dillon. God, she hoped Stonecoat wasn't a Geronimo wanna-be.

Both her sex and her profession irked the captain, but she didn't work for him, not strictly speaking, and while she hadn't wanted to go over his head—another cop taboo— Phil didn't exactly leave her with any choice. She was damned if she did and damned if she didn't, but also damned if she'd sit another day in her office while Lawrence casually, unassumingly, even cunningly assured his men that appointments with her were made to be broken—despite his lip service, despite what he called policy, as when he'd told Lucas to submit to her scrutiny on a routine basis. It was all hogwash.

She realized that Texas was part of the Bible Belt, that it was ten, maybe twenty years behind in both the civil rights movement and in women's rights issues, and that men like Lawrence were on every old-boy circuit in the bloody state, but it was high time someone explained the facts of life to "Cap'n Phil," as his boys called him. She'd gone to top brass officials and had quoted their offical manuals to them. She had not only blown the whistle on Captain Lawrence's out-of-date practices, but had also pointed a finger at his ineptness and incompetence. She had gone out on a lengthy, shaky, narrow limb.

She still fumed from what he'd said to her behind the closed door of his office this morning. After getting assurances that he wasn't being put on tape by a hidden recording device, he had half-kiddingly and sanctimoniously dared ask her if she'd take exception to his frisking her. She did take exception and promised their discussion was strictly private. "Good," he'd replied to this, coming around his desk and pressing his body close to hers, searching her eyes for a rise. She instead glared and stepped back, giving off no uncertain signs.

"Look," he said, his voice quivering, "no pussy with a Ph.D. is going to screw me over in my own department and get away with it."

"Is that a threat, Captain?"

"Consider it fair warning."

"Consider this, then. I'll file charges against you if you so much as come near me again."

She'd stormed from Lawrence's office, driven by anger and frustration to chase out after the only man in the department who didn't appear to be under Lawrence's thumb, yet—Lucas Stonecoat.

"Right, you are," a small voice told her. "He's not under Phil's thumb now, but give him time." She realized the bastard had gotten to her, that she was talking to herself now.

She didn't know precisely how Lucas Stonecoat and Lawrence were getting on, but she knew Lawrence was just bigoted enough to rub Lucas the wrong way. A feud between them was as likely as water rolling down a rocky slope. Perhaps she could usher in the feud between them a little sooner with a few well-placed words, all to her advantage. It wasn't a pleasant alternative and certainly called her ethics into question, but it was feminine, after all, and she damned sure had to do something. She was grasping at straws, and the largest one to come along in some time was the tall, imposing Lucas Stonecoat.

She considered his size as he climbed from the car across

and down from her. She thought Lucas strong looking, handsome, save for the scar, but even this added an element of mystery that lured her on. His voice, so like a whiskey-drinking blues singer, reminded her of her father's cracked tones.

Maybe she'd best get to know Lucas Stonecoat, she thought, see if he could provide some assistance. After all, he'd once been a detective. His insights on the Mootry case might prove invaluable.

To this end, she'd stalked him from the precinct like a cub following a lumbering grizzly bear. This grizzly drove like a crazy man, a good deal more fleet of wheel than he was of foot, given the pronounced limp. He was already ducking out of sight ahead of her. Damn, he really was going into a bar this time of day, while on duty. What kind of a fool was he?

She hesitated now, debating with herself. Should she boldly go inside, confront him, or see him another time? Time was a luxury she could ill afford, especially now that Lawrence had taken off the gloves. At bedrock of all the rumors she'd heard about Lucas Stonecoat, there seemed a grudging admiration on the part of others that Lucas was a badger once he clamped down on a case, the kind of tenacious, tough detective who'd make for a useful ally, if only she could get him to listen to her.

She pulled up, passing his vehicle, U-turning and placing her own car right in behind his. Taking a deep breath, thinking of all that had brought her to this time and place—her father, her mother, her uncle Bill, all pushing her to be the best at whatever she chose to do in life—she got out of the car and marched in to find this supposedly crazy Indian cop to learn firsthand his story, tired of the secondhand crap she'd been handed. All this effort put forth, all this dangerous activity in which she risked so much, she thought. Perhaps she liked it, the intrigue; perhaps it was just what Lawrence had said it was, "A self-serving attempt to further your career."

"No, no!" she'd fended off the allegation. "It's to build a bridge of connections between the Mootry case and case files I've found in the Cold Room dating back some ten years, possibly more."

The old pain had come back like a rodent sniffing out prey: quietly at first, before pouncing. It was the pain that made his already pronounced limp, due to the stiffness in his hip, even more pronounced. He wondered how he'd ever hidden the true extent of his continuing physical ailments from the training officers all through his trainee period. It hadn't been easy, relying on painkillers and trying to remain alert at the same time. In the end, he'd made it, and despite the hellhole to which he'd been assigned, he was, at the very least, carrying a shield again. It wasn't a detective's shield, not even second-class; it was the silver of the uniformed street cop, but it was something.

Still, Lucas did have his first-class Dallas gold shield, along with the gold watch they'd foisted upon him . . . along with his damnable disability retirement. And although being reactivated to duty in Houston meant the loss of his retirement funds from Dallas, his forced departure and the endless days back home on the reservation had been driving him insane, so coming out of retirement was worth it at any price.

He opened his wallet and placed his two badges onto the bar side by side, the gold and the silver, weighing them out in his mind as he sipped at his bourbon.

He lifted and studied the Dallas gold shield, which looked liked most any gold shield in any city in America, save for the lettering. He superstitiously rubbed it between his large fingers for good luck before tossing it faceup on the bar, where he stared into its gleaming, reflective light.

His silver HPD shield was better than no shield at all, he rationalized; it had gotten him in charge of the damn Cold Room, hadn't it? It gave him slightly more weight than status as a former Dallas Police Department cripple with three-quarter Texas Cherokee premium red pumping through his battered body. Hadn't it?

He couldn't let them see his pain, so he forced it back with a second shot of bourbon where he stood at the bar, not anxious to sit again for some time. He took the bourbon straight up and neat—best way for the pain, he kept telling himself. But also for the pain that claimed him and told him daily it'd be with him until his grave, Lucas knew to utilize that strict code of the ancient Zen-like masters of his tobacco-twisting, magic-making race.

He just had to control it.

Had to be smart.

Had to second-guess the department. Beat them at their so-called spot-testing program.

He could do it. If anyone could. He was smart.

When he lowered the shot glass and saw her in the mirror, standing in the middle of the bar behind him, he brought the tumbler down with the sound of a gunshot. He wheeled, and his anger shone as thunderbolts flitting maniacally across each dark iris.

"What're you, following me?"

"I had to," she pleaded, her arms wide, palms up as she approached.

"Did that bastard, Lawrence, sic you on me?"

"Christ, Stonecoat, I'm not an attack dog! And no, quite the contrary; he warned me to steer clear of you."

"Said that, did he?"

"That's right," she lied, but it felt right.

"So you disobey him, like—"

"Disobey? I'm not a child, and I don't take orders from the likes of Phil Lawrence. Technically speaking, I'm a civilian and not part of his paramilitary organization."

"Who do you report to, then?"

"Commander Andrew Bryce, or at least his office. That's where my reports go."

"And Bryce is over the division?"

"You got it." Good, she told herself, now you've got him interested.

"You followed me here from the station house? Last time we talked, you said you weren't interested in me. What's with you, Dr. Sanger?"

"What I said was, I don't need another wigged-out cop on my couch, if you'll recall."

"Then what do you want from me?"

"Buy me a drink, and we'll talk," she offered.

"Like to play the bad girl? Is that it? This your way of getting back at Lawrence for some slight?"

"Bad girl?"

"Madonna, all that."

"Jesus, you're hard to talk to. You always so hard to approach, Stonecoat?"

"No, only when I'm expected to perform, and I've got a notion you're looking for a performance of some sort."

"Please, Lucas . . . can I call you Lucas?"

When he failed to answer, she stared into his eyes, finding herself swimming in a deep brown warmth and hidden hurt for a moment before she barreled on. "I think we could help each other out."

"I really don't recall asking for your help, Doctor!"

The bartender, without shouting, demanded, "Either take it to a booth or outside, but keep it down, will you? I run a quiet joint here."

"So," he said to her, indicating the second bourbon in his hand and leading her to a booth, "now you know my secret."

One of them, perhaps, she thought, carefully considering her words. "One of them is painfully obvious, but listen here, Lucas, I see a lot of cops with hard-core problems every day, problems you don't come near, so . . ." She paused, picking her way over the minefield of his emotions. "Fact is, there's very little I haven't seen on this job. So what if you drink while on duty? Half or more of the force does. I'm not here as a police shrink or to pass—"

"Sit," he ordered. She silenced herself and slid into the corner booth. "What'll you have?"

"A Coca-Cola's all."

"Coke," he shouted to the bartender. "Make it two. Wouldn't want you drinking alone in a bar."

"I'm sorry if I startled you, but—"

"Startled me?" He half grinned, and this made his face more handsome, the scar more easily tolerated. He tried a flagrantly lazy laugh, repeating the word *startled* as if the sheer impossibility of his being startled by her was as remote as finding a winning lottery ticket in this place. He turned his eyes and his scar tissue away from view in a practiced, now habitual fashion.

"I'm not exactly on Lawrence's guest list for the Christmas party, believe me," she continued again. "I guess I came after you because . . . because I need a . . . an ally, a professional connection, and because your record indicates a distinguished career."

Now he did laugh openly.

"You won two medals for valor before the accident."

"I don't want to talk about medals or accidents."

"All right, but what about it? I could use a friend, someone who—"

"A friend?"

"—somebody who hates that bastard Lawrence as much or more than I do, and I figure you're it."

"How do you figure that? Lawrence hasn't done anything to me."

"Are you kidding? He's a racist, for one. How do you imagine you wound up in the Cold Room in the first place, Lucas?"

"By his request?"

"It wasn't via lottery."

Lucas breathed this information in. "He heard plenty about me in Dallas, didn't he?"

"Everybody knows about Dallas, about John F. Kennedy's assassination there and about your accident there, but with Lawrence, when you went after the city in that court battle, that was enough to destroy any chance you had on his force."

"Whataya know . . . it all goes back to Dallas, doesn't it? They warned me that Houston's still a small town in many ways."

"Most Texas cities are. . . ."

He raised a hand to his chin and nodded in silent agreement.

"And everything about a police department is small-town," she added. "A lot of cable's been laid between here and Dallas, and you're something of an infamous fellow. And here you are, pretty much alone, and I'm . . . well, I'm pretty far out on a limb with Captain Lawrence, too." She now stared purposefully once more into the rippling and layered pools of his marble-hard brown eyes. This time, he held her stare as if daring her to break it off, as if studying her level of intensity, or sincerity, or both. Or was he thinking sex? She did not know.

"How do you know I'm not a racist or a sexist?" he asked her. "Many Indian men are proud to be both, you know. . . ."

She laughed lightly at this, realizing that he was kidding for the first time with her. Maybe the bourbon wasn't such a bad idea, after all.

"Seriously, Dr. Sanger, just what is it you want from me? You certainly didn't come here to warn me about Phil Lawrence."

She snatched a notepad from her purse and slipped on a pair of reading glasses that made her look like a schoolteacher, he thought. "What I'm going to tell you, Lucas, must remain confidential if—"

"So long as this entire meeting remains confidential, I think I could agree to that," he countered with a snakelike reaction.

She looked from her notepad over her glasses and across at him. "Agreed. Like I said, I've got more important fish to fry than your ass over an indiscretion more suited to the concerns of Internal Affairs."

"But don't you work closely with IAD?"

"IAD doesn't work closely with anyone. Listen, I am not your enemy."

"Shall we shake on it, to ensure the bond?" he suggested, still unsure of her motives, still not certain he could trust her.

"God, next you'll be asking me to slit my wrist and mingle my blood with yours in some pagan ritual out of—"

"Not a bad idea either."

"Okay, all right already." She reached across the rough, scarred tabletop, and he firmly took her hand in his, testing her strength for a moment, allowing his hand to linger in hers as they shook. She frowned, tugged her hand from his and turned her attention back to the notepad now lying between them. "I've mapped out my suspicions for several weeks now, all brought on by the Mootry killing."

A glazed, unknowing blink was quickly masked, even as he said, "Okay . . ."

"A brutal mutilation murder like that doesn't go unnoticed and—"

"Then this isn't a dead file case? It's not something out of the Cold Room?"

"Well, it is and isn't."

"What's that supposed to mean?"

"Well, let me finish. The Mootry case is current, but a less recent killing, a senseless murder here ten years ago come Friday, held some fascinating similarities. I wasn't on staff here then, but I read about it in the Seattle papers."

"You've only been here how long?"

"Four months come Tuesday."

"And you're from Seattle?"

"Yes."

"Your people all there?"

"Yes, now let me finish. Anyway, it occurred to me . . . I mean, I . . . the Mootry murder immediately brought back memories of similar deaths both here and elsewhere. I wondered if the three crimes could possibly have been connected. So I did some checking."

"I don't get it. Why didn't you just turn your suspicions over to the detective bureau?"

"That's just it. I did, but no one's taking me seriously, least of all Lawrence."

"Well, you are sticking your nose into his territory when you—"

"God, I hate that kind of thinking."

"Whataya mean? What kind of thinking?" he countered.

"We're going to let macho shit-head territorialism come before the truth?"

"It usually does."

"With men, yes."

He smiled. "You got me there. Something to do with the testosterone levels, I believe."

Well spoken, well read, fast on his feet, she thought. "Will you just listen?" she suggested.

"Shoot, Doc."

"I've found several suspiciously similar former cases, some of the information coming out of your dead file room down in the basement."

"Well, from all appearances, a lot of cases wind up in that twilight zone."

"One was the file I just gave back to you this morning."

"Really?"

"Yes, really. Have you reshelved it yet?"

"No."

"Good, then read it; see what you think. Then go back and check out the others I've read over the past few weeks. That's all I ask, Lucas."

"The way I had to remind you to check that file in this morning? How am I going to know which ones you've checked out before?"

"I checked 'em all back in, in order."

"You mean you were just a little flustered this morning?" he teased.

She managed a smile. "You might say that."

"All right, so what if these cases are linked?"

"What?" She gave him a confused stare.

"If they're in the Cold Room, they're like me."

"Come again?"

"They're not likely to be of any great interest to Lawrence or anyone out ranking him."

"They will now . . . or should."

"Meaning?"

"Where've you been, Chief?" She realized now that he had no notion of the enormity of the Mootry case. "The

Mootry case, the one that's been front page for the past week?"

"I don't read the newspapers. They depress me. Besides, I've been working my tail off night and day as a rookie, remember? Work detail by day, classwork by night."

"Couldn't've been easy after the years of rehab you've gone through," she replied, her tone consolatory, sincere.

"No one said it was going to be easy. . . ."

"Tell me about the most important single event in your life, the accident," she blurted out, her training as a psychiatrist getting the best of her, coloring her tone with condescension, making her immediately sorry, wishing she'd found a smoother transition into this touchy, obviously unhealed wound. "I know you want to talk about it to someone. . . ." she said, trying to repair the damage done by the blatant nosiness that accompanied her profession.

"I'm going to make you work hard for this," he said, his smile a curling snake.

"So I've noticed. Look, I'm sorry if I've overstepped my bounds. I must appear nosy, but in fact I'm . . . well, just . . ."

"Inner-rested?"

She nodded, smiling. "Yes, interested."

He shook his head like a big dog and then fixed his eyes on her. "I talk to the One God, the Great Spirit, about it. That's enough."

"Bullshit. Tell me about it; trust me, it'll only make you feel better."

"Me? Feel better? Not ever going to happen in this life, Doctor. Maybe when the Great Spirit comes for me, but not on this plane ever again. Besides, I had a shrink on my case, along with six physical therapists."

"Yours is a real success story. Surprised the movie people haven't sought you out for one of those—"

"They did and I refused. It wasn't exactly Robert Ze-meckis and DeNiro beating down my door to make the offer."

He dropped his gaze, staring through the solid oak table, and he began to tell her the story in as brief a clip as possible, knowing that if he fed her this, maybe she'd see him as more than the cripple he'd become, and perhaps she'd better understand why he was here now, downing whiskey. She listened without interruption.

"My partner, Jackson, and I, we had just gone off duty. We had hoisted a few when we heard the radio call on a heist nearby. In fact, we believed it had to do with a case we'd been working for months, so we responded." He explained that the car accident had happened while he was on what had begun as a rather routine call, since it appeared the gunman had abandoned the scene long before they'd arrived.

"So at this point it'd become a routine investigation of a robbery at a downtown liquor store in Dallas. The scene had actually been secured, cordoned off. It should've been routine. But it ended in a high-speed chase gone bad. Thanks to my now dead partner, who was a worthless drunk, a rotten wheel man, and the best cop that I've ever known."

"He was your senior partner?"

"The best. Learned so much from Wallace Jackson, but the crazy bastard got himself killed and very nearly killed me with him."

"Stonecoat, you aren't still angry at Jackson, are you?"

"Hell, yes . . . Hell, yes . . . All right, hell, no . . . whichever answer keeps me off your office couch."

She gave a little shake of the head, her silver-blond hair caught in the breeze created by the wafting overhead fan.

"Anyway, Dallas PD was embarrassed to its shorts by a press corps that'd already been vilifying them on an 'inside' investigation of the 'excessive number' of high-speed chases in the Dallas area resulting in the deaths of civilians and officers."

"I get the picture." She drank from her fizzling Coca-Cola.

"So the force was sorry for the loss of their black detective—one of a handful—and neither were they crazy about the idea of returning their Indian back to active duty."

"You realize, don't you, that Captain Lawrence can't look favorably on a detective who sues his own department?"

"I dropped the damned suit before it ever got to court."

"You dealt it out, I hear. You walked away without a fight."

"Let's put it this way, Doctor. I wasn't walking, period, at the time."

"I only meant that they paid you off without a fight."

"And I'm telling you, I fought from my hospital bed, on my back, like a goddamned overturned turtle. And trust me, I had a greater enemy to fight than with the Dallas Police Department."

"You'd have won a much heftier settlement. You had a good case. Obviously, no one was looking after your interests. What about the Police Benevolent League, what about the Patrolman's Fund, what about—"

"I started an action against the force. Lawyers got involved and fees got too heavy and too many for me. Still payin' 'em each month, along with rent."

"But you won?"

"Won the right to sit home and wait for a check, yeah. It took two years and a divorce for me to find a new situation while I lived on disability checks and TV dinners and beer. My so-called wife didn't even bother to come down to the hospital; said she'd had enough of life as a cop's wife. Meantime, the problem I was having with my own department in Dallas was due to a bureaucracy mired in itself, along with my police superintendent, who sold me and Jackson out. This creep was worried about his own job, so he just made certain that the redskin would stay off the payroll, nailing the coffin shut on the Indian problem he'd had all along."

"Nothing like having your superior go to bat for you," she commiserated.

"The bastard was nobody's superior. His main interests were his own interests," he replied. "But it taught me a valuable lesson."

"Oh, and what's that?"

"Never get blindsided. Never assume anything, and never underestimate the depths to which human nature sinks."

"So, you rehabilitated yourself physically, but it sounds to me as though you have a ways to come back emotionally. I mean, you've got to learn to trust again if you're ever to fully—"

"As you have seen, and so you shall see, this man is fully recovered in every way. I wear more body armor, sure, and I like it that way!" he said with a flourish of his large right hand, tipping his bottle at her and downing the drink in a final gulp. "Thank the Great Spirit, Houston wasn't being too choosy. That explains why Lawrence was saddled with the likes of me, wouldn't you say?"

"With a mandate and a federally funded program to train one thousand new foot soldiers in President Clinton's war against crime, and given your experience on the force, I really shouldn't—"

"Wonder? The redskin is put to great use now. . . . Some help I'll be in the war against crime here in Houston, sitting down in that hole Lawrence has found for me. Then the bastard has the balls to pretend he likes me by telling jokes about . . . well, never mind." He leaned back in the cushion, uncomfortable now.

"You okay, Lucas?"

"Can't sit in one place too long. Insides start to act up on me. A pain that is coming from deep within is always also a going-back pain, so it hurts both ways."

An old Indian expression, she guessed. "Want to get out of here?"

"Yeah, any ideas?"

"Park's not far from here."

"Park?"

"Municipal Zoo."

"Animals . . . I love animals," he replied. "They never ask anything from you, never take anything from you, and they never lie to you."

She eyeballed him, wondering about the double entendre of his words. "That's certainly true, and lovely in the way you express it," she finally agreed.

"So, let's do it. Let's go see some honest citizens of Houston. All in the zoo, right?"

She wondered just how seriously to take him. Was he kidding, half kidding, or deadly serious? Did he know that she'd told a few lies to get his attention? Was he including her in with all the dishonest citizens of the city, everyone outside of a cell? Was he saying that people in prison were more straightforward and honest than the average citizen, or was he just talking about animals? His mind seemed as agile as a fox's.

She grabbed the check, but not quickly enough. He grabbed her hand, pried the check from her and plunked a twenty over it. "This'll take care of everything," he said.

Machismo in a cripple, she thought. Kind of nice, far more so than in others. He was on his feet and offering a hand to her as she slid out of the booth. She sensed that it was important to him that she accept his helping hand. She imagined how difficult it must be for him to begin his career over again here in Houston, only to find the same foot on his neck as he'd had in Dallas.

$\mathscr{F}$IVE

Peace

They took her car, and while she drove, he continued to talk more freely, as if a floodgate had been opened. He cursed the duty he'd pulled, paperwork, mold and ancient files. "Everything about Dallas has become a curse then, hasn't it, Doctor? As a result of my prior experience in Dallas–Fort Worth as a detective, Lawrence assigned me to the Cold File Room, the pits, the bottom basement of police work here."

"But he's familiar with your record, so he has to know you were a good detective. Maybe somewhere in the back of that thick skull of his, he's thinking why not put a man in the Cold Room who has the aptitude to do more than clerk the files?"

"Now that's some kind of wishful logic, Doctor," he replied as they passed row upon row of dilapidated shops and abandoned houses. He wondered how much of his past she actually knew. She sounded as if she'd rummaged around in his personnel files, but if so, she'd have to have done so before they met in the Cold Room. She'd been setting him up from the beginning.

"He's got to know that you possess a good mind and a talent for detection," she continued her lame attempt at bolstering his ego.

"I've got no such illusions, Dr. Sanger."

"Meredyth."

"What?"

"Call me Meredyth."

He gulped and nodded and said, "I'm in the Cold Room for one reason. It's a convenience for the department, a place to put the cripple."

"Well, you can't let them get away with it, now, can you?"

"What can I do about it? I'm just a rookie, on probation status. Hell, I haven't even finished all my classwork yet."

"You're still taking classes?"

"I'm finishing up with my last evening course. The one I kept putting off."

"Which is?"

"Street Courtesy, or as the cadets call it, Bull on the Boulevard. Most of it amounts to filling in garbage in a little workbook that has absolutely no bearing on the real world."

"Hey, you do what you have to do."

He slapped the dashboard with both hands, creating a rifleshot of noise, making her start. At the same time, he nearly shouted, "I hate the classroom nonsense. Pretending to believe the crap the instructors hand out, pretending to like and respect both instructor and subject, when in fact I know they're generally full of it."

"So, you think you know more than they do?" She managed a laugh.

"Fortunately, I do."

She stared across the gulf between them.

"I tell you, it's true. Most of 'em have had no more than a year on the street, but because they couldn't cut it there, they teach. Those who can't do, teach."

"That's a nasty bit of bumper-sticker logic. God, Lucas, I can just see you seething in the classroom like some overheated radiator about to explode. I hate those types in my class sessions."

"But lives depend on what these teachers feed these rookies, so . . . so somebody's got to set them straight."

"Set who straight? The rookies or the teachers?"

"Both, if the situation warrants."

"Then maybe you should put in to teach rookies yourself, if you believe you can do a better job of it. You've got a hell of a chip on your shoulder. Not sure I'd want to see you in a class of mine."

He thought about this even as he countered, saying, "I just bet you're holy hell to please as a teacher." He saw an image of himself before his instructors, and he didn't like what he saw. He must project to his instructors the image of a wiseass, did-it-yesterday, know-it-all hard case. But he went on defending himself to her for some unaccountable reason. "Occasionally, I have lost it while sitting straight-backed in one of those damnably uncomfortable desks."

"It must be hard for you," she patronized as the cityscape passed by their windows on either side.

"And I've often taken exception to something either written on the board, in the book, or spoken by an instructor."

"Oh, Lord," she muttered.

They were entering the zoo grounds, and this time she was too fast for him, paying the parking fee.

"For instance, there's no such thing as a polite shake-down," he continued lecturing as the car pulled through the gates.

"But there is such a thing as proper protocol."

He ignored her, continuing on. "Nor can there be a friendly rapport with street lowlife at three in the morning when your mind's got to be focused every second on the possibility of some truly evil thing exploding in your face—maybe the kid you're making jokes with turns out to be on PCP. He might turn out to have an IQ of eleven and a half."

"Yeah, I've heard all the jokes," she replied sarcastically. "Luis has an AK-47 with a thirty-round clip."

"If Luis misses four of every ten shots and fires sixteen times at each drive-by shooting—"

"How many drive-bys can be attempted before he has to reload," she finished the tasteless but sadly poignant, all-too-familiar urban tale.

After they laughed together and turned off the ignition, she asked, "Is that what happened with Wallace Jackson?"

"Killer's street name was Red-X. Time we got near him, he'd colored his hair something approximating green." Lucas painfully flashed anew on what had happened in Dallas when his partner, Jackson, had been interrogating a punk one second and suddenly hitting the pavement the next when the kid pulled a gun to open fire. The cretin had realized his own stupid ploy to step in as an eyewitness to the very crime he'd committed was going haywire under Jackson's scorching interrogation of him at the scene. Jackson was so good at what he did that even though the kid had worn a mask during the holdup, Wallace had actually gotten a voice identification on the creep even as he spoke.

Lucas found himself telling her every detail as he had never told the story before.

"The kid who pulled the job returned to mingle in the crowd and then stepped forward claiming to be a witness. Jackson was immediately, instinctively suspicious. He told the kid to hold still and that he'd get back to him, asked me to keep the kid company, to ask him a few questions. Which I did. Then Jackson goes to the store owner, his wife and son, and asks them to listen in when he returns to ask the punk more questions."

"So, the kid's voice was recognized by the shop owner?" she asked, pulling the car into a vacant spot.

"Rule number one in crime: Crime makes you stupid," Stonecoat summarized for her now as he had for all the rookies in his class the night before. The others had politely listened to his story before he realized his classroom etiquette error. He had then turned the floor back over to the instructor, Officer Pete Jenkins, who obviously lived by the book and was likely going to get some of these rookies killed by the book.

"So, the kid realizes it at the last minute and opens fire?"

"Fires warning shots over the heads of everyone. We all hit the ground and he disappears down the street, brandishing his weapon. Jackson and I hopped in our car and gave pursuit. The rest is history, or bad karma, as they say. . . ."

During their stroll through the zoo and as they fed the animals, he confided in her that he still liked to think of himself as Detective First Class Lucas Stonecoat, even though he no longer enjoyed that rank. He'd held on to his shield, however—a keepsake from the old days with his buddy Wallace Layfette Jackson. "One crazy nigger teamed with a war-whooping Indian," he said, and then burst into laughter over pleasant memories that rose up from deep within his soul.

She strolled alongside him in a leisurely manner, allowing him to continue. "Sometimes I'll flash my old shield—you know, like in a bar—when I think it'd do me or the situation some good . . . Criminy, I sound like one of those old men who've turned into living Buddhas who squat around and tell stories to people who aren't listening."

"Oh, I'm listening to every word. I suppose you really flash that gold shield to impress the ladies, right?"

This made him laugh again, and he had a wonderful, warm laugh. "Sometimes, sometimes maybe I do. You're pretty smart, Doctor . . . ahh, Meredyth."

"For a white woman, you mean?"

He laughed again and tossed a handful of food pellets to monkeys roaming the other side of the fence. They didn't react, bored with their onlookers and their diet. The animals felt the heat, too. The mercury was already climbing through the nineties at eleven A.M., and Lucas felt the perspiration trickling even as he wondered how she managed to appear so cool.

"I bet you're the type that takes risks with that Dallas badge," she said, having pegged him as a risk-taker.

"Risks?" he asked sheepishly. "Me?"

"Like most cops."

He nodded. "Yeah, my own people . . . they say I'm more cop than I am Cherokee."

"Do you like to take risks with other cops?"

He stopped to stare at her, finding her eyes inviting. "Whataya talking about?"

"Other cops . . . from other precincts, of course, where they don't know your face. Do you like to pretend around them that you're still a detective?"

"Of course."

"Just to let them know that there're Dallas cops on the prowl here, too."

He nodded appreciatively, adding, "Or simply to get past a door as a detective, just to look in on a crime scene, to get the adrenaline rush going again."

"So, you've done that? Just for the rush?"

He only smiled.

"Here? As a civilian? Now, I'd say that's taking a big risk."

The smile only widened.

"You are a bit . . ." She searched for the word.

"Loco?"

"No! I wasn't going to say that!"

"Crazy, wacko? It's okay to say it."

She lied. "I was going to say brave, gutsy."

"So, you're not above lying to save someone's feelings, Doctor. Your profession hasn't thoroughly claimed you?"

She retorted with, "So, you're not above using your old badge to gain a confidence. I'll have to remember that."

"Call it my outlaw badge."

$\mathscr{S}$ IX

Ward off evil spirits

```
764LT1:\C42119\Category 42 . . . Topic
159LOG . . . Message 294 . . . Sun.
July 21, 1996 . . . 9:00:00
Questor 3 . . . Helsinger's Pit . . .
```

Q3: Problem with New Cain here resolved.
Altar prizes on the way. Enjoy and bask in
knowledge of the sacrifices. END TRANSMISSION,
Category 42, Topic 159LOG . . . 9:02:00

```
Category 42 . . . Topic 159LOG . . . Mes-
sage 295 . . . Sun. July 21, 1996 . . .
3:29:05
Questor 1
```

Q1: I look forward to the prize. You have
proved a true crusader and savior, my
knight. END TRANSMISSION, Category 42, Topic
159LOG . . . 3:30:01

•   •   •

Captain Phillip Lawrence's phone rang and he answered it,
knowing from his superior's strange habit of letting dead air
follow instead of announcing himself right away that it was
Commander Bryce. "Are you aware, Phil, that your precinct
shrink is looking into the Mootry killings on her own,
freelancing?"

"*I* told *you*, Commander, remember?"

"Oh, yeah . . . you did, didn't you."

"At the time, I thought like you. She's got a personal
stake, back off. But she's gotten everybody on the case
scratching at themselves. My detectives hate her guts."

Lawrence could almost see Bryce frowning, and he heard
the other man's groan clear enough. "What do you want me
to do that I haven't already done, Commander?"

"She gets in the way again, let me know. I'll give it some
thought from this end."

"Gotcha, will do."

"So, how're the kids, Phil?"

For some time, they talked of personal matters, ranging
from Lawrence's family to Andrew Bryce's wife to sports.
Bryce was always quick to put a man at ease, Lawrence
thought, although he hadn't known the commander long,
only since taking over as captain here at the Thirty-first, a
job Bryce might easily have awarded to another man. Yeah,
Bryce always put a man at ease . . . just before he handed
him an impossible task, thought Phil Lawrence as he waited
for the other shoe to drop. "I'm sorry, Phil, but until some
additional funds come in, we're going to have to refuse your
last budget request for more manpower. After all, the
academy just sent you fourteen additional foot soldiers and
this former detective, what's his name . . . Stonecoat?"

"Yeah, but I need additional detectives, Commander."

Bryce sighed, conveying a sense of defeat. "You understand, I hope."

"Sure . . . sure, sir . . . but I hope when cases go unsolved . . ." He thought better of it, letting it go as Bryce murmured sympathetically.

Lawrence heard the click at the other end. Bryce always did it the same way. Always hung up as if in the middle of a thought, no good-byes, no take cares, no see ya rounds. Was it bad manners or simply a man without enough time in the day?

Lawrence leaned back in his chair, placing his hands behind his head, giving further thought to Dr. Sanger. That bitch was single-handedly causing an uproar in Donavan's division over at the Twenty-second Precinct, where Detectives Amelford and Pardee were in charge of the Mootry murder investigation. Lawrence's department was unofficially being held accountable for the problems across town, thanks to Meredyth Sanger, who had caused the kind of uproar that was impossible to keep in-house. No doubt one or more of the detectives working the Mootry case had gone to Commander Bryce; more likely, one of them simply slipped him an anonymous note. Detectives, more so than any other breed, hated being shadowed or second-guessed. And Phil had not been out of it long, so he, too, understood the contempt with which Sanger was regarded by the detectives on the case.

"God, I wish I could control that nosy bitch," he muttered to the empty room. Giving it some thought, he was soon graced by a tight smile that spread across his lips. Maybe there was a way . . . a way that Andrew Bryce had himself suggested without realizing it. *Maybe she needs a scare thrown into her. If I weren't so constrained by my position . . .* He gave it some thought, and then quickly lifted the phone again and made a call.

•   •   •

Commander Bryce's secretary had interrupted his call to Phil Lawrence, stepping into the room. He didn't want anyone, including his trusted secretary, knowing about his interference with Lawrence's operation; it could look unseemly, politically incorrect for him to make any movement that could influence Lawrence's handling of the Mootry case. Mootry had been a judge and prominent figure in the area, as well as a friend, after all, and it would not sit well should some ambitious, hotshot reporter doing investigative work uncover the fact that Commander Bryce had a personal stake in the outcome of the Mootry investigation.

It was as his long-dead daddy had always told him: "The appearance of impropriety, son, is just as deadly as the impropriety itself." They were words to live by if you were in a political seat, and the job of commander of the Houston Police Department was only a few political rungs below the mayor. He equally believed in the notion that whether or not you knew what you were doing, you had to present yourself in action, word and deed as one who knew what he was doing, that looking like you were an expert was as important as being an expert. It was on such principles that he had conducted himself thus far in the public eye, and it had worked in ingenious fashion for him. So why change now?

Clarice, his secretary, a middle-aged but still handsome woman who'd been with him for years, urgently reminded him of his luncheon meeting with the deputy mayor, who would be interested in knowing the current dispensation of the Mootry matter. Donovan had given him all the data necessary to sound informed for the deputy mayor's benefit. Unfortunately, it appeared a case that might never be solved, as the killer or killers had left absolutely nothing in the way of useful clues.

He thanked Clarice, dismissed her and again sat in the silence of his enormous office. He'd worked extremely hard to be in this chair. Mootry's death was hardly cause for great alarm at this time, but he meant to monitor the case every step of the way. He momentarily wondered if he shouldn't reconsider Phil Lawrence's appointment as captain. He wasn't sure exactly why, but it had to do with competence or incompetence, one or the other outweighing all else. But who did he have to replace Phil with? Who could he trust . . . who could he really, truly trust?

He'd had to claw his way to the top of the crab heap, the others snatching, pinching, tearing at him the entire way. He had enemies in all the precincts, people who thought him inept, wrong for the job, dangerous, all manner of things, but none of them knew him; no one could ever know him entirely. Certainly not Phil Lawrence, Donovan, or any of his captains.

Bryce had friends, but no one in police circles, not anymore. It was the price he'd paid.

He snatched at the notes he meant to take to the deputy mayor, stood, and went for the door. He waved perfunctorily in Clarice's direction. Their affair had cooled many years before. He'd been good to her, keeping her on with him as he rose through the ranks, due in large measure to the fact that she respected his privacy and need for meditation. She had been like a rock and still remained a rock. Maybe he could trust her, but no one else on the inside, not anymore . . . not ever. . . . Everybody wanted to bring him down, and he must accept that fact, live with it or die (in the political sense and perhaps every other sense) ignoring it.

"Commander Bryce," Clarice called out. "Sergeant Kelton's on line three."

"Kelton, huh?" Kelton was his eyes and ears in Lawrence's

precinct. He needed to take this call, but he was running late.

"Shall I take a message?" Clarice politely asked.

"Tell 'im I'll call after one."

"Yes, sir . . . understood. . . ."

Bryce marched out and Clarice forwarded his message word for word.

$\mathcal{S}$EVEN

Coyote track

On their way back to pick up his car, Meredyth Sanger explained to Lucas Stonecoat what she'd gotten herself involved in, bringing him up to date on the Mootry investigation. As they drove, the images of the city floated by the car windows, rolled up tightly against the heat and city noise. He noticed that she ran her AC at full-tilt, so that her police band radio crackled with static as loud as a child's popgun.

"Hobby?" he foolishly asked.

"Business. Never know when you might be needed. The movies are the movies, the streets quite another."

He groaned. "How I know that."

"Anyway, when a first-timer discharges his weapon, we know he's going to have to talk to the likes of me. And sometimes . . . many times, in fact, even a vet needs my help. Sometimes I'm called in to help a victim or a family member, sometimes children who're involved."

"I guess you've seen a lot here, more so than in Washington?"

"I saw my fill in Seattle, but yeah . . . this place is wild."

"So, fill me in more on this Mootry case."

"Mootry was a rarity, a well-liked Texas politician for most of his life, more recently a retired appellate court judge, although from a close scrutiny of his dealings, you might say he pretty much bought his way into the appellate court. He had amassed a fortune, led something of a Ross Perot life. A generous man, though."

"Where were his views on abortion?"

"I've thought about that. He took the unpopular view that a woman's decision was a woman's decision where her body was concerned. He hedged a bit, calling the fetus a seed before the end of the first trimester. Anyway, I don't think he was killed by fanatical pro-lifers. His body was found mutilated, the head severed and taken away, along with other parts of him. I've never heard of an abortion-related murderer also being a hacker."

"Sex organs?"

"Among other things."

"What other things are there?"

Damn, even his dark humor is subtle, she told herself. "His hands and feet."

"Both hands, both feet?"

"You got it."

"Cut at the wrists?"

"Forearms, actually."

"Feet?"

"At the calf."

"Somebody really wanted this dead man hobbled. You're the shrink, maybe you can help me."

She smiled, nodding. "However I can."

"I'll never fully understand hacking up the body in such a way after the guy's dead."

"Indians did it."

"Sioux, Cheyenne, and other Plains Indians did it to mark a kill during a battle to send a message, to demonstrate to all other enemies just who had sent this particular enemy—say George Custer—over to the other side. So why do white murderers do it?"

She shrugged. "An FBI profile would likely come to the same conclusion as it might in a lovers' quarrel, that such an overkill means only one thing: that the killer knew his victim, had a vested, highly charged emotional interest in mutilating the body."

"Yeah, so the killer loved Judge Charles Mootry?"

"Loved him or hated him. The emotions are, while opposites on the spectrum, extremely close if the spectrum is a circle."

"So, in any case, the killer wanted Mootry deader than dead. By eating an enemy's heart, a warrior takes on the courage of his enemy. Taking his head, I don't begin to understand, nor his hands or feet, unless . . ."

"Go on," she encouraged.

"Old and foolish notions come to mind."

"I'm listening."

He shrugged. "There are ancient tribal stories among the Alabama that speak of supernatural creatures that fed on men; they were like vampires, and the only way to kill one was to strike it through the heart with a stake or spear." He paused to look up at her, to see if she was getting this.

"I'm with you so far," she said, as if reading his mind.

"It's foolish, but the old ones say you then cut off the monster's feet, so it can't walk, and the hands so it can't crawl, the head so it can't see, and the genitals so it can't reproduce."

She nodded. "All very sound reasoning when dealing with a supernatural enemy, I would think. Meanwhile, we're left with the torso sporting a high-tech, high-density, huge aluminum crossbow arrow straight through the heart. He died on impact."

Lucas's eyes widened, his breath coming short in a dry mouth. "He was killed by a . . . a crossbow, really?"

"Really."

"I guess I should've heard about this, if nowhere else than in the locker room. Where'd it happen?"

"In his bed."

"In his bed? Whereabouts?"

"At his home in the Bay area, where the killer somehow gained entry without using so much as a screwdriver."

"Another indication the killer knew the man . . ." Lucas lingered over the suggestion, finding himself naturally caught up in the mystery.

"It was believed he either forced his way in at gunpoint or talked his way past the threshold. Or he was someone known by the judge. Other than these possible scenarios . . . well, there's the sexual proclivities angle. Was the judge into sex games, autoerotica, anything of that nature? But this monster arrow made for one pretty deadly toy, if that's what was going on."

"Assuming it wasn't a lover of one sort or another, what's left? Who had reason to kill the judge? Was he a sentencing judge?"

"He had some big and well-known cases, but he was one of a number of judges on the court, so really, he had no known enemies. He adjudicated cases all his life, both criminal and civil offenses, nothing major except for the money involved."

"Until he bought his way into the hearts of the rich and powerful and found a seat on the appellate court, you mean?

People who lose appeals are generally at the end of a long rope. Good enough reason for most people to take a life."

She tried to steer him back on course even as she steered the car. "The brutalization of the body . . . you see, there were no signs whatsoever of a struggle, or that Judge Mootry had the remotest chance of escaping, since he'd made no attempt to do so."

"No signs of a struggle? No blood trails? Coroner puts it as death first, mutilation afterwards," he stated.

"You hit the nail right on the head."

"So, how did the killer waltz in with a speargun?"

"Crossbow, actually," she corrected him. "Very expensive, very high-tech. Sort you find in gun magazines for collectors."

"Sure, I've seen some at the gun shops. I've even hunted deer with one."

"Nobody knows for sure just how the killer got in or out. He got past Mootry's gates, his guard dogs, his alarm. Nothing, it seems, could save the judge that night. It's as if it were fated."

"Or well executed . . ."

"Another pun and I'll execute you."

"Certainly must have known the place well. I don't suppose anything useful was left at the crime scene by the killer?"

"Only a message written in the judge's blood."

"Really? What, on a wall?"

"No, with pen on paper."

"Really? Interesting . . ."

"It figures to be an old quill pen, according to the guys in Documents. They're studying the wording, the handwriting, everything."

"What'd the message say?"

"It's pretty straightforward: 'Cut off the limb of Satan.'"

"Sounds biblical."

"They're running it down, but I have a girlfriend who is a biblical scholar, and she tells me it's not a direct quote from any of the various translations of the Old or New Testament."

"That's interesting."

"Joanna says that although the sentiment sounds Christian enough, it's not specific to any texts she knows. Still, I'm guessing that this guy has some kind of fixation on himself being some sort of savior, and that for some reason, he singled out Mootry as one of the demons he is meant to destroy—the so-called limb of Satan, maybe . . . you see?"

"Or someone wants the authorities to believe it's all part of some bizarre shit."

"I knew you'd love it."

"You did, huh?" She had indeed read his record, he surmised. She simply knew too much about him. From the start, she had known all about Dallas as well. She was playing him like a fiddle, and he liked it.

They were back at Tank's Place, the shabby little neighborhood bar with the unlit neon Schlitz sign in the window and the peeling tiles and the raunchy awning. Meredyth pulled in beside Lucas's car, an olive-green, departmental issue, unremarkable, and unmarked Ford. Lucas remained cautious, unsure of her motives or if he ought to get involved, so he promised that he'd make no promises beyond going over the files she'd logged in and out during the past week. "Can't promise you much beyond that, since all I am is a rookie in care of dead files in the necromancy chamber."

"Thanks, that's all I ask, Lucas."

"Until I scan the files, I'll reserve judgment."

"Fair enough."

He slid from her car and closed the door and leaned in

when she automatically lowered the window. "My ancestors teach me caution in all matters. . . ."

"Oh, in all matters, no exceptions?"

"A careless step can leave a man without a moccasin and perhaps some other vital items," he joked.

She liked his easy way, how he joked about his heritage. "Such as?"

A heart, he wanted to say. "You name it," he said. "All things in moderation, angels rush in where fools fear to tread . . ."

"Now I know that's not sage Cherokee wisdom." She smiled wryly. "And besides, you've got it backwards. Fools rush in where angels fear to tread."

"Maybe it's not so backwards."

"What're you giving me, a compliment and a lecture? Rather backhanded of you."

"Did I say all that?" He quickly stepped away from her car and limped to his own.

Something about him made the limp almost admirable, certainly distinguishable; he wore it like a badge of honor, something he'd earned, she thought, despite the fact that in earning it, he'd almost died, and he had lost a partner, a wife, a home, and a career in one fell swoop. The facial scar, too, disappeared once she'd gotten to know him a little better, and she had enjoyed watching this big, powerful man talk to the animals as he doled out tiny food pellets like a Scrooge. She liked the way he had shown respect for the trapped, domesticated zoo animals, as if each had a soul.

Meredyth now watched his car pull from the curb, allowing Lucas to move off well ahead before she pulled into traffic. She wasn't any more anxious for people to see her with him than he was to be seen with her. She certainly didn't want anyone at the station house to see them returning together. God only knew what great palaver that'd create around the watercooler. Besides, the less others knew of her plans at this point, the better, including Lucas Stonecoat. "And another besides," she told herself and the empty car, "he's dangerous."

She had heard and read enough about his accident, and his run at suing the City of Dallas for damages, to know that he was indeed a dangerous ally, and she knew enough about herself to know that she liked having a little danger in her life. She knew that this particular, tall, handsome Cherokee man was a tinderbox ready to explode at the slightest provocation. If rumors started flying that he was seeing her personally, there was little telling what might happen. One thing was certain. She didn't want to frighten him off now.

Despite the automobile accident that had nearly cost him his life, Lucas Stonecoat barked his tires and rammed home his fist into his horn at every turn. He drove with the abandon of a man who truly believed that every other driver on the road was completely insane, and that to escape any injury or accident, he must race ahead or around the maniacs surrounding him. He had long since lost any sight of Dr. Sanger's vehicle.

Lucas thought about Dr. Meredyth Sanger all the way back to the Thirty-first Precinct house. Meeting her in a social setting, opening up to her, strolling about the city zoo alongside her . . . it almost made going back to his cell bearable. The two bourbons hadn't harmed him any, either. Maybe there was hope for him here in Houston, despite the shock of the Cold Room and the rather nasty possibility that Phil Lawrence had placed him there due to both his past history and his genes.

But it had to figure that Dr. Meredyth Sanger—Mere, as he liked to think of her—also had her ulterior motives, since she was both white and a shrink. He'd had his fill of shrinks and others who talked in riddles and circles and never-ending meanderings, their meaningless loops like so many petroglyphs so far as he was concerned. Not that his own race wasn't guilty of the same. Some of his grandfather's talk was like falling into a bottomless spiral, the riddles within riddles endless. When it confused an enemy, true Indian gibberish was a thing of beauty, he told himself now.

Maybe Sanger was different, maybe not. Either way, she certainly seemed to delight in challenging him at every turn, and how gracefully she carried that disquieting little smirk which magically turned into a disarming smile whenever she wanted her way. *As charming as a multicolored diamondback rattler,* he thought. The more colorful, the more poisonous, and she could mean plenty more trouble than he'd been looking to find—in more ways than one.

Maybe if she wasn't a psychiatrist . . . then there might be a snowflake's chance; since she was, he wondered why the question was even wafting through his head. It was a preposterous notion, that maybe he and Dr. Sanger could be more than just friends, when in fact they weren't even friends and weren't likely to become friends . . . ever.

Still, she wanted an alliance against Phil Lawrence, who represented a threat to her. "And that's all she wants, you fool," he told himself, "an alliance, backup, to build her case . . . possibly a fall guy if things go badly, and that's all she's interested in."

He wheeled the car sharply at the next corner, squealing already burning tires. The police band calls rattled about the cab, still nothing he might reasonably respond to.

Lucas was just glad that he'd remained cautiously aloof, and wary of her motives—the reserved Indian. There was little telling what her hidden agenda might be.

He didn't care for her constant need to know everything about him, her prying questions, yet he'd volunteered much. Still, what was there to volunteer? She had known it all before in one form or another. On the drive back to the bar, she'd asked him where he had grown up.

"Born and raised on the Coushatta Indian Reserve," he had replied.

"But you got out . . . ahh, off, I mean?"

"Scholarship to Yale," he'd joked, making her laugh again. He liked teasing a laugh from her.

"You'll have to tell me about it sometime." Which translated to: You'll have to tell me the truth sometime.

He made no such promises.

For all he knew now, an alliance of any sort with Meredyth Sanger could make matters worse for them both, and he was particularly concerned about his rookie standing, and the fact that one day he wanted very much to get shed of the Cold Room and all the duties that went along with it. After all, Lawrence was holding the cards, yanking the chains, in charge in toto, so pissing the man off would be sheer suicide. Maybe if he played by the rules for a while . . . maybe if he could impress Lawrence . . .

Obviously, he wasn't going to impress Lawrence by joining Meredyth Sanger in some crusade to declare Mootry's death one of several in a series, the work of the same killer.

Dr. Sanger had obviously never been turned down by a man before, or perhaps she'd never known a real man before. Most certainly she'd never lost a fight—or perhaps anything else, for that matter—in her life. He guessed she came from money; old or new, it mattered little to him. She was white and upper-crust. Used to getting her way, having others do what she said was best. Spoiled, well-off, no dirt ever beneath the nails.

Lucas thought momentarily of his parents, an alcoholic father who provided nothing and a mother who slaved at two jobs to provide Lucas with creature comforts and books to feed his insatiable appetite. They had little else besides corn and books in the house, and one day his father, in a drunken rage, made a bonfire of Lucas's books. It was then, after he'd struck his father and almost killed him with a single blow, that the nearly full grown Lucas knew it was time to leave the reserve and his home, his mother and his grandfather, to seek a new life in the larger world. He found himself in downtown Dallas, where he applied to the police academy, sailed through the tests, and was soon a rookie in a patrol car.

At that time, the Dallas PD had been delighted to place an Indian on the force: It looked good on the books, having a Native American alongside the Chicano and Black officers. After a series of failed partnerships, he was put into a car with Wallace Jackson.

Lucas now spied a Texaco gas station, pulled over, and went inside, asking for the newspapers. He wanted any back issues the Star Mart might carry, as well as today's paper. They had two back issues and today's. He purchased them, along with a bag of chips, and stared out at a rust bucket just pulling into the station. Something told him that the two characters inside the car were hardened rednecks who were out for more than just a pleasant drive this morning.

He'd already paid, and the cashier looked curiously at him now, wondering what else he wanted. "I'm with the Houston police, son," he told the young man behind the counter. "You got a couple of toughs coming through the door who look a bit suspicious to me. Don't argue with them if they want you to open the cash box. Got it?"

"Yes, sir."

"You got a back room, a john, anything where I can duck outta sight?"

"Yeah, straight back," came the nervous reply. "Should I call the cops?"

"Not yet. No crime's been committed," Lucas replied over his shoulder as he went for the back room. He positioned himself behind the door.

The two scruffy-looking men who came through the door looked as if they'd stepped from a bayou swamp. Each wandered different aisles and sections of the store, one passing near where Stonecoat lay in wait. The man reeked of booze and looked as if he'd been snaking or frog-gigging or involved in an old-fashioned crawdad hunt the night before. Both men had forgotten how to bathe or shave or trim hair. But it was more than their appearance and smell that alerted Lucas to their purpose; it had been their actions, the way they moved, the shifting of their eyes since the moment they had driven up. Best-case scenario, they'd come in to shoplift, he told himself now, since they were browsing. Worst case—but the thought remained incomplete when the man closest to the register suddenly pulled out a .22 and shouted for the money. The second man was hopping, hyper, a gun in his hand, too. It looked like his first job ever. He let his partner do all the talking while he grabbed at the bills in the register.

"On the floor, faggot! Now!" ordered the guy in charge.

Both men were white. The younger one called the boss Gerald, asking if they should rifle the clerk's pockets, saying there looked to be only a few hundred dollars in the register.

"Do it, pinhead!" shouted the boss.

Stonecoat saw this as his chance. He silently moved to within inches of the brains of the outfit and leveled his gun against the man's temple.

"Tell your pal to toss his gun over the counter and squat back there, friend. Police! Now do it!"

"Jesus, Joseph, and Mary."

"Shut up and do as I said!"

"Mickey . . . Mickey, some cop out here's got a gun at my freaking brain, so do what he says!"

But Mickey had other ideas. He rose with the clerk held in front of him, his gun at the young man's head. He somehow had gotten some nerve. "Looks like a Mexican standoff. You blow Gerald away, I kill the kid," he said. "Otherwise, you drop it and you let us walk out of here."

"No way I'm dropping my weapon, mister," replied Stonecoat. "You let the kid go, and I'll let you two walk, but I'm not so trusting that I'm going to be at the mercy of you two without my weapon. Is that clear?"

"You mean that?" asked Gerald.

"We can't believe he's going to just let us go, Gerald," replied Mickey, whose gun hand was shaky at best.

"I'll lower my gun," suggested Stonecoat. "And you let the kid go, and you two can get back in your car and go."

"With the money," negotiated Mickey.

Lucas hesitated, pretending to give this serious thought. "Okay . . . all right, with the money."

"Deal . . . deal," shouted Gerald, reaching about the floor for his gun, which Lucas held firmly beneath his boot.

"Let it up, man!" Gerald ordered.

"No, I can't have two guns trained on me," Lucas coolly answered.

Gerald raised up again and shouted, "Come on, Mickey, let's get out of here. Now!"

Gerald hurried over to the counter, shoved the kid away, scooped up all the money, and started out, while Mickey's gun remained firmly trained on Lucas, who had lowered his own weapon. For a second, Mickey stared down the top of the barrel, itching to fire, to kill the obstacle before him.

Lucas calmly said, "Don't do anything stupid, Mickey. Don't do anything you'll regret for the rest of—"

"Shut up! Just shut up, man!"

"Lucas. My name's—"

"Shut up!"

"Come on, Mickey! Let's go, damn you!" cried Gerald, who was halfway out the door as another patrol car approached.

"Give Gerald his gun back, now!" shouted Mickey at Lucas.

"All right . . . all right, kid." Lucas booted the .22 across the floor toward the door and Gerald, who crouched for it, his hands already full. At the instant he kicked, Lucas brought his gun up and Mickey fired, the bullet creasing Lucas's ear, bloodying his shoulder, while Lucas's bullet sent Mickey sprawling into the cigarette display behind him.

Gerald, still crouching for his gun, was now frozen in that crouch, looking like some stone gargoyle.

"Go ahead, Gerald," said Stonecoat. "It's your turn now."

Gerald's mouth had fallen open after repeated shouts of Mickey's name. It was almost certain they were related, perhaps cousins, down on their luck. Gerald had gotten himself into much more than he'd bargained for, and young Mickey had "proven" himself a man—proven nothing, in the phony ritual of the street.

Gerald crawled toward his friend or relative, whimpering, but Lucas grabbed him and yanked viciously, sending him far across the room and ordering him to stay put there on the floor. He had taken charge of Gerald's gun again, and he wasn't sure what he might find behind the counter. The clerk had raced from the store and across the street to a Jiffy Mart to dial 911 there.

"Now, Mickey, if you can hear me," began Stonecoat, "I don't want to hurt you anymore, so don't do anything more stupid than you already have here this afternoon. You got that? Answer me! Answer me!"

But only silence answered from behind the counter.

Lucas rounded the counter with great care and caution; Mickey still had a gun back there with him somewhere. But one look told him that the young man was unconscious and bleeding profusely from his shoulder, where the bullet from Stonecoat's .38 had penetrated and exited his back.

"Damn it, Gerald, he's bleeding to death! Get me one of those trash bags off the shelf! Hurry!"

Gerald instantly reacted, racing over with a box of bags.

"Open 'em, damn it!"

Gerald slammed a fist into the box and tore out a large plastic bag, black and shimmering. "Whataya doing?"

"Locate some string, rope, fishing string, anything we can use to tie with."

Gerald did as instructed, racing about the store for the needed items even as a siren blew into the lot outside. He rushed back to Lucas with a large ball of twine, kite string.

By now Stonecoat had ripped the bag with his Bowie knife, which he kept in a scabbard in the middle of his back, and he now quickly forced a large section of the black vinyl into both the front and back wounds to stanch the flow of blood. He now worked furiously to tie the string round and round the shoulder to hold the plastic pads in place.

"Whataya doing?" Gerald asked again.

"This will help keep the blood flow in check, help the coagulation."

"Damn, you sure shot hell out of my brother-in-law; why'd you have to shoot him? All over a measly hundred dollars! You had to force it, didn't you? Damn you cops. Is he going to die?"

"You two come in here using deadly force, placing people's lives in danger, and you're shifting the blame for your friend's condition onto me? Listen, Gerald, you got no one but yourselves to blame for this goddamned mess."

"How'd he miss you at such close range?" Gerald wondered aloud.

"His hand was shaking like a leaf when he pulled the trigger. He might just as well have put a bullet through my head or heart. Did you talk him into this stupid business?"

Now the paramedics rushed in alongside uniformed police, who ordered Stonecoat up and away from the shooting victim.

"I'm a cop with the Thirty-first," he announced, flashing his badge. "Best call my captain, Phil Lawrence, and he'll take it from there. You men want to take this punk into custody for attempted armed robbery?" He shoved Gerald toward the uniformed men.

"Be glad to."

"Hey, you're new with the Thirty-first, aren't you?" asked the other.

"Yeah, first year."

"Way to go, rookie. Looks like a righteous collar and shoot. You keep up the good work and you'll see promotion soon."

"Just happened to be in the right place at the right time."

The clerk had returned through the other side door and he piped up, saying, "He saved my life, and he read these goons like a book; he knew they were going to rob the place before they ever got into the store, before they ever got out of their car out there."

"Impound the vehicle, will you?" Stonecoat asked the two uniformed cops, who appeared to be unsure about what to do next.

The paramedics shouted for everyone to get out of their

way as they hoisted Mickey from the ground on a stretcher and carried him from the store, one of them congratulating Stonecoat on saving the kid's life. "Good improvised dressing! Did the trick. His vitals aren't great, but they're better than they might have been."

The two uniformed cops took Gerald toward their waiting squad car. Other police vehicles had arrived, strobe lights flashing. One patrol sergeant, who apparently knew the terrain well, huddled with the cops in the know, then he came into the store to find Lucas.

"I'm Brady, Jim Brady," he told Stonecoat. "Watch commander for this area. Seems you're a little ways off from the Thirty-first, officer. What's your name, officer?"

"Lucas, Lucas Stonecoat."

"Rookie with the Thirty-first, my men tell me. Oh, yeah . . . think I've heard some talk about you. Used to be in the Dallas–Fort Worth area, didn't you?"

"Yeah, yeah . . . that's right, Sergeant, but I don't see where that has anything to do with this occurrence here today."

"I sure hope not." He sized up Lucas, circling him and talking the whole time. "IAD's on the way. Your captain's on his way, too."

"It was a righteous shoot, sir," replied Lucas, knowing the man wanted to hear him say the word *sir*.

$\mathcal{E}$IGHT

Hogan: home, permanence

Lucas had to admit that what had begun as a dismal, uneventful day had quickly transmogrified into an exciting, exhilarating and challenging day after all. He'd met a vivacious woman who was passionate about her work— perhaps too passionate about her work—had visited the animals in the zoo, had foiled a robbery attempt by two other animals, and what's more, he had been cheered to see his captain come straight to the Texaco station and back him one hundred percent. Lawrence had done all he could to shield his new recruit from the onslaught of Internal Affairs detectives, a breed of cop always anxious for a scandal. It appeared that Captain Lawrence wasn't half so bad as Dr. Sanger had made him out to be. Whatever personal and professional differences existed between Sanger and Lawrence, Lucas was sure of one thing: He didn't want to get in between a rock and a hard place.

Lucas now pulled into a parking spot at the rear of the

Thirty-first, near a back door that would take him into the precinct without his having to pass either the sergeant's cage or the squad room. He wasn't anxious to face his big Irish sergeant just now, nor the detectives and officers who would want all the dope on what went down at the gas station. Word got around a precinct faster than a hairdresser's.

Lucas now scooped up his assorted newspapers and headed toward the building and back to the Cold Room, where he had a couple more hours to kill before going off duty. The newspaper stories on the Mootry case would keep him occupied till then, he was sure. Maybe he'd get through this day after all.

He quickly located the staircase that took him down into the bowels of the old structure and to the Cold Room, the stack of *Houston Chronicle*s and *Star-Standard*s under his arm.

Reopening the dank room, he found it a stone coffin. Looking around at his small kingdom, a dungeon in the belly of the Thirty-first Precinct, wondering if every god-damned precinct in the lousy city had a Cold Room, he mentally reconsidered Dr. Sanger's offer with a glacial, determined eye. On the one hand, he told himself, he had a great deal more to lose than did Dr. Sanger in sticking his neck out on a case he had no business on; on the other hand, what had he to lose? His dark little castle of moldy case files, the faceless, lost orphans of murder dating back to the turn of the century?

Still, it would require some quiet deliberation. He'd have to weigh all the facts, review the information on the Mootry case, see what if anything it had to do with the case files Dr. Sanger had mentioned. Still, he was no one's fool. He realized how crazy it'd be to team up with Meredyth Sanger. "What does she know about criminal investigation any-way?" he asked himself. Still, she could be his ticket out of here, if not for good, then at least during their investigation into this matter together. *And what might that lead to?* he wondered. There was no telling.

He suddenly slumped into the shocked and protesting chair, its piercing wail an ear-shattering banshee scream that could curdle the blood of the toughest cop in the precinct. He imagined it must be echoing through the heart of the old building and hurting everyone else's ears and teeth as much as his own. *Christ, am I getting that heavy?* he silently wondered.

As comfortable as he was going to get, he flicked on the swivel lamp and scanned the papers for all the news on Charles D. Mootry, Esquire, now deceased. After three-quarters of an hour spent scanning the various articles he'd collected, he decided aloud, "Not much more than what Meredyth had to say has gotten into the press." This was true so far as he could determine from the articles read, but the case itself was rather an incredible one, something for Gary Larson's *Far Side* or Ripley's *Believe It or Not*.

It had all the earmarks of a Movie of the Week, too.

He next dug out the file that Dr. Sanger had carelessly tossed below his desk lamp early that morning. At first he just picked at the file the way he might a blemish on his skin, and he helplessly wondered how much of the file material she'd duplicated on the station Xerox. He finally, without enthusiasm, thumbed the file open and peered at the police reports and ghastly photos she had been playing with. Inside the innocent-looking, cream-colored manila folder, now yellow with age, an abhorrent world of black-and-white crime scene photos stared back, like grinning devils, displaying broken and irreparable lives; lives lost to the ultimate discontinuity: murder.

The older case file held a nightmare similar to the Mootry affair; in fact, it was shockingly similar to what had

occurred in Baytown, where Mootry's body had been
discovered, but this was a case in Sugar Land, and this one
was—by police file standards—ancient, dated 1986. One
of the ads clinging to the news clippings he found said that
gasoline was eighty-seven cents a gallon. President Ronald
Reagan was in office; the paper was filled with news of an
armed U.S. strike against Libya, this after several terrorist
bombings Libya was believed connected to. *Ferris Bueller's
Day Off* was playing at the movies and *Me and My Girl*
topped the musicals list. The largest U.S. corporation
according to *Fortune* was General Motors, and a dispute
was waged over AIDS virus research in which the Patent
and Trademark office designated the Pasteur Institute of
Paris as the senior party rather than the U.S. National
Institutes of Health, in the matter of the first AIDS blood
test. At stake were millions of royalty dollars to be earned
by the use of the test.

Stonecoat could only recall that it was the year that the
North American Soccer League went belly-up with great
financial losses to all involved. This memory triggered his
recollection of several more events in '86 that he had taken
particular note of. It was the year the Chicago Bears
defeated the New England Patriots to become world cham-
pions in Super Bowl XX. It was the year Ivan Boesky
agreed to pay the government one hundred million dollars
as a penalty for illegal insider trading, while Congress voted
to make the rose the official U.S. flower, a choice debated
off and on for a hundred years. Roger Clemens, pitcher for
the Boston Red Sox, started the season with thirteen straight
wins—only the seventh man in history to do so; the World
Series was lost by the Boston Red Sox, won by the New
York Mets in a stunning upset. Len Bias, star forward for the
University of Maryland, died of a heart attack reportedly
brought on by the use of cocaine at a party celebrating his

signing a contract with the Boston Celtics; the space shuttle Challenger exploded seventy-four seconds after liftoff at Cape Canaveral, Florida, killing all seven astronauts aboard, including civilian Christa McAuliffe, thirty-seven, a Concord, New Hampshire, schoolteacher, the first private citizen chosen for a space shuttle flight. On August 20 the third worst murder spree in U.S. history took place in Edmond, Oklahoma, when Patrick Henry Sherrill shot and killed fourteen of his former coworkers, wounded six others, and then killed himself, after losing his post office job. In Leicestershire, England, Dr. Alec Jeffreys had discovered genetic fingerprinting, and the test for DNA evidence was put to work for the first time on a criminal case the following year. And the first American Indian to become a Roman Catholic bishop, the Reverend Donald E. Pelotte, forty-one, was ordained in Gallup, New Mexico.

Among law enforcement officials, 1986 was also remembered as the year crack cocaine came on the scene.

Stonecoat brought his mind back to the man for whom the death file was named. He knew he must go slow and easy to fully appreciate just how similar these two deaths were: Mootry today and this professional man, this medical doctor, some ten years before. Dr. Wesley Palmer had been murdered in his bed in the same brutal fashion, a steel arrow through his chest, his head severed, along with hands, feet, penis and testicles. These body parts were carried off by the madman. This had occurred at the doctor's home some six months after his arrival in the area.

The maniac had coolly gained entry to the house, found the doctor asleep in his bed, and mercilessly fired an arrow from a crossbow. As indicated in the report, the hundred pounds plus pressure behind the arrow was enough power to split apart the man's heart and send the arrow cleanly through to the floor beneath the bed.

The forensics report read like déjà vu: The arrow in each case had been placed point-blank at a location that assured the heart would burst immediately. In each case, Mootry's and the older case, the deadly arrow had in fact been recovered from *below* each of the dead men's beds. This suggested that one, the killer had no trouble gaining entry or getting close to his victim with a large and deadly weapon, and two, perhaps the killer had some working knowledge of anatomy, since in both cases the killer had obviously managed to avoid both breastbone and ribs. According to the records, the arrow had slammed into and run completely through each victim's heart as if that were the practiced purpose.

And if the killer knew something of anatomy, then perhaps he shared the same profession as Dr. Wesley Palmer, the 1986 victim. After all, deadly doctors abounded in the annals of crime.

Lucas was now thoroughly entranced.

He went back and forth between the fresh ink of today's news clippings and a musty handful that had remained all these years in the Palmer file. He pored over the police reports and FBI reports, all of which led to so many dead ends. Usually serial killings with such a closely linked pattern happened within months, often weeks, of one another, sometimes days of one another, but these two killings were separated by ten years. It didn't figure.

According to the record, Dr. Wesley J. Palmer, like Judge Mootry, had been clean. No ties to organized crime, no outstanding gambling debts, no angry clients or customers, no relatives or others with a grudge. In fact, like Mootry, the man had been well liked, well respected, apparently by all who knew him, save a pair of would-be in-laws, parents to a young lady the doctor had planned to marry when the young woman's untimely death had ended all such plans. The woman's death was some sort of mystery in itself, and her parents had concocted the idea that Dr. Palmer had somehow caused her death. Lucas made a mental note to check more deeply into the young fiancée's death, but however bitter her parents were at the time of her death, they were, in 1986, completely absolved of any wrongdoing surrounding Dr. Palmer, their alibi standing despite a vigorous effort on the part of police to bring a charge of murder. Lucas's eyes widened at the reason investigators were convinced, for a time, that the elderly couple had acted on a revenge motive: Palmer had been dispatched in identical fashion as his fiancée! Lucas dropped his feet from his desk and rode his squealing chair to an upright position on seeing this.

How had she died? He searched the report for more information. It was vital to know how the fiancée had died the year before; what did the '86 coppers mean by "dispatched in identical fashion"? Did they actually mean by bow and arrow?

He could find but scant details of the earlier death filed with Palmer's paperwork. What he found was far too sketchy. Still, he read all there was on the 1985 Alisha Reynolds, Marietta, Georgia, case mentioned in the file. The information about the previous murder of the doctor's fiancée in Palmer's former palatial home in Georgia was teeth-gnashingly superficial and insufficient.

Lucas searched high and low for more information on the dead fiancée, but there was no more here. Had Meredyth Sanger lifted it? There had to be more. How precisely did Dr. Palmer's fiancée die? Was there some revenge motive in the Palmer case that involved the dead girl? Had the parents hired a hit man in retaliation after the courts found Dr.

Wesley Palmer innocent in the wrongful death of his intended bride? Had she been strangled, shot, poisoned? Had she been given too many barbiturates or uppers? Had she stumbled off a balcony? The damned reports were infuriatingly silent on exact cause of the woman's death, as if details of her death had been ripped from the file and tossed out as unimportant, the only tantalizing smidgen of detail left the single phrase "dispatched in identical fashion" to Palmer's own death. Could he trust this image? And if so, did this mean there were three intended victims of the crossbow killer? Or had the fiancée stepped into the crossfire?

Was it possible that the parents, a year later, still filled with grief over the loss of their daughter, hired a professional who preferred the sound of an arrow to the sound of a gun? That could explain the coincidence of a ten-year separation in "jobs" for this killer, but it wouldn't explain who killed the daughter.

Lucas made another notation to check the national crime files for any information on professional hits or hit men who used a crossbow or bow and arrow. It seemed as far-fetched as finding an alien hit man or a Geronimo out of time, but it could sound off some bleeps and alarms, so he'd give it a try. But then, perhaps Dr. Sanger had already done as much. He didn't want to ask her, however. Instead, he wanted to dig a little deeper before committing himself to her little covert operation.

Just as in the hit movie *Pulp Fiction*, hit men did come in all sizes, shapes, colors, sexes, and brainpan sizes these days; perhaps there was one out there with a Robin Hood fetish? Maybe he or she even wore tights? If it was a she, that might explain how she had gotten so close to two men—at their bedsides—with a deadly weapon the size of a shotgun.

Lucas needed a break. The information was coming in too fast for him, and his legs needed stretching, and his back was beginning to trouble him again. If he was going to be behind a desk for as many hours as this a day, he would have to get a contoured, expensive-as-hell chair like the one Johnnie Cochran and the rest of the O. J. dream team had had for the duration of what had become the longest trial in the history of jurisprudence in America and the world.

On a notepad, he jotted down the name of Palmer's fiancée—Alisha Reynolds—along with a note about her parents, Dick and Mildred Reynolds of 1224 Cherry Lane Drive, Marietta, Georgia. By now they could have moved out of the country, or out of life, he reminded himself even as he wrote. Still, he'd have to find out what he could about the would-be in-laws. Most crime started in the home, in one fashion or another.

Lucas pondered further what he'd learned about the similarities in the Mootry and Palmer cases. Why were these supposed good men, pillars of the community, targeted for murder in such heinous fashion? What did both men have in common? What clubs did they belong to? Did Mootry know something about the Palmer case? Had he known Dr. Palmer? Had he known of Palmer's murder? What did he know about the earlier problem in Georgia, when Palmer's fiancée was killed? Was Mootry dispatched for what he knew about Palmer? Had the judge ever been to Georgia? Did the judge know Alisha Reynolds's parents, perhaps? Perhaps.

While the cleanly efficient method of dispatching both men seemed wholly practiced and professional, why decapitate and remove hands and feet and private parts? That was not the sort of work your usual hit man bought into. He didn't want to leave the scene covered in blood; he didn't want to make a mess. So why the mutilation of the two bodies? It certainly didn't seem to be for reasons a hit man would enjoy. Hit men and women worked on one principle and it was called lucrative payment. They were mercenaries, pure and simple. Lucas had a hard time imagining a pro who would have anything to do with gratuitous bloodletting, unless . . . unless he was paid a great deal more for the extra show?

Whether a hired killer or just a nutcase, was the after-death mutilation an effort on the part of the murderer to shock authorities, confuse or slow the process of identification? If so, why leave the torso in the dead man's home? And how did the killer gain entrance? And did his victim know him, even trust him?

"Damn that Meredyth Sanger," he muttered to himself. Without knowing it, she had hooked him like a marlin.

He wondered if he ought to simply call her and tell her that he knew she was withholding information about Palmer's fiancée and facts surrounding that case just to keep him on her damned string.

Instead, Lucas stood now, stretched, and decided that since it couldn't be Miller time yet, he'd locate the coffee station upstairs, take a break and come back at this thing fresh. It hadn't surprised him that neither Captain Phillip Lawrence, Duty Sergeant Stanley Kelton, nor anyone else for that matter, had interrupted him all afternoon. This place was not inviting; in fact, it was ignored, the pretense being that it didn't exist, and by extension, neither did he.

He went for that coffee.

The coffee station stood alongside the active homicide board, on which the names of victims were placed in red ink alongside the name of the detective in charge of the case. Cases in red ink meant they were open; cases placed on the left-hand side of the board, scripted in black ink, meant they were closed. There was no pen color or place on the board

for the cases that went unsolved. They merely disappeared
from the board when Lawrence decided it was time to call
a halt to the "waste of taxpayers' money" on a case that
wasn't ever going to be solved, usually when it was two or
three years old. Many cases came in with the name of the
perpetrator all but emblazoned on them, but what cops
termed a stone-hard mystery was that rare case in which
whodunit is unclear and sometimes completely invisible.
Sometimes, many times, even the stone-hard mystery could
be solved, but often it took years to do so. More and more,
departments were unwilling or unable to apportion manpower and man hours of that duration to a single case, so
that rooms like Lucas's had begun to swell at the seams.

Every city in America had such cases; every precinct in
the city had such cases. For the Thirty-first Precinct, such
homicides wound up as dust collectors in what was now
Lucas Stonecoat's necromancy collection. It had always
been referred to as the Dungeon, the Graveyard and the
Cold Room, but already the cops upstairs were referring to
it in various cute ways for Lucas's benefit, names such as
Lucas's Lodge and, Stonecoat's *X-Files*. They were also
calling Lucas "Spooky" just to further annoy him.

Nine

Lightning & lightning arrow: fast, swift

A LONELY STRETCH OF INTERSTATE 5 OUTSIDE ROGUE RIVER, OREGON

Timothy Kenneth Little felt a dull, pounding throb tolling with the rhythmic back-and-forth of a bell against his temple. It'd been a trying day, and the long trip to the Rogue River plant had required a two-junket flight that got him only as far as Medford's little municipal airport. Eugene, Oregon, was just too bloody far from the plant to be of any damned use whatsoever, and he cursed himself these days for not having had the foresight to've leased a similar parcel of property in Eugene in the early days rather than taking the cheaper route and building in Rogue River. But back then every dollar had to be accounted for. End result? A plantful of people in Rogue River had jobs, thanks to him, and there was no taking those jobs elsewhere now. Bottom line? He now had one *helluva* long, difficult drive ahead of him, and his back was acting up, and his neck was killing him. Turning fifty was a bitch, and that, too, was preying on his mind.

At least he'd done something with his life. Not like his brother, Thom, who was still cutting other people's lawns and frying eggs, bacon and ham as a short-order cook in San Francisco, where when he wasn't working he was catching the latest wave, a ridiculous, aging surfer.

Timothy Little had never stood a surfboard, had never been athletic at anything in his life, but he had been a careful investor, and now he owned sixteen plants around the nation, plants that made aircraft parts which were always in demand—the convenient little kitchen apparatuses needed aboard every jet airliner. He'd tried to get Thom interested in the business, but Thom declared he'd go homeless before he'd take charity from his little brother.

He wasn't by any stretch the wealthiest man on the continent, but if this were France, maybe. . . . Still, his loved ones didn't want for a thing. All the boys were grown up, following careers of their own, each with a family of his own, nice houses and cars, and they all owed it to their pop, a man who'd been as a pre-teen and teen what all the other kids in school called a pencil-carrying nerd. Thank God his interest in science and gadgetry never waned, paying off handsomely in the long run. Where were the jocks who'd bullied him throughout high school now? he curiously wondered as yet another discourteous driver the other side of the highway blinded him with high beams.

"Bastard!" he uselessly shouted while flipping his own brights on and off—another useless gesture.

The brights hitting his eyes conspired with the thumping headache to make him feel a creeping nausea rising within him. He tried to concentrate on the importance of the trip, the big merger with ASCAN, and how best to break it to the people at the plant, put the most positive spin on it.

Hell, he wasn't getting any younger. And if something should happen to him, God forbid, say a heart attack?

Where would it leave the company? If he sold out, and if ASCAN followed through on its promises, everyone—not just him—would benefit in the long run. It would mean more overtime, more money for everyone all around, and he could retire, begin to enjoy the fruits of all the years of intensive labor he'd put in.

He felt good about himself and the direction his life had taken him. Thought briefly about Lenore back in California, waiting for his call, no doubt. They had had another argument about money. He had wanted to, as they say, "give some back," and Lenore had always supported him in his charitable donations in the past, but for some reason she had had a strange and urgent dislike for an old acquaintance from college who had contacted him for a donation, suggesting that he leave part of his estate to the religious organization his old friend now represented.

Timothy and Lenore Little were of the same faith, after all, and so why shouldn't he be charitable toward his church? Lenore simply didn't like the approach his college friend had taken.

Without telling Lenore, he'd gone ahead and made the donation, along with others to organizations he believed in and supported. For his old friend, he had gone a step further, signing over one of his many life insurance policies to the friend, who was now a Jesuit priest in Texas. His friend had contacted him via computer modem to tell him of their needs in Texas.

The dusk of evening was giving way to that twilight moment when visibility was at its worst. Timothy Little kept his eyes on the road, popped a cassette of relaxing, old-time piano music by Billy Vaughn into the player, and took a deep, long breath of air. On his left, on the grass median between the divided highway, he noticed a silver-gray van that might be in trouble. But what next caught his attention was the man atop the van on his belly. He was dressed all in black, like someone out of a Bruce Willis *Die Hard* film, like someone wanting to blend in with the night.

"My God, if he doesn't look like some sort of commando sniper preparing to fire," Little said to himself.

Then Timothy saw movement at the base of the van on either side, two additional black-clad men. They truly did look like bloody assassins out of a Hollywood action-hero movie or something. Each man was holding up some sort of telescope or weapon; he could not tell for sure. He was moving sixty miles per hour, the car on cruise control, careful at all times to obey the traffic laws and speed limits, but now for some insane reason, he thought these strange, alien-looking creatures on the grassy knoll ahead were going to fire high-powered rifles at him. So he instantly forced the gas pedal to the floor.

The speedometer on the Olds Cutlass immediately rose to sixty-five, then seventy. Suddenly the windshield shattered in front of Timothy, glass and blood showering his line of vision, his right arm throbbing, but a second powerful blow like a fist to his chest negated all sight and feeling, save the cold numbness and dark blindness that spread through him like a moving current.

My God, he thought, *they've killed me . . . but who . . . who are they?*

He didn't know that his car was skidding off the road or that he'd blacked out all in the space of a nanosecond.

One of two arrows pierced his heart, which sprayed forth blood across the wheel and dash as the car careened out of control, first veering into the median, heading straight for the van, just barely missing it and sheering off before bumping back up onto the shoulder tarmac from which it had come, decelerating as it went into the right-hand ditch, bumping along this trench for another forty yards before coming to an abrupt, dead standstill, thanks to a tree. The impact sent Timothy Little's body lurching forward, but the body was saved any meeting with the jagged, shattered windshield not by the air bag or the seat belt but by the two steel arrows that had pinned him in place like a marionette.

The assassins brought the van around behind the wrecked vehicle, and like dark vultures they descended on Timothy Little. They had to wrench him from the car seat, where both his chest and an arm were pinned to the cushions by the steel shafts of the arrows that'd killed him. His heart was still pumping blood, but he was in such a state of shock and dying that he didn't feel a thing when they tore him from the cab, laid him out across the hood, and efficiently went to work on removing his extremities.

One of the assassins worked to decapitate Little's head, with its bulging eyes and grimacing teeth, necessarily causing a great gout of blood in the process. The blood ran in many small rivers over contours of the rental car, and several unusual dents across the hood of the car were left where the meat cleavers had done their work.

A passing motorist's lights momentarily shone on them, but the driver, speeding at well over sixty-five, didn't give them a thought beyond the minimal, *Car trouble . . . glad it's not me . . . .*

Meanwhile, Timothy Little's feet, hands and head were bagged in two separate large plastic Hefty bags. These were thrown into the back of the van as one of the assassins climbed in.

The other two climbed into the cab, the engine still running. Cigarettes were lit, great breaths of relief were taken, and finally a cheer went up among them. It had been a job well-timed and well-executed. Helsinger 1 would be proud.

With a last look at Little's now limbless torso sprawled

across the hood of his midnight-blue, regal-looking rental, a shining steel shaft sticking straight up into the air from his chest, the other shaft still in the car, the black-hooded killers congratulated one another, one taking credit for the direct hit on Timothy's heart.

They then disappeared down the highway toward Rogue River, leaving the silence of night and the body behind them. Only the absolute stillness and Timothy's mangled remains, sliding down the hood now, were left when the raccoons came to investigate the pungent odor left in the wake of the passing humans.

TEN

Days & nights: time

Lucas Stonecoat looked up, thinking he had heard someone quietly snooping at the door to the Cold Room, but there was no one there. The room had filled with dark men, hunched forms, gargoyles—all shadows. He glanced across the room at the cubed and barred single window, finding it had been painted vermilion on this side, black on the other.

Night had come on and he hadn't been aware of it, so enthralled had he become in some of the other files Dr. Meredyth Sanger had checked out of the Cold Room over the past two weeks. Apparently, she had already run a computer check on cases involving arrows and had done the research, casting out many an archery accident to find these cases where an arrow was used with deadly intent.

He hadn't gotten very far into the other files Meredyth had logged out when he realized he'd put in overtime. Neither Kelton nor Lawrence would appreciate him putting in for overtime his first day on the job, not after all the paperwork he'd already cost them with his field trip to the Texaco station.

Lucas had lost track of time, and his black coffee had turned to cold mud while he had scanned the month's roster to locate the ID numbers of other files borrowed on Meredyth Sanger's name. Except for the dust kicked up and the allergy itch running along the canals of his nose, he effortlessly found these ancient files as well, long forgotten by all but a lone police shrink, and now him.

The dust was not so thick or undisturbed on these folders, making it obvious they'd recently been fanned and scanned. He piled them atop one another, four in all, and placed them into a battered briefcase he'd been using for his classes. Not bothering to log the fact, not wanting to leave the kind of tracks Dr. Sanger was leaving in her wake, he pushed the files into his case, intending to study them overnight. Switching off the light, he limped from the exit of his monastic hole in the wall, his leg killing him from having sat so long in one position.

Locking up, he turned to the service elevator and waited for the damned pachyderm to come get him.

More coffee, Stonecoat told himself, pouring the last of the pot, long cold, into his cup. Instead of going to class as he should have, Lucas had spent a restless and long evening with the remaining files, holed up in his bare apartment in an effort to follow in Meredyth Sanger's curious footsteps along the convoluted trail she had blazed. He was trying his damnedest to punch holes into her reasoning and the stubbornness with which she had come down this path in the first place. But he wasn't having much luck in doing so.

He paced what little space remained here for him to walk, what with the files strewn about the floor, along with boxes yet to be emptied since his move. He was using unopened boxes as chairs and tables for the moment, as he'd taken the unfurnished apartment with the desire and design that he would decorate in a manner suiting himself. So far his interior decorations amounted to a handful of prints of noble Indian faces and early tribal life, which adorned the walls along with an authentic Cherokee blanket his aunt had sent him during his convalescence in Dallas. Lucas had moments before risen with some difficulty from the floor, where he'd been splayed out for an hour now, going over the final papers of the final file he'd taken from the Cold Room. He didn't own a table, so the papers were spread across boxes.

Going for the refrigerator, which was owned by the super, along with all the other appliances in the flat, he located a cold Coors and drank long and deeply, savoring the cool feel of the liquid and its bite as it slid familiarly and easily down his throat. Earlier, he'd ordered Pizza Hut's complete spaghetti meal, along with a small pizza, and what remained of the pizza sat on one edge of two unopened cardboard boxes that he'd been meaning to get to but was now using as a makeshift tray table in his nearly empty flat.

The chief features of the place were the hardwood floor, the poster bed he'd bought for the bedroom, and a pair of first-model Colt .45's he'd hung in a special place above his bed. Lucas hadn't had the time required to do the place up right. And if he followed Sanger down the primrose path she wanted him to take, there'd be less time than ever to pursue personal interests, such as making a suitable home for himself, fishing, boating, diving or hunting. One of the allures of Houston was its proximity to the ocean on the one hand and to good hunting grounds on the other. Houston itself had very few lures. It was, like all cities its size, an abominable place to be if you were poor, a lovely place to be if you were rich. But within a two-hour drive, out beyond the last development, Lucas knew he could find the trailways of his ancestors alongside those of Sam Houston, Davy Crockett, Austin, and Travis. He could canoe through a primeval swamp, angle for a free crab dinner or go sailing. There were ferries to ride to distant destinations, beaches to walk, and quiet country roads to drive. There were horse farms and sugarcane mills in every direction. It just took a little effort and looking to find sea-rimmed marshes and wilderness trails. And despite all of his physical problems, Lucas Stonecoat had dedicated himself to returning one hundred percent to the man he once was, a man who loved the outdoors and the open prairie.

He continued to pace, to think, and to become angry all over again at the circumstances closing in around him. Dr. Sanger was no fool; she knew he'd do almost anything to get reassigned out of the Cold Room. And damned if he didn't want it both ways—wanted her to be wrong about the files, about the connections she'd perceived, so he could safely bow out, and yet he wanted her to be right, so he could get excited about something and go back to being who and what he was before the accident. But that renegade was hardly more than a faint memory now, a shadow puppet in the theater of remorse. Still, he had promised the God who daily moved him that one day he would return to full health and vigor, and perhaps by getting involved here and now, getting excited about his work, this case . . . then perhaps.

Still, he found himself as curious about Meredyth as the journey she'd been on, forged as it was from tantalizing footprints which, while timeworn and wholly spectral, had roused his most basic instinct for the hunt. Indeed, he wished very much to understand her motives as best he might, and to determine if he really wanted to get any deeper into this figurative hotbed with her, aligned as she was against the one man in the department who could most easily make his life miserable. Of course, Phil Lawrence's decision to place him in the Cold Room had pretty well created a hell from which there appeared no escape, save perhaps Dr. Meredyth Sanger's plans for Lucas, anyway. . . .

It was a convoluted mess already, and he hadn't done a thing beyond reading the files. So he worked, trying to see all she saw in the files, hoping to learn what, by God, had alerted her to the similarities in the first place—such as they were. Some of the answers, particularly regarding her, eluded him like a trout in two feet of water. He could see the prize, but picking it up was going to be near impossible, like falling in love with a woman who had devoted herself to a lifetime of love for a mission, a spirit, or God. He may as well declare it a useless enterprise and "step back," as the rappers would say.

"Maybe it's me," he told himself, sipping at what remained of his beer, wondering if he ought to spike it with some Red Label. He would have to use some sort of drug or drink to get any sleep tonight, to get past the three-pronged problem of pain, insomnia and loneliness.

Sure, there was a great deal of similarity between the other cases, beyond the obvious fact that they remained unsolved: The victims had all died of a massive blow to the heart or chest with a spear or arrow. Once again, semantic errors abounded in the reports, arrow and spear being confused. A spear was a lance, sometimes six times the size of an arrow, but these were white cops filling out reports at two and three in the morning, and words like spear and arrow were interchangeable in a brain of putty. But there were also distinctly dissimilar crime scene facts here. Not all the victims had been mutilated after the initial kill, and some only partially, but none perfectly matched the extensive mutilation damage done in the more recent cases of Palmer and Mootry.

Maybe Palmer and Mootry were connected, and the

connections seemed clear, but not so with the other bodies, at least not on paper.

A fellow by the name of Bennislowe—poor slob—along with his wife and daughter were all slain in brutal fashion, all three with metal arrows fired nastily through their hearts, but their bodies were not mutilated—no chopping off of hands, feet, head, or private parts. Also, this awful occurrence had taken place many years before, in 1981 in the Brier Forest area, the outskirts of Harris County. When it had been unofficially closed and detectives put to other duties—murder cases technically remained open for ten years—relegated to the Cold Room, in 1984, with no likely suspects, the Palmer killing had been less than two years off.

Were the HPD cops at the time blind, careless, stupid or all of the above? A careful check showed that each case had been handled by different detectives in differing precincts. Lucas wondered how many had retired between these incidents and gone to Florida or California. In any event, no one save Meredyth Sanger had considered the cases together, as a whole. He again wondered why her . . . why had Meredyth of all people come upon this startling string of events? What had been her springboard? What had first prompted her to ask, *What if?*

Prior cases also involved high-tech, tempered-steel arrow shafts, one of these again fired through a window—an open window this time—directly into the victim's chest, missing the heart but causing such trauma as to leave him dead nonetheless. This fellow's name was Charlton Whitaker, and his head had been lopped off and carried away by the ghoul who'd killed him. The head had never been recovered, the killer never found. Sometime later, Whitaker's grave was disturbed, his family crypt opened, and additional mutilation to the body occurred: hands and feet fiendishly severed and carted off, along with private parts.

Lucas winced at the thought of lying peacefully in a grave somewhere, already missing his head, and here come grave-robbing ghouls to take his privates and extremities— why and for what purpose? It sounded cultish, and certainly these days there were enough cults to choose from. However, the records showed that police investigated every known cult in the area for any hint of involvement, only to come up completely empty-handed.

Whitaker's wife, parents, and all others in the crypt were disturbed in the process, arrows placed through the corpses at the heart as well, the "dead victims" left like so many staked vampires.

The trail of Whitaker's killer or killers led detectives down multiple paths and directions ending in frustration, making some believe that the death of the wealthy financier had been tied into some sort of international intrigue beyond the kin and scope of the Houston Police Department. A second theory involved neo-Nazis and hatred of Jews, as Bennislowe was Jewish. Another theory had Charlton Whitaker somehow mixed up in a weird religious cult of some sort which had exacted this ritual vengeance on him. None of these theories had gotten detectives anywhere.

The phone rang, and he had to search a moment to find it among the debris of boxes. Picking it up, he asked, "Yes?"

"Stonecoat?" It was Meredyth Sanger. "Have you had an opportunity to look over some of the files I suggested?"

"You don't waste time, I see." A quick glance at his watch showed him it was almost two A.M.

"So, whataya think?"

"I think you're reaching."

"Maybe . . . or maybe you don't want to see what's before your eyes? I know it will mean bucking some broncos, cowboy, and maybe you're not quite up for that these days? Perhaps you prefer a quiet little desk job in the base—"

"Hold on, there, Dr. Sanger. Hell." Lucas stopped himself, covering the mouthpiece in order to mutter to himself, "Damn, but she's got some nerve." Then he said to her, "Look, if the goddamned detectives who handled the cases at the time, the men who were that close to the case and time frame of the murder couldn't do anything about it, what kind of fool am I to think that I can step in and pick up a scent on this, after all these years."

"Still, there's the Mootry case."

"What about it?"

"It's still warm and palpitating."

He involuntarily nodded and thought, *Yeah, and for some unknown reason, it has enticed Dr. Meredyth Sanger to all these additional gruesome events.*

He finally said, "Taken separately, these cases might simply be random acts of violence."

She seemed to agree, saying, "The mindless work of the inhuman types who walk upright and look like men, but whose minds are those of monsters, their occupation that of stalking the streets of every city in America, the kind of men police routinely call depraved, self-indulgent animals."

She was speaking of a sort Stonecoat had seen time and again in his long years as a peace officer. The sort who— having had a few snorts of cocaine—decide to pull into any driveway, scale any wall to attack the nearest man, woman or child they could lay their bestial hands on just for the sheer hell of it, for a thrill only the truly criminal-minded understood, as kicks to ward off the boredom and monotony which so characterized their otherwise dull and miserable lives.

Lucas said, "So far as I can make out, neither Whitaker

nor Bennislowe had anything remotely in common with either Palmer or Mootry, save strong ties to the community and an upstanding and exemplary life. Tying the cases together in one neat package just isn't going to happen, Dr. Sanger."

"Meredyth," she mildly corrected him.

"I mean, you've got a retired judge, a surgeon, a real-estate broker, a car salesman turned megabucks-filthy-rich when a theme park bought up his family's old homestead to build on. The other victims seem only afterthoughts, incidentals who happened to be in the . . . the way when . . . when—"

"When the random act of violence was in full swing?" she facetiously asked.

"All right, I admit there are some questions, lingering doubts, loose ends," he replied.

"Look, would you mind terribly if I came up to your place and we talked further about this?"

"Where are you?"

"At a place called Bonevey's, across the street."

Bonevey's was the all-night diner across the street. He could see the place from his window.

"How did you know where I live? Never mind. You ever been under psychiatric care, Doctor?"

"Whataya mean, physician heal thyself?"

"I'm just not sure I care to be stalked, even if you are—"

"Are what?"

"—a beautiful woman."

"Trust me, Lucas Stonecoat. My interest in you is purely professional."

He hesitated a moment before saying, "I'll put some coffee on."

"Don't go to any trouble on my account."

This made him laugh. "I'm apartment 15B, but then you know that. Come on up."

He looked around at his place; it was a shambles of opened and unopened boxes. He had never fully relaxed here, wasn't one hundred percent sure he meant to stay. There was a guy across the hall who sometimes sent out banshee wails when he went into delirium tremens, a real alcoholic of the old school: He lived on booze alone. The man looked like death walking. Fleckner was his name, and every time Stonecoat looked into his dead eyes, he feared the reflection, knowing that he himself could be Fleckner at any time, anytime he wanted to give up and give in. . . .

ℰLEVEN

Rain clouds: prospective

Over a shared pot of black coffee, the former detective and the police psychiatrist stared at one another. Meredyth got up from the single chair in the apartment, which he'd graciously offered her, to walk about the place and comment on its hardwood floors, and the pictures he'd hung, and the Cherokee blanket hanging from one wall. She began to think aloud as she gazed about the place, saying, "Your Indian bearing, your surroundings, and your natural good looks remind me of Lou Diamond Phillips, the actor, but you're taller, more broad-shouldered."

Lucas remained stonily cool to all her remarks, some of which were designed to bring him out, to relax him. He knew what she was trying to do. "So," she finally said, "what'd you think of the fifth case, the Gunther case?"

This case took place back in 1979, and it involved a younger man who really seemed to have nothing whatever in common with the other victims, as he was not a home owner or successful or wealthy in any sense of the word. In fact, he was a metalworker, something to do with automotive bodywork. His name was David Ryan Gunther, but he'd been somewhat new to the greater Houston area, and no one knew from where he had arrived. His body, or what little remained of it, had been discovered in a wooded area, in a little pit hastily covered over by brush and stone and earth, the head severed and missing while all other limbs and parts and members had remained intact. His name was known because of an ID found in the shallow grave. But after repeated police requests for help, including an appearance on the tube by cartoon Officer Take-a-bite-outta-crime, no one had ever come forward to claim the young man's remains.

The only thing remotely linking David Ryan Gunther to the other deaths was the large Bowie knife sunk to its hilt that—according to the coroner's report—had been driven in with such force as to pin the body to the ground. The huge blade had been discovered still straight up after some eight years, while the body had decayed around the knife and bones. And with the cranium missing, there wasn't an opportunity to even guess at his facial features. It was presumed that the skull was either pulled off by animals and taken to a den somewhere, or that the killer had taken Gunther's head away with him for some bizarre ritual or dark purpose. With no one claiming the body or coming forward with any information, the remains were buried in a city cemetery at cost to the taxpayers.

Again she asked, "What do you think about the Gunther body being discovered where it was, as it was?"

He gave her a deprecating shrug. "Obviously, there are a few tenuous links that you've already examined and judged. Obviously, you've buzzed about on the VICAP and other computer systems in your search for similarities in killer

MO and victim profile, and the big bulletin board must have alerted you to the Gunther case along with the others. Then, for a closer and more personal and detailed look-see, you found your way down to the Cold Room for the actual files."

"But?"

"But I don't think it washes, especially in the Gunther case."

"Still, what about the link between the Gunther kid's body and where it was unearthed? I mean, someone had him dig his own shallow grave, lie down in it, and take a hit from that Bowie knife that pinned him to the grave. After which his head was removed, and he was covered over."

Lucas threw up both hands. "Whoa, you're making twenty assumptions there, none of which you know for sure."

"His body was unearthed by a dog out on a walk in the woods very near the Charlton Whitaker estate. This geographical link seems a bit eerie and uncanny."

"Yeah, but Whitaker's murder and the subsequent destruction of the Whitaker family crypt came much later in time. It's most likely just a curious coincidence, coincidences being more common now that computers and computer cross-referencing are a fact of life. More coffee?"

"No, thank you."

"A beer?"

She shook her head no.

"Well, if you'll excuse me a moment." Lucas went to the bathroom and splashed cold water into his eyes and face, staring for a long moment at what remained of his youth and vigor in the mirror, seeing the scars, incised worry lines and crow's feet instead. Since the accident, gray strands of hair had become his, entwined amid the thick black weave, finding a permanent home now at each temple. Some people said it gave him more character, others called it credibility, as if the gray meant more wisdom or vision, and this, along with his Indian blood, had had the naive among the white rookies at the academy coming to him for advice! Advice ranging from money matters and relationships to the best scoped rifle to use on a deer hunt. He doubted that hair of any color had much to do with wisdom or power, but the illusion certainly was there. And as every good magician or Indian shaman or good cop knew, mirage, mirrors and chimera—the appearance of things—usually meant far more to people than the reality behind a fantasy. But no amount of phantasm was going to be of any help here and now as he weighed the relative wisdom or foolishness of either accepting or turning down Meredyth Sanger's request for assistance. She was not likely to be taken in by anyone's hocus-pocus.

She was waiting in the next room for an unequivocal answer.

He toweled off. There was more to sift through waiting for him in the other room. He returned to it, sitting cross-legged in the middle of the floor, his resolve to remain objective stronger than his resolve to remain awake.

"I need to look a little deeper," he told her, stalling for time.

She began pointing items out to him, facts he had already considered. It became annoying. A few minutes later, he stood and paced, went for a hefty tumbler of whiskey, offered her some, which she declined, and drank long and sighed heavily afterward.

He saw that she watched him with one eye—the eye of retribution and rebuke—while her other eye filled with a pleading appeal. She felt like, smelled like, sounded like, and probably would taste like Katharine Hepburn in *African Queen*, he thought. Given half a chance to get near his kitchen, she'd likely pour out every ounce of booze he owned and tell him it was better than Drano for the pipes.

"You took some documents from the Palmer file," he accused.

She dropped her gaze. "I haven't been completely forthcoming, no."

"No, you haven't. Now, do you want to tell me why?"

They were both seated again now, she leaning in toward him as if she must whisper what would come next. "I left the Gunther report in to test you; see if you were as good as they say."

"As good as who says? My superiors in Dallas weren't exactly handing out laurels when I left."

"No, but you had a number of supervisors up till then, and no one could change your record."

"You sure do your homework, lady. So, Gunther was a ringer? To see if I was paying attention."

"Not at first, but I decided to use it as such. See what you had to say about it."

"And what about information on Alisha Reynolds? Or do I have to call Atlanta for that tomorrow?"

She snatched her purse to her and rummaged through it, pulling forth a folded cache of papers. "Here's all that was in the file. I didn't have time to make you a copy, too."

"These are the originals? Police property . . ."

She frowned. "They are and you know it. Read them over."

Lucas first stared at the ceiling overhead. *Do I really want to get into this any deeper than I already am?* he wondered.

"Just look them over," she urged. "Then we'll talk about threads and coincidences, Lucas."

The police report on Palmer's fiancée, Alisha Reynolds, was a fax some ten plus years old, dated as it was 1985. Atlanta and Houston obviously were ahead of the times, having faxes so early on in the game. At that time, many law enforcement officials used a nearby college or university in faxing information back and forth. The report wasn't as detailed as it might have been, but close enough attention was given to Alisha Reynolds's death to sort out a few things in Lucas's mind. The woman's death was ruled a murder in the first, and it had taken place at Palmer's home just after the breakup of a party that evening. Alisha Reynolds had actually been cut down by a steel-shafted arrow fired from a crossbow through a closed window.

"The dead woman's name—Alisha Reynolds—corresponded with the would-be in-laws, who became suspects in Palmer's death the next year," said Meredyth, her voice like a narrator of some dark documentary. "Very little was done in the way of background on her here in Houston. She was an Atlanta socialite, expecting to marry well, and all seemed right with her world when a mindless *random act of violence* took her."

"Could there have been a jealous suitor? Someone smart as well as enraged? Someone who wanted to make it look like a maniac had done Palmer and his intended in, in order to cast the shadow of suspicion away from himself? Perhaps another doctor who worked alongside Palmer at Georgia Baptist Memorial Hospital in Atlanta? Did Palmer engage in crossbow hunting? Did anyone, friend or acquaintance, ever take up the weapon?" All these questions escaped Lucas's mouth, and he could see that she could see that his mind raced with curiosity over the oddities here.

Just how much of me are you wanting to take, Dr. Sanger? Lucas wondered. He had on occasion used a crossbow himself on deer hunting excursions, but she probably had unearthed that bit of information as well.

The high-tech crossbow weapons of today were damnably, horribly accurate and cleanly deadly.

In what seemed an attempt to explain why the similarities in the cases had been overlooked, she said, "In one of the earlier case files, some fool with no knowledge of crossbows quickly characterized the arrow as having come from a speargun, and so the word speargun had continued to be carried over from protocol to protocol until the M.E. got hold of it and declared it an arrow from a crossbow."

"The M.E.?"

"He's something of a hunter himself. He'd seen crossbows and crossbow arrows before."

"And you?"

"Yes, I had. The M.E.'s my uncle, and he's been retired, encouraged to take a pension. He hunts with a member of a hunt club."

"Ahh, I see, and so that's how you got started on this trail?"

"That and the fact I knew Alisha Reynolds when I was a child, growing up. I summered in Georgia, where my mother lived at the time. I was going to be one of Alisha's bridesmaids. Her parents were like my own for a time, and when they were under investigation for Palmer's murder, it brought it all back like a nightmare that never left us."

"Funny, you don't look old enough . . ."

She smiled at the compliment. "In any case, I never forgot how awfully she died. When Palmer was killed, I was away at college and hadn't heard anything of it, but when Mootry was killed, I was reminded of Alisha, so I went back in time, searching in Georgia first, and getting very little help. It was, after all, a dead file."

"No wonder you want an Indian on the case," he managed to mutter to her now.

She managed a light laugh, which brightened the dark room. "Whatever can you mean by that, Lucas?"

"An Indian knows the difference between a spear and an arrow, and besides, an Indian never forgets an enemy."

She indulged him with a broad smile now. "Truly, I hadn't given it any consideration."

"So were any of Alisha's former lovers or suitors ever traced? Anyone jet to Atlanta to check firsthand on the situation there?" He riffled through the additional pages she'd provided but found nothing of great import on the Atlanta murder.

"With so little in the file, your guess is as good as mine," she replied, "but it appears the detectives in charge didn't follow Atlanta up, or *someone* didn't get back with more than what you have there in your hands, Lucas."

"Appears that Palmer's murder here in Houston PD's jurisdiction was given far more attention than the dead socialite in Atlanta."

"It was already old news. He had moved on to wooing women here in Houston high society."

Stonecoat nodded. "And since he had become so prominent here—"

"He was originally from here and had returned to get away from the morbid curiosity surrounding the death of his fiancée in Georgia."

Lucas nodded and said, "Since he was so big here, his case file actually carried an asterisk, indicating that it required a box of its own."

"The single folder I pulled is just the proverbial tip of the iceberg," she agreed, adding, "the HPD swarmed over this case, turned it into a special task force operation with forty detectives working around the clock. Palmer's family was well connected. They even got TV time on *America's Most Wanted*, but nothing—absolutely nothing—came of it."

Lucas may've heard vague rumblings about the case, but in Dallas at the time, he'd had his own problems as a first-year cop in a mean town. He was filled to overflowing with an unbridled energy that kept his paperwork cryptic and his time on the street twice that of any other cop. He and Jackson hadn't yet been teamed, and no other cop in the precinct could stand being around him. He was too gung ho, the others said of him. He had made few friends in or out of the department. He was hard to get to know because he was always so fired up and anxious. Soon it was rumored he was doing drugs, which he wasn't; but he was called in for a spot drug test. He passed with flying colors. Still, not even his captain could keep him in one place long enough to explain the simplest of *regs* to him. He couldn't sit in a chair without rocking, couldn't stand in a doorway without bouncing off the facings. When he had been on his back, facing rehabilitation and a grand jury probe and his superiors, the worst part of that hell was being immobile.

"Yeah, I seem to recall something about the case when it broke," he managed. "It might be interesting to see the episode that aired on it."

"I've seen it, and it is; in fact, I had a copy made. I'll gladly share it with you." She went on to explain, "The HPD detectives working the case had spared no one in '86: not Palmer's shrink, not his personal physician, not his attorney, not his servants; they even went so far as to question the doctor's minister at his church. My uncle used to joke that they even brought in a psychic to talk to Palmer's dog. They were that hard up for a lead that had never been forthcoming."

"Your uncle sounds like a smart man."

"He thinks he got on everyone's nerves too much."

"Oh?"

"He was—still is—something of a perfectionist. Things never sat well with him with the Palmer case."

"Retired, you say? So, where'd he retire to?"

"South of Galveston on the bay. Has a great place. Visit there whenever I can, but he doesn't like me just dropping in."

"Oh, why's that?" Lucas didn't expect an answer, and his thoughts were running toward the old guy's having plenty of girlfriends in.

"He's writing up his memoirs and it's making him a real bastard. Ask him to tell a story and he's masterful; ask him to put it in permanent ink and he chokes like a dog on peanut butter. I got him a tape recorder for his birthday and told him to just speak the damned book and let someone else transcribe it. I hear now it's going well, but for a time, God!"

When she finished, he said, "It's hard for a man to speak his heart."

"More Indian wisdom?"

"Fact, is all. Like the detectives at the Thirty-first who joked about dropping a match on the Cold Room. It's easier than speaking their hearts about cases they couldn't solve."

"Well, sure . . . The place houses mistakes, over-sights . . . doubts and regrets."

"Being the designated curator of such a museum isn't likely to win me any friends. The other guys are already calling it Indian Affairs."

"As opposed to Internal Affairs?" She smiled and laughed.

He joined her, his laugh so loud that someone in the apartment overhead beat the floor to silence him.

"So what will it be, Stonecoat? Are we a team or aren't we?" she finally asked point-blank.

"I'll have to sleep on it."

"And if you never get to sleep?"

"You know about my insomnia, too? You've been all over

my medical file, and you've been all over the computer Internet trying to locate all kinds of conspiracies. I'm not so sure I trust you, Doctor."

"Don't be ridiculous. I'm only interested in the truth."

"Yeah, well, perhaps you should heed some of your own Anglo advice."

"Which is?"

"Careful of what you wish for . . . you may get it."

She bit her lip and nodded. "Tomorrow, then, without fail, you will let me know, one way or the other."

"I will."

She stood up, took his hand and shook it firmly. "Thank you."

He held on to her hand, enjoying the warmth of touch. It had been a long time since he had held a woman's hand. "For what?"

"For being the first man to listen to me on this, to take me seriously on this, and to see that there is something quite odd going on here."

"Did you take all you have to Captain Lawrence?"

"I did."

"Withholding nothing? Not even the Gunther file or the added info from Atlanta on Reynolds?"

"Well, he never gave me a chance to get that far. He's so negative and so insufferable."

"Funny, I haven't found him to be either."

"That's because you're a man. He doesn't treat you like a . . . a goddamned Barbie doll or a bug."

She made her way toward the door.

"You sure you don't want to stay a little longer?" he asked, afraid to let her go and afraid she might hear the panic in his voice as well. The moment she stepped out the door, the place wrapped itself again in that deafening silence it wore before she'd brought her fire inside. It was a fire he both admired and remembered; it was the fire he had once carried.

"Lucas, it's going on three A.M.; I've got to get some sleep, and you'd better do the same. Have you tried some of that whiskey in a tall glass of warm milk?"

"Milk?" He almost spat the word. "I don't have any milk in the apartment."

"Then I take that as a *no*?"

"That's right."

She could only frown. They said a final good night.

But ten minutes later there came a knock at his door, and when he opened it, there she was, extending a pint of milk to him. "Try the milk-and-whiskey toddy. There's something released in warm milk that'll help you sleep. Trust me."

He stood astonished, not remembering how the pint of milk got into his hands. "Thank you. I will try your remedy."

"That's all I ask. Just a try." Her smile warmed him. "Now, good night, I hope!"

She was rushing away again.

"Are you sure you're safe out this late alone?" he asked her as she disappeared into the shadows of the hallway for the elevator.

He next saw her silhouetted against the light of the elevator when the door opened. Someone in a nearby room was shouting through the wall for quiet.

"I know how to take care of myself, thank you. And Lucas," she paused, and just as the elevator door closed, added, "I do hope we can be partners."

Lucas stared down at the cold pint of milk in the green-and-white carton she'd handed him. The slogan on the milk proclaimed it to be WINS DAIRY MILK—THE VERY BEST OF LIFE IN A CREAMY CASCADE OF WHITE ENERGY.

"Give me white lightning any day," he muttered to himself.

TWELVE

Snake: wise, defying

His warm milk and whiskey in hand, a full glass of it, Lucas now lowered himself into Sears' poor excuse for a La-Z-Boy, as he had no sofa yet, and found the TV remote and a cold piece of pizza. He tossed aside the pizza, finding it a poor complement to the hot toddy.

Fatigued, feeling spent, he flipped on the TV and channel-surfed, stopping to stare with wonder at a QVC-style television evangelist who was going to save him from himself, from wild, wild women, from anything smokable or pokable, from anything he might guzzle, such as whiskey, from Satan, and from an eternity in Satan's last resort. The TV evangelist whooped as well as the best Baptist minister in all of Texas and made as much sound and fury and promise as a used-car salesman with a sledgehammer in hand.

Unable to stomach another word, Lucas switched on an old western with Jimmy Stewart in the lead role opposite bad guy Arthur Kennedy. Lucas closed his eyes and allowed the dialogue, voices and music to wash over him. It was nearing three-thirty in the morning, the dementia hour, and he dozed, semiconsciously wondering if the white medicine woman's remedy acted as placebo more than anything else, wondering if his sleep was helped by the drink, or if it had come on simply due to exhaustion, or a combination of both. Either way, he knew he'd sleep more soundly if he stopped worrying about how he had gotten here. . . .

He awoke with a knife to his heart, but the startled moment came to an abrupt end the instant his eyes leapt open. Those damned Cold Room files had brought on a nightmare. He surveyed the apartment, a barren, stark personality, this place, without warmth or color. Meredyth could not have approved of the place or liked it. He had to do something about that, had some ideas, wondered when he'd find the time. He wanted very much to get some rich, vibrant desert earth colors to surround himself with—reds, browns, ochres, umbers, perhaps a few Arizona or Texas landscapes with towering mountains. He loved the Painted Desert and Grand Canyon scenes. Yes, that would work.

He'd work on it. For now, he shuffled off to the shower, painfully stripping away his clothes, the old injuries firing up anew, a punishment for falling asleep in the old chair. In his medicine cabinet, he found some horse-sized pain pills left over from his days at the hospital in Dallas. The pill bottle ought to've been emptied months before, but he'd weaned himself off traditional medications, taking the big brown things only sparingly, relying more and more on tribal medicines forwarded by his grandfather, as well as smoking the root. The root gave him a greater high than any bourbon or marijuana might. The herbal medicine, also known as locoweed, was as old as his tribal people. This and meditation were now his constants, his caregivers, his doctors.

Still, since he'd not smoked anything tonight, he popped one of the white man's remedies and got under the soothing hot spray of the shower. Afterward, he quickly toweled down and found his soft mattress. The bed comforted him back to a deep slumber, his greatest regret at the moment being that Meredyth Sanger wasn't lying beside him, and secondly that she'd have absolutely no reason to ever speak to him again—not after what he had to say to her in the morning.

But liking her wasn't enough reason to get involved with her harebrained scheme of building a case for a serial killer going about with steel-tipped arrows over a period of almost twenty years. Besides, there were just too damned many loose odds and ends.

Still, linking the two most recent cases, Mootry and Palmer, might have merit, and there damned well could be a serial killer on the warpath in the greater Houston metropolitan area. But such cases were out of Lucas's hands, beyond any reach of either him or Dr. Sanger, so far as he could tell.

He fumbled for the card she'd left him, which he had placed next to his phone, and for a long moment, he focused on her melodic name. "Oh, hell," he announced to the empty room. "Might jus' 's well get it over with."

He began dialing her number, not worried about waking her. "Damnation and hell, she's kept me up all night with this crazy shit, not that I could sleep anyway, given all my givens."

His was an impossible situation. He understood the need for a Dr. Jack Kevorkian in the lives—or rather deaths—of many people. Insomnia alone was hell, but coupled with agonizing and torturous pain, that was quite a bit more. He silently meditated as the phone rang at the other end.

The phone rang six times before he heard her knock it to the floor, retrieve it and find the mouthpiece. Obviously, she was having no trouble sleeping. Maybe she had taken her own remedy. She now found the presence of mind to speak clearly. "Ellowww? What time is it?"

"Near four-thirty."

"Stonecoat . . ."

He lied. "I've gone over the files again and—"

"Again? So, you see the similarities!" she said, excited, instantly awake.

"Listen to me, Dr. Sanger," he began.

"You'd have to be blind not to see the connection, the pattern."

"Will you listen to me?" he commanded.

Her silence was her reply.

"Now look, we both know that these back cases . . . well, that nobody gives a damn about the Cold Room files, but you go poking your nose into an ongoing case like the Mootry matter, and people go ape shit, especially detectives working the case."

"So what's your point?"

"Point is, I'm in no position to piss off my superiors."

"Lucas, we have to. . . . We can make a difference together if you'd only give it a—"

"I need my job, Doctor, not just for the money . . . I need the work. Some people would say I have no business carrying a badge; most departments in this country would not have hired me, given my record."

"Have you tried other departments?"

"I wanted to stay in Texas."

"Then you're whining, Lucas. Come on, I need your expertise, and I need an ally."

"There're plenty of guys down there who'd like nothing more than to help out a . . . help you out. I'm just not the guy. Sorry, Doctor. I'll keep your confidences. You needn't worry about that, and—"

"How can you do that?"

"What? Keep your secrets?"

"Turn your back on the evidence."

"What evidence? We're talking about a handful of similarities and your . . . assumptions, Doctor."

"Arrows don't show up in bodies every day, Lucas. Not even in the Wild West of Texas, not anymore."

"I agree there's a possible, perhaps probable connection between Palmer and Mootry, and possibly Whitaker, but the others I'm not sold on."

"But that's enough to start a real investigation."

"For you, maybe. Look, I'm sorry but—"

"I thought you were different, Stonecoat."

"Different how?"

"I thought you had some guts, that you weren't afraid to go after the truth."

"What I'm afraid of, Doctor, is being used by a woman."

"Go to hell." She hung up on him, hurting his ear with the resounding gavel of the receiver.

"Have a nice day. . . ." he grumbled to the dead phone. "Now that went well," he told the room. He also told the room that he wasn't going to jump up and down and walk on the ceiling for her. And he didn't want her making a lot of assumptions about him, as she'd obviously already done. He told himself all of this as he dozed more readily toward much needed slumber; two hours before alarm bells would peal. Still, if the Mootry and the Palmer cases alone were unmistakably linked, maybe it was his duty to pursue the matter a little further, discreetly and on his own. Telling her of his plan to do so would be less than discreet.

Vacant of substance, smoke and mirror images and shadowy figures now danced about a roaring fire on the ceiling before dancing inside Lucas's mind as he again found sleep. The final image to come before his closed eyelids was of an impatient and angry Captain Phil Lawrence, reaching out to tear the buttons off Lucas's shirt in a theatrical display of disgust and unbridled hatred. The buttons bounced and rolled away from Lucas's dream self like enormous black tires off a DC-7, and suddenly a howling wind blew a fierce fire over Lucas's badge, melting it. Looking over his shoulder, Lucas located the dripping, molten gold of his badge as it seeped downward from the branches of a twisted and scorched oak, where the badge had taken a Dali pose amid the charred limbs, like one of those melting clocks the artist was so curiously fond of.

```
764LT1:\C42119\Category 42 . . . Topic
159LOG . . . Message 302 . . . Tues.
July 23, 1996 . . . 4:03:05
Questor 3 . . . Helsinger's Pit . . .


Q3: Problem north of Eden resolved. Altar
prizes on the way. Enjoy and appreciate
efforts here to gain sacrifices to Hels-
inger. END TRANSMISSION, Category 42, Topic
159LOG . . . 4:05:02



Category 42 . . . Topic 159LOG . . . Mes-
sage 303 . . . Tues. July 23, 1996 . . .
4:05:07
Questor 1


Q1: Again you have proven your worth,
Questor 3. I look forward to the prize. END
TRANSMISSION, Category 42, Topic 159LOG,
4:07:00
```

• • •

Meredyth Sanger couldn't believe what Lucas Stonecoat had left her with—nothing, no way to turn. Damn him. Maybe it had all been a stupid play from the beginning, she rationalized. Maybe he wasn't the man she had thought, or perhaps since Dallas and all that horrible trouble, he simply wasn't the same man Dave Cass had known. Cass was the police shrink in Dallas, and they had been friends for six years, seeing one another at various conventions and conferences over the years. Cass had not blinked when she asked him for whatever records on Stonecoat he might possess when she told him that she would be taking over his case from here on out, now that Lucas was a Houston cop. Cass had held back nothing.

Meredyth couldn't go back to sleep now. She felt like an army of one, as though everyone down at the precinct was against her. Only Cass from afar and young Randy Oglesby, her computer-wise male secretary, had given her any help whatsoever. She had really been counting on Stonecoat, and she had put in a lot of time courting the bastard.

She climbed from bed and replaced the receiver on the phone. She had slam-dunked it when she had hung up on Lucas, and while it had hit squarely on the cradle, it bounced a foot away like an errant basketball shot. She went for the kitchen where she thought she might scramble some eggs, make coffee for one, get an early-bird start on the day. As she did so, she tried to get Lucas Stonecoat and the shameless way in which she had pursued him out of her mind. The man no doubt thought she needed psychiatric care. Still, how could he ignore the evidence before his very eyes? How could he ignore Alisha Reynolds and Dr. Palmer and the way they had died? How could any rational man?

Of course, he hadn't known Alisha. She'd been a wonderful friend. She would have given Meredyth anything, and they had shared two wonderful summers together between her mother's farmhouse and Alisha's ranch. Together they had tried out every horse on every path and every ridge of the Georgia estate. Meredyth had been much younger than Alisha, but Alisha had treated her as an equal, and when she confided through correspondence that she was marrying a doctor, she begged Meredyth to return to be her maid of honor. Meredyth had not responded one way or another before she got the horrid news that her longtime friend had been the victim of a homicide.

The incident changed Meredyth's life forever. It wasn't that she was obsessed with her friend's death, but it did take her in the direction of criminal psychology and away from a more conservative area of medicine.

Her Uncle Howard's influence encouraged her to break away from the traditions of the family, a tradition that would have had her married off to a "proper young man" years ago. Uncle Howard, something of a black sheep, had played a large role, but she had never once considered following in any way, shape, or form his footsteps. Autopsies and death investigation simply were not a calling for her, that is until Alisha Reynolds was so brutally murdered.

Captain Phil Lawrence and others had dismissed her before all the evidence was in, before she had gathered all that she now had, and so for them, there was no turning back, no way to say, *Sorry, Dr. Sanger, we were wrong about you; we perhaps rushed to judgment, failing to weigh the obvious merits of your arguments and the evidence you have brought to bear on this matter.* No, no way in hell she'd ever hear those words from a jerk like Lawrence.

"The matter is under investigation by those in charge, men better suited to criminal investigation than you, Doctor," Lawrence kept snidely saying, the words now like a mantra, a chorus of nonsense. So typical of men—unable to admit a mistake or make an apology, so what was left but to withdraw?

She had once approached the team of Fred Amelford and James Pardee, the principal investigators on the Mootry case, only to find them as narrow-minded and as paranoid about her wanting to help as Lawrence had been. The good old boy network just closed right down on her.

So she had moved on to Lucas Stonecoat, an outsider and a loner. And she had expected more, better perhaps, from Stonecoat. She didn't know why, but she had. His phone call tonight was crushing.

When she got settled at the small kitchen table, eggs, toast, and coffee in hand, she saw that Lucas's medical file was still there on the tabletop from the previous day. She lifted it and flipped through it, staring again at the Dallas Memorial Operative Report. It read like a medical dictionary, a What's What of medical jargon:

DALLAS MEMORIAL HOSPITAL
Operative Report

Date of Operation: 01/6/92

Operation: Multiple trauma, craniocerebral trauma, and respiratory failure.

Postoperative Diagnosis: Same as above.

Procedure: Laparotomy; tracheostomy; Swan-Ganz placement; bladder repair; cystostomy; reduction of respiratory difficulty.

Meredyth went on to read the procedure as described and attached by the physician who'd overseen Lucas's multiple operations. It read:

Procedure: With patient in supine position and with hyper-extension of the neck, the anterior cervical area was pre-pared and draped. 1% Xylocaine anesthesia administered at all levels for a total of 8 ccs.

With adequate anesthesia established, a midline incision was made and deepened down through subcutaneous layer to the cervical fascia. Subcutaneous homeostasis achieved with a Bovie. The deep cervical fascia was next incised. A large venous channel was ligated with a #3-0 black silk and divided. Dissection was then carried down the midline incision to the pretracheal fascia, which was incised. Tracheal cartilages were immediately apparent. Using a hook, trachea was grasped and a window inferior to the hook was excised.

At this juncture, thirteen minutes into operation, a #6 soft pressure Shiley tube was inserted into the trachea and immediate functioning was successfully begun. The tube was attached to the ventilator and skin closure instituted with #3–0 silk sutures. Routine dressings with KY gauze and 4 x 4s applied. The tracheostomy tube secured around the neck with umbilical tape.

The patient tolerated procedure well, considering earlier head injuries and operations to reduce pressure on the brain. Patient went back into ICU with stable vital signs.

Dr. Daniel Garvey, M.D.
01/6/92 Attending

Patient Name: *Stonecoat, Lucas*

The bullet lodged in Lucas's right upper chest was near the heart and quite life-threatening, and at first it appeared his severe burns might be beyond help. Certainly, witnessing the burning death of his partner, trapped in the car beside him, must have left psychological scars as well. The removal of the bullet and the work of Lucas's skin grafts came later. Meredyth Sanger once again found Stonecoat's medical records both heart-wrenching and astounding. It was truly astounding that he showed such determination, first to live and secondly to rebuild a life.

Despite all this, and despite the fact she realized anew just how much he had gone through, and that most men who had managed to live beyond such an incident as he had faced would have long before retired from active duty, Meredyth was now in the unhappy position of having to blackmail Lucas into cooperating with her. She wondered if she could do it, use his medical records against him in so foul a manner. It was either that or drop the Mootry-Palmer connection and go back to administering to the needs of officers on the force, her Rorschach tests and filling in reports. If anyone knew about Hermann Rorschach's imaging tests, in which the patient was asked to project his feelings into an ink splat, it was Meredyth Sanger. And if anyone knew how to skew results on an ink test . . .

And sometimes she wondered, Why not? Why not simply forget about what she knew? Why not return to the staid lifestyle of before? It would demand a great deal less of her, and Lawrence would be a great deal happier with her.

Stonecoat surely would detest her if and when she lowered the boom on him. It wouldn't take much for her to see that he came under such close scrutiny that he could hardly survive as an officer in the HPD; his hopes of ever becoming a detective again could so easily be denied him if she were to do a psychiatric investigation. Add to this what she knew of his personal habits, his health record, his getting involved in a shooting his first day back on the job . . .

No, getting Lucas Stonecoat into deep shit would be as simple as making a phone call. In fact, Lucas did it to himself; he made it so easy. Maybe teaming with him had been a ridiculous notion to begin with, so why had his turning her down made her so bloody angry? Still, how could he—a detective—ignore the importance of the cases she'd so painstakingly brought to his attention?

Like most men, he needed a good swift kick. "Where the sun don't shine," she muttered to herself. She had thought that kick would have come in the form of information carefully fed him by her. She'd thought manipulating the big lug would be a simple enough matter, but obviously the man was not so easily manipulated. She supposed that was normally a good quality, his thinking for himself, but not when it affected her this way.

"Damn you, Stonecoat," she vowed to the empty apartment, which in comparison to Lucas's seemed overfurnished with its huge winter-white sofa and cool gray carpet, its glass surfaces and paintings of the blue Adirondacks and the even darker blues of the Smoky Mountains all around. Her place was perfectly suited to her, she believed: cool and blue and icy. She'd have to be all three where Stonecoat was concerned.

There had to be a way to make the deaths of Mootry, Palmer and Alisha Reynolds as important to Lucas Stonecoat as they were to her; she must find that way no matter what it took.

$\mathcal{T}$HIRTEEN

Thunderbird track: bright prospect

Lucas's day had gone by uneventfully; surprisingly, he hadn't again been bothered by either Dr. Sanger, who obviously knew how to take a hint, or IAD. Internal Affairs officers were either lying low and in wait for him, or they had decided that his handling of the problem at the Texaco station the other day had been well within proper procedures. But with Internal Affairs, one could never be certain or sure. It had been an IAD unit's unflattering investigation of both Lucas and Wallace Jackson after the deadly accident in Dallas that had given the department all the excuses they needed to wash their hands of Detective Lucas Stonecoat.

Lucas had all day silently thanked Meredyth for allowing him to bow out at this point without pursuing or attacking further, or making further attempts to persuade him. With IAD still investigating the Texaco shoot-out, with Captain Lawrence giving him the watchful evil eye, he had hoped

for and had gotten a day without stress or pressure. In large
part, this was made possible by the Cold Room.

One advantage was becoming clear: He could retreat to
his "office" and no one would follow. It was as popular a
place as a funeral parlor, the city morgue or the cemetery.

Tonight he had no class to attend, so he found himself
here, sitting outside the gated home of Judge Charles
Darwin Mootry, the man whose murder had been so
sensational no newspaperman in town could ignore it. The
police were doing an excellent job of keeping the prying,
curious eyes and cameras off the grounds, however, and so
it appeared Stonecoat might have a difficult time getting
beyond the yellow and black ribbons himself.

"Do I wanna do this?" he asked himself now in the empty
cab of his car while staring down the street at the gates
ahead. Police vehicles and a gray van marked CORONER had
come and gone, not for the first and perhaps not for the last
time in this bizarre case. But for the past hour, the place had
fallen into a relative calm, and even the news media had
disappeared. For this latter fact, Lucas was grateful. He
didn't want anyone videotaping his going up to the gate,
didn't want his license number on the eleven o'clock news.

A guard at the gate seemed both sleepy and bored. With
a little Cherokee chutzpah, Lucas believed he could bully
his way inside.

His air conditioner blowing in his face, lifting his long
strands of hair, he dropped the car into drive and motored
ahead for the gates. The place was palatial. The judge
obviously had made wise investments of one sort or another
over the years. Maybe he was crooked. . . . Maybe he was
into mob business, racketeering, fixing big-ticket items for
serious wise guys who played hardball if they felt the least
slighted by you. Maybe they arranged for the sensational
way in which the judge met his maker. They—the mob—

certainly had the talent and the muscle for all of the above, but Lucas didn't want to lock down too soon on any one theory or suspect.

He had given the judge's case a great deal of thought throughout the day, despite what he'd told Meredyth. While he didn't particularly relish the idea of teaming up with a female police shrink on the case, he did know that cracking such a high-profile case meant promotion through the ranks, and he had asked himself over and again, Why not me, why not now?

He'd have to run his investigation the way a private eye might, outside police circles, and he couldn't expect this guy, Fred Amelford, or his partner, Jim Pardee, to be especially happy to learn of his interest in *their* case any more than they were when they no doubt learned from Lawrence about Dr. Sanger's interest. While Amelford and Pardee were working out of the Twenty-second, there seemed little doubt in Stonecoat's mind that the captain of the Thirty-first would not have talked to the captain of the Twenty-second about Meredyth's interest in the case. There was no reason to suspect otherwise.

So, if he were to pursue this matter, he knew it would be risky and problematic at best. Cops working a case didn't want other cops shadowing their efforts. It was as old as the Texas Rangers, probably older, this unspoken law. It was a white cop's way, a white man's path, which no doubt served Allan Pinkerton and his first secret-servicemen well during the Civil War. No, the two cops working the case would really be pissed off to learn he was here snooping around in their territory, sleuthing their case tonight.

He knew all this, and he also knew that if he were to pursue this matter, it'd have to be on his own time for the most part; however, given his insomnia problems, his own time meant a lot of time, so he believed if he could get nearer the crime scene and the crime scene evidence, perhaps he might find an angle others had overlooked.

Only then, when he had something tangible to take to Lawrence, might he tip his hand. The Cherokees hadn't invented poker, but they had invented the poker face.

And if he had to fall back on someone for help, for inside assistance, for whatever, then and only then would he go crawling back to Dr. Meredyth Sanger.

Lucas brought the automatic window down, and he slowly allowed his solemn features to be softened by a wide smile, asking the guard what he thought of the Houston Astros' chances this year, all the while flashing his gold shield from Dallas.

"Those bums?" replied the officer in blue, frowning sourly over the mention of the baseball team. "What can I do for you?"

"We got a call about some of the particulars in the Mootry case, how they might match a similar crime up in Dallas-Fort Worth area, you know?"

"Oh, yeah? Really? I hadn't heard. . . ."

"Just speculation for the moment."

The uniformed cop nodded as he took it all in. "I see."

Stonecoat quickly added, "They asked me to come have a look."

"Who asked you?"

Lucas saw it as his password. "Some guy on the case named Amelford, another one named Hardy—no, Pardee; you know, the guys whose case it is?"

The guard eased his stance, a good sign. "All right, and you'd be?"

"Detective Plumber, Dallas PD."

"All right, go on through. But I don't know what you expect to find."

"How's that?"

"Coroner and his sister and everybody else have been through the scene twice already."

"Well, let's just say I want to get a general feel for the place, where it happened, exactly how, so I can compare it to what happened up in—"

"All right, save me the details. Go on through. . . ."

"Thanks."

He was invited in, but he expected to be challenged again at the door. Rounding the large, circular drive, he parked some distance from the house. He didn't want anyone reading his tags, and later, on exiting, it might be wise to be as discreet as possible. To his right, some bushes protected windows on the ground floor. He noted their proximity to his car before walking back toward the main entrance, where as expected there stood another uniformed cop, who asked, "Can I help you, sir?" in a tone that revealed his weariness.

There were only a few lights on inside the mansion, and the guard was munching on a sandwich he'd likely put together for himself from what he could find on the inside, using whatever mayonnaise, mustard and cold cuts he could locate in the deceased's refrigerator. Here on the porch, the light subdued by a moonless night, Lucas's skin tone went unnoticed by the guard.

For the occasion, Lucas had found one of his old sports coats and a tie, and now he once again flashed his huge Dallas gold shield. But not to belabor this formality, he quickly began playing with a pair of latex gloves, cursing as he tried to pull them over his large, hairy hands—the show entirely for the guard. Still, the guard radioed his companion at the gate, asking, "This guy check out?"

He got an affirmative reply. "Amelford sent 'im over."

Now the uniformed man simply nodded and gestured for

him to go on through. Lucas wasted no time. Now he was really inside.

He had read enough about the case to know that forensics investigators with the HPD crime lab had thoroughly gone over the bedroom where the body was discovered, but he still felt a need to see the area just the same.

Bedsheets had been removed, leaving only the mattress and the gaping hole that would have been aligned perfectly with the old man's heart.

It was a remarkable sight. No doubt about it. The killer leaned in over the victim where he lay motionless, asleep or helplessly tied down—his eyes wide open perhaps? God forbid—and when the killer placed the crossbow directly against the chest, he or she fired, sending the arrow clean through the heart, out the back, and through mattress and box spring, the shaft being driven into the floor below the bed where it had been recovered by Houston detectives, the body staked to the bed.

Not much detection necessary to know what killed Mootry, but plenty of detection required to learn why and by whose hand he was murdered.

The tunnel or bore created through the mattress was neat, like a bullet hole, the weapon cutting a prim and straight-arrow incision through the material. A wedge of the surface had been dug out, most certainly by the medical examiner or one of his people. Talk about care and overkill in evidence collection. They would examine the blood in the fibers of the mattress to be certain it was Mootry's, even though he obviously bled out his back here where the arrow opened up a hole through him and his heart.

Why the heart? Lucas wondered. Was there a great significance placed on destroying the heart in the mind of the killer? Like a deer hunter, the killer wanted an instant kill, instant results. If the M.E. found no marks on the wrists or ankles to indicate Mootry had been bound and had fought against his restraints, then this would further prove out the fact his killer was not interested in any sort of sadistic torture of the victim. Then what was to be made of the attack on the body after death? The insane mutilation and the missing body parts?

The killer was skilled, practiced, most assuredly a hunter of one sort or another. The killer was quite capable of getting within inches of his prey. The killer might be a trusted person, someone close to Mootry.

Lucas lay down on the bed, placing his heart over the position of the hole created by the killer's arrow. He stared around the room, taking it in from this unusual vantage point. The walls were covered with expensive paintings, etchings, prints of all sort, mostly of historical themes relating to Texas and her birth. None of the old etchings and paintings lining the walls were disturbed, not so much as by a hair. Forensics investigators obviously found no blood on the framed pictures.

Everything was in its place as if nothing bad had ever happened here. Family photos still stood on the bureau top. Prized collectibles—again the prizes of one deeply interested in his roots and those of his community—littered the mantel over the fireplace, where an ancient flintlock musket hung.

There was much of value remaining on the property worth stealing, and neither the two uniformed guards nor the killer seemed the least interested in these valuable collectibles. There were some areas around the bed where the carpet had been cut away, where bloodstains—perhaps bloody shoe stains—had been collected by the evidence techs, but not a single indication that any of the walls were smeared with blood, that any large artery was spurting a trajectory of blood that might hit and trail down the walls. As mutilated as the body had been, it had been a controlled mutilation, each cut done by someone knowledgeable in applying the right tool to the right joint and in the right manner, in a clearly surgical manner—a doctor, a butcher? From what he could see of the room, Lucas guessed that this had to be what the coroner and the lead detectives on the case must be thinking. They no doubt had evidence that the killer knew precisely where to make the cuts to disjoint Mootry's arms and legs as one might a roasting chicken, with the least effort and the most efficiency. The killer may even have used an electric saw as his carving knife.

Lucas sat up now and reached for his large knife, examining the gleaming long blade. He stood up and once again leaned in over the hole in the mattress, which to him looked like a winking eye.

By using his Bowie knife, which he carried in a holster below his coat at the small of the back, Lucas could see where brown bloodstains trailed through the matted material and clung to the springs below, as if in search of a life force. But he had to dig about the hole to see this. It was as if mattress and material had closed ranks over the wound and what remained of the blood the coroner's people had left behind.

Lucas next moved the large four-poster bed aside just enough to get at the spot below where the arrow had embedded into the plush and expensively carpeted floor. Here, too, the M.E. had been at work, cutting out a swath of the warm brown-and-beige-flecked carpet. Lucas stared down at the hole cut through the carpeting, finding it impossible to tell how large the hole had been before the coroner had gotten at it. Fortunately, no one had actually ripped up the floor beneath, and it was here, using the tip of his own knife, that Lucas investigated the hole in the masonry floor. Again, the force of the arrow was evident, in that it had penetrated concrete. The M.E. must have had photos taken of the hole. Lucas now made a quick guesstimate of the size of the arrow tip. It was as wide as two and a half, possibly three centimeters, plenty wide enough to cause great damage, large enough to bring down a moose in the wild.

"One hundred fifty pounds of pressure on the bow," he said aloud now, more for the benefit of the man standing behind him in the doorway than for himself. He didn't know whether it was the guard who had followed him in or someone else. He only knew—sensed, rather—there was someone at his back.

"Heard you movin' things around. We were told everything . . . that is, nothing's to be touched. The ET's mayn't be completely through in here."

"Oh, sorry. Want to help me put this bed back, then?" Lucas remained calm.

"Sure, no problem."

"Just wanted a look at the results . . ."

"You all done in here now, Detective—Ahh? What'd you say your name was?"

"Plumber, Jack Plumber."

"Plumber, huh?" The uniformed officer helped replace the bed and seemed appeased when Lucas said that he was through in the bedroom.

"But I'd like to look around the rest of the house, get a feel for the way Mootry lived, you know."

"He lived damned well."

"I can see that . . . but he also died damned badly."

There was the unspoken reply lingering on the officer's lips: *Then why in hell do you need to stomp around here any more if you know all that?* But all he said was, "Do what you gotta do, Detective. You come all the way from Dallas, you sure don't want to have to make a second trip down here."

Obviously, the cop at the gate had told this man that Plumber was with the Dallas PD. There *was* a detective with DPD named Jack Plumber. A phone call to the right precinct, and they could check up on Lucas's alias.

Lucas thanked the other man and started out across the great expanses of the palatial home. He doubted he'd dare take time to get to the second floor, much less the third or the fourth. "No one was staying with the judge when he was killed?" he asked the cop, who was heading back to his post.

"Not a soul. Didn't have any family, but when he threw a party, word is everybody stayed over. He got his kicks that way, they say."

"Great Gatsby, huh?"

"Who?"

"Never mind . . ."

"Whatever you say, Detective."

"One question, officer."

"Shoot."

"Have you or your partner at the gate used any of the facilities inside here?"

"Facilities, sir?"

"Bathroom toilet, telephone, fridge?"

His slight hesitation gave him away. "No, no, sir."

"No drinks from the icebox, nothing? It's important. Save me a lot of time if you'll be honest with me. Besides, I'm sure the coroner took your prints to rule out any they find on the inside."

"Well, we got a little hungry earlier," he confessed.

"Well, I noticed the sandwich. Any drinks?"

"Just a Pepsi, two, we pulled from one of the 'frigerators."

"One of the refrigerators?"

"There's two in the kitchen."

Stonecoat nodded. "I see. Did you and your partner use glasses?"

"No, we just took the cans and that's all we touched."

"And you disposed of the cans?"

"In the trash, yeah."

"In the trash inside or outside the house?"

"Tossed 'em into our vehicle, so's nothing would be disturbed, ahh, sir."

Both the men were relatively young, likely no more than a year or two out of the academy. "Okay, good, and thanks for your honesty. We'll keep it between us."

This seemed to appease the guard, who quickly returned to the front entrance. Lucas's questions had gone a long way toward keeping the other man at bay. Lucas knew he was walking a tightrope; he knew he hadn't much time alone here before someone close to the investigation might waltz in. Either one of the two guards could at this moment be checking up on him. A single call to Fred Amelford, chief investigator on the case, could send squad cars squealing in from all directions to end this night with his arrest. Maybe he ought to get out of here while the getting was good, he cautioned himself. But then, what risk was there in that?

He instead began to look over the living room area, where he found a pair of coasters on a marble table—one of those tables held up on the back of a jade elephant that must weigh a ton. Other than the two elegant coasters, there was nothing else out of place in the room. He wondered if the cop had lied to him, if he and his partner hadn't had a drink of some sort here amid the splendor of the old man's estate, using the marble table and coasters.

He went through an enormous ballroom, which was "put up" in neat order. From there he found a lavatory large enough to put his entire apartment into, with room to spare.

He moved on to a relatively small and cozy dining room, which was still large enough for a football squad to practice plays in. Nothing untoward here.

Another door off this area led him into the spacious kitchen area, large enough to accommodate twelve chefs, if you could keep them from cutting one another's throats.

The kitchen was also home to an enormous walk-in freezer, as well as two jumbo refrigerators, all stocked to bulging; there were large stainless steel cabinets with a huge chopping block running down the center, below which were additional cabinets and not two but three dishwashers.

Apparently, the judge enjoyed lavishing his wealth about on others who came here for gala events and parties. Lucas recalled something in the news accounts about his employing his home as a place for fund-raising events on a grand scale, with such guests as Willie Nelson, Kris Kristofferson, and Merle Haggard as his draws. One paper called him the most beloved benefactor in all of Houston, an altruistic horn-blower and enthusiastic supporter of the human spirit. People high up in such organizations as the March of Dimes, the American Diabetes Association, Al-Anon, Alzheimer's Research, AIDS Research, Cancer Research, Farm Aid, the Red Cross, Disaster Relief Fund of Greater Houston, Advocates for the Homeless—"You name it," said one official.

So, who could hate a guy like this? wondered Stonecoat as he moved about the kitchen, looking for exactly what he didn't know.

Hate was the operative word—passionate hatred or fear.

You didn't dismember someone after blowing a three-centimeter hole through his heart because you liked the guy. Maybe there was some irrational maniac involved, one whose fear of Mootry was so great that he must completely and utterly destroy the man to be free of his hatred or fear or both. In the legends spoken of by old men of his tribe, Lucas knew the steps one took to completely annihilate an enemy. You cut out his heart, you take his vital power—the privates—and you lay waste to his limbs and head, and to be doubly sure such a powerful enemy could not resurface, you buried each part in separate secret locations.

Lucas Stonecoat wondered if he might be seeing the work of another Indian. There were all manner of American Indians living in the Southwest and Texas vicinity. There were, besides those on his home reservation, the Tonkawa, Tawakoni, Atakapa, Karankawa, and Coahiltec to the south, the Kichai and Waco to the north, the Apache, Commanche and Llanero all to the west, small pockets of all these peoples having at one time or another found their way back to Texas lands they considered theirs. This being the case, was one of Mootry's big fund-raising efforts in any way attached to a cause that might have embraced or disowned the American Indian?

At any rate, Mootry had to have had some contact previously with his killer. It was looking more and more to Lucas like a family thing or a revenge killing, but Mootry's "family" extended to an untold number of guests regularly invited into his home.

According to reports, police and servants, nothing was removed from the mansion, which ruled out theft as a motive. Besides, how many second-story men carried crossbows around with them? Lucas wondered who most benefited from the old man's demise; to whom did his estate and holdings fall? He made a mental note to check into this, a simple enough matter if he could get his hands on the case file, as it would likely finger the same recipient as Amelford's chief suspect at the moment: he who benefits most from another's death. A standard procedure in wrongful deaths and homicides.

Still, something didn't smell right, feel right or taste right about this case; this didn't seem a standard case, so following standard measures might be a waste of time and effort.

One thing was obvious. It was a premeditated homicide, quite possibly a contract killing. The question was, who took out the contract and who carried it out?

Lucas looked about the kitchen just as he had the other rooms, even glancing into the large walk-in freezer, primarily concerned with eyeballing anything out of the ordinary. Nothing looked amiss. He saw no glasses, silverware or dishes in any of the seven or eight sinks. He next opened one of the dishwashers. It was completely empty, as was the second he glanced into. Opening the third, it too appeared empty, except for two glasses with long stems. They were, in fact, crystal goblets, most likely used for sipping brandy or wine. On closer inspection, they appeared to be ornate Waterford crystal, born in fire.

This reminded him of the two coasters in the living room that were not stacked with their counterparts. Lucas began searching the cabinets for the most expensive glassware, and when he came to one cabinet, he found a set of twenty-two goblets identical to the two in the dishwasher.

Most people, even the idle rich, knew better than to place such expensive glassware into an automatic machine; most such easily breakable glassware was cleaned and polished by hand. Would a servant working for Judge Mootry make such a mistake?

If Mootry knew his killer, and if he actually had shared wine or brandy with the assailant, then perhaps he was immobilized by something placed in his drink. After the killing, the assailant may have wiped the goblets clean of any fingerprints and placed them out of sight by putting them into the dishwasher. Even this, if it were true, told

Lucas something about the killer: that he was of a cool mind when he left, that he went about his work in a methodical manner, that he was no young street punk or disorderly minded individual who stumbled in for sex with the judge and in a moment of passion decided to kill him. In the bowl of one of the goblets, there might remain trace residue of a sleeping potion.

Lucas heard the sound of a number of voices filtering through the huge house. He found a window that looked out over the drive and saw that there were new arrivals; possibly Amelford, his partner, more evidence techs with their electronic Magna brushes and infrared cameras in search of a blood trail or a usable print. Or the newcomers might be all of the above, returning from dinner together. Whoever it was, he didn't want to meet them, not here and not like this. The guy at the door had by now mentioned the fact that Jack Plumber had arrived from Dallas.

His hands still gloved, Lucas quickly but carefully pinched first one and then the other crystal goblet between his finger and thumb, delicately placing each into its own plastic bag, which he'd found in one of the cabinet drawers. He concealed each goblet in his sports coat pockets.

The others were coming, he could hear their approach, the sound like a replay of his pounding heart. He enjoyed the moment.

He quickly replaced everything and shut all cabinets and the dishwasher; next he located a back door out of the kitchen, which freed him into a series of other rooms and passageways until he was returned to the ballroom. There he rushed for the curtained windows, and behind the heavy burgundy drapes, unlatched one of the doors, praying no alarm would be set off, certain the fools had been sure to turn off any alarms before they'd begun their investigation—if any had been turned on by the killer.

No alarm sounded, and he felt the rush of Houston's hot, humid wall of air rush in at him as if its life depended upon getting inside. He held firm to the door and carefully eased it closed. Silently, he moved away from the house, taking a shadowed path around to where he'd left his car.

It looked as if he'd make it out of here, if the cop at the house hadn't yet radioed ahead to his partner at the gate.

He made a long sweep around the premises, and he could see that the search for him had advanced through the house; lights were going on even in some upstairs rooms.

Hearing a footfall, knowing someone was skirting the perimeter in search of him now, Lucas crouched beside a hedgerow. When the man came into view, Lucas recognized him as the uniformed young man at the door. As soon as he was near enough, Lucas placed the cold steel of his .38 against the nape of the kid's neck, making him start.

"Shut up and listen."

"Are you nuts, Plumber?"

"Shut up, I said."

The kid complied.

"Drop your weapon and kick it away."

He did as told once again.

"Radio the gate that everything is okay here, and your pal's to let Plumber exit peacefully."

The kid hesitated.

"Do it, damn you!" He cocked his weapon and rested it again at the base of the kid's brain. He intentionally allowed the weapon to shiver as if he were nervous. The feel of the muzzle lightly shaking and raising the kid's hairs was enough to convince him.

"All right, all right . . ." The young cop made the call and repeated precisely what Stonecoat wanted without hesitation or a quiver in his voice.

"Well done and good night," Stonecoat pronounced,

striking a blow that sent the kid into unconsciousness. "Sorry, kid," he apologized as he stepped over the young man.

He quickly made his way to his car, got in, and started away, bringing his headlights up on the gate, where already the partner had hit the electronic gate opener. The gates rolled back, the open streets of Houston welcoming Lucas back into their anonymity.

He casually waved to the gatekeeper, who waved back, and Lucas felt the weight of the crystal wine goblets in each pocket. They felt good, he felt great, better than he had in a long, long time. He thought of how much more fun and how much more dangerous tonight would have been if Wallace Jackson had been with him.

$\mathcal{F}$OURTEEN

Morning stars: to direct, guide

Lucas lay on his own bed now in his own small apartment, feeling foolish and harebrained and thinking now just how small his place was compared to how the rich lived, and he stared the whole while across the room at the two crystal goblets still in their cellophane sheaths. He'd placed them on his dresser, where they were busy catching and reflecting the light, the colors bouncing off the mirror in a variegated, miniature world of crazy mazes, dancing about the walls as if some spectral campfire from an ancient time had invaded Lucas's room.

The goblets' jewel-like multifaceted cuts were like fire in more ways than one. They would fetch a few good bucks at any of the hundreds of pawnshops in the city or in nearby Galveston. They could also bring him suspension, sanctions, possible other disciplinary action. He was angry with himself for having gotten sucked into this by Sanger, and even angrier at himself for having foolishly lifted these glasses from a taped crime scene. It was enough, alongside striking another officer, to get him thrown off the force.

He momentarily wondered if subconsciously the shining fire glass had symbolized for him his former self, his burning flame—lost for some years now; it also represented his old idiocy. Perhaps it was an idiocy handed down from former generations, an idiocy of the genetic kind, one he could never truly hope to escape. He had heard stories all his life of Indian ancestors who "counted coup," men who dared death, flaunted their prowess as warriors, even brave Cherokee women of the Wolf clan and other clans, known as War Women, who fought alongside their men in battles lost to time and oblivion. But the Cherokee did not make war for territorial or political reasons; they made war for one reason only, to restore the natural order of the universe when one of their brothers was killed. They made war only in retaliation for murder, in order to avenge fallen brothers of the same fire. This thought, as always, made him curious about a missing people who called themselves the *Ani-yun-wiya*, the Principal People who were at the known center of the world, and about Kana'ti and Selu, the first man and woman, who most certainly faced enormous obstacles in their lifetimes.

As with all life, change came, sometimes violently, with the clash of cultures, and so came war and reasons for war with it, along with the Cherokee idea of what constituted bravery. As Cherokees were pushed westward, first to Oklahoma Territory on the Trail of Tears, some later migrating from there to Texas, they adapted many of the Plains Indians ideas of war and bravery, learning that bravery could mean making a fool of a white man, sometimes simply by stepping into an enemy camp, slapping an enemy's face, and escaping with his horses to return to a village as a hero.

Stonecoat's very name had come about on one such foray

into the camp of a sleeping band of conquistadors. His ancient ancestor had led a band of Cherokee into an enemy stronghold, surprising the "stonecoated" one in his sleep, attacking and wiping out the Spanish detachment in retaliation for earlier wrongs. When his renowned ancestor had killed the leader of these men, he had taken the man's breastplate and henceforth worn it in battle, and so his followers came to call him Stonecoat. The first Stonecoat survived many battles and died in old age, probably forty or forty-five, and was buried with his silver breastplate as a warrior. Lucas had always wondered if the man, like Lucas, might not have simply been crazy.

Lucas wondered now if Meredyth Sanger was, in a sense, a War Woman, if she wouldn't fit right in with the Wolf clan. He admired her tenacity, but he also wished now he had never met the woman. He recalled at the same time their stroll through the Houston city zoo, what a wonderful time he had had with her, and how lovely a person she actually was, and how he had liked having her sitting across from him in his apartment, and how that was likely something he'd never see again. At the same time his mind raced with the question of how he was going to find an independent lab in this town that could discreetly analyze the fire glasses for fingerprints and chemical residue. At the same instant, another voice in his head told him not to bother, that no prints would be found on the glasses, that he killer was too damned smart for that, that he would have wiped them clean of prints before putting them into the dishwasher, and he'd have cleansed them of any chemical residue.

"Then why didn't he put them up with the other twenty-two goblets on the shelf?" Lucas asked the room.

"He couldn't find the others. He was in a rush, so he shoved them into the machine just to get them out of sight," he answered himself.

He nodded to his own inner counsel and replied, "You know something, Indian man? You're probably right."

So, if there wasn't so much as a damned trace of a print on the goblets, why'd I steal them? he wondered. *Am I that hard up for trouble?*

He got up, went to the mirror, and stared at his reflection before answering himself.

"I borrowed them as evidence," he tried to convince himself, "because . . . if they are thoroughly and absolutely clean, then the glasses were wiped clean and shoved into the dishwasher. Why? This means the killer was careful to clean up after himself."

Stonecoat paced the floor until someone below banged on the ceiling, sending him back to his bed where he placed his hands behind his head and resumed thinking and talking to himself. "After he drank wine with the judge, he killed the old man and then took great pains to clean up the evidence. He knew his victim. If that's the case, the old man went to bed with the killer, slept with him or her? Or allowed the killer to take a bed just down the hall from him, likely in one of his guest rooms, where the killer patiently waited for the old man to nod off, as in Poe's story *The Tell-Tale Heart*."

Like *The Tell-Tale Heart*, this crime involved hearts, but unlike Poe's story of guilt and anxiety and stress overcoming the murderer, Lucas didn't expect to hear of anyone's claiming responsibility for Judge Charles D. Mootry's murder—save the habitual lunatic confessors found in every major metropolitan city. No . . . no sociopath who might be psychotic enough to drive a steel stake through the heart of the judge was likely to unburden himself at having killed old Uncle Charlie.

This thought brought him back around full circle to himself and self-protection and a concern for self-preservation. What kind of fool—or rather, how many kinds of fools—had he played tonight? He hadn't taken such risks since . . . since before the death of Wallace Jackson, since before the accident nearly costing him his own life as well as Jackson's. The night had been great, uplifting, filled with risks. It had rejuvenated him in many ways, and he had Sanger to curse or to thank for his troubles now.

Had Dr. Sanger known of his buried need for a life of risk-taking? Had she read him so thoroughly and easily?

But perhaps the risks were too great, too gaping huge should he tumble. He had so much to lose, and what was in it for him if he went out of his way to solve the Mootry case, anyway?

Certainly there were no guarantees. The department, once they learned of how he had approached this case, how he had circumvented the law, would not look kindly on his intervention, despite a favorable outcome. He knew this all too clearly. Even if he did succeed, there would be sanctions.

So what's in it for me? he silently asked himself, his room, the goblets, the dead judge, his own ancestors.

At near two A.M., he closed his eyes on the madness he'd become a part of. He was only certain of one thing at the moment of sleep. He did not wish to get any more involved with either the Mootry case or Dr. Meredyth Sanger.

He wanted rather to crawl back into that safe place where he had been before meeting her. But that meant returning like a dog with his tail between his legs to the goddamned Cold Room and pretending nothing had changed. He wasn't completely convinced he could do that, but a stern and cautionary voice deep within told him he bloody well had no other choice.

Meredyth Sanger had tried to sleep, but her frustration and her feeling of resentment toward everyone associated with the Houston Police Department—and especially Lucas Stonecoat now—had boiled anew to the surface and had actually awakened her in the night. A look at her clock told her that it was 3:11 A.M. The entire day before, she had hoped to hear from Lucas Stonecoat, that he had had time to really think things through, and that he realized his earlier mistake in not instantly and readily joining forces with her. It all seemed so obviously the right thing to do, at least in her mind's eye. Besides, what better offer was he holding out for?

She sat upright in bed, feeling like a windswept prairie, her throat parched. She reached for the water beside her bed and gulped at it. She mentally began to browbeat herself for having sunk so low as to go out stalking and pleading with the big bear for his help. "To hell with him," she reiterated for the hundredth time since he'd declined helping her in her quest.

"As a trained psychiatrist," she told herself aloud, "you should've known better. You'd think you would be a better judge of character after all this time, dealing with the abnormal, the aberrant, the psychos."

Part of her work took her into jail cells and courtrooms, where she ran tests and conducted interviews to determine whether or not a man was legally sane or medically insane, competent to stand trial or not.

"So, why couldn't I have seen the truth about Stonecoat?" she wondered aloud.

Like any man who faced extreme trauma, pain, and suffering, he had a right to the armor he had built up around himself, his protective coat. Stonecoat was an apt name for the man. Trauma permanently changed a man, any man. Why should Lucas Stonecoat be any different? Nowadays, he naturally leaned more toward a conservative and safe lifestyle. Naturally he did not want to go out of his way to risk himself. Unfortunately, his reaction to her and her offer was all too normal.

In her profession, she saw all the wide spectrum of machismo in the male cop—and in many a female cop as well. She saw the gung-ho, anxious to face down death and prove some private code of valor, and she saw those who feared not only the street and the job they had committed themselves to, but their own shadows after a brush with death. She saw some ruthless cops, some reckless cops, and others who were careless and foolish, while some were careful and cautious to a fault, a fault that could get a partner killed.

Every man reacted to the streets differently, and little wonder, given the variety of experience of each new recruit.

So maybe the Cold Room was easy for Lucas Stonecoat, a haven of a place to spend his second career as a cop in absolute safety, without risks and far removed from the trauma of his past in Dallas. She had thought the Cold Room her ally in fetching him to her side. The Cold Room, with its walls closing in on his Indian soul, she had believed, must convince Lucas that if he did not join forces with her, his spirit would wither and die.

But perhaps that spirit she had heard about had already died, back in Dallas.

She knew the Cold Room might easily drive any man crazy, but once more, Lucas was not just any man.

Despite it all, despite his turning her down, there remained a gentle intrigue surrounding this man, with his tough guy exterior and hidden hurts. There was a mystery about the pained expression—the knowing eyes that seared another's soul. There was a fire, like embers that might burn on forever, deep within the luminous brown eyes of this man, and this mystery had leapt out at her like a cougar and had touched her as she had not been touched by anyone in a long time. He was, clinically speaking, a fascinating case study.

At the same time, she knew she could not allow this man too close. He was nothing if not dangerous; he was, rightly or wrongly, filled with paranoia and phobias, not to mention his physical problems and the abuse of alcohol and drugs that were all too often the aftermath of a yearlong hospital stay. Besides, she had Conrad McThuen to think of. She and Conrad had been working up to a total commitment now for too long, and she loved Conrad, who was a real estate acquirer and market analyst for the University of Texas at Houston, a man who was outside police and legal circles— and she thanked God for that.

Conrad's duties with the university had sent him on an extended trip to Italy, of all places. Conrad had pleaded with her to take some time, come away with him, but she had been too obsessed with her recent discoveries to back off now, and so she had declined a romantic getaway with her lover in favor of beating her head against the stone wall of Captain Lawrence's prejudice and attempting headway with Stonecoat, and nothing guaranteed.

"So what does that say about you, Doctor? Maybe the redskin was right: 'Heal thyself'?" she muttered to the empty bed.

Maybe she needed to soften the Indian up, but how? She could fix him up with a girlfriend. He did great with the zoo animals; maybe he could be half as charming toward Carrie or Dana? Or perhaps the more exotic Abigail?

She lay back against her pillows, contemplating her role as Cupid, soon allowing sleep to reclaim her, the thought of playing matchmaker to Lucas Stonecoat swirling about her brain like a whirling dervish, perhaps determined to find an alternative to the idea of matchmaking—maybe blackmail?

It wasn't an idea she relished, and it certainly wouldn't enhance her already shaky beginning with Stonecoat, but if it was all she had . . . maybe . . .

FIFTEEN

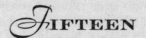

Saddle bags: journey

A fire raged in the gaping, open mouth of the giant incinerator, the resultant heat singeing the hair on the thick arms of the man standing before it. With a grunt, he lifted a final shovelful of black coal and tossed the black rock and ash to feed the fire even further. He stared at the gauge, which was nearing nine hundred degrees Fahrenheit.

"Close enough," he told himself.

The room was hot with the furnace's maw. The fire inside the furnace licked out at the surrounding world like a living creature in search of prey.

Carefully placing the now-hot shovel against the ancient stone walls of his dungeon, the big man reached next for one of two black polyethylene Hefty bags that had been left against the wall as well. With friends looking on, the bare-chested fire-feeder lifted one of the bags and slowly approached the furnace mouth. But before he could fully swing the bag and its deadweight contents into the raging fire, the heat melted the facing side of the bag, causing its heavy and bulky contents to spill out over the filthy bare concrete floor here, creating a kind of sticky gruel of the ancient dust on the stone floor and bodily fluids spilling from the human body parts that the fire-feeder had spilt.

The man stared down at the head, eyes, nose, ears, hair and the left leg once attached to Timothy Kenneth Little.

"Damn you, Little," cursed one of the other men looking on, whose face was hidden in shadow, lit now and again by the licking flames from the incinerator. "You'll not escape so easily as that. You're in Helsinger's Pit now. . . ."

"Toss the bastard in, eyes directed at the flames," said another of the onlookers. "So the evil bastard can see the flames as they lick him up."

The others agreed with a hearty alcoholic cheer, and the bare-chested, sweating fire-feeder did as instructed.

The leg followed.

The second bag was pushed into the fire-feeder's hands after this, and he was told, "Be a little more careful with the rest of him."

The booming voice of their leader, still in shadow, called out, "Sure beats burying his parts all over the country, wouldn't you say, gentlemen?"

The others laughed and agreed.

"And stoke that fire up to a thousand. I want nothing left to chance; not a trace of Little's head or privates or limbs or bones is to be left. Only ashes."

The second bag, containing Little's private parts, his other leg, and his two arms, was tossed into the inferno. The flames spit out at the men surrounding the furnace as the feeder began shoveling more coal into the mix.

The dark dungeon was alight with a warm glow, and this glow filled the small ministry, who together began a mantra: "Helsinger . . . Helsinger . . . Helsinger . . . sing. Sing for me . . . sing for we . . . We provide you with this demonic and foul creature. Banish him forever to the pit. We do your bidding, our God. . . ."

"Some things you can't do on-line," muttered their leader through clenched teeth.

Lucas was already late for roll call, and he knew he'd be in trouble with Sergeant Kelton, because Lucas's absence had caused a gaping hole in Stanley Kelton's log entry, and Stan didn't like big holes in his little square boxes. However, since he was already late, he swung by Renquist Laboratories, Inc., an independent biochemical and DNA lab in downtown Houston.

He walked in with the two Waterford crystal goblets in their cellophane wraps, each labeled with dated evidence labels which he had snatched from his detective's kit at home. They looked official enough, and he signed as Det. James Pardee, giving them a number where he couldn't possibly be reached, since it was the number for the Houston Rockets ticket office. His plan was to check back with them hourly until they had some results for him, so he would be doing the calling.

"Where is your paperwork on this?" asked the clerk.

"It'll be coming."

"Coming? We need it with the item to be analyzed."

"It's forthcoming. My partner'll bring it over this afternoon. Trust me."

"This is highly irregular."

"I didn't want to waste any time."

"We'll at the very least have to tag it." She typed up a label and placed it over the plastic covering each goblet. "There's no way I can assure you that these items, without the proper paperwork, will not be lost in the . . . along the system here. You'll have to sign here to release the items into our custody and sign this waiver form, which relieves Renquist of any responsibility for loss or damage."

"Understood." He signed everything as James Pardee.

"Then the City of Houston Police Department precinct number that will be paying for these tests?"

"The Twenty-second Precinct," he replied, giving them Amelford and Pardee's precinct number. "Paper's on its way; you'll get paid."

She stared back at him, an owl of a woman, her glasses larger than her face. "All right, Detective—ahh—Pardee. We'll begin to process your request, but without the paperwork, it could get held up. I warn you in advance."

"It's been a while since I've done this. Can you give me the blank forms? Maybe I can speed up the process at our end if I have them."

She frowned and her eyes sent shards into him, but finally she relented, nodded, thinking this a sound idea, and with the speed of a Musketeer whipping out a sword, she presented the forms to him.

They exchanged pleasantries and Lucas was on his way, the staid clerk staring suspiciously after him, marking him.

He could feel her eyes on him all the way out the door.

As soon as Lucas stepped inside the precinct house, Stan Kelton was on him like a tick, asking him, "Mister, who do you think you are? Mister, what gives you the right to waltz in and out of here anytime you feel like? Mister, tell me this: What rank are you, mister?" Kelton's eyes grew ablaze.

Kelton never called an officer an officer when he was angry with the officer.

Lawrence burst forth from his office, shouting for Stonecoat to come into his sanctuary immediately. He'd obviously heard Kelton dressing him down, and now it appeared Lawrence wanted the privilege himself.

"Sorry, Sarge," said Lucas. "You'll have to get in line."

"Now," ordered Lawrence.

When Lucas stepped through the door and saw Meredyth, he assumed that Dr. Sanger was once more driving Lawrence up the wall. But Commander Andrew Bryce, seated at Lawrence's desk, suddenly shredded Lucas's assumptions when he held up a police fax alert, saying, "I got this on my machine this morning."

"What is it?"

"Some disturbing news out of Oregon, a carbon copy killing in the style of our Judge Mootry. Some poor slob named Little, Timothy Little."

Stonecoat stared at the fax and then across at Meredyth. "Arrows?"

"Two recovered at the scene this time," she replied.

"And the body?"

"One torso, clothes and all identity taken off, along with arms, legs, head and private parts," began Commander Bryce, gritting his teeth and shaking his head. "And damned if this isn't beginning to make us look a bit bad, gentlemen, Dr. Sanger. And since it appears you, Dr. Sanger, have shown a hell of a lot more initiative and gumption than some people around here"—he viciously raked Lawrence with his eyes—"I'm having Phil here send you up to this place . . . Medford, Oregon, to have a look. And as for you, Stonecoat, or should we call you Jack? Jack Plumber?"

"Sir? Plumber, sir?" Lucas feigned ignorance.

"We got a pretty good description on the intruder at the Mootry crime scene, Officer Stonecoat. I don't think we need to play games, do you?"

"Well, sir . . . no, sir," stammered Lucas, unsure what to say next.

"At any rate, what we have up north may just be one of those damned copycat things or . . ."

"Or the same guy at work," Meredyth eagerly finished for Bryce.

Captain Lawrence interrupted. "Commander Bryce seems to feel that we should send someone up to investigate, Stonecoat, and he suggested that it be you. I have to say, I haven't approved of the way you and Dr. Sanger have gone about this, and I certainly wouldn't send you two to cover traffic at the rodeo, but—"

"But, hell, Phil," cried Bryce. "You didn't think there was much to this serial killer conspiracy thing. What'd you call it, a *cum laude* conspiracy angle that Dr. Sanger has put together with earlier cases from the Cold Files, and now this thing in Oregon. Hell, man, it puts a whole new kink into the starch." Andrew Bryce was boiling over, filling the room with his large, commanding form. He had sharp gray eyes, flinty and hard. Lucas thought him direct and energetic and a leader of men. He liked him. "Now, I want you, Stonecoat, to accompany Dr. Sanger to Medford. See what the two of you can find out up there. See if it has any bearing on us here."

"You want me to go have a look at what they've got in Oregon?" He wondered why the brass were being so generous to make such an offer. Did they expect it to be a wild-goose chase? Did they expect, even want Lucas to fail along with Dr. Sanger on this?

"Well, sir, if you want me to go, then I'm on my way." He thought of the crystal goblets and cringed inside.

"Good, then it's settled. Dr. Sanger, Officer Stonecoat, there's a military transport waiting for you at Houston Intercontinental Airport. Pack a bag out of your locker and be on your way," Commander Bryce replied. "They won't hold on to this guy Little's body long up there. They've already held off a day, trying to decide what in hell they've got. Apparently, they've got their hands more than full and haven't had much experience with such problems in the past. For that matter, neither have we."

Meredyth added, "They contacted VICAP, reported what they had to the FBI, everybody, in hopes someone would come in and give them a hand."

Stonecoat nodded. "And we're it?"

"Sanger here put out a nationwide alert on anything resembling Mootry," grumbled Lawrence.

Lucas countered with, "I'd have thought the detectives on the case would've done that."

"No, they hadn't got round to it, it appears!" bellowed Bryce, his darting eyes finding Lucas.

"Meanwhile, these hicks in Oregon want to call out the National Guard," added Lawrence.

"Why the overreaction?"

Meredyth explained. "Turns out he's a millionaire two or three times over, something to do with jet airline appliances and solutions. I don't know, but the family'll be wanting to feel some closure as soon as possible, and that'll mean releasing the body—or what's left of it—over to them."

"I see." Murder always left more victims than the dead one.

"And if it is connected to Mootry and Palmer and Reynolds," she added, "the man's immediate family could also be in danger."

"Mootry didn't have any immediate family, but if what Dr. Sanger has uncovered has any validity, apparently family members of victims have also been targeted by this creep, so we're letting authorities in this guy's hometown know what's going down as well. Meantime, Stonecoat, you're our guy in Oregon, along with—"

"Yes, sir, Commander."

"—Dr. Sanger here, and I want you two to report directly to Phil. Anything I need to know, he will in turn report to me. No more going over Phil's head, either, young lady. I'm not in the least impressed by that sort of thing, you understand? I want you three to work together!"

"Yes, sir," she replied, obviously happy with having been vindicated, but Lucas wasn't yet sure. It might well be that what had occurred in Oregon had next to nothing to do with Palmer or Mootry or the other cases they had examined. He would keep his counsel and withhold judgment.

Together, Lucas and Meredyth left Lawrence's office, and when the door closed behind them, she gave him the high-five sign, but he only frowned, refusing to return it.

She was surprised by his reaction. "What's wrong with you? Don't you get it? This assignment gets you out of the Cold Room."

"For how long?"

"For as long as it takes; hopefully for good, if we do well in Oregon."

"Well, I've got a smoldering little problem of my own right here," he replied, taking her aside, locating the stairwell.

"Are you crazy, Andrew?" asked Lawrence, the moment Sanger and Stonecoat were out of the room.

Bryce remained impassive, silently moving about the room, lifting little knickknacks and items from Lawrence's shelves, staring at the other man's family photos, pictures of Lawrence as a much younger man in a football uniform and then a Marine Corps uniform. Bryce then stated the obvious. "You were a marine, once, I see."

You know that from my goddamned record, Lawrence's mind screamed. "Wellllll, yeah . . . but what's that got to do with anything?" he replied.

"Put in for the Marine Corps once myself, but had trouble getting in. I was too young at the time. Moved on from there . . . A boy grows up . . . puts wild notions aside. . . ."

What's that supposed to mean? wondered Lawrence. It wasn't like Bryce to wax philosophical. "You going to answer me, Commander?"

"Oh, about sending those two to Oregon? It seems the logical thing to do, wouldn't you agree? I mean, what'll they find in Oregon? Meanwhile, it might keep them out of the way of the Mootry investigation."

"Then you don't believe they'll find any connection in Oregon? You're hoping that they'll become discouraged with this serial killer notion?"

"Maybe . . . Meantime, Pardee and Amelford aren't hindered."

Lawrence wondered about the wisdom of this, but he kept silent on that, merely replying, "Yes, sir." God, he had to bite back bile to show this man respect, he thought. What had Andrew Bryce done to earn anyone's respect? Yes, he had come up through the ranks, but when was the last time he was on the street, the last time he risked a hair on his politically correct head? Bastard.

Bryce seemed to sense his animosity. He grinned at Lawrence. "Give it all time, Phil. Time is a wonderful solvent for many nasty stains we encounter."

On that note, Commander Bryce abruptly turned and disappeared, leaving Lawrence alone with his office and his own counsel. He turned to the PC behind his desk and called up a bulletin board he liked to play around with; he found it helped him to unwind. Maybe he'd go searching for some familiar log-ins and friends on the Internet. Friends and acquaintances on the Internet seemed controllable, predictable even. These people in the real world, especially those he was supposed to supervise, caused him so much dull pain, he could easily lose control and use his gun on them, or on himself, he thought now.

In the stairwell now where Lucas had taken Meredyth, the two waited for a passing pair of blue-uniformed cops before they spoke.

"Precisely what kind of a problem do you have, Lucas? This is great, what Bryce has done. He's giving us a chance to prove what we know."

He didn't readily answer, beginning to pace instead.

"Spit it out, Stonecoat."

He told her of how he'd gone to Mootry's mansion home, and how he'd finagled his way into the crime scene.

"Damn! Then it *was* you! When? How?" She was full of questions.

He gave her the details, including his theory about the cutter being clever in knowing precisely where to cut.

"No, the autopsy reports were sealed to protect the integrity of the evidence collection process and to help the detectives. How could you know that?"

"The lack of blood evidence."

"I see you've gotten down to it, and here I thought you weren't interested. Silly me."

"I just went to get the feel of the place."

"So, whataya think?"

"What do you mean, what do I think? He was murdered, and not in a kind way."

"Yeah, everybody knows that, Ace Ventura, but you must've come away with more than that."

"Well, I did . . . and that's my problem."

"What do I need here, pliers? What're you talking about, Lucas?"

He told her how he had lain in Charles Mootry's bed, over the very spot where the arrow had gone through the man's heart. "I wanted to become him for that moment," he explained. He told her how he'd wandered the house and noticed a pair of errant coasters and the two goblets he'd discovered in the dishwasher.

"Wait a minute . . . are you saying that you took them?"

"They're at Renquist as we speak."

"The labs?"

"And I need these forms filled out and initialed and stamped by the captain over at the Twenty-second Precinct to get the results and the goblets back."

"Damn, I knew you were a little loco, Lucas, but this . . ."

He gave her a self-deprecating little shrug, like a boy, she thought. Then he asked, "What can I say? More to the point, what can I do?"

"I've got a secretary who can help us."

"A secretary? How's she going to help?"

"You wait and see how *he's* going to help."

She guided him to her office two flights up where they found her secretary on the computer. The young man turned and beamed at Dr. Sanger and smiled at Lucas, extending a hand. He was clean-cut and clear-eyed behind a pair of fashionable half-tinted glasses.

"Officer Lucas Stonecoat, this is Randy Oglesby, the best man I ever saw with a computer. If he can't fix your little problem, Lucas, no one can."

"Maybe, but what I'm asking could get you both into deep . . . trouble. Are you sure you want to go through with this?"

"Tell Randy your problem, and we'll take it from there. Meantime, I've got to grab a few items from my office in preparation for our trip."

"Trip?" asked Randy. "What trip, Doctor?"

She explained they must be in Oregon this afternoon. "There's been another crossbow killing, Randy."

"Jesus God, another one? That's so . . . so weird, so out there, you know?"

"Yeah, we know what's out there, don't we, Lucas?"

"I wish we knew a little more about what's out there, exactly what we're looking for," he replied, but she rushed off, only half listening to his complaint. Lucas then turned to the eager young male secretary and explained to Randy about the Twenty-second Precinct voucher forms, finishing with, "I'm sure you can't do a thing about it, so thanks anyway. . . ."

"You mean even if you could overlook the dangers of hacking into the Twenty-second's accounts receivable's routing problem, could I put aside my petty morality and conscience? Is that all?"

"Something like that." Lucas instantly liked the kid with the lopsided grin.

"Hacking. I live for it, officer, so I'll see what I can do."

"In that case, I'll need one more favor."

He nodded, his red hair bouncing. "If I can, sure."

Lucas asked him if he'd act as a courier when the results were in, fetching them from Renquist Labs and keeping the results in a safe place until his return.

"Anything else?" the kid half joked.

"As a matter of fact, yes."

"You don't ask much." Again it was in a kidding tone.

"You may have to use an alias to get the results. They may ask you to sign, also."

"What's my name?"

"Pardee, Detective Jim Pardee. And if that's a problem for whatever reason, use Detective Fred Amelford."

The kid smiled up from his computer, even his eyeglasses alight with the possibilities of intrigue. "I've always wanted to be a detective."

"It's not a game. This is very serious. If you're caught—"

"I say I was working under Dr. Sanger's orders," he finished as she emerged.

Stonecoat laughed. "You're a fast learner."

"That's what I noticed about Randy the moment I hired him," Meredyth added. "Just what've you two cooked up? No, don't tell me. I really don't think I want to know."

"I'll fill you in on the ride over to your place and on the plane," Lucas suggested, and they were off, leaving Randy Oglesby to stare after the couple. He wondered what Stonecoat expected to lift from the goblets he'd mentioned.

"This guy's got balls," Randy told his computer as the screen flashed before him with the information needed to forward a voucher to Renquist from the Twenty-second Precinct. "Piece of cake. Give me something challenging, people!" he said to himself, recalling his darkest secret, something he'd never told anyone, not even his parents. When he was still just a kid in high school, he had hacked his way into HBO, and it was he who was responsible for the 1986 interference with the HBO signal. He had sent his own signal over nationwide television at HBO's expense, and it had read: *I'll never pay for free airwaves.* After that, he had avoided electronic capture by downloading everything, completely gutting his system, and starting all over again. He had simply pulled the plug on any possible investigation that could lead back to his PC in Steubenville, California, where he had grown up.

Randy had very much liked the mission Dr. Sanger had last put him on: sending out a request on the law enforcement Internet regarding any and all unsolved murders in which crossbow-styled weapons or arrows were used. The notion had tickled him at first, and then it revived some old memories of a game of cat and mouse played out on the video screen between the forces of good and evil, but the forces had become blurred with a madman named Helsinger and his henchmen each in turn taking on the name and the ritualistic quest of their leader to seek out and destroy evil. But it was evil as defined by the original game-player, Helsinger 1, who could be anybody who initiated the game. It was a lot like Dungeons and Dragons, but all mixed up with Ravenloft and vampires and vampire-stalkers, as well. It got a lot of play back then, Helsinger's Pit as it was called, because eventually the evil one's hacked-up parts were returned to the so-called pit from which they had emerged—Satan's underworld.

Randy had quit playing the game years before, having become bored with it, having graduated to more sophisticated software. Still, he thought it odd how so often life imitated art, for then only comic characters were firing harmless arrows from crossbows at imaginary, albeit human, targets, but here and now, some damned fool was out there in real time and in real space butchering men like Judge Charles Mootry, and now some guy in Oregon, in the same or similar fashion as in the game he'd nearly forgotten.

He was reminded of the song lyrics, "It's a strange, strange world we live in, Master Jack. . . ."

He wondered when, if ever, Dr. Sanger was going to share what they had learned on the Internet regarding bow-and-arrow deaths across the nation and throughout the world. They were more common than first thought might allow. Most were hunting accidents, granted, and some were speargun accidents between diving buddies, but others had gone down as outright murders, most remaining unsolved, and some were as far away as Spain and Great Britain and Prague, while others were closer to home: Washington State, L.A., Nebraska, Oklahoma, Miami, Chicago.

Dr. Sanger hadn't told Randy what she'd done with the list, but from what he'd gathered, he knew she hadn't initially shared it with Captain Phillip Lawrence, that she more likely took it over his head, possibly to Commander Andrew Bryce. Then all of a sudden everything was popping and stripping. She was now headed for Oregon, where the latest crossbow killing had taken place.

Fascinating stuff, and he was proud to've played his small role. Dr. Sanger had also confided somewhat about Lucas Stonecoat and how hard she had worked to get the former detective, now in the Cold Room, to work alongside her on uncovering the truth out there. Maybe by Randy's helping Stonecoat with his problem, the favor would bounce back someday.

He sent the electronic impulses that would fax Renquist all they needed from the Twenty-second Precinct to arrange billing for the work on the goblets.

Sixteen

Medicine man's eye: vigilant, wise

764LT1:\C42119\Category 42 . . . Topic
49LOG . . . Message 438 . . . Thurs.
July 28, 1996 . . . 1:10:01
Questor 1 . . . Helsinger's Pit . . .

Q1: There is a threat. A new enemy has
risen and has flown from the Star Kingdom,
49th Realm. These are two enforcer demons—
male and female. They must be stopped. They
go now to where you last traveled. Take all
necessary precautions and take as much
help as you require. All details await your
departure. Reply this board 0700. Good
luck. Questor 1 . . . END TRANSMISSION, Category 42, Topic 49LOG . . . 1:13:06

Category 42 . . . Topic 49LOG . . . Message 439 . . . Thurs. July 28, 1996 . . .
1:51:02

```
Questor 2 . . . from the Pit . . .

Q2: Understood. Will take all necessary
precautions and resources. Will follow
instructions to letter. END TRANSMISSION, Cat-
egory 42, Topic 49LOG . . . 1:52:00



Category 42 . . . Topic 49LOG . . . Mes-
sage 440 . . . Thurs. July 28, 1996 . . .
2:05
Questor 3 . . .


Q3: Agreed. Will locate alien beings in
NorthStar quadrant. Will dissuade all
misguided creatures there. END TRANSMISSION,
Category 42, Topic 49LOG . . . 2:06:01
```

Lucas and Meredyth had first gone to her apartment, where she quickly stuffed a flexible bag with whatever she felt essential for an overnight stay—which apparently meant quite a lot, Lucas thought when he looked at the time. Still, he knew that their trip could last through an extra day. While he waited for her to pack, Lucas looked about her neatly arranged, beautifully decorated apartment, feeling the lightness of it, the soft hues—her corner of paradise, it would appear. She was well dug in here, had put a small fortune into the upscale apartment. The place appeared all her.

"Make yourself at home," she called out from the bedroom, where she'd disappeared moments before. "There's some soft drinks in the fridge and some leftovers if you're hungry."

He was more interested in snooping.

He looked at her paintings, the soft blues of mountains seemingly her favorite view. Some of the soft hues matched her intelligent blue eyes. He picked over a handful of photos she had displayed over a mantel, one of an older couple, their arms about one another—no doubt Meredyth's parents. They looked, from their clothing and the trappings around them, well-off indeed, their station somewhere south of filthy rich, but quite comfortable. They appeared to be rather bookish types, he likely a college dean and she likely a banker, if she worked at all. The father looked like a stern and intelligent man, possibly a scientist, possibly into psychiatry like his daughter, Lucas guessed from the disheveled way he wore his expensive, Ivy League clothes; perhaps he taught psychiatry at one of the local colleges and had invested well. Her mother looked the picture of comfort and caring, and had a dimpled face like Meredyth's own. Another picture showed a youngster in the couple's arms, but here the parents were decidedly younger, straighter, and the child was a little girl dressed in her best—Meredyth as a child. A third photo was of a handsome, square-jawed, dark-haired man, perhaps Meredyth's current age or a bit older. He was no doubt her current boyfriend. The name *Conrad* was scrawled carelessly across the picture with the words *Love and Devotion.*

Lucas went to the large balcony windows which looked out over greater Houston, and he stared long at the clean, straight, even geometry of the skyline where Houston's greatest pinnacles stood like lances pointed to the sun. *It must be a magnificent view at night,* he thought. It was a terrific, first-class, lush, and expensive apartment.

As she packed, Meredyth called out again from the other room. "So, you went to see the judge's digs?"

"I did."

"You might've had the decency to ask me along."

"Getting myself past the guards was hard enough. How would I have explained you?"

"You seem quite clever enough to explain away most

anything. I heard about your little incident at that gas station the other day."

"I did what I had to do," he called back, walking toward her bedroom now and standing in the doorway.

She was leaning in over her suitcase, packing a final cache of underwear. She looked up at him but resumed packing as she spoke. "So, are you going to tell me what you found at the judge's place or not? And what gives with those goblets you took?"

"I'll tell you what I think if you'll tell me how they ID'ed the victim in Oregon, since they had no hands for prints, no head for teeth or features."

"Birthmark, lower back, right-hand side, a little cherry the family knew about. Besides, everyone in Rogue River was expecting him. Had a picket line waiting. Word had gotten out."

"Word had gotten out about what?"

"He was planning to merge with a company called ASCAN."

"And the judge, Mootry, how was he ID'ed? Aside from the fact the carcass was found in his bed, I mean . . ."

"Photographs, scars from the war. He was in Korea. Verified by a family member."

"Whoa, I thought he had no family."

"No one close, but a cousin twice removed or something flew in from Chicago, I think it was. You know his estate had a lock on it until he could be identified, so all of his charitable donations were cut off immediately, and his will was frozen."

"Hmm, so all of a sudden this unknown relative shows up, ID's the body, and all the funds are liquid again?"

"He left a fortune to charitable organizations. Everybody's happy." She zipped and snapped the suitcase closed. "Ready."

"Let me take that for you."

"How about you? You can't have enough in that little bag you brought from the precinct house to carry you all the way through tomorrow."

"I'm fine. We'd best not waste more time."

She nodded. "If you're sure. The plane's not leaving without us."

He carried the bag to the door, saying, "Let's be on our way."

Downstairs they packed her car and headed for Houston Intercontinental Airport. Traffic was hellacious even at mid-morning when most people in downtown Houston were behind a desk somewhere. Lucas wondered where all these people were going, and if they wanted to get there any more than he wanted to get to this small town in Oregon.

Meredyth's police dispatch radio crackled to life. Captain Lawrence was calling her. She lifted the receiver and said, "Dr. Sanger, here, Captain."

"Is he with you?"

"Stonecoat? Right beside me. We're on our way to the airport."

"I want to talk to Stonecoat, now!"

Lucas frowned, raised his shoulders in a clownish shrug, and took the receiver. "Yes, sir, Captain Lawrence?"

"Stonecoat, I just got a very disturbing call from a Detective Amelford over at the Twenty-second Precinct."

Oh, hell, Lucas thought. *They've already learned about my impersonating Pardee at the lab.* Still, Lucas bluffed. "Sir, I'm sorry, but I truly have never heard of anyone by the name of . . . Detective Abelford, sir?"

"The hell you haven't, and it's Amelford. You know perfectly well he's lead investigator on the Mootry case. You learned as much from Dr. Sanger. What pisses me off, Stonecoat, is that you had the unmitigated gall to cross a yellow line, walk all over a crime scene, and God knows what you disturbed out at Mootry's, and to knock a man unconscious on your way out! I don't know why Commander Bryce chose to overlook your transgressions, Stonecoat, but believe me, I am not looking the other way on—"

"Sir, I swear to you, I don't know what you're talking about."

"As Bryce said, the intruder's description matches you absolutely to a T, Stonecoat, and now—"

"I'll be happy to stand a lineup, sir, when I get back."

"If it comes to that, yes, you damned well will, and you'd better have a damned surefire alibi!"

"I do, sir . . . I do. . . ."

"And?"

"I was with Dr. Sanger all last evening, sir . . . ahh, going over the case."

He saw Meredyth visibly stiffen at the suggestion they'd spent the entire night together. She punched him.

"You don't cut any corners, Stonecoat. You go by the book up there in Oregon. You understand me?"

"Absolutely, sir."

Lawrence cut off the conversation without fanfare, his anger still electrifying the receiver.

"Did you have to tell him you spent the night with me?" she demanded. "He already thinks the worst of me."

"Oh, cheap shot, Doctor." But at least he had dodged the bullet on the lab. Obviously, Lawrence knew nothing about that part of his "transgressions" yet.

He offered verbal salve for her wounded ego. "Well, if Captain Lawrence already thinks the worst of you . . . what harm can it do for him to think you spent the night with me?"

"Damn it, Lucas, I do have a life outside police circles which I would like to protect."

"Cops don't get to have personal lives. Why should you?"

"Cops don't want personal lives."

He nodded. "Yeah, I saw Conrad on your mantel."

"Good, then you see why I don't want Lawrence or anyone else down at the precinct to get the wrong idea— about us, I mean."

"All I said was we were going over the case files together."

"I don't think that's what he heard."

They were in the airport traffic now, exiting 59 at North Sam Houston. She drove for John F. Kennedy Boulevard, which was flanked on either side by runways. They need now only get a parking stub and slot and locate the hangar where military planes flew in and out.

"I'm still angry you *didn't* spend the evening with me," she said now.

"Really?"

"What I mean to say is . . . well, the least you could've done was call me after you went out there to the judge's place to tell me what you found. You didn't even bother doing that."

"I still hadn't made up my mind at that point I wanted to get this . . . this involved."

She stared across at him, studying his inscrutable Indian features. "With the case, I hope you mean?"

"Yeah, with the case."

"So why'd you jump at the chance today when Commander Bryce said to get on a plane with me?"

"An old Indian trick."

"What's that?"

"Know when to surrender. I was surrounded, wasn't I? And what kind of choice was I faced with? Disobey my superior and go back to the Cold Room, or obey and see the skies over Oregon? What kind of incentive is that? I mean, you did orchestrate that whole thing back there in his office, and don't deny it. You went directly to Bryce, didn't you? Embarrassed hell out of Phil. And by the way, it appears— even though I missed the main event—you did a lovely bit of maneuvering back there. How'd you get the commander so agreeable in the first place?"

"Call it a little extra incentive I brought to the party. Reach back there in the back seat and grab that file folder. I was going to save this for the plane trip, but since you're interested . . ."

Lucas reached into the back of the small car and almost spilled the pages of the computer printout from the manila folder.

"Go ahead, take a good, long look," she said as if it were a dare.

Lucas stared down at a list of other deaths caused by arrows across the nation, going back several years. Many were crossed out as if unimportant, but others were not. "Damn, this is impressive. Is this what got to Bryce and Lawrence? Why didn't you show it to me before?"

"I didn't have it before."

"Randy Oglesby?"

She nodded.

"You just waved this in front of Bryce, and that's all it took? I don't buy it."

They had found a dark little parking spot inside the towering parking garage fronting the terminals. She pulled the key and looked him in the eye. "I can play hardball, too. I'd warned Lawrence earlier. I made it clear that if we weren't allowed to pursue leads on this angle of the investigation with his approval, then this and all my notes that are currently sealed and safely put away would go directly to Commander Andrew Bryce. Phil called my bluff and so . . ."

"Lawrence's boss. You cut the man deeply with your . . . blackmail."

"Call it what you like."

He laughed inwardly. "I kinda like calling it what it is, blackmail."

She laughed now. "The man left me very little choice, and you . . . you weren't any help. Now tell me, honestly, why'd you go over there to Mootry's? What got you moving? And why didn't you call me to help? With my badge, I could've gotten us past the guards easily enough."

"I didn't want you getting into trouble."

"Bull. Typical male crap. You thought because I'm a woman I'd slow you down somehow."

"Whoa, wait up now!"

"Isn't that it?"

"No, I—"

"That maybe I couldn't climb a fence or run fast enough. But if I'd been with you, there would have been no call for climbing in and out of windows, running or hitting some poor schlepp over the head."

He held up his hands as if under arrest. "I just wanted to check things out for myself. You should be grateful." He was instantly sorry he'd used the word, but it was too fast off his tongue and too late to exchange if for another.

"Grateful? Grateful . . . Just like a man."

"For all you knew, I had canned any thought of getting involved. I had turned you down, remember? And meantime, you're working to tie me to the case anyway, so what is that if it's not typical female . . . procedure?"

She hesitated a bit, pursed her lips and took in a deep breath. He smelled less of alcohol today and more of cologne. "All right, but on the plane, I want to hear everything in detail."

"Everything?"

"Everything you saw, heard, touched, felt, smelt, and tasted out there. I know you're an intuitive cop, a good investigator. I don't want any secrets between us, Lucas."

"All right. Then afterwards, you can tell me all about Conrad."

"Conrad's got nothing to do with the case. That's private life, and it remains private. Let's go."

They located a burly skycap, and he found a maintenance crewman to take them and their bags on a cart across the airport taxi strips to a row of Quonset huts and hangars set apart from the commercial passenger terminals. Some of the huts and hangars here housed UPS, FedEx, Flying Tigers Cargo, and other businesses, but there was one large hangar marked U.S. Army Corps. It was here they were deposited.

They easily located the pilot waiting for them, and after quick introductions, boarded the plane. The pilot wasted no time in getting clearance, and they were airborne within minutes, while passenger planes were jammed like so many pachyderms along a water route.

Stonecoat hadn't flown too often, and each time he did it was both an exhilarating experience and one that filled him with awe. He still could not believe that a building could fly, and the military jet was the size of a small office building.

It was equipped with a small conference area complete with table and comfortable chairs—unusual for military transport, but on boarding, their pilot had explained that the local FBI often engaged their services, so the plane was modified for in-flight conferencing.

"Hell," he had bragged, "we once had none other than Dr. Jessica Coran aboard."

"Who?" Meredyth had replied.

"You know, the federal M.E. who solved the Queen of Hearts killings over in New Orleans? We were part of a search party for an escaped madman who was believed to be in the Oklahoma vicinity at the time. The feds got him, too."

After takeoff and leveling, they availed themselves of coffee, the cushioned chairs, and the conference table.

"So, tell me about Mootry's," she pressed Lucas.

"But I already told you everything."

"I want a play-by-play; every detail, Detective."

He corrected her. "I'm no longer a detective, Doctor, and you know that."

"If you don't mind, I chose your help on the basis of your record as a detective, Detective, and if it helps my confidence in you to call you a detective, then I'm going to go right ahead and do so, Detective."

"Helps you, huh?"

"Yeah, me."

He dropped his gaze, guffawed, and said, "All right."

"Now give me every detail; leave nothing out."

He began at Judge Mootry's gate and told her how he had gained entrance. He found talking to her was easy, even cathartic somehow. She eagerly hung on his every word, fascinated by his having lain down in the exact spot where the judge had died in order to get a fix on the room. Then he explained why he had taken the two glasses from the kitchen.

"Let me get this straight, Lucas," she stopped him. "You took the two goblets *believing* you'd find no prints on them? You took them anyway?"

"I did."

The look of sheer incredibility on her face spoke volumes. "Amelford and Pardee may've seen them, too. May have assumed the same as you, but they left them. But not you . . ."

"I had my reasons."

Her look said, *I'm sure you did.* But she remained silent.

"Well, would you like to hear them?"

"If I don't, I'll go on wondering what made me believe you were some sort of Cherokee Sherlock Holmes. Please, do go on."

He explained his convoluted reasoning. "Whoever killed Mootry knew him."

"You got that from the no prints on the glass?"

"If no prints show, yes. The killer knew Mootry well."

"Well? How well?"

"Perhaps intimately."

"Intimately sexually or intimately intimately alone?"

"Intimately enough to have had a drink with him before tucking him in, I believe."

"Whoa-up there. You mean, from what little you evidenced there, you somehow have come to the conclusion that Mootry trundled off to bed with the killer in the house with him, knowing he was not alone."

"I believe so, yes."

The look of incredulity began to cloud her face again.

"Well, I will say the case has to date lacked a certain imaginative input by the detectives working it."

"That's the problem with a lot of cops," he agreed. "No imagination . . ." He then changed the direction of their discussion. "What do you hope to find in Oregon?"

"I don't know. Use your imagination."

Randy Oglesby was in Muncie's New York Style Deli, awaiting his pastrami on rye and currently on the telephone. He was also in seventh heaven, getting to play a mole within the system, getting to play one cop—Lucas Stonecoat—pretending to be another cop—Jim Pardee. This was like a complex computer game to him, pretense heaped upon pretense, circles within circles, and the result would please the beautiful, talented lady he worked for, Dr. Meredyth Sanger. He was up for it.

From his desk, he had done as the mysterious Lucas Stonecoat had requested, telephoning Renquist Labs hourly for an update on the progress of the testing they were doing for him—Detective James Pardee. He laid it on thick, saying it was possibly the most important case in Texas history since John F. Kennedy was gunned down in Dallas, certainly more important than the Sydney Fielding socialite killing in which her doctor husband had been indicted.

The technician he finally got through to ate it all up, and why not? They had said they would hustle on this one now that the paperwork had been forwarded, and they had.

"So, what're the results?" he asked. "Any usable, clean prints, Darlene?"

Darlene, the technician, her voice an octave lower than the last time Randy called, now replied, "I'm sorry, there was nothing."

"Nothing? Whataya mean, nothing?"

"Detective Pardee," she said in a tone that implied she might as well say, *What part of nothing don't you understand?* "There were no prints on either glass."

"None?"

"Crystal is difficult anyway, the many surfaces, you know, but—"

"Sounds like you guys blew it."

"No, no, sir, no one blew anything. There was not one trace of any human secretions whatever on the glass surfaces. Soap residue, wine residue in the bowls, some sleep-inducing drugs, but no prints whatever."

"Whoa, hold up there. Sleep-inducing drugs?"

"A mild sedative, probably harmless, but in such trace elements, nothing could really be determined. Like the prints you apparently thought would be there."

"Yeah, I see. . . . Thanks, Darlene. Didn't mean to get my back up. It's just . . . just . . . well, I don't admit to cop stress, but maybe this time I will."

"A frustrating case, Detective?"

"Yeah, very."

"It sounds like you are a very dedicated man."

She sounded Oriental, he thought, but with a name like Darlene, he wondered. "You sound very hardworking and dedicated yourself, Darlene, and I want to thank you for being so"—he gulped as if it might help him find the word he wanted—"thorough and professional in getting this information for me in such a . . . a timely manner."

"I only wish that it could be better news for you, but you know we can't . . . fabricate"—she had a little trouble pronouncing the word, and Randy thought it cute—"evidence, you know. We must be finding the truth only."

"Yeah, sure . . . I understand that. Look, about the sleeping drug."

"Yes?"

"Was it detected in both goblets or just one?"

"Just one."

"Thanks, that may be of some help," he replied. "Later on in the investigation, you know?"

She promised to send the results to him.

"Oh, tell you what. Have them sent directly to Detective Lucas Stonecoat, Thirty-first Precinct."

"But I thought they go to you."

"Detective Stonecoat is overseeing this part of the investigation after today, you see."

"Lucas Stone Coat?" she repeated as if writing it down. "Very well." She was saying good-bye now, about to hang up.

He wondered if he dared ask her for a date, but as *who*?

Randy Oglesby or Jim Pardee? Lucas Stonecoat, maybe? He let the phone go dead.

His thoughts and imaginations regarding Darlene and her exquisite voice quickly faded with the realization that Lucas Stonecoat had placed him, his computer, and Dr. Sanger in jeopardy for what? *For absolutely nothing.* Still, there *were* traces of sedatives in the bowl of one goblet.

However, as Darlene had said, it was most likely simply mild sleeping pills. Now he couldn't help but wonder at the costs involved in the useless testing of those goblets taken from the Mootry crime scene. He wondered about Stonecoat's legendary reputation, wondered if it hadn't gone by the wayside, along with a few other things about him since Dallas. He had seen the files on Dr. Sanger's desk, and while he had not read them word for word, he had gotten some feel for what was going on, and he had heard about Lucas Stonecoat through the police grapevine and the support services grapevine as well.

While Randy was no cop, unable to pass muster in the academy, he had determined to remain as close to police work as he could get and utilize his specialized knowledge as best he might for crime fighting. He hadn't planned on working in the Thirty-first Precinct alongside Dr. Meredyth Sanger, and at first he hadn't liked the idea of working so far from the action, for a police shrink instead of a police captain, perhaps. But Dr. Sanger, whose name ought rather be Dr. Danger, had changed his mind about police psychiatry. It was often quite dangerous. She had to deal not only with cops who walked into her office with their guns strapped to their hips, cops who might or might not be mentally unstable, but she had to go down to the jails and face the criminals, too; many of whom were of the criminally insane variety. She often had Randy come along to take dictation if the case warranted it.

Randy was fleet of finger, capable of typing and computing 130 words a minute. He was also an expert on the Net, and he'd proven his worth to Dr. Sanger with the "list," the one she had used as leverage this morning with Captain Lawrence.

If Lawrence had any brains, he'd transfer Randy down to his division, but he wasn't that smart.

Randy's sandwich and drink arrived at his table. He started to go for the food, his stomach growling for it, but on impulse, he rang Renquist once again and asked for Darlene.

She came right on, as if waiting for his call. "Yes, this is Darlene Muentes."

"South American, maybe?" he asked.

"What?"

"This is—"

"I know it's you, Detective."

"I was just guessing that maybe you were from South America? You have a lovely accent."

"I work hard to be rid of my accent."

"You shouldn't hide it. I like it. Everybody else talks the same; it gets boring. Your voice is not . . . boring."

"Is there something else I can do for you, Detective?"

"Ahh, the bill. Can you tell me how much?"

"Oh, well . . . with lab time and testing, let me see. I can give you a rough estimate, but the actual bill, it does not come from here, my lab, I mean."

"How old are you?"

"What?"

"How much?"

"Ahh, maybe seven, seven-fifty."

"Seven hundred dollars for nada?"

"Nada? It took a lot of work to find nada!" she replied.

He nodded into the phone. "Sorry, it's just my boss is not going to be terribly pleased."

"I . . . sorry for that, and I am twenty-three."

It was his first indication she was interested. "I'm twenty-two," he replied. "Look, I'm having lunch at the grill on Elgin, not far from the university, and I know your lab's nearby, so what do you say? Are you hungry?"

"Where is this place?"

He gave her the name and location, and she recognized it. "I can be there in fifteen minutes. How will I know you?"

"Last booth on the left as you walk in. I'll order for us."

"That sounds delightful. See you then, Detective."

"James . . . call me Jim," he lied. Returning the phone to the wall, he cursed his situation. But then again, Detective Jim might be a great deal more relaxed and in control than would be comp-nerd Randy, so maybe he had made the right choice after all. Besides, she could turn out to be anything but what he imagined.

Play it out. Play out the game. But this was no ordinary game. This was real life, with real consequences. A part of him didn't feel comfortable playing with people's feelings and emotions. It was anathema to all that was positive on the Internet, where such things didn't routinely exist. Sure, you heard of the occasional Net partners making a random date, falling in love in the real world and getting married, but you never heard of the statistics on the divorce rate for such Net surfers.

Still, he had committed to the game in this world now.

"Play it out," he told himself again. Risk it all, he added as he found his way back to his booth, called the waiter back, asked the other man to deep-six the sandwich in favor of two veal scallopini lunches and a dark cabernet, or Chianti, perhaps.

This was going to set him back some, but it was what

Detective James "Bond" Pardee would do, right? he asked himself.

The waiter only shrugged, lifted the sandwich plate, and made a beeline for the kitchen. Meanwhile, Randy awaited Darlene's appearance.

SEVENTEEN

Gila monster: desert sign

"Now it's your turn," Lucas said to Meredyth. "How come we know so much already about the victim in Oregon, his name, his line of business? How did you first hear of him?"

"Randy."

"Really?"

"He saw something come in over the computer on it."

"So, what else do we know about the victim?"

"We don't know enough about Little. We need to know a great deal more about him," she suggested. "I understand he's originally from Texas—not far from Houston, in fact, a town called Sealy, where he grew up. He owns—owned—a mansion estate there, but he also maintains a house in Malibu, California. He was a man building a fortune, obsessed by work, was the way his wife put it."

"Who supplied all the details? You didn't get all that from a birthmark or from Randy."

"A sheriff's deputy found his wallet at the crime scene."

"Really? An oversight on the killer's part, perhaps? Especially if this has anything to do with Mootry, which I rather doubt. . . ."

She frowned in response, asking, "Do you always have to be so damned negative, Stonecoat?"

He shrugged this away. "So . . . what'd they do, notify next of kin, put out an APB for information on the guy, what?"

"Seems everyone in Oregon, or at least this area of the state, knew the victim well, at least by reputation. So they contacted his wife. She and their children are all torn up about it, they say. She had to be hospitalized after they told her. Still haven't officially identified the body beyond what was found at the scene."

"They found his wallet? But he wasn't wearing any clothes?"

, "It must've fallen. Got kicked up underneath the car, where an alert deputy found it."

A signal bell overhead pinged and lit up, telling them to fasten their seat belts for landing. The military jet touched down in Oregon with the ease of a glider, the expert pilot making it look easy. There wasn't much here, a small terminal and two strips of asphalt for an airport with a handful of the big carriers coming and going. The highway murder had occurred somewhere between Medford and Rogue River.

They were immediately met by the local deputy, Harold Lempel, who had been sent to greet them, to take them first to the morgue and then out to the crime scene on Interstate 5 just outside Rogue River, Oregon. Harold was big at six feet three, his shoulders wide and thick as cinder blocks, his face about the same, with an affable smile and how-kin-I-hep-y'all-folks attitude.

In the squad car, Lucas asked, "Are you the deputy who found the wallet?"

Harold beamed. "Yes, sir, that'd be me."

"Was there anything else found at the scene?"

"Just the worst nightmare I ever witnessed, and I've seen some roadkills that involved power lines and bodies up trees, sir."

At the morgue, they were ushered into a deathly silent room where the victim—or rather what little remained of the victim—had been placed beneath a sheet, the arrow still protruding from the chest, creating a small teepee effect over the torso. The man who led them in was the local pathologist working for the Rogue River hospital. The nearest medical examiner was in Eugene, Oregon, and so far, no one from his office had come down. It was quite possibly a stroke of good luck for Dr. Sanger and Lucas that no official coroner had yet examined the body, since everything had been carefully preserved intact for the man or woman coming from Eugene.

"FBI may be coming in this afternoon to have a look-see also," said the doe-eyed, middle-aged pathologist. "Damnedest bit of grief I ever come across in all my years, I can tell you."

Thus far, there seemed little interest in the death of Timothy Little in any place other than Rogue River. Speculation about the killing ran high there. Little was killed by renegade union men who got wind that he was going to sell the local plant. Word had it that some of the meanest of the homeboys just got together, got liquored up for courage, dug out their hunting bows, and went after Mr. Little, literally cutting him off at the pass.

Meredyth instinctively pulled back when the sheet was pulled away. She and Lucas were treated to a Judge Mootry look-alike murder victim, a hacked-up torso—no head, no limbs, and no private parts. A thick titanium metal shaft, looking like a sleek metal post, with a stylized, aluminum-feathered end, protruded straight up and out from the heart, a direct hit.

"Whoever this guy is, he sure as hell shoots straight," said Lucas, more to hear his own voice than anything else.

Harold, from a dark corner, said, "They say the car had to be moving at between sixty-five and seventy when it left the road, and that the arrows—two of them—came straight through the windshield."

Meredyth was gasping for air, wanting to get out, and she did so. Lucas nodded to the little pathologist and said thanks before allowing Meredyth out. The place reeked from the indescribable fleshy items put up in formaldehyde-filled jars.

"Seen enough to convince you there's something very bizarre going on?" she asked.

"I have, but we're going to need pictures to convince Lawrence and the others back in Houston."

"Don't worry. I intend to get a copy of every photo they've taken here."

Harold had stayed back long enough for his third look at the body. He went past them now in search of a Pepsi-Cola machine down the hall, where he inhaled what was in the can in his bearlike claw.

Meredyth said to Harold, "Take us to the scene, where it happened."

"Well, maybe first you'll want to see the car."

"You impounded it?" asked Lucas.

"Had to get it outta there."

"You moved it."

"Don't worry," he assured them. "We marked where it was, where it left the road, all that."

"Did you drive all over the surrounding area? Park your squad cars over vital evidence?" pressed Stonecoat.

"We obscured some tire prints, but there wasn't much in the way of evidence found out there."

"Where's the sheriff? Why isn't he talking to us?"

"Lowell . . . Sheriff Barnette's a busy man," replied Deputy Harold Lempel. "He's up at the courthouse right now, dealing with news media, all that. He thought you'd appreciate his keeping the media off your backs."

Lucas wondered if the local sheriff thought there might possibly be a book or movie deal in it for him. "So you're our escort?"

"'Fraid you're stuck with me. But the sheriff'll see you later on."

"Okay, take us to the vehicle."

Meredyth asked Harold, "Does the sheriff believe it was the act of local men?"

"He has taken to the theory, yes'm. He knows . . . well, we all of us know some boys here capable of such if they get swimming in their booze."

"But you said yourself it'd take a hell of a shot to hit a moving target at seventy miles an hour."

"We figure those boys just musta come right up on the car, right next to it, passed it a bit, and fired through the windshield, looks like . . . Looks to us like getting their game man was all they could think of."

"Their game man?" repeated Meredyth.

Lucas poked a large finger at the deputy and asked, "And you believe that?"

"Well, sir . . . what else might explain Mr. Little's getting himself killed like this?"

"Did you know Little?" asked Meredyth.

"Everybody in these parts knows *of* Mr. Little."

Lucas asked, "A lot of people owed him big-time?"

"Yes, sir, they did. Owed him their livelihoods."

Meredyth seized on this. "And owing sometimes breeds contempt, doesn't it, Deputy?"

"That's sometimes so, Doctor, yes."

"Was there any show of this contempt before now?" she added.

"None beyond the usual palaver, no."

"Palaver?"

"You know, beer-stool talk. Mostly nonsense, but that nonsense has some men behind bars this mornin', ma'am."

"Still, your sheriff here thinks there was sufficient animosity toward Little to see him murdered in this brutal a fashion?" Meredyth pressed.

"Well, talk around Medford was he—Mr. Little, that is—was going to close down the plant."

She shook her head. "I thought there was a planned buyout."

"Some figured it was one step removed from a shutdown, that the buyout was ASCAN's way to write off tax losses, or so I'm told. That at the very least, they would move the plant elsewhere, to some big industrial park outside Kansas City, I think."

"Still makes a weak argument for murder, Deputy Lempel."

"Gotta agree with you, sir, but Sheriff Barnette's got to do what he's got to do, I reckon."

"Gotcha," added Lucas, knowing that in the face of publicity doing nothing could be lethal. Lucas again said, "Let's have a look at the car."

The deputy gestured for them to follow him, and behind his back they had a quick powwow, Lucas saying in a whisper, "Still, if this guy was about to cut off everybody's livelihood . . ."

"Whataya saying, Lucas? That news of the Houston

arrow murderer has spread, and that the killer or killers here – "

"A copycat can't be ruled out. Not on what little we've seen."

She silently but reluctantly had to agree. "You think Lawrence already knew as much? That he sent us on this wild-goose chase just to get me off his back for a while?"

"Maybe . . . maybe not."

"Can't you make up your mind?"

"Can't say . . . Too little to go on."

"God, you can be exasperating with that."

"Caution is a pill you may wish to try yourself, Doctor."

She only gritted her teeth and continued on, following Deputy Lempel through a pair of double doors, across a parking lot, and to an impound lot.

The clean two- and three-centimeter holes in the windshield looked like large, oversized bullet holes, and they told the whole story. Even safety glass, designed to hold in place like a shaky spiderweb, was no match for the crossbow arrow when the arrow was traveling at something upwards of 115 miles per hour and the car at seventy, and given the impact that must have occurred. What car manufacturer's test involved steel-shafted arrows at such speeds? If Little was traveling at sixty-five miles an hour, and two arrows came careening through his front windshield, he was headed for disaster even had they missed his vital organs.

Lucas's high whistle filled the impound yard where he stood, staring at the damage. "The crossbow had to be high-powered with a scope to make this kind of hit, and it'd be pulling upwards of two or three hundred pounds, depending on the distance the sharpshooter took. Maybe the killer *did* come up close on the vehicle."

"Then perhaps the sheriff was right, that some good

ol' boys drove right up to the vehicle, and in a drunken state, someone fired."

Lucas and Meredyth considered the possibilities as they looked over the Alamo rental, a once beautiful 1995 Olds Cutlass, midnight-blue with ocean-blue interior now stained with an ugly brown-purple, the sort of hue you got by mixing all the Easter egg colors together, Meredyth thought.

Lucas thought the bloodstains looked like bear paw tracks in the mud.

The passenger-side seat was untouched, but the driver's seat was ripped and bloody, and here one of the two arrows remained embedded in the cushion.

"What do you make of this?" she asked Lucas.

"The man was hit by two arrows."

"No, only one in his body out on the hood where we found it," said the deputy. "Damnedest sight I ever seen."

"The second arrow had to've hit him, too," countered Lucas.

"How can you tell?" she asked.

"At the speed this second arrow was traveling—to cleanly slide through the glass"—Lucas's partitioned mind thought how carmakers would now have to design tests to ward off crossbow attacks—"this cushion wouldn't be enough to stop its progression into the backseat," he explained as he climbed about the interior, pointing. "So, it had to be intercepted by something far more substantial than the cushion, most probably Mr. Little's arm, from the look of these blood spatters. See how they fan out in rays in this direction. There on the passenger-side panel and window as well."

Meredyth shook her head in disbelief and confusion. "But if he was traveling at seventy miles an hour when the damned arrow hit, how could the killer have placed a second one into his heart with the car careening all over the road?"

Stonecoat looked her in the eye. "There were two arrows, fired simultaneously. Now, unless the bowman was using a double crossbow . . ."

"Two assassins?" She nodded. "My God."

"There had to be two bows fired at the same instant, and that meant two sharpshooters, two assassins at minimum."

It made them each rethink the Mootry killing while Harold gulped, burped, and exclaimed, "Damn, you think so? That'd fit the sheriff's suspicions."

"The blood here, I take it, has been determined to be that of the victim?"

"According to tests," replied Deputy Lempel.

"We'll want copies of any and all tests and photos your department has shot, Deputy," said Meredyth, a sense of gloom invading her heart.

"Yes, sir, ma'am, Dr. Sanger."

"Now, will you take us out to the crime scene?" she asked, trying to quell her nerves.

"Right away, at your service. The Medford Police Department is at your service," he repeated it like a well-rehearsed line.

Stonecoat whispered in her ear. "You okay? You look a bit pale-faced."

"I'm fine. Let's get on with it."

ℰIGHTEEN

Deer track: ample game

They stood on the lonely stretch of Interstate 5 outside Rogue River, Oregon, where Timothy Little had met his death, dusk just beginning her first warnings, the western sky enormous, entertaining no clouds, stern and grim and going on forever. This particular stretch of highway was all loneliness and silence, alloyed with the vague and trivial life of insects. The roadbed here rose ahead of them on a slant that took a sharp curve and a hill ahead. In the median there were trees, a thick copse of jack pine and fir wherein black holes peeped out at them. Anyone or anything could be hidden in the dense woods around the scene of the murder.

If it were a setup, there could be no better isolated spot to attack long-awaited prey. Other than the black tire marks of the single vehicle, there was no indication a chase took place, no second set of squealing tires.

"If we're here, looking at where the car came to rest,"

Lucas said to Harold Lempel, "then whereabouts did you decide Little first lost control of the car?"

"Back up yonder," Harold pointed.

"Take us back there, please."

There was nothing save a police marker to indicate what horror had taken place here two nights before. Harold backed the squad car along the shoulder. Passing motorists, seeing his flashing lights, slowed, but not by much, children in back seats waving naively and wildly at them.

In a moment, they came to the spot where Little's tire marks indicated he was first in trouble. Lucas and Meredyth climbed from the squad car to have a cursory look at the black tire marks snaking all over the road.

Meredyth asked Deputy Lempel, "Your office has gotten no calls from witnesses; absolutely no one saw anything?"

"Not squat, Doctor. People must've seen something, flashing lights twirling with the car, something, but no . . . nobody wants to get involved."

Lucas looked up and down the roadbed, his attention again going to the median across from them. Once more a stand of trees provided a dark cave in the crook of a bend just before the motorist would reach the bridge up ahead. Lucas walked across the asphalt to the median, stepped past roadkill, and walked toward the trees, while the others stared after him. He pointed toward the trees ahead and shouted across the roadway, saying, "I'm going down there to have a look."

Two cars sped by, making it impossible to hear him. He went toward the grassy tree oasis some hundred or so yards off to the left.

"What's your friend doing?" Harold asked Meredyth.

"He's part Indian," she said with a shrug, which seemed to say it all.

"A tracker, you mean?"

She had read somewhere in Stonecoat's file that he listed among his abilities hunting and trapping and tracking, all lessons learned from his days on the reservation near Huntsville, Texas, where he had grown up.

"We scoured the whole area. He ain't going to find anything in the median anyway."

Both the deputy and Meredyth put their dark glasses on. It had been a brilliant morning in which white struggled against the blue sky of an Oregon afternoon, one of those days when the wind tells you you're lucky to be alive so you can breathe it in, and now the sun in the west blinded them with golden plumes, making it difficult to see just what Stonecoat was up to. In fact, it was as if the Indian had walked into a time warp. He had essentially disappeared. Meredyth could just barely pick out his form. He was camouflaged by the stand of trees he now knelt among.

She studied Lucas, thinking how changed he seemed since that day she had followed him into the bar where he was drinking on duty, the same day he had taken on two would-be robbers at a gas station. He was a crazy man.

Kneeling at a spot just in front of the trees at a crook in the road, just ahead of the bridge overpass where cars sent jeweled reflections back at her, the Indian seemed to be praying. Lucas was staring hard at the ground, almost sniffing it the way a hunting dog might.

"He's found something. Come on," she told Harold.

When they caught up to Stonecoat, he was sitting cross-legged in the grass, a faint smile on his smug face, his hands extended to cover his find. "Tire marks, clean and untouched. The killers fired from this position, no doubt about it. And if you search the woods over there, you might even find a third arrow shaft, one that missed the car completely."

"Hell," complained Harold, "anybody might've pulled in

here for a rest or a camp. How can you know what you're saying is even half true?"

"Not just anybody carries these," he countered, lifting a steel arrow shaft between two fingers at the feathers.

"God Almighty . . ."

"They left tracks this time," said Meredyth.

Lucas quietly agreed. "Many more tracks here than at the butchering sight." He pointed out three separate, distinct shoe prints. "It's a bit more soggy here from the rains. When did it last rain hereabouts, Deputy?"

Harold looked at the evidence of at least three sets of footprints here, all male, all adult. He shrugged off the question about rain.

"Now it looks like the work of at least three men," said Lucas.

Harold scratched the back of his head, staring at the shoe prints in the mud here. "Damn, maybe Sheriff's right . . . maybe it was our local union boys."

"Drunks aren't going to hit that target down there," said Lucas, pointing back to the deputy's windshield.

Meredyth had to agree. "Whoever did this was stone sober and very, very good. . . ."

"Very good with a high-powered, scoped crossbow with infrared targeting equipment, top of the line." Lucas stood up, grimacing with a sudden stab of pain, hiding it by averting his face. He then asked Harold, "At least two hundred fifty, maybe three hundred pounds on the bows. That kind of power means high-tech equipment. Do you know anybody around here with that kind of hunting equipment?"

"Couple of folks, maybe. 'Course, Billings's old hunt club store carries some pretty high-tech items. We could start there."

The quick trip around town to the people who might

know something about high-tech crossbows proved a monumental waste of time. They were all Disney characters, as if they'd stepped out of another time period, their smiling, ingratiating ways making them either Stepford Wives or simply pure and honest village folk. Everywhere the Houston authorities went, they heard the same lament about Timothy Little. "Just awful, and him such a fine man who done so much for our area. . . ."

To save time and taxpayers' money, they decided to fly back late the same night, allowing the locals to run their string of arrests out on their own. Harold's boss, Sheriff Lowell Barnette, only surfaced at the airport to see them off. He remained convinced that the killers were a pack of local boys who had it in for Little.

Barnette was a huge man, intimidating, with leather for skin. He looked genetically suited to the hardships of the outdoors. Robust and powerful, his forehead massive, creating a hanging cliff over his dark, brooding eyes, the man merely shook his head over Stonecoat and Meredyth, apologizing brusquely for not having had time to monkey-cart them around all day, as he put it, punctuating with the phrase "damn that, damn that," and finishing with, "But, by God, I have a hell of a situation on my hands here, folks, and I'm 'specting the FBI in any time, and there's some confessions to get before then. But I know what I can do for you . . ."

"What's that, Sheriff?"

"I can give you a crack at these boys we got locked up."

"Is that right? Well, we'd like to, but we got folks waiting for us in Houston," countered Stonecoat. "Thanks all the same."

"You got some pure Injun blood in you, don't you, boy?"

Meredyth watched Lucas's reaction to this with interest. He showed no sign of displeasure.

"Some of the best," replied Lucas.

"What're you, then? Coming from Texas, does that make you Coushatta," he massacred the name, "Apache, a li'l of both?"

"Cherokee, but I break bread from time to time with the Coushatta and the Apache—what's left of them."

"Damn that, what our race done to yours, son. I'm truly sorry for history. Damn that, for sure."

Nice way to view it, as history, Lucas thought—*the white man's history was the red man's demise.* "It's ancient history, and certainly not for you to worry about, Sheriff. Sounds like you got your hands full with those *white devils* in your cell."

The sheriff stared for a moment, uneasy at the remark, then decided it was meant in jest, so he let out with a western whoop and a laugh. "Sorry I didn't have more time with you and the doctor, here," he finally said before they began boarding. "Have a safe trip back now, you hear?"

Once on the plane, Meredyth summed Barnette up as the most purely Neanderthal individual she had ever met outside of a museum showcase. "He really didn't want us involved in his big show, did he?"

"Probably an election coming up." Lucas grinned, then added in response to her remark, "He does look like a meat eater."

Lucas quickly stowed his bag. "I sure do pity those local boys he's got in lockup."

"You sure we shouldn't have talked to those boys?"

"Waste of time."

"You sure are . . . sure of yourself. I'll give you that, Lucas Stonecoat."

"This was a professional hit."

"Professional. Like hired mob types?"

"Well-trained commando types; it was set up so neatly

the whole thing was done in a matter of five to ten minutes, including the butchering."

"God."

"It looked very familiar, wouldn't you agree?"

"You mean like Mootry?"

"Precisely."

"Then I was right? All along, I was right?"

"Yes, yes, yes, you were."

She could hardly contain herself, so Lucas sat her down and locked her seat belt around her. "I knew it! I just knew it!" She beamed up at him. "What's our next step?"

"We go see Covey."

"Covey? Jack Covey?"

"He was working the Palmer case, remember? Early in the investigation."

"The cop pedophile serving time for abduction and child molestation?"

"He was working the Palmer case when he was put away on the charge. He's likely mellowed out some by now. In any case, we need to know what he knows."

"What do you hope to learn from him?"

"Why he was caught."

She glowered at him. "What kind of game are you playing, Stonecoat?"

"One as old as time. I have twenty questions for Mr. Covey."

"Beginning with?"

Lucas strapped himself into his seat. "Who was behind his capture and arrest?"

"But what does that have to do with . . . with this?"

"Maybe nothing . . . maybe everything."

"Damn it, I hate it when you revert to Indian glibness and cryptograms. Will you please tell me what you hope to gain from this filthy individual whose arrest brought down the image of every cop in Houston with it?"

"He may be dirty, he may crawl on the earth as a snake, but why was the snake beheaded just as he was about to uncover evidence in the Whitaker case?"

"What evidence? I saw no evidence of evidence coming out of Covey's involvement. Where'd you get that?"

"I read between the lines in the file. Covey was one of the two investigators on the case. One, Pete Felipe, a Spanish cop, was killed in what was described as a random act of violence outside a liquor store the night before his partner, Covey, was picked up on charges he abducted, molested, and filmed sexual acts with a number of minors."

"All true, and a court of law put the man away."

"Precisely."

"Precisely what?"

"The judge who put Covey away?"

She stared hard into Lucas's eyes. "No. Charles Mootry?"

"One and the same."

"Damn that! As Sheriff Barnette would say."

"Something big and dark like an ugly cougar is roamin' about, and it has large claws and bigger fangs, Doctor, and if we continue to scratch at it, it's going to turn on us. Maybe now's a good time to ask yourself just how far you're willing to take this thing."

"What're you talking about? Quitting now? That's nonsense!"

"When white men tell lies, they are often lies within lies, and I've heard it said that a cautious man is careful for what he wishes. Can you face the truth in the end if the truth may reach out and kill you or harm those in your family, Meredyth?"

She thought about this warning well. She said nothing, leaning back in her seat instead. They'd left the ground. "We've unearthed irrefutable evidence that some sort of hit men or hit squad is operating across state lines. We could turn what we have over to the FBI, pass the standard, make it someone else's nightmare. We could let it silently sink back into the quiet cemetery of the Cold Room from where it all came. But that wouldn't avenge Alisha Reynolds, now, would it?"

"Think long on it," he said.

She shook her head. "I don't have to think long on it. I'll go with you to see Covey. We'll find out what he knows, or what he thought he knew when Mootry and the system put him away."

"It may be he knows nothing."

"I'm aware of that."

"Then again, it may be that he was set up."

"And his partner murdered? How did his partner die, exactly?"

"Stabbed repeatedly through the heart by what was described as a trio of street toughs."

"Anyone charged with the stabbing?"

"They were never caught, never identified. One eyewitness said they were dressed entirely in black to blend in with the night, and apparently, they did."

"Where did you learn of all this?"

"Insomnia gives a man time. I saw that Covey and Felipe were suddenly no longer on the case."

She nodded. "Yeah, I noticed that, too, but I didn't pay much attention. I just figured administrative shuffle since they were getting nowhere on the case."

"That's the difference between us, Doctor."

"What's that?"

"I see conspiracies everywhere; you're too trusting."

"Well, maybe . . . perhaps . . . but . . ."

"Covey and Felipe were probably warned in one fashion or another to let up on the case, to lighten up; it was probably suggested to them that it wasn't worth pursuing, but they continued to pursue, and look where it got them."

She swallowed hard. "Are you suggesting . . . that we're Covey and Felipe now?"

"I'm suggesting that we're in danger."

"Now that's carrying things a bit far, Lucas. The next thing you'll be suggesting is that Phil Lawrence is somehow involved, and that's why he's stood in my way all this time."

"Just watch your back, Meredyth."

She tried a joke. "I thought you'd do that for me."

"You need somebody to do it for you. Obviously, you're no good at it," he tried joking back, but then his tone hardened. "In all sincerity, we may be dealing with people who view life, your life and mine and anyone else's who stands to unmask them, as having very little worth, and frankly—"

"You mean like the mob, the Mafia?"

"—and frankly, at the moment, I don't know anyone we can trust."

The plane banked a bit. She stared once more into his deep-set, sure brown eyes, the centers filled with dread. She found her mouth dry and her palms sweating, her heart rate having jumped. "I'll see this thing through with or without you, you know."

He frowned and dropped his gaze and shook his head. "Perhaps that is the one thing of which I have been certain all along."

The plane continued to bank, smoothed out, played tiddledywinks with the air and their stomachs, the purr of the engine continuous and loud.

"You were good back there," she told him.

"Just good? I thought I was a regular Columbo."

"All you needed was the raincoat."

He shook his head in amazement. "You know what I can't fathom?"

"What's that?"

"I can't believe those fools in Oregon overlooked so much."

She shrugged. "Not everyone's got the gift. Hell, it was weird the way you did that. It was as if you knew the exact spot to go, the exact angle the killers used against Little."

He realized she was looking at him with those blue-green eyes in a strange new light. "Hey, when I said we can't know who to trust, I meant people other than the two of us, Meredyth. You can trust me, and I can trust you, right?"

She hesitated only slightly, but enough that he noticed, she feared. "Sure . . . sure, I know I can trust you."

"And I'm going to trust you."

She managed a smile. "Big step in a . . . relationship."

"Yeah, don't I know it. And don't forget, when this is over, you promised to get me out of the Cold Room permanently, right?"

"Yeah . . . sure, I'll do everything in my power."

Why didn't it sound like enough? he wondered.

NINETEEN

Teepee: home, temporary

It was extremely late when they arrived in Houston. Even the airport was deserted. They shared a cab into the city, and Stonecoat's place being closer, he said good night to her on the street. She had taken custody of all the information and photos they'd brought back with them. Tomorrow, they would share it all with Lawrence, who would in turn provide Bryce with the information.

Lucas waved the cab off and strolled for his door, swinging his small bag. He placed the key into a locked gate that surrounded the building, stepped through, and found himself caught off guard when someone in the shadows between the building and the gate grabbed him about the neck, toying with a huge knife at his Adam's apple, using it to make like a violin, the knife the bow, playing it back and forth, creating little rivulets of blood and telling him to shut up and listen. Lucas dropped the bag to free both hands, but he was in a helpless situation. He dared not attempt a fight.

"You get yourself free of this case you're pursuing, son, or you and your girlfriend are dead. You understand that, *kimosabe*?"

"I-I-I . . ." He couldn't nod for fear the razor-sharp knife would cut a major artery, and he couldn't find the words in his suddenly parched throat. He imagined what the world would be like tomorrow without him in it.

"That's what we think, son, exactly. Now, you just come to your fucking senses, boy."

Lucas felt a double-fisted hammer-blow to the base of his skull just as the knife was lifted away from his throat. His last thoughts were twofold: The attack on him was the work of *two* assailants, and Meredyth was in danger as well. But Stonecoat was in a black world now, the dirty cement his pillow. Through a fog, he thought he heard one of his assailants say, "We should just kill the bastard here and now."

The words filtered through Lucas's fog in broken slow motion.

"No, not—now—and—not—here."

A sudden, teeth-jarring kick struck Lucas in the side. "Why're—we—screwing—with—him?"

The other man answered, "That's—'nough. We—do—it—the—way—we're—told."

Another vicious kick, same exact spot. "Damn. It's—a'ways—hell—Sanger's—way, isn't—it?"

"Orders—is—orders."

"Our—lives—on—the—line."

"Damn it. Part—ner, we're—all—in—this-t'gether."

"Bas—tard!"

Stonecoat felt a third sharp pain in his ribs where one of the apes again savagely kicked out at him. Fighting it every step of the way, Lucas then went into complete unconsciousness.

Blood seeped into the pavement where he lay from the open wounds on his neck, wounds that were cautionary and formed a pair of miniature but painful rents like railroad lines along the throat, parallel to one another.

A passerby on the street saw the assailants leaving through the front gates, looking as if they lived there. The passerby, walking his dog, saw next that someone lay between the building and the lock gate, realizing only now that he was witness to what appeared a horrible, gruesome murder. His first impulse was to turn and step quickly the way he'd come, to hide himself and his dog away, not because he feared the fleeing pair of killers, but because he didn't want to get involved. A thing like this, he reasoned, could take years to resolve, and the authorities could make his life hell. He'd seen it happen before. He'd seen it happen in the movies and on Court TV.

Lucas awoke with a terrible headache, scratched about to locate his bag, wondered how long he'd been lying here, and tried desperately to focus his eyes. Eyeballing the bag, he focused on it until it came into clear view. He wondered now just how many people—neighbors—had walked by, offering no help. He was angry to've been caught so totally off guard. He hadn't imagined they'd come after him this way, and certainly not this soon. Whoever they were, they seemed clued into his and Dr. Sanger's movements.

He tried to assess who in the city knew of his returning from Oregon tonight; who knew where he lived; who knew how to get through the damned gate, and that he'd be stepping through it at just that moment?

Maybe it was just retaliation between cops.

Maybe it had been Fred Amelford and Jim Pardee. In Texas, every cop liked to think he was a Texas Ranger—a judge, jury, and executioner all in one.

They were smart cops. They had asked around, gotten the answers they wanted, learned that the guy out at Mootry's the other night had to be Lucas Stonecoat. Hell, even Phil Lawrence might have supplied them with the information. Pissed off at him for stepping in where he wasn't wanted, sure. When the guy with the knife said to butt out of the case, he was talking as one cop to another. Maybe it wasn't the crossbow mob at all. He rifled his memory for every word the knife wielder had said in his ear as he played the blade across his now burning, still bleeding throat. Not much there: "You get yourself free of this case, son, or you and your girlfriend are dead."

Damned nasty enough threat, he thought. But cops who've felt wronged had been known to use strong language. The other guy wanted to do him in, but the more controlled guy, the one who held the knife and kept calling him son, had balked at actually sticking Lucas with the pitchfork he was waving about.

Fred Amelford was a lanky giant, a senior detective at the Twenty-second Precinct, and the apelike arms that'd draped over Lucas could've been his. The phantom in the dark had called his accomplice by the term *partner*, or had Lucas heard it wrong, had he said Pardee? And there was another word they used that sounded like a name, Sanger. But that must've been the daze talking.

Pardee and Amelford. Fill in the blanks, he told himself now. Most likely a strong dose of warning to butt out of the Mootry investigation, to stay off their turf. He had imagined they would be pissed, but he hadn't bargained on this pissed.

He had managed to pull to his knees and pull his bag to him, holding it now like a shield against the pain and humiliation they had visited upon him tonight. He prayed they had not gone from here to Meredyth's place, but he rather doubted this.

He had to get to his feet, get his door opened, find the elevator and his apartment, telephone to be certain she was all right.

It seemed simple enough, but it took him fifteen minutes to manage what was normally done in an easy three. Once inside the hallway, he'd collapsed again. Whoever hit him had used a military blow, the kind that could stop a Mack truck. He managed to get to the elevator but couldn't focus on the buttons. He played with them for quite some time before he found his floor.

Once he got to his door, he began having more trouble fitting the key into the lock when a neighbor stepped out to ask if he was all right. The neighbor took him for drunk, came over and sorted out his problem for him and got him through the door and stretched out on the couch. The man was known only by his last name, Fleckner, a thin, raggedy man with beady eyes and the snout of a Manhattan rat, the smell of cheap whiskey lifting off him like heat off a Texas blacktop. In fact, he looked like someone on the run, and each time Lucas had seen him in the past, he'd seemed to skulk down the hallway rather than walk. Still, tonight he was welcome help.

"You okay, pal?" he asked when Lucas was laid out on his bed. "Christ, you're bleeding. I'll get a towel."

Fleckner was as good as his word, finding a towel and stanching the flesh wounds. "Damn, somebody's took a knife to your throat. We gotta call 911 or an ambulance or something."

"No, no calls, no doctors, but if you could drag the phone over here, I'd appreciate it."

Fleckner was standing over Lucas in only his underwear. "Sure . . . sure, if that's the way you want it, but if you go and bleed to death, it ain't Morris Fleckner's fault."

"The phone, please."

Fleckner frowned, chewed his gums a bit, and finally nodded. "It's your funeral." He mumbled disapproving words under his breath.

Stonecoat thanked his neighbor and told him he'd be fine, and that Fleckner shouldn't bother himself a moment more with him. "Please, just go now. I'm fine, really."

"You don't want to call the cops ner nothin'?"

"I . . . I am a cop."

"Geezus, I didn't know. Damn, you, you sure don't look like no cop I ever saw."

He said it as if, had he known, he might not have offered help to begin with. As if he might be a fugitive whose face had appeared on *America's Most Wanted.*

"Thanks again," Lucas called out to the retreating ghostly figure.

Morris Fleckner's only reply was the closing of the door behind him as the ill-looking, hungry-eyed man left.

Lucas quickly telephoned Meredyth, who picked up on the third ring.

"It's me, Lucas," he muttered.

"This is getting to be a bad habit with you," she responded. "I thought you said you were bushed. You know, your insomnia shouldn't have to involve me, and another thing—"

"Are you all right?"

"I'm fine. Why shouldn't I be?"

"I had a little visit from the boys working the Mootry case. Least, I think it was them." He coughed uncontrollably, the pain in his ribs excruciating.

"Oh, no. I hope there wasn't any trouble."

He managed to get control. "Not too terribly much."

"But there was some?"

"I just wanted to be sure they . . . they weren't harassing you tonight, too."

"Me? Why should they? I didn't break their yellow tape."

"No, but they mentioned you prominently when they threatened my life."

"Holy . . . they threatened your life? Those creeps. Are you hurt?"

"Not too."

"How about them? Did you hurt them good?"

He would have liked to answer in the affirmative. Instead, he stuck with, "Not too."

"Aren't you going to give me any of the details? What is it with you and details?"

"Mere . . . think I'm go . . . ing . . . hang up now."

"Are you okay?"

"Fine. Good"—he held himself together—"night." He quickly hung up. In a few minutes, he passed out again, thinking, *Damn, that SOB hits harder than a tree falling, and my neck's going to be as stiff as a pine tomorrow—if I ever wake up again.*

Earlier in the evening, Randy Oglesby had telephoned Dr. Sanger, but he'd gotten no answer. He didn't want to leave a message of such importance as he had on her answering machine, so he cut off before the beep. He tried Stonecoat at home, having gotten his number from the personnel files on the Net. Once again, no answer, and this time no answering machine.

He had made second and third attempts to get in touch, finally assuming that so much work had confronted them in Oregon that they had had to stay over. He wondered if anything of a romantic nature was taking place between them, but rather doubted this since Dr. Sanger was always and forever talking about her beau—her swain, her suitor, her escort, her fiancée, Conrad, ugh! Conrad could, according to Dr. Sanger, become the next Newton or Einstein or Stephen Hawking, he was that brilliant. Bullshit.

But he didn't care tonight one way or the other about Dr. Sanger's boyfriend, because he couldn't believe his own great fortune. Not only had Darlene Muentes been petite, beautiful, and exotic, but she had laughed at all his stories *in the right places,* had gone somber during all his stories *at the right moments,* and had thrilled to the adventure of his police detective's life. She was so enthralled that she wanted to see him again. Life was grand as Jim Pardee.

Darlene, to save time, had brought the two goblets and the bill directly to him when they met for lunch. It had been an exquisite lunch meeting. God, he thought now, what a rush!

Randy had praised Darlene for her sense of duty in getting the evidence back into his hands as quickly as she had. She shyly accepted the compliment, eating like a butterfly trying on a horse's appetite. She was so well-mannered and delicate, but she certainly could pack the food away. There was something about that he liked.

He had been pleasantly surprised that she found him good-looking—a real "hunk," as she'd put it. She had confessed to having never met anyone over the phone before. He told her he had never met anyone in any "blind" way before, but that her voice just rang so pure and clear, like a bell in a wooded glen. She giggled at the image and wondered if he was lying.

She had no idea, not a clue.

It was great, Detective Randy Jim Pardee Oglesby thought now as he made his way to dreamland and found Darlene Muentes waiting there for him. Their next date was for Saturday night. He could hardly wait.

He gave a momentary thought to Dr. Meredyth Sanger, to whom he owed so much for getting him placed in the hierarchy of the support staff at the station. He had secretly admired her all the time they'd been together, but she was way out of his league and much older, which meant about ten years his senior. Still, he knew the odds of his ever interesting her romantically were as astronomical as winning the Texas State Lottery or of the Houston Astros ever again having a pitcher as good as Nolan Ryan, the first man in history to strike out four thousand batters.

Surrounded by this swirl of thought, light and apprehension, Randy Oglesby slept, Judge Mootry's goblets sitting atop his bookcase, the lab results beside the glasses, the bill below this.

TWENTY

Water house

A little makeup applied professionally by the barber down the street, and Lucas's unkind wounds were made to pretty well disappear. It beat a giant Band-Aid, he decided. The neck was, as he'd predicted, stiff as a board, and his head still ached somewhat dully, but he was otherwise well. It had been the massive, bearlike blow to the back of his head that had wreaked most of the havoc. When he had stepped over his blood in the gutter this morning, the sight made him boil and seethe with anger.

He wasn't used to being taken so easily. Maybe he should let it go, but his pride was bruised along with his neck.

He and Sanger were to have met with Lawrence at nine, which time had come and gone an hour ago. He supposed that now not only would Sergeant Kelton be pissed, but the captain and Sanger as well; but there was no reason Mere couldn't advise Phil on her own about what they'd found in Medford, Oregon.

He had slept until the phone rang. It was Kelton who had made the wake-up call, saying that Dr. Sanger was worried about him when he didn't show up at nine, and that if it wasn't bothering Stonecoat too awfully, would he get his bloody arse up and onto his duties! The last phrase was delivered in an earsplitting, painful war cry.

"I'm on my way. I had a little medical emergency last night, Sarge," he had replied.

Now he was stepping through the doors to face Kelton, Lawrence and Sanger together. He hoped none would see the fresh wounds on his neck.

Kelton immediately and silently, his anger rising off him like steam, escorted Lucas to Lawrence's door, announcing him as if he were the king of Siam, bowing loudly and exaggeratedly, making Stonecoat frown and blush at once.

"That's not necessary, Sergeant," said Phil Lawrence, dismissing Kelton. Meredyth stood in one corner of the room. "I'm told by Dr. Sanger you had some sort of brush last night with Pardee and Amelford from the Twenty-second. Is that right?"

"Yeah, a slight brush, sir."

"Those boys can get rough."

"So I've noticed, sir."

"Have a seat, Lucas."

Lucas did as told.

"Dr. Sanger here's brought me up to speed on what you two found up in Medford. Damned strange business . . . damned strange, wouldn't you say? Insane, really. What do you make of it?"

"Like you say, sir, insane."

"Some kind of sociopath on the loose?"

"If so, there're more than one."

He nodded. "Yes, Dr. Sanger told me about your theory. Well, there's no shortage of sociopaths who meet in prison, team up after they're released to work in tandem. The literature of crime is filled with team killers. What's next, you two?"

"We're not sure just yet, sir, what our next step will be," Lucas quickly said, "but I think we'll start talking to some of the hunting goods outlets and maybe some of the hunt club types around Houston, if that meets with your approval, sir."

"Hunt clubs? You know that involves some big muckety-muck types. No lowlife joins a Houston hunt club that I know of."

"No, sir, I mean, yes, sir, I know. Have it in my head, sir, that we're not dealing with the usual criminal element, sir."

"Really, now. Then what kind of criminal element are we dealing with, Lucas?"

"High rollers, sir. Timothy Little was a rich man, and so was Mootry. They traveled in different circles, sir, but one thing they had in common was a lot of money to leave behind. Dr. Sanger's promised to look into their wills and scour for who stood to gain the most on their parting, Captain. Meanwhile, I thought I'd ask around at the local hunting goods outlets and clubs about members who prefer the crossbow to, say, a Remington automatic, sir."

"Sounds like a plan. Okay, you two . . . keep on it, run with it, and keep me apprised every step of the way. Do you understand that? I'll talk to the twenty-second guys."

After the perfunctory yes, sirs, bowing, and scraping, Lucas and Meredyth emerged. Meredyth was wearing a lime-green suit that made her look more youthful and beautiful than ever, he thought.

"What is our next move?" Lucas asked.

"Randy's got something for us," she said, "on the goblets."

"Oh, yeah? What'd he find out?"

"The goblets were returned to him."

"Returned to him?" Lucas was amazed, nonplussed.

"Whoever gave him the goblets thought he was Detective Pardee."

He joked, "Who could possibly make such a mistake?"

"In any case, there were trace elements of sedatives, nothing particularly potent, but alongside the brandy, enough to induce sleep."

"And fingerprints?"

"Just as you predicted, wiped completely clean."

"And the paperwork, the bill from the lab?"

She fetched it from her purse. "It's all yours. Do with it what you like."

He grimaced.

"Don't be silly. I'm just teasing. Randy's already put it into the electronic maze. No one will ever know."

"So, where do we go from here?" Stonecoat asked.

"I'm going to see Covey. I've already arranged it with him. He's anxious for company."

He darkened his gaze. "I'll bet he is. You weren't going to go see him alone this morning, without me, were you?"

"He sounded real nice over the phone," she said defensively.

"I'll bet he did."

"Come on, Lucas. He's incarcerated."

"Exactly where is he being held?"

"The new state pen at Hempstead. It's an hour's drive west."

"Hempstead, really? I thought he'd be in Huntsville. Damn, I was planning to introduce you to my folks out at the res."

"Huntsville's become too overcrowded. They opened a new state facility in Hempstead, much to the displeasure of the locals there."

"You driving?"

"I know the way."

"Let's go see Mr. Covey, then."

"I got to thinking over what you said about Covey and Felipe, and it makes sense to see what we can shake loose from the man."

"Damn it, you *were* planning to go see him without me, weren't you?"

"I wasn't going to wait around all morning for you, no." She frowned and relented somewhat, adding, "Just where've you been, anyway? I telephoned your place this morning, but there was no answer."

Apparently, he had slept through the ringing phone, or else she had called while he was out having his neck wounds cosmetically covered at the barber's. "Let's just say I was out. . . ."

"Lucas, you wearing makeup? You don't have a secret life I don't know about, do you? What're those marks on your throat?" she asked.

"God, you can be so nosy." He grimaced and swore again. He'd paid the barber well, but apparently it was for naught.

"I thought we were just getting to the point where we could be open and honest with one another, partner," she complained.

"I'll tell you about it on the way to Hempstead."

"Deal."

As they were about to leave, Sergeant Kelton stopped Stonecoat in his tracks. "We got some settling up to do, mister."

"Sergeant," began Dr. Sanger.

"Ma'am, this is between Officer Stonecoat and me, ma'am."

"It's Doctor, Sergeant," she countered, "and at the moment, Officer Stonecoat and I are working on special assignment for Captain Lawrence. If you've got a beef, take it up with Lawrence."

He just stared at her, chewing on his next move. Then he stepped aside and watched them, his intent narrow eyes never leaving them as they disappeared out the door.

Damn it, thought Kelton, *this means I gotta find someone else to hold the keys to the Cold Room today. I wonder if Lawrence has a clue to the workload that goes by the wayside when he does shit like this. I wonder if Commander Bryce has any idea what goes on. Wonder if I should call Bryce on such petty matters.* Maybe he'd give it some thought over a cup of coffee.

But the coffee didn't help Kelton's disposition any. Soon after, he stalked off to see if he could shake anything loose from Captain Lawrence as to what gives with letting the Indian run in and out as freely as if he were a full-blown detective. Besides, he didn't like things going on in the precinct he knew nothing about.

For one, it wasn't fair—not if he was responsible for the duty logs.

Hempstead in Waller County was a picture-perfect, quiet little town with white picket fences, red mailboxes, lovely farms, schools and churches, not a one of which was in ill repair or need of painting. It was as if the town provided the paint. There were no overturned trash cans, discarded sofas, abandoned bikes, or a scrap of paper out of place, and this without a single warning sign about littering. The grass was greener, the sky bluer, the paint on the homes newer than any place Lucas Stonecoat had ever seen. There were no broken-down hovels, no ramshackle shacks, no ancient automobile relics or appliances on people's lawns or porches. It was as if those who'd dared these transgressions in the past were immediately run out of town. The main roads were narrow and the lines freshly painted.

Only the state penitentiary on the outskirts of town detracted from the Disney appearance of the place.

"You'd never know the place was once called Six-shooter Junction, would you?" she asked.

"No, but I've heard that it once was. That it was a wild and woolly place for decades after the Civil War."

The rolling hills south of Hempstead were settled as early as 1821, but today only scattered historical markers, many hidden by time, told the story. In 1857 it became the terminus for the Houston & Texas Central Railroad, an early small-gauge train line that tooted across much of Waller County before expanding north to Bryan-College Station. During the Civil War, the railroad made Hempstead a major supply and troop depot for Confederate brigades, and at the cessation of hostilities, Confederate soldiers made their long walk home from Hempstead. Hempstead had also been the geographical turning point in Texas's war for independence from Mexico. Sam Houston's retreating forces camped and regrouped here from March 31 to April 14, 1836, before beginning their final aggressive march on San Jacinto and ultimate victory over Santa Ana and the Mexican army.

Hempstead had obviously awakened to its past, all the historical houses, buildings, and the old railroad station having been refurbished and freshly decked out, some now open to the public, some soon to be.

As they found Junction T-6 at US 290, they saw the old railroad hotel, the Hempstead Inn, originally built in 1901, now fully restored and open for business and serving lunch and dinner. The old place beckoned as they passed by.

The only blot on the entire area was the dull red-bricked, looming fortress and guard towers of the newly constructed penitentiary, which came into sight on the horizon after acres upon acres of fenced-in land that the state had bought up as a kind of buffer zone between Hempstead and its new neighbor.

It was to the gates of the medieval-looking yet modern brick facility that they drove. They were stopped at the guard station, where a display of their credentials got them waved through.

On the inside, they waited impatiently, anxiously for John "Jack" T. Covey, former Houston cop now serving time for abduction, lewd and lascivious acts with a minor, pornography, and child abuse. The man had been close to retirement, a life-crisis period for all cops, Meredyth told Lucas in a feeble attempt to explain his reckless lifestyle when he was apprehended. A good pension and clean record, all lost, everything having blown up in his face due to his sexual addiction and proclivities, or so it went. Lucas wasn't so sure that justice had been served in the case, finding Covey's partner's death, atop all else, rather a strange coincidence, both men conveniently out of the way, perhaps so that someone, somewhere could sleep better at night.

The moment Covey stepped into the interrogation room, he went on the defensive. A big bull of a man, he looked like King Rat here, his muscles bulging so that his prison shirt pulled and tugged with each movement he made. He obviously took great care of his physical health, and for a man his age, he seemed incredibly fit. His eyes were an icy gray steel, and they bored into Lucas as he asked Meredyth, "What's he for? I thought you wanted to talk cozy-like, just the two of us. Jack don't fancy talking to no one else. Get 'im outta here, or Jack don't talk." He referred to himself in the third person.

"We're partners," she countered. "This is Detective Lucas Stonecoat."

"HPD? I don't deal with HPD, no, never."

"Dallas," lied Lucas, quickly showing his gold shield from Dallas.

"DPD, HPD . . . where's the difference? You're all scum."

"Hold on, there." Lucas's voice rose an octave, but Meredyth stood and stepped between the two men.

"Now look here, Mr. Covey."

"Jack, he likes to be called Jack," Covey replied, "sweetheart. What's wrong, you afraid to be in a room alone with Jack?"

"No, Jack, but my partner has to know what I know. You've got to remember how it was with you and Felipe."

"Felipe got himself killed knowing what I know. You want me killed?"

"You help us, Jack," she countered, "and we'll see your sentence is reduced, and you'll be out of here a great deal sooner than you could ever hope for through any other avenue."

"I'd be out by now if Jack hadn't made that stupid getaway attempt." He grinned at her, searching for some sign of understanding.

She tried to assure him that she was on his side. "I know that, but this is no stupid getaway attempt. Work with us."

He again suspiciously eyed Stonecoat.

"Sit down," she suggested.

"I could be murdered in my sleep just for talking to you people," he muttered. "I told everyone inside that Jack was talking to a shrink about his problem. Jack even showed around a picture of you, darling."

"A picture of me?" She was surprised, and Stonecoat was equally surprised.

"I still get the *Police Gazette*, sweetheart, and Jack can read. Read it from cover to cover. Guys in the joint think he's screwy, but we all know better, don't we, Doctor? Jack tells 'em on the inside that there's a lot to learn from the *Gazette*, and I particularly enjoyed your article on—"

" 'The Psychology of Pedophiles and Interrogation Techniques,' yes."

"Yeah, gave him a thrill, a whole new insight."

"Insight into himself, or how better to behave during an inquiry, you mean?"

Covey gave a broken-toothed, tobacco-stained, loose-lipped laugh as his response. He appeared to have disgusting habits, despite an otherwise solid, masterful physique. He looked as if he'd had his nose broken on more than one occasion. Stonecoat sensed it was best to keep silent, to let Meredyth work her unique magic with this cretin.

"The article gave Jack plenty of insight—insight into you, Meredyth." He looked up at Stonecoat, glaring, still feeling he'd been cheated of his private moment with this celebrity, Meredyth Sanger. "You show guys like Jack a great deal of . . . of genuine . . . compassion. Jack likes a girl with compassion, understanding, you know?"

"That article was about cop psychology and how foolishly some cops treat pedophiles, that in treating them as untouchable monsters, they easily lose the upper hand in interrogating the pedophile. It was about a cop's need to distance himself from the emotional constraints of a crime that involves children, not about—"

"It spoke volumes to Jack," he countered, his hand having almost imperceptibly slithered across the table toward her.

Except for the bad teeth and scars, Covey was not unattractive for a man his age, and she could see how he might easily lure a young person, boy or girl, into his warped world of sexual deviancy. His size, his stature, his badge. His eyes and his firm features and granite build could mesmerize, never mind the fact that he was a "Blue

Centurion," with all the trappings of authority. It wasn't hard to understand how young people might find him charismatic. His allure had surely tarnished by now, but apparently Jack didn't think so.

"Jack likes you, Meredyth, very much," he cooed, his hand closer now.

She backed her seat away, the chair screeching in response. She was glad Stonecoat was nearby, but she wondered if Lucas were any match for the huge man, despite the age difference, should Covey come over the table at her.

"You told 'em," he said, "you told 'em all that it was an uncontrollable sickness, what people like Jack have. You told 'em it wasn't some habit like smoking or drinking, that it ran deeper than a conditioned habit. You told 'em that Jack's brain, his genetic makeup, was as much to blame as his upbringing, didn't you? You told the world that Jack was not responsible for the stripes God put on his back."

She hadn't exactly exonerated him as much as he had exonerated himself, but for the sake of keeping on Covey's good side, she nodded. "Yeah, Jack, that's what I said."

She heard Lucas groan, as if to say, *Oh, brother*. But fortunately he kept his feelings to himself.

"Jack likes your savvy, Meredyth. The way you called him up, the way you come to see him. Now, ain't it funny, Jack already knew who you were when you told him who you were on the phone. Jack thinks it's like that kismet thing, you know, fate. You think you could learn to like Jack? Maybe come to visit him on a routine basis, without a reason and without your friend here?" Covey sneered up at Lucas, who kept his stony Indian features set.

The man made her skin crawl. She knew now he was put away for exactly what he was, and that she was experiencing the same emotions she had preached against in her article in the *Gazette* about interrogating a child molester.

Covey smiled a rotten-toothed smile at her, his wrinkles causing his jaw to sag. "Jack's quite taken with you. Jack knows you understand him completely. No woman's ever done that for Jack before. . . ." The man's hand snaked forward quickly now, taking hers in his.

Stonecoat came off the wall, shouting, "Take your hand off Dr. Sanger!"

Meredyth shouted, "Shut up, Lucas! If Jack wants to hold my hand, then Jack holds my damned hand!"

Covey growled a bearlike sound at Stonecoat and held firm to Meredyth's hand. "God . . . been so long since Jack's touched a woman. . . ."

He closed his eyes and savored the feel of her hand as it throbbed in his.

"We're here to talk to you about the Palmer investigation, Jack. When you were a cop, doing a job, remember? Remember Dr. Wesley Palmer?"

"'Course I do. Got me in here, it did, and my name's John. Jack's the bastard controls my dick, but I'm the brains here." He dashed her hand down as if it burned his.

She wondered if the man was play-acting for them or if he'd ever been diagnosed as having a split personality.

"Palmer case got Felipe killed and got me shut up like a goddamned animal, in more ways than one." He guffawed until he coughed and spit.

"Tell us about that, John," she suggested.

"Felipe was knifed, assassinated really. He was coming from a neighborhood grocery story with two bags, one in each arm, when they jumped him. Felipe wasn't a bad guy; made a good partner. Stayed out of my business."

"Go on, tell us how he was killed."

"Three, maybe four thugs dressed in black, according to witnesses. They took his wallet to make it look like a street mugging, but there were four puncture wounds direct to the man's heart, six to the lungs, twelve in all in the space of seconds. I'm telling you, they descended on him like locusts."

"Who were they?"

"I don't know. I never got the chance to find out. Next thing I know, they got me on trumped-up charges, things Jack was into. They set Jack up, suckered him right in. You find that girl they gave Jack to play with, and maybe she can tell you who they were. They musta paid her plenty."

"Did you rape this girl?"

He reluctantly answered. "Ask Jack."

"I see."

"Sounds like they played you like a fiddle," replied Lucas.

He glared up at Lucas. "That they did. That they did. Played on my weakness for little blond ones." Covey gave Meredyth another of his crooked, leering grins.

"Who . . . who do you suspect?"

"Who do you suspect?" Covey countered.

"This is a waste of time, Dr. Sanger," Lucas sullenly replied. "Let's go have lunch at that nice inn down the road, shall we?"

"Look!" Covey exploded, standing, dropping his guard, "Just check out the facts. One day Felipe and me, we put it together. We struck a nerve with somebody high up! I mean, just a few days after we drew some simple conclusions about the similarities in the Palmer and Whitaker cases, whammo! they came for us."

"Who?" persisted Lucas. "Who came for you?"

"Street thugs for Felipe, the State of Texas for me. The whole story on Jack was given to the D.A. by someone, someone who hired that girl to wear a wire which I only found when I tore her clothes off. That's when they stormed in, cops—cops I'd thought were my buddies. But they all knew I was into child porn for years before and nothing, nothing ever happened to me before then, before Felipe and me got involved in the Palmer case. So now, talking about it all these years later, I could still get myself killed."

"Nobody has to know what we're here for," she assured him.

"You can't be that naive, lady. Somebody knows why you're here, and that means anybody could know. If I cooperate, I want protection, a private cell, a TV like O.J. got, double meals, stuff like that, and if you ever get this thing together so there's a trial, I'll want amnesty, witness relocation, a new life, the whole damned nine yards."

"So far you've given us crap, Covey," countered Lucas. "So don't count on any help from us. Come on, Dr. Sanger. Let's get out of here."

"But I'm telling you, a whole damned tactical unit came busting into my place that night they took me. They had warrants to search everything, my house, my car. Busted down my front door. Scared hell out of my—Jack's harem, poor kids. This the same night as Felipe got his. Now, if that ain't goddamned coincidence, then I don't know what is."

"We'll keep you posted, Mr. Covey," Meredyth began.

"Jack, you . . . you can call me Jack."

She nodded, "We'll be in touch."

"In touch . . . that's all I want."

Stonecoat buzzed the waiting guard, who came in and removed Covey, leaving Lucas and Meredyth to stare at one another.

"Whataya think?" she asked.

"The guy's all creep-oid, that's what I think."

"But if what he says is true . . ."

"Big if, first, and secondly, he was a cop who used his position to get lost and homeless kids into his little sexual fantasyland! He disgusts me. Doesn't he disgust you?"

"Whether he does or not, that's not the point," she replied. "The point is, if he and Felipe were onto something, and they were both silenced, then we are dealing with some heavy hitters here, some truly influential killers. I keep coming back to how Felipe was killed, and when it happened, as they were on the verge of connecting up the two cases."

"Who was conducting the Whitaker investigation?"

"Pardee and Amelford, remember? They were there from the beginning. Coincidence?"

He recalled the records he'd read, and she was right. "Those two bastards have got to see the similarities in the Mootry killing. Maybe it's time we paid them a little visit."

"And what do you expect to get from such a visit, after the two played chopping block with your throat last night, Lucas? They're not going to share what they've turned up with either of us."

"Why weren't they silenced ten years ago along with Felipe and Covey?"

"They didn't make the connection between Palmer and Whitaker, Felipe and Covey did."

"Either that or think the unthinkable."

"What? That Pardee and Amelford were part of Felipe's and Covey's downfall? That they were interested in some sort of cover-up in the Palmer and Whitaker deaths?"

"Well, you saw how scant the file information was."

"Wheeew, that's quite a stretch."

"It might explain why they were so testy with me."

"They could have killed you last night, and if they are as deeply involved in some sort of conspiracy as you say, maybe they would have."

"One of them wanted to finish me off; Pardee, I think. Said as much."

"What precisely did he say?"

"I don't know. I was half unconscious from the blow he'd delivered."

"They knocked you unconscious? You didn't say that before."

"I didn't want to worry you."

"Goddamn your stubborn, prideful hide."

"I got the distinct impression they felt more than a little threatened by my having stepped into the Mootry crime scene."

"What else did they say?"

"I was in a hell of a daze when they started conversing with one another. Hell, they thought I was completely out."

"I think we could refresh your memory with a bit of regression therapy. Would you sit still long enough for me to hypnotize you?"

His eyes widened. "You can do that?"

"I can. I'm fully trained. We might get some interesting bits of . . . insight."

"All right, but I don't want you digging around for anything but last night," he commanded.

"What do you think I am? Some sort of psychic vamp? I'm only interested in helping your recall of the isolated event."

He nodded. "Good . . . good, then we'll do it."

They left the prison, going down its stark corridors, past the rattling bars and the whistles, finally out into the courtyard and the parking lot. The place seemed like some sort of hell on earth, like one of the rungs in Dante's *Inferno*, she thought.

Twenty-One

Fence: guarding good luck

Randy Oglesby had gotten a call from Dr. Sanger, who was still out at Hempstead with Stonecoat; in fact, she said they were having lunch at the Hempstead Inn. Randy wondered if all they were having there was on a plate.

"Randy, I want you to push hard for any computer crosses that might link Judge Charles Mootry with Dr. Wesley Palmer and/or Whitaker. Can you do that, Randy?"

"Sure, but what kind of links are we talking?"

"Anything whatsoever. Credit references, organizations they belonged to, schools they attended, you name it."

"That'll take some time, but sure, I'll get on it."

"That's why I called you, Randy. I knew you'd be game."

"This is really big, isn't it, Doctor?"

"I don't know yet."

"Today's trip of any help?"

"Don't know yet."

"Gotcha . . . I'll get right on it."

And Randy Oglesby was a young man of his word. He had spent several hours after that telephone call running down crosses—cross-references between Mootry, Palmer, and Whitaker—without any clear-cut satisfaction. Some of the information came over while he was on break. He had simply let the machines talk to one another while he grabbed a Snickers and a cup of coffee. When transmission had ended, He stored the new information without going through it. He had a lot of other jobs to attend to today, and it was getting later and later.

An hour later, he sat before his terminal at the Thirty-first, chipping away at the deluge of work left him from previous days. There were notes, articles, and other items to electronically file away. But he quickly grew tired of the case studies and the usual materials coming out of Dr. Sanger's office. In a moment, bored, he was surfing the Internet for news bulletins on deaths by strange arrows around the nation. While he had earlier checked with all police agencies worldwide, including Interpol and the FBI and Scotland Yard, he wondered with fresh eyes if there could be people out there on the Net who might know of any additional bizarre stories involving bows and arrows and murder.

He soon found himself inundated with stories, many of which he recognized for the bullshit they were; some of them were reminiscent of Dungeons and Dragons, Doom, and Helsinger's Pit, all games he had played as a child. People out there weren't taking him seriously.

"Oh, yeah, sure, get real," ridiculed some of the electronic responses. "Hey, Cochise," shouted another. "Way to go, Geronimo!" came a third.

One message he got was strange and crude. "Keep fucking around with this stuff, Mr. Squeegee," someone responded to his electronic handle, with no clue as to where his request had originated from, "and you'll get a tempered steel arrow through your goddamned evil heart and another up your ass."

A second vulgar message said, "We'll scalp your head and your prick, punk."

Just the ramblings of assholes hanging out their entire lives on the Net, seeking identity, seeking validation, seeking kicks, highs, and even sex in a world of silicone and bytes rather than in a real bed with a real woman, he told himself, shrugging off the threats as childish bullshit.

He turned his mind instead to Darlene and the problem of having discovered that he liked her too much to go on lying to her. Still, he feared what she'd think now if he told the truth, once she learned he was just a computer support person in the department working for Dr. Sanger, and not a detective at all. It was a quandary that had been taking up much of his time lately, and there didn't seem any solution but to tell her the truth, but when, where, and how? he wondered.

He surfed off the Net and got back to his duties. But halfway through a routine case study Dr. Sanger wanted all her notes organized on, his screen went blank. There was no explanation for the interruption. A few bleeps and grinds later, a handful of words suddenly flashed across his screen.

The flashing few words were scary words. They read: You'll pay dearly, with your heart's blood. . . .

Randy swallowed hard. It was one thing to be threatened by computer nerds on the Net; it happened every day. But this was different. Someone had hacked their way into his system. They knew who he was, where he was, and the threat, using the words *heart's blood*, was a little too close to home, with all these crossbow murders Dr. Sanger and Stonecoat were investigating.

Just as suddenly as the message appeared, it disintegrated

into black and the program he had been working on re-appeared.

Randy steeled his nerves and tried desperately to trace the break-in, but whoever it was, he was clever, leaving false trails and no true tracks. Now Randy felt electronically vulnerable for the first time in his life. He felt vulnerable in the real world, too, looking around himself for any sign of intruders who might storm in. He wondered if the place was bugged. He knew that his computer was being monitored.

"Damn," he cursed. He had a great deal of work to do, and he must do it quickly. He began to make disk copies of all the investigative work he'd done thus far for Dr. Sanger in relation to the crossbow murders. He named the file Crossfire, labeled the two disks he'd filled, and collected them up. He gathered the rest of his things and made his way to the door, prepared to leave the office, taking the disks with him. His feelings of paranoia were running rampant, while one voice in his brain kept saying, "Hey, man, you wanted intrigue; you wanted to be Detective Pardee, asshole."

Maybe it was just another prank from good ol' Terry and Stephen downstairs in programming and research. Those jerks had too much time on their hands. Yeah, perhaps it was just those two clowns. Maybe he was just overreacting.

But before he turned the doorknob, before he walked out, he decided to take one more step, just for insurance. He returned to his desk, placed the computer disks in a Jiffy Pak, labeled it in longhand, and walked it down to the mailroom. There he found Barney, the affable mailroom guy, and he got the proper postage on the envelope addressed to Dr. Sanger's home.

Barney said he'd shove it in the outgoing mail, but Randy said that he needed to put another item inside, just a note, so he'd take it with him.

Barney waved him good night. Outside the station house,

he found the nearest mailbox and mailed the package to Meredyth Sanger, a small voice in his mind saying, *I hope this isn't my last natural act on this planet.*

"Don't be so dramatic," he told himself aloud, dropping the package into the slot.

Still, as he walked to his car, he couldn't shake the feeling that people who normally didn't pay him any attention were interested in his every footfall. When he climbed into his car, he snatched out the two disks out of his jacket pocket—he'd only pretended to mail them—and when he put the keys into the ignition, sitting there in the sauna left by day's end, he hesitated, staring at the key. He foolishly wondered if anyone might have placed a car bomb below his little '84 Le Mans. He pleaded with himself to cut it out, to stop this nonsensical paranoia. He wondered if he had the stomach for this James Bond crap.

He bit his lip, grimaced, and manfully turned the key and cranked Lucy—the name he'd playfully given his car after a squat little Aunt Lucy—and expected it to explode in a ball of flame in his face, but nothing of the kind happened.

Maybe it had just been those goof-offs in programming. Sons of bitches . . .

Dr. Sanger used Lucas's telephone in the Cold Room to ring Randy, but she'd apparently just missed him. She cursed the time. Where had the day gone? She and Lucas had returned to the files here in the Cold Room to look for the tenuous threads between the cases they suspected were related.

But it was late and they'd been frustrated by the lack of connection between the judge, the doctor and the stockbroker.

"It's time to give it up here. Damn," she muttered. "I hope Randy has more for us from his computer searches."

"He's bound to. Do you know where he lives?"

"I've got his address, but if all the information is upstairs in the computer, that's not going to help us much."

"How safe is it, in the computer, I mean?"

"It's coded; has a lock on it."

"Do you know the code?"

"Yeah, sure I do."

"Let's have a look-see, then."

They found their way to Dr. Sanger's office. The lights were out, and with a dark, rumbling storm blanketing the city now, the place was like a cave. But there was a light on. Randy's computer screen.

"Randy? Are you still here?" she called out.

Silence was their only response. A window in her office was open, the rain seeping in. Outside, a fire escape revealed nothing. They turned on lights and went to the computer screen. It was blank, filling now with an automatic screen saver, fishes in a coral sea.

"This is just not like Randy, to leave his computer on, and to leave my window open."

"Maybe it wasn't Randy who left it on."

"Well, if he rushed out in a hurry . . ."

"We should locate him."

She nodded, a ball of gnawing, gloomy concern forming in the pit of her stomach. "Yeah, let's do that."

```
764LT1:\C42119\Category   42 . . . Topic
49LOG . . . Message 440 . . . Sat.
July 30, 1996 . . . 2:10:21
Questor 1 . . . Helsinger's Pit . . .
```

```
Q1: There is a further threat. A new enemy
has risen in perdition, this realm. These
are two enforcer demons—male and female.
They must be stopped. Do all necessary to
protect the brothers and sisters and
children of Helsinger. Reply this board
```

after evil is wiped out. God's speed to you. Questor 1 . . . END TRANSMISSION. Category 42, Topic 49LOG . . . 2:13:26

Category 42 . . . Topic 49LOG . . . Message 441 . . . Sat. July 30, 1996 . . . 3:55:20
Questor 2 . . . from the Pit . . .

Q2: Understood. Will take care of perdition's problem. END TRANSMISSION, Category 42, Topic 49LOG . . . 3:57:02

Category 42 . . . Topic 49LOG . . . Message 442 . . . Sun. July 31, 1996 . . . 8:10:01
Questor 1 . . .

Time to take out all threats. Set trap and exterminate the mice. No more fun and games. Eliminate the leaders of our enemy. See message drop, new station . . . END FINAL TRANSMISSION THIS E-MAIL.

TWENTY-TWO

Cactus flower: courtship

Once at home, Randy snatched a frozen pizza from the freezer and slid it unceremoniously into his microwave, careful to follow the convoluted but well-remembered instructions on the box. He fed his fish, petted his cat and stretched out on his sofa, the disks having been safely tucked away. Maybe later he would bring up the stored information on his machine, have a closer look. Maybe he'd struck a sensitive nerve with someone, but he was damned if he'd noticed anything of worth in all the material flowing through earlier in the day.

Still, he might've missed something.

He turned on the TV, listened to a little MTV. He was nearly dozing when something awakened him. It sounded like a gunshot, but it was just the cat, who'd somehow gotten into the metal trays and pots and pans below the sink. He must have left the pantry door open for Muriel to discover.

Muriel had frightened herself and came racing out of the kitchen. At first he thought she'd been frightened by something other than inanimate objects, but no, Muriel was true to form.

As he began to wash and dry pans and trays that Muriel had left marked with her fur, he heard the noisy elevator moving up the shaft, which was adjacent to his apartment.

The damned thing went up and down all night. There was nothing unusual in hearing it now, but for some reason, tonight it sounded more ominous. He listened to hear what floor it would stop at, hoping it would stop on the floor below or above, but no, it stopped on his floor.

This was followed by silence, pure and deep and foreboding, filling Randy with an ancient gloom he must surely have shared with ancestors who stalked saber-toothed tigers and woolly mammoths. He could only imagine who was out there, who had gotten off the elevator. There was not a sound, no footsteps, no laughter or talking, just the damnable silence.

They were coming for him. He just knew it. And him without so much as a cap pistol for protection. Damn, he'd electronically painted himself into a corner, a corner where he could get seriously hurt, maybe busted ribs, maybe worse, maybe killed, maybe . . . maybe . . .

There came a knock on the door.

He pretended to not be home as Muriel welcomed the guest with a startlingly high-pitched cry.

Another knock and Randy was sweating in the kitchen, his pizza beginning to smell from the heat.

"Randy? You in there?"

God, it was Dr. Sanger's voice.

"Open up! We've got to talk."

She'd never seen his place, never been here before. It was a shambles. Damn, why hadn't she called to give him some warning? "Dr. Sanger," he called out. "Just . . . just a minute." He futilely went about picking up, giving up after a few tosses.

He pulled the door wide to find Meredyth with Lucas Stonecoat beside her.

"Hi, Randy," she said, smiling. "I'm sorry I didn't get back to you today, but when I called you were gone."

"That's all right, Dr. Sanger. Hi, Detective . . . Officer Stonecoat."

"Why don't you call me Lucas."

"All right, Lucas."

"We came into the office and found your monitor on, Randy."

"What? No way, I shut it down. I never leave it up, Doctor, never."

"And a window was left open in Dr. Sanger's office."

"No, no way, I swear."

"We got a little worried about . . . things," she said.

"You don't know the half," Randy replied.

"Meaning?"

Randy gave them a complete rundown on what had occurred late this afternoon. He located the disks and showed the others.

"Better get your dinner," she warned. "It'll be burnt."

"Looks like we've got work ahead of us," said Lucas. "Why don't we order out for three? I'm buying."

With that, they settled in around the computer and brought up the material Randy had copied to disk. After a time, they began taking turns, watching the screen as the material scrolled by.

"There," said Meredyth, pointing.

The others joined her. "They all belonged to the Houston Hunt Club. They all contributed heavily to a number of charities, church organizations."

"All rather harmless enough in and of itself," suggested Lucas.

"They both contributed to the Church of the Sepulcher, located in a poor section of Houston, Texas, where a monastic order of brothers did all in their power to help out troubled youth. And they both likely knew the pastor there."

"Maybe he gave them both last rites?" Lucas wondered aloud.

"And look, they both went to the same college, Texas Christian University. . . ."

"But they attended different years."

"I wonder where Timothy Little attended college," Meredyth pondered aloud.

"Geezus, man . . . wow, what do you think?" Randy was asking.

"There's another cross here," said Meredyth, pointing to the screen.

Lucas leaned in to read it for himself. "They shared the same doctor?"

"Coincidence?"

"Or plan? Remember, whoever filleted the bodies knew anatomy, and whoever got close enough to tuck Mootry in was likely a trusted friend." Lucas began to pace the room, trying to consider all sides.

"Meantime, someone's getting damned nervous about what we know. Someone broke into my office and was rifling through Randy's computer."

"Why weren't these simple connections made on the earlier investigations?" Randy wondered aloud. "Why weren't they in the Cold Room files?"

"Removed?" suggested Meredyth.

"Maybe this was the connection that got Felipe and Covey put away so permanently."

Meredyth looked from Lucas to Randy and back again. "You think it's now our turn?"

"We could call a halt to it. Tell Lawrence we've got zip. Go our own ways, maybe live longer," he suggested.

"Hell, Lucas, we can't do that."

"To buy time, we can, until we know more."

"Besides," she suggested, "who's to say that Phil Lawrence isn't behind the cover-up?"

"We've got to be smarter than Covey. He gave them the wherewithal to silence him. We can't be so careless."

The elevator disturbed the silence now creeping over them, and for a long and sullen moment, they all stared across at one another, each sizing up the weighty aroma of paranoia they all inhaled. It was a potent and sensuous thing they shared, spooning up great gobs like an acrid and pasty oatmeal. Lucas located his gun and stepped to the door, where the pizza deliveryman pounded on the other side and shouted in his best business voice, "Delivery for Lucas Stonecoat!"

After gulping down Pepsi and pizza, Lucas agreed to submit to a hypnotism session with Meredyth Sanger. Randy agreed to remain as a witness to the session. Meredyth's voice was soothing, like a prairie wind, he thought, and he easily allowed himself to fall under her direction. He was soon relaxed; in fact, he could hardly recall a time when he'd felt more relaxed. Under hypnotism, he felt none of the usual bodily constraints or relentless pain that stalked him under normal circumstances.

But all freedom from pain was lost when he found himself reliving the events of the mugging he had suffered. He saw it all through a teasing fog and heard through a filter that created a slow motion of all speech. He didn't hear himself as he mimicked the voice of the man he had judged to be Fred Amelford: "You get yourself free of this case you're pursuing, son, or you and your girlfriend are dead. You understand that, *kimosabe*?"

"I-I-I . . ." He couldn't nod for fear the razor-sharp knife would cut a major artery, and now his body was frozen stiff on the couch where he lay. He couldn't find the words in his suddenly parched throat. He imagined what the world would be like tomorrow without him in it.

"That's what we think, son, exactly. Now, you just come to your fucking senses, boy," the supposed Amelford voice continued.

Lucas felt a huge, doubled-up fist chop away at the base of his skull, just as it had happened, and he sensed that the knife was lifted away from his throat in the same fluid motion. He guessed that one of his assailants had had combat training. His last thoughts were twofold: The attack on him was the work of two assailants, and Meredyth was in danger as well. But Stonecoat was in a black world now, the concrete walk his pillow. The words of his second attacker filtered through Lucas's fogbound mind now, the words of Jim Pardee, he assumed, tumbling out in broken slow motion. "We should just kill the bastard here and now."

"No, not—now—and—not—here."

A sudden, teeth-jarring kick struck Lucas in the side. On the couch where he lay, he flinched in pain. "Why're— we—screwing—with—him?"

The other man answered, "That's—'nough. We—do— it—the—way—we're—told."

"Damn . . . damn . . . It's—a'ways—hell—Sanger's— way, isn't—it?"

"Orders—is—orders."

"Our—lives—on—the—line."

"Damn it. Partner, we're—all—in—this—t'gether."

"Bas—tard!"

Stonecoat felt another sharp pain in his ribs when one of the apes viciously kicked out at him again. He flinched where he lay on the couch. He fought the pain every step of the way, then fell into complete unconsciousness. But now, under hypnosis, he could contemplate his own unconscious state. It was strange, like being on locoweed.

Then he was brought out of it, thinking it hadn't worked, that he was incapable of being hypnotized, and that only a moment's time had elapsed. He hadn't heard a word or felt a thing during the session, according to his conscious mind.

Meredyth looked grimly down on him, much disturbed, and Randy's mouth hung open until he finally said, "Must be his thoughts are all jumbled up, Dr. Sanger."

"What's wrong? What'd I say?"

"You accused Dr. Sanger of siccing those goons on you!"

"What? That's nonsense," he instantly replied. "Why would I think that, even in an unconscious state?"

"Well, in a sense, I got you into this," she countered. And in her most professional manner, she continued, saying, "You have every right to subconsciously explore your animosity toward—"

"Whoa-up there. Hold on . . ."

"To point a finger of blame at me," she groped for simple terms, "for having gotten you nearly killed. After all, I did—"

"I wasn't nearly killed, and why are you saying that I blame you? I'm a grown man, capable of making my own decisions, and I decided I wanted in, as I recall."

"No, I manipulated you."

"You did no such thing. I don't get manipulated."

"I put your back to the wall in your own captain's office before Commander Bryce if you recall, so don't tell me

about who's at fault and who's not." Her voice rose
wavelike, cresting and washing anger over him.

"Damn it, woman, I decide when I go forward and when
I go backward. My mother's name was Goingback."

"Really? I don't see where that has any bearing."

Randy attempted a timid truce, his hands waving as he
dared step between the cop and the shrink, saying, "Let's
run the tape, okay?" He had tape-recorded the session, using
a small recorder from Dr. Sanger's purse.

"Good idea," agreed Lucas, his eyes never leaving
Meredyth. "I'd like to know exactly what I said to so upset
you."

She dropped her gaze, shook her head, as if to say
everything he did upset her. Randy clicked on the tape.
Meredyth's voice crisply explained what the session en-
tailed, who she was, who the subject and witness were, and
the date; the tape then continued into the hypnosis itself.
Lucas thought she sounded like any other psychiatrist at this
point. Then, after a few questions posed by Meredyth to set
the scene, he heard himself, speaking in the voices of the
two thugs who'd jumped him. He soon realized why she had
become so defensive and self-conscious about her role in
dragging him into the case. It did sound as if he had
subconsciously blamed her for the beating as he as much as
said in his hypnotic state that the men had been sent by her.
The one goon wanted it done *Sanger's way*.

The phone rang, shaking Lucas from his despair at the
evidence brought to bear against him. He shrugged in an
apologetic manner toward Meredyth, a gesture he knew to
be too little, too late. Maybe subconsciously he did conceal
some dark caves of hatred for the doctor. Maybe he was
upset with her for having gotten him so deeply involved in
a case that could easily boomerang on them all.

Randy picked up the phone on the third ring, his eyes

never leaving the other two. "Yeah, yes, sir . . . matter of fact, he's . . . he's right here, Captain Lawrence," sputtered Randy. He carried the phone over to Lucas and added, "It's for you." He gestured to Meredyth after relinquishing the phone to Lucas, as if to say, *Don't ask me how he knew you were here.*

"Yeah, Stonecoat here. Can I help you, Captain?"

"We got another brutal killing up north, Lucas." Captain Lawrence's voice seemed a fix of fatigue and angst.

"Same M.O.?"

"Sounds to be, yes."

"Where exactly?"

"Rapid City, South Dakota—outskirts, actually."

"Outskirts? North, south, east, or west outskirts?"

"West, I'm told. We got you booked in a place called the Wagon Wheel."

"Same M.O., using a crossbow?" he repeated, hardly believing it.

"Near as authorities up there can tell. Some poor bastard and his woman, both with arrows through their hearts. That close enough?"

"Execution-style murders? Mutilated corpses?"

"You got it. Hands, heads, feet, sexual organs."

Lucas saw that Meredyth was listening intently. "Bloody business. Nothing but the torsos remaining?"

"I've been trying to locate Dr. Sanger. You two are booked on a red-eye flight leaving tonight, but I haven't been able to locate her."

"I'll let her know."

"You know where she is, then?"

"She's having dinner with her boyfriend at the Marriott, so I'll have her paged there."

"Her boyfriend? She's got a boyfriend?"

"A nice guy named Conrad. Why not, Captain?"

"Way she drives a man . . . just surprises me." He laughed at his own feeble joke. "Anyhow, a plane will be waiting for you two at the same military hangar you left from last time."

"Roger that, Captain."

He hung up and informed the others of the horrid yet half-expected news.

"Why have the killers stepped up their pace?" Meredyth wondered aloud.

"I don't know, but at this rate, their dirty little activities are going to be front-page national headlines soon."

"Let's get out to the airport. Run me by my place, Lucas." She then turned to the younger man. "Randy, it's important that you go on as if nothing's happened. Just maintain."

"Got it, Dr. Sanger."

Lucas threw together a set of clothes and items for the trip nearly identical to what he'd taken on the last one to Oregon. He made a quick telephone call, getting reservations at a place he called the Prairie Wind Lodge in Black Hawk. After he dropped the phone back onto its cradle, she instantly asked, "Black Hawk?"

"Near Custer State Park, in the Badlands area. Kinda rustic."

"Meaning?"

"Meaning friends of mine operate the place," he told her. "I've hunted elk and deer in the area myself. Have even used a crossbow. May as well throw them some business."

She nodded. "So long as it's not so rustic we can't get separate rooms, fine."

"They're Indians, Sioux, a little Shoshoni mixed in. They had parts in *Dances with Wolves*."

"Really?" From her tone, he could not tell if she was amused or curious.

"Their accommodations weren't good enough for Kevin Costner. He stayed at the Alex Johnson, downtown Rapid City, the presidential suite. But for you and me, we'll be fine at the Wind."

"Sioux, really . . . sounds interesting."

"Don't worry. Pawnees were the bad guys. Sioux were the good guys in the movie." He left unspoken the suspicion he couldn't completely trust Phil Lawrence, nor did he feel comfortable bedding down in a place that was procured by Lawrence for Stonecoat's comfort. He wasn't altogether sure why he distrusted Lawrence, but sometimes an itch had best be scratched, he told himself now.

Twenty-Three

Horse: travel

A case file was waiting for them on the plane when they boarded, couriered to them by none other than the real Jim Pardee, who shook Lucas's hand and wished them success, explaining that his captain had spoken to Lucas's captain, and that while he and Amelford felt they should be going to South Dakota, politics within the department were politics. "All the same," he finished, "safe trip, and we'll be interested to hear about your findings when you get back, Stonecoat, Dr. Sanger." He tipped his fifties-style hat and waved as he left the boarding area on the tarmac.

The flight gave them ample time to review what they were in for. The information was sketchy, but detailed enough to tell them that it appeared the murders were the work of the same assassins.

"Strange send-off," she'd suggested as they lifted off.

"Why, I thought Pardee was playing nice this time."

"At least he didn't kick you."

"Or put a knife to my throat."

The moonless, uncaring South Dakota night cloaked the land around Rapid City, but Lucas told Meredyth of its beauty, that it was wild and uninhabitable, nowadays serving as a playground for summer tourists in buses and by the carload. Every twist and turn in the highway here presented people with an awe-inspiring panoramic view of waterfalls and mountain peaks.

It was just past three A.M. when they touched down at Rapid City, where they looked for a cab to take them out to Black Hawk.

"Why don't we just stay at that Wagon Wheel place where Lawrence got us reservations?" she asked. "You know, no surprises . . ."

"Too many people know about us coming up here."

"Such as?"

"Pilot, clerks, Pardee, Lawrence, who knows who else? I'd just as soon they not know where I am when my eyes are closed."

"I thought you were easing off that paranoia kick."

"Who? Me? Paranoia's good defense against dead, Mere."

She secretly liked the way he shortened her name. No one else called her Mere. "Do you really think Pardee and Amelford might . . . ambush us?"

"At this point? I think anything's possible. Come on. There's a cab."

They went the extra several miles the other side of Rapid City, and on arriving at the Prairie Wind Lodge, Meredyth found herself pleasantly surprised. It was a beautifully tasteful, extremely well constructed, authentic looking cabin village and main lodge made from what appeared to be native trees. Everything was clean and pleasant, even to a city girl like her.

"We'll get some rest here tonight. I'll ring your room

around nine, nine-thirty, we'll have breakfast, and then
we'll arrange for a rental car."

She agreed. "Not much we can do in a half-sleep state.
I'm exhausted."

He signed for the rooms, chatting with a kindly old Indian
behind the counter who recognized Lucas. The man had
come around the counter to give Lucas a bear hug. He was
Lucas's size, perhaps sixty or sixty-five years old. *Hard to
tell with Native Americans,* she thought.

The man called to his wife and she appeared from a room
in back, followed by two younger men, all of them greeting
Lucas as if he were a long-lost brother. Even now in the
middle of the night. They had been expecting Stonecoat,
and had obviously either stayed up late or gotten up early to
welcome him. Lucas introduced Meredyth to the Sioux men
and mother, all of them smiling at her as if there were no
intrusion and no bother. They wanted Lucas to enjoy some
fresh-baked bread and a drink, and perhaps some wild Rapid
City nightlife if it could be located, but he begged off,
indicating Meredyth and saying they were both tired and
needed two rooms.

This request seemed to please them all, as if there might
yet be hope of converting Lucas to their tribe. Their oldest
daughter had joined them in the lobby, and was now staring
out from behind jet-black hair that veiled her eyes. Perhaps
they had hopes of Lucas joining their family, since they
knew he had been divorced from a witchy white woman in
Dallas.

Meredyth was sure they liked the idea that she and Lucas
were not sharing the same lodging. They went straight to
work, assigning them rooms, taking Meredyth's bag and
leading the way. Soon, with a few handshakes and pleasantries, Lucas and Meredyth found themselves in their

rooms—special accommodations here in the main lodge that had been readied for their arrival.

The interior was modern rustic, the walls filled with Indian primitive art, men hunting buffalo, wolves racing through the night in packs, antelope and elk and warfare scenes. There was no air-conditioning, so Meredyth decided this must have been what Lucas meant by rustic. Still, the air was cool and a lazy, serpentine breeze filtered through the open windows.

She took a pleasant shower, and when she returned to the room, she realized just how richly warm were the colors of the wood. But most of all, the bed was soft and inviting and Meredyth quickly, easily found sleep.

She didn't know why, but she felt safe here with Lucas Stonecoat in the room just across the hall from her, in the midst of the Badlands of South Dakota.

Meredyth had eaten lightly, despite the sumptuous outlay of food on the buffet the lodge offered its guests by way of breakfast. She opted for cold cereal because she knew what lay ahead for her viewing pleasure. Stonecoat, on the other hand, sampled everything on the buffet, including buffalo sausage, grits, biscuits, biscuit gravy, scrambled eggs, hash brown potatoes, and something called French and Indian toast.

Now they were at a place called Buck Mountain, elevation five thousand something feet, population fifty-three, now fifty-one, with the deaths of two of its summer residents. The victims were a surgeon named Maurice T. Shirley, near the pinnacle of his career and life at thirty-five, and his wife, Emily, who had recently married Shirley in a civil ceremony that had been kept hush-hush. Buck Mountain and Rapid City were summer home to Shirley, who was described in his usual home of Fort Worth, Texas, as a pillar of the community and an up-and-coming political force, as he was heavily into politics and very much the liberal Democrat. But on entering the Buck Mountain estate, a palatial playground overlooking vast reaches of the Badlands' surreal beauty, Lucas and Meredyth found little remaining of the former power in Fort Worth or his recent bride.

Their lifeless, bloodied torsos seemed posed like grisly, gruesome artworks on a single wall before a three-sided window that gave a panoramic view of the surrounding foothills and rainbow-colored mountains and buttes shimmering in the morning sun beyond, undisturbed by the human tragedy. Meredyth looked from the awful bodies to the distant mountain walls and found herself questioning her own eyes. She knew the mountains were real, she was looking at them, but at the same time, her mind kept saying nothing could be so beautiful in the sight of such horror as that a few feet behind her.

Miraculously, the press had not been alerted, so there were no cameras flashing other than police photographers and a man with the FBI. They found the place abuzz with police officials from Rapid City as well as the county sheriff's office, and uniformed men who were introduced as FBI agents who'd come in from Pierre, the state capital, at the request of Rapid City officials.

"Agent Bullock, Agent Price," said Sheriff Walter Hindman, a garrulous, large man with thick, animated hands and a perpetual smile. "This here is Dr. Meredyth Sanger and Detective Lucas Stonecoat, Houston, Texas. They're here 'cause they've been shadowing a similar killing, as I understand it, that happened in their neck of the woods."

Bullock and Price were tall, tanned, strong young men, polished. They wore ties and dark Brooks Brothers suits.

"What's the FBI interest?" asked Lucas, knowing the FBI

didn't investigate murder unless requested by local authorities to do so. All the same, Price read them the standard line.

"We're here at the request of local law enforcement. Same as you. Maybe you'd like to tell us more about why you're here?"

Meredyth launched into a full explanation, detailing their involvement, concentrating mostly on the murder of Judge Mootry, but laying out the trail of other deaths.

"That's what took us to Oregon," she finished.

"Oregon?" Bullock and Price looked at one another.

"You can't seriously be denying the connection," Meredyth blurted.

"We haven't heard anything about Oregon," replied Price in a cool and controlled voice.

Lucas shook his head. "Every man for himself, huh? There was talk there of FBI on the way when we left a kill scene very similar to this one."

"Damn, really?" Bullock for the first time looked shaken.

Price and Bullock conferred in a corner about this development.

Lucas said to Meredyth, "These two are full of it."

"Whataya mean?"

"They're lying. They're putting on an act for us."

"You really think so?"

"Body language gives 'em away. They knew about Oregon; that's why they're here."

Price returned to them alone. "We'll happily share what we know if you're willing to pool your knowledge. We need to know everything, just how far you've gotten to date."

"Hell, that sounds rather lopsided," replied Lucas. "I mean, you guys don't even have anything on Oregon."

Price's face hardened and Bullock came forward, hearing what Lucas had said. "Forget it, Price. We don't need these amateurs."

"Yeah, forget it, Price," agreed Stonecoat.

"You're a damned Indian, aren't you, Stonecoat? You don't particularly like the FBI, do you?"

"Not much to like about a tail-wagging-the-dog agency that tramples on human rights and breaks up Indian families, no. You are, after all, part of the history of the extermination of Indian rights and lives."

Meredyth was trying to snatch him away, but he stood up to the FBI men.

"We'll keep our own counsel then, and you keep yours, Mr. Stonecoat."

"Okay, if that's how you want to play this thing out. Fine with us."

"Lucas!" Meredyth hardly agreed.

"If we wanted to, we could bar you from these premises," countered an angry Bullock, who was easily Lucas's size and obviously in much better condition. "I'd say we're being fair, Detective. Now make your sweep. Come on, Stu. We've seen enough."

When the FBI men disappeared through the door, Meredyth hit him.

"Ouch! What's that for?"

"Your stubbornness."

"They had nothing we could use."

"You don't know that."

"They're at least as perplexed as we are as to motive and understanding of these brutal attacks."

"How do you know that?"

"I just know."

"What is it, some kind of mystical thing? You can look into their souls because they don't know how to hide their souls from your gaze? Give me some reason to trust you on this, Lucas."

"I know what I know, and those two were just in the way.

Now, if you don't mind, there's a lot of work to do here."
Lucas stepped away, going for the ghastly torsos on the
wall, examining each more closely. Wearing latex gloves, he
studied the metal shafts that pinned the bodies to the wall.
On either side of the metal shafts, the weight of the torsos
was pulling them down, enlarging the entry wounds.

The sheriff wanted very much to take the bodies down
and wrap them in body bags for the coroner, who had come
and gone, and be done with this day's work. Meredyth could
hardly blame him. He had been the force here that had kept
the crime scene intact to this point, and he wasn't winning
any prizes for his decision to do so.

But Lucas wanted to take some measurements. He
created a hooked line to fit through the holes in the window
where the arrows had penetrated. The string was then
attached to the ends of each arrow still protruding from the
decaying white torsos. Each arrow had hit its mark, directly
through the heart. A side window had been smashed and a
dirt trail led from there to the phone and to the torsos.

Walter Hindman, the local sheriff, walking them through,
said, "The alarm was set off at exactly 10:49 P.M. the night
before the bodies were discovered. But the alarm company
got a call from the doctor's wife at 10:53 to say it was
triggered accidentally, so nobody came out here."

"It was a woman's voice on the phone?"

"Yes, sir."

"Who discovered the bodies?"

"Tourists . . . day after the alarm call."

"Tourists?" asked Meredyth, swinging around, confronted
by the awful torsos.

"Well, actually, it was one tourist at first, one tourist with
a pair of expensive binoculars. There's a favored picture
stop and scenic viewing area riiight over there, if you look
just beyond that stand of juniper trees. Anyway, this fella

from New York, eighty-one years old he was—traveling by bus coach—he'd decided to use his binoculars this way, to take in the house. When he sees what he sees, he tells the tour guide, a fellow I know who comes through all the time. Anyway, Tony contacts me, tells me this bizarre story, and, of course, I don't believe him for one moment, because Tony's forever pulling my leg. But he pleaded so much, I told him I'd come out and have a look, let him have his fun, you see."

"But it didn't work out that way," finished Stonecoat.

"You got that right, son."

Lucas again studied the two shiny, steel-alloyed shafts. They were of the same make as those found in Oregon.

"Don't touch nothing," suggested the sheriff.

"Rule number one of criminal detection," countered Lucas.

"And rule number two?" asked the sheriff.

"Don't touch nothing."

This made the sheriff laugh for the first and only time during their meeting.

Lucas saw that Meredyth was turning pale as she stared at the filthy work of the crazed killers, one now possibly a female.

"You okay, Dr. Sanger?" he asked.

She swallowed as if unable to get air. "Fi-fine."

"Return those sheets to the bodies and get 'em to the coroner," suggested Lucas.

"Yeah, well, FBI's done finished, too, so you're right."

"How long has the FBI been here?"

"Very interested in the case. They came straightaway when I called, yes, sir."

"When did they arrive?"

"Yesterday. Seems they were in Wyoming on some other

matter. Said their Pierre office buzzed them to make the stop."

Lucas mentally chewed on this information before saying, "Nothing more we can do here. We've got the angle at which the arrows entered. We trace that back, we might find the spot where the assassins were standing when they fired." This meant outdoors and air. Meredyth was pleased, and she was the first to go through the door, but the stench of death had already permeated her nostrils and clung to her hair, and not even the cleansing South Dakota winds, so clear and sweet, could eliminate the odors now clinging to them both.

"Don't you find it curious that the FBI has become so interested in our cases?" he asked her.

"Well, the sensational nature of the killings . . . might attract any law enforcement agency."

"I wonder."

"You wonder what?"

"I wonder what they know?"

"Probably about as much as we do, like you said. Why? Are you having second thoughts now about pooling our resources and information with Bullock and Price?"

He grunted and began his search for the position from which the arrows began their journey, once again figuring on more than one assassin.

She followed, anxious to get away from the house. Looking back over her shoulder, she saw the sheriff's men and paramedics working to remove the arrow shafts and placing the headless, handless, footless torsos into body bags.

"Why do you suppose they cut them up so?" she asked Lucas.

"No feet, the dead can't walk. Old Indian belief."

"Really?"

"It's also true of Transylvanians, so . . . take it for what it's worth. Still, if you cut off an enemy's head, hands, feet and genitals, it's for a purpose. Whoever's behind this may be involved in some sort of cult that believes an enemy's power can only be eliminated by scattering his parts to the four winds. I dunno."

"It makes sense. There's something there. Always strike the heart, like a stake through a vampire's heart, then dismantle the pieces. Isn't that how the belief goes?"

"You think we're dealing with vampire-hunters?"

"I dunno. I don't know much of anything anymore."

"Hang in there," he said, placing a firm hand on her arm. She nodded. "I'm okay."

"Here, right here, is where they stood when they fired. They had a direct shot, and those two inside never knew what hit them."

She looked up and saw that it was true. This was the perfect angle from which to fire. It was close enough, within range, and all the killers needed to do was step from behind the boulders to their left, where crushed cigarettes told the story of how long the assassins had waited for just the right moment. Meredyth thought this must have been exactly how Alisha Reynolds was killed in Georgia.

Lucas began scooping up butts into a plastic bag. "Maybe we'll get lucky. Maybe we'll get a print."

"But you doubt it."

"Yeah, I do."

"Why didn't the FBI take the butts?"

"Because they know it'd be a useless waste of time, most likely. These guys don't leave prints."

They walked back toward the house, the cars and the waiting sheriff.

On their way back to their hotel, Lucas asked her what kind of weapon she carried.

"Weapon? You mean gun?"

"Yeah, what caliber? A .38 or what?"

"I'm a police psychiatrist, not a police officer. I don't carry a gun."

"What?" He was amazed. "You're tracking killers—predators—without a gun? I thought so, when I saw no sign of a bulge under your arm. Who do you think you are, Jessica Fletcher of *Murder, She Wrote*? Get real. If these assassins decide to turn on us, how do you hope to defend yourself?"

Frankly, she told herself, she hadn't given it a thought, but she wasn't about to tell him that. "That's what I have *you* for."

He smiled at her little joke and then suddenly turned off onto a solitary, winding, and isolated dirt road. The sky was a deep cerulean blue, like the bluest of oceans, the sun brilliant, and the thick clouds like whipped cream piled high. It was what every boundless western sky in every Gregory Peck western was supposed to look like. The clouds seemed posed, even fake, yet they were real, and the mountain backdrop appeared painted on, yet it was actually there, not to be denied.

The road snaked like a river, deeper and deeper into a hidden crevasse, and soon they were driving alongside a sparkling river that cascaded over a rocky bottom. Nature here was rampant with casual beauty, so that even the leaves on the trees fluttered enchantingly elf-like in the sunlight.

"This place is lovely, beautiful."

"I know. I own a little piece of it, kind of a retirement place. One day, I plan to build on it, if I don't die first."

She recognized the fatalism of both Indian and cop. "One day? Why not now?"

"Perhaps you hadn't noticed, but currently my cash flow is not quite as strong as the creek there."

"What's it called? The creek, I mean."

"Elk . . . Elk Creek. There are several reservations around here, and I'd be welcomed on any one of them, but I don't want to spend my retirement on a reservation; I'd like to own my own place."

"That's a fine goal."

He pulled the car to a halt just off the road on an overlook near the creek. He got out and stretched. He seemed in his element here, she thought.

When she got out of the car, he pointed to a clearing opposite her. "There is where I'd put the house."

"It is beautiful, really."

"I'd be snowed in winters, but I could handle that."

"I'm sure you could."

He walked around to her, and for a moment she worried he was going to propose she spend those winters here with him, too; instead, he surprised her with a gun, pushing it into her hands. "This is yours. I'm going to teach you how to load it, how to handle it, how to fire and hit your target."

It wasn't a matter of what she wanted; it was what he wanted. Still, she held the gun up by the trigger guard and said, "I don't know about this."

"You will, when I'm finished with you. Now, let's get started. If you're going to be my partner, I need to know I can count on you in a fight."

This challenge issued, she grimly brought the gun back under her control and said, "All right. Show me."

"That's the spirit. Now, this gun is what we call a police special, a .38-caliber weapon. Very efficient and light-weight."

"Lightweight? I'd hate to see what you call hefty."

He offered her his Browning automatic, his hand almost large enough to conceal the big weapon, and she compared the two firearms, saying, "I see."

"Now, let's talk about how you load a .38," he suggested.

"Yeah, please, begin with the basics."

"Before we leave here, I'll have you shooting with some grace and ease," he tried to assure her.

"I'm just not certain I could shoot another human being, ever," she confessed.

"You will if your life depends on it."

Maybe . . . maybe not, she mused as he thundered the words, "Pay attention, now!"

When they got back to the lodge, there was a message light blinking on Meredyth's phone. The message was left by Randy Oglesby. She made the call, using her calling card, and when Randy came on, he sounded out of breath and excited.

"What's up, Randy?"

"Something big, really big, Doctor."

"Tell me about it."

She listened in rapt attention, her eyes widening with the new information.

"I know it sounds crazy, but when I was a kid, we played this computer game called Helsinger's Pit. Remember Stonecoat's having told us the guy said it had to be Sanger's way? Well, I listened to the tape again, and he actually might have said, Hell-singer's way. . . . Get it? Helsinger's way, Helsinger's Pit, the computer game I told you about? It got me to thinking and muddling over that game, and damned if that game isn't precisely what's happening— murder by crossbow. It's a game that sets you up as a kind of religious fanatic, out to rid the world of . . . of vampires, you see?"

"Vampires? No, I don't see. . . ." She didn't want to believe it, but at the same time, she recalled the earlier discussion she'd shared with Lucas on vampires. In the car coming back to the hotel, he'd also added that vampires existed in every culture as part of the antireligious icons necessary to preserving order.

"The hero, this Helsinger guy, and his followers tracked down and killed practicing vampires. It was the hottest role-playing game around after Doom. Lotta demonology stuff, very hostile environment, easy to get whacked either by the vampires or by law enforcement."

"Law enforcement?"

"Yeah. According to the game rules, no self-respecting cop's going to believe in vampires, see? That's how come it's so easy for them to get away with murder, but it makes it tough when the good guys kill a vampire, because they're taken as citizens, so the cops intervene wrongly all the time throughout the game."

"Back up there a second, Randy. What'd you mean when you said locating *practicing* vampires?"

"Sure. FBI keeps a knowns list on people who claim ties to the vampire life."

"People who claim ties to the vampire life?" She realized that she was repeating everything Randy was saying, but she couldn't help herself. This sounded simply too off the wall.

"Sure! Even if you're just a kid on a PC, you start talking that you're a vampire, enjoy nightlife, shun the light, crap like that, and then you start keeping vampire hours and drinking goat's blood or some such shit, and they begin to track you."

"They?"

"FBI."

She wondered anew about Bullock and Price, and their business in all of this. Maybe they had long since seen the vampiric nature of the killings? Maybe they were well aware of this bizarre computer game called Helsinger's Pit . . . perhaps?

Randy continued. "Anyway, the object of the game was to hunt down and destroy these self-professed demon types, to kill them before they could completely taint the world. But it wasn't easy, because they had demonic powers."

"Sort of an electronic witch-hunt, you mean?" she suggested.

"As a kid, you'd get addicted to it."

"You played the game, then, a lot?"

"I got so into it, I became a screen zombie for one entire summer. My parents had to literally dismantle my computer to detox me. It was that mesmerizing."

"What're you saying, Randy? That there's some connection between these murders and a . . . a computer game?"

"You got to play the good, pure guy, the avenging angel, the soldier of God, while at the same time—"

"You got to destroy all these evil characters."

"Yeah. At the outset, you have a list of vile characteristics to choose from to create the most awful creatures ever to masquerade as human beings. You gave them careers, traits, families, but they were all, you know, devil worshippers, cultists, vampire types who made their fortunes and got their kicks, you know, from feeding off others. So, you always got this double rush: You got to waste people, like Rambo, or G. I. Joe, but you sorta got God's pat on the back for fighting His war."

"Electronic vindication from God, huh? Justifiable homicide."

"Well, it was only a game, but I'm telling you, the overtones, the similarities to the crossbow deaths are unreal."

"What similarities besides the crossbow?"

Lucas knocked at her door, asking if she'd like to join him for dinner. She moved to the door, phone in hand; she then told Lucas to come in and sit, and then she returned to Randy. "Well? I'm listening."

"There were scenes in the game where the stalker fired directly through a window, and the target was always the vampire's heart."

She looked up at Lucas, recalling his earlier, cogent comment about the hearts of the victims here having the look of stalked vampires. "Go on," she said.

"You only scored if it struck the monster's heart."

"I see."

"Furthermore, you had to dismember the parts and bury them in secret places so the demon could not collect up its parts and revive itself and come for you."

"It's too mad, too far out," she told Randy. "Perhaps one person might fall prey to the game, confusing virtual reality with reality, but now we know there is more than one assassin at work."

"But there's only one spiritual leader guiding them," countered Randy. "Every cult has a leader, and nowadays every PC in the country can be turned into a pulpit or altar from which any maniac can rant. Oddly enough, Helsinger's Pit was a networking game. No one played it alone."

Meredyth was having trouble taking all of it in. "I see . . ."

"Thousands upon thousands, hell, hundreds of thousands of kids were playing that game, and part of the game was this conspiracy of sorts to . . . to—"

"Conspiracy?"

"Yeah, to reintroduce the world to the power and wrath of the god of the Old Testament, you know, the God of Abraham, the one who believed in an eye for an eye, a tooth for a tooth, all that, a god less forgiving."

She repeated his words, shadowing him thus, trying to

follow Randy's convoluted, Generation X, paranoia-laden thinking. "A god less forgiving of what?"

"In particular? Less forgiving of lesser gods to which some mortals prayed, say like coin and money, arrogance and pride, sloth, gluttony, Satan and Satan's minions, you name it."

"I can't buy this, Randy. It's just too damned . . . weird and unimaginable."

"All I can say to that, Doctor, is think the unthinkable. I knew some guys so plugged into this game they never came out. Then imagine some nutcase, religious gung-ho type who decides there are real vampires screwing around among us, having their way with our women and spawning little devils everywhere they go. Get the picture?"

"But Mootry and Palmer and these others . . . they weren't practicing witchcraft or vampirism or anything. Nothing points to any sort of occult connection with the victims."

"They're all on the list."

"What list?" she asked, blinking, wondering what else Randy had to pull forth in his magician's manner.

"It's a list compiled by the FBI."

"What FBI list?"

"FBI started doing checks on professed vampires and practicing demonologists over forty years ago. J. Edgar was fascinated by it; believed it was a communist plot to infiltrate and weaken the moral fiber of the country from within."

Meredyth held her breath. "My God . . . How many people are on this witch-hunt list?"

"It varies from year to year, but usually in the neighborhood of three hundred."

"Three hundred?"

Randy almost asked about the echo he was getting over

the wire, but thought better of it. "There are, of course, thousands, but the ones who make the list have, you know, gotten in trouble with the law at one time or another by taking their beliefs too far."

"Do you have a copy of the list?"

"I do."

"God, how'd you get it?"

"I used a computer at Circuit City. The salesman really wanted me to buy."

"And you're saying Mootry's name is on that list?"

"A young Mootry dabbled in the occult, yes. Maybe he got over it, maybe he secretly continued with it, I don't know, but yes, he's on the FBI's list of three hundred and nine practicing vampires. Don't ask me how often the FBI updates the list."

"Not soon enough for Little."

By now Lucas was leaning into the conversation, trying to hear what Randy was saying while enjoying the smell of Meredyth.

"Little's on the list," replied Randy.

"And Maurice and Emily Shirley?"

"Ahh . . . ahh . . . no, not on the list, but Palmer's there, and so is Whitaker and some of Whitaker's family."

Lucas interrupted, telling her to ask about Bennislowe.

She asked and turned to him, her face stark. "Yes, he's listed."

"And David Ryan Gunther, the kid whose skeleton was found close to Whitaker's estate but whose head was never found."

"No, not listed," replied Meredyth after passing along the inquiry. She then asked Randy, "But why target these particular men for . . . for e-mail murder?"

"That's just it. Nowadays, if they have your social security number, they can tap into your financial status, your inheritance, how much you paid for your house, the details of your divorce. It's only a keystroke away."

Meredyth thought about this for several lengthy moments, about how easily young people were led astray, how easily minds were warped and put under the control of some guru or another, anyone with a platform from the racial hatred doctrines preached by the KKK to the cult dicta of a Jim Jones of Guyana infamy.

"God, still, you're talking cyberspace murder, Randy, and I'm just not sure I'm ready to accept that."

"But we've got FBI crawling all over this case," added Lucas into the mouthpiece.

"Damn, then that cinches it," Randy shouted. "They've got to know something screwy's going on with their vampire list."

"Maybe you're right. We'll talk to them about it."

"Tread lightly. No one's supposed to have access to the list."

"Then how did you get it?"

"Illegally."

"Of course . . ."

"Be careful out there, Meredyth."

"I will . . . we will."

Randy hung up, leaving Meredyth and Lucas to puzzle over all that he had left them to ponder: an FBI demonology list, the fact several men who'd died so horribly were coincidentally on this hit list? Murder by computer e-mail, the fact the arrows were the tip of the iceberg. Could someone in the FBI be involved? Was the paranoid ghost of J. Edgar working through some brash young Republican elite guard in the FBI? Were Bullock and Price the vanguard of these driven fanatics? The questions continued into the night.

ᎢᏪNTY-ᎶOUR

Crossed arrows: friendship

After Meredyth and Lucas had discussed every detail of Randy's call and their debate wound to a close, Lucas began pacing the small hotel room like a nervous puma, and she complained, "Will you sit down; light somewhere."

He turned in mid-stride, his eyes clear and malevolent, but the malevolence was not directed at her, she knew. "Maybe we'd better find Bullock and Price, put it to them. See their reaction, you know, face-to-face, man-to-man, all that."

"Yeah, and maybe with a woman present, we just might get a read on 'em, you mean?" she replied with a smile. "It might prove interesting. Still, I'm having a hard time believing that murder could be committed by an electronic cult over the Internet. Talk about *wired* . . . wired for murder . . ."

"Every other crime in the country has gone high-tech, so why not murder?"

Lucas telephoned Sheriff Hindman, who put him in touch with Bullock and Price, who agreed to meet them for dinner to talk over mutual interests in the case. The FBI men were staying at the landmark hotel, Alex Johnson, in downtown Rapid City. Lucas got the sense the men were counting coup. Bullock didn't rub it in or even say it aloud, but he and Price had been expecting their call.

"We'll be there by seven."

"Meet us in the restaurant. We'll dine together on Uncle Sam," offered Bullock.

"Yeah, well, Uncle Sam does owe my people a few meals," Lucas said, trying to keep it light, gaining a grunt of understanding from Bullock before the man hung up.

Lucas and Meredyth stepped into the beautifully refurbished, turn-of-the-century hotel exactly at seven. The decor was rustic, early western, so much so that Meredyth felt strange to be walking on the carpet. It looked handmade, something that ought to be hanging in a museum. The same applied to the American Indian designs and paintings adorning the walls. Antlers and moose heads and stuffed deer, cougar and other animals also stared down from on high. Meredyth expected to see Teddy Roosevelt step through the next doorway.

They located the FBI men in the restaurant off the lobby. Bullock and Price looked as stiff and formal as ever, but they seemed pleased that the Texas authorities had come groveling to them. There were handshakes all around, and after ordering drinks and a look over the menu, Lucas brought up the possibility that some nutcases had formed an Internet club through which members were controlled and selected and told to murder people on an FBI list of cultists or vampire worshippers.

Bullock laughed in Lucas's face.

Price's frown deepened his wrinkles. "Give us a break, Stonecoat."

"I thought we were here to share information, gentlemen," Meredyth instantly reacted. "Now, it's no secret you're here because of the list, the Vampire List, and the fact that people on that list are being murdered by self-appointed vampire stalkers and demon killers. Isn't that right?"

Bullock bit his tongue and finally released the air he had inhaled, instantly dropping his poker face. "How the hell did you get that information?"

"Are we on the same side or not, Agent Bullock? Are you guys onto some sort of weird *X-Files* kinda case here or not?" pressed Lucas.

"All right . . . all right, we deal. You tell us what you know, we'll level with you about our interest."

Between them, Lucas and Meredyth filled in the blanks for the FBI men. Both Price and Bullock listened with rapt attention, amazed at the amount of information pulled together by the duo.

By now the waiters had delivered four sumptuous dinners, two of stuffed salmon, two roast buffalo plates, Lucas having talked Meredyth into trying the unusual. She was pleased with the sweet flavor and that it was not tough, as she'd imagined, or fatty or greasy.

"We've been trying to locate these cultists on the Internet," said Price, "have a team of the best minds in computerland working on it day and night, but we're dealing with people who really know how to hide their tracks."

Bullock quickly added, "They're not sloppy like you see with the porno freaks on the Internet. They close up holes as they go, plugging us out. They're cleverly disguised bastards, these people."

"At the same time, they have access to . . . to anyone," Price assured.

Bullock added, "Anyone with a public persona. Anyone with a birth certificate, a driver's license, car registration, voter's registration, if you license your pet, get a divorce, file for bankruptcy, inherit property, they know about you, and they can stalk you."

"The average person on a PC could build a whopping good picture of your life and your financial transactions for just a little trouble," commented Price.

"Hell, nowadays, a single stop at a data company like CDB Infotek, for a five or twenty subscription rate you can scan hundreds of thousands of public record databases— electronic versions of county, state and federal court files," continued Bullock.

"Matter of fact, there's a private investigation firm in your own city of Houston, Intertect, that can do in one hour what ten years ago would've taken a week," agreed Price. "Employers hire these guys to check on prospective employees. But then again, Intertect isn't too particular who they take on as clients."

"They can tell if you've ever been charged with fraud, were ever sued, or had ever sued anyone else. A nationwide search can quickly turn up assets, hidden or otherwise, such as a second home, luxury car or boat," added Bullock.

Lucas understood completely, saying, "If you're in an auto accident or injured in some other way, a lawyer might want to check you out to know how deep your pockets are."

"Even information supposedly not available to the public is floating around out there on you," added Price. "Your bank account and credit card numbers, your brokerage records—"

"Social security recs and tax returns," offered Bullock.

"It's all an impostor needs to check your balances."

"Despite federal law that restricts access to those with a . . . a legitimate need to know," began Bullock.

"Such as prospective creditors, insurers, or employers," added Price.

Lucas groaned and rolled his eyes. "But all anyone has to

say is that they intend using the information for a legitimate purpose, and they're in, right?"

"So anyone answering yes can get the files?" asked Meredyth.

Bullock confessed with a rueful smile, "That's how Dan Quayle's credit history wound up in *Business Week* in 1989, yeah."

"People, strangers to you, nowadays can turn up anything on you—the fact your home has a pool, the number of vehicles you drive, your political party affiliation, what charities you donate to, the magazines you subscribe to," Price further explained.

"Not like the FBI would consider such tactics," grumbled Lucas.

"All right, true, touché as they say. We led the way in this kind of surveillance, but now it's out there. Anyone surfing the Internet can play FBI," countered Bullock. "Look, I was a special agent in the division of the Secret Service that investigates electronic financial crimes for seven years, and I don't trust my account number in Internet providers' files."

"Hell," grunted Price, opening up wider now, "there's fifty-six thousand IRS employees alone who have access to the computer system where taxpayer records are stored. Thirteen hundred of them were investigated in 1994 for snooping violations in the confidential records of their neighbors, friends and celebrities."

"Some altered files to generate higher tax refunds for their friends," volunteered Bullock.

"All the gibberish you see on an e-mail map . . . it maps out the path the commands have gone through. A system administrator or hacker—like the one you obviously have working for you"—Price pointed a finger—"at any way station can read a copy of your message, so it's downright insane to send information naked over the Internet."

"Price means unencrypted."

"Downloads leave footprints in the computer system through which they pass, too," added Price, a statement that made Meredyth and Lucas think of Randy Oglesby's safety. Still, Meredyth had told Lucas that Randy was taking extreme precautions, explaining that for his last "break-in" he'd used a PC at a Circuit City in a downtown Houston mall. "Try and trace that," she'd said to Lucas.

"Banks and financial institutions are now using encryption to protect transactions," Bullock told them. "Encryption scrambles the data much like airwaves are scrambled on pay TV, and for the same reason, to protect against voyeurs as info travels the Internet. If it's not encrypted, it's not taken seriously."

"Once you're on the Internet, you're open to theft unless you've set up a fire wall," Price explained.

"Fire wall?" asked Lucas.

Price frowned and said, "A security technique that isolates that part of the computer system accessible by modem."

"Hell, I found out about this stuff early on, went home and removed the checking account numbers from the Quicken files on my home computer," observed Bullock.

"Well, that's overkill, Tim," Price argued.

"I don't think so."

"Unless some hacker's got a specific reason to target you, your hard drive is probably not so tempting a target compared to large corporate and governmental databases." Price looked into Meredyth's eyes and added, "I would not spend time worrying that someone's breaking into your PC through a phone line. It would take a lot of time, and there's not much upside."

"Unless maybe the guy's a creep and is stalking her," challenged Bullock.

"You miss the point, Tim. Hell, InfoBase in Conway, Arkansas, claims to have data on ninety-five percent of the

U.S. households, all compiled from public records, credit bureaus, consumer questionnaires, telemarketing and mail order companies' files. The hacker or stalker or stalker-hacker doesn't need to tap into the lady's machine; he can do it through the third party and do it more safely."

"Sounds like anybody can play Big Brother; sounds like *Brave New World*," said Meredyth, a bit shaken.

"For sale: your estimated income, your home's market value, your available home equity, what merchandise you buy, donations you make, your marital status, occupation, and children's ages, your hobbies and interests. Now imagine a con man who is interested in your money."

"Hobbies and interests?" She was dumbfounded.

"The information requested on those little cards you fill out called warranties and guarantees puts you on InfoBases's Chiphead list."

"A stranger can easily learn what you buy and what you read."

"That is scary," she agreed.

"The benefits of staying off modems and out of Nets," replied Lucas. "Sometimes the old ways are better . . . or at least safer?"

Meredyth and Lucas conferred quickly and just as quickly agreed to share everything they knew about the series of killings they had been pursuing from their home base in Houston. They described the Cold Room files she had unearthed, the similarities in the string of deaths going back so many years, and the fact no one had to date put them together, and now this—the obviously hacked or stolen FBI list of self-proclaimed vampires and demon worshippers.

"What do you know about the Vampire List?" asked Meredyth of the FBI men.

"It was discovered that the list was tapped into, hacked

into, but only recently. Fact is, the list hadn't been updated or kept in serious repair for ten, maybe twenty years. A lot of nonsense associated with the list."

"Whataya mean, nonsense? If it's nonsense, then why's the Federal Bureau of Investigation interested?" asked Lucas.

"Well, it started with the Hoover Administration, and you know what kind of paranoia ran rampant in the agency then," began Bullock, whose eyes followed people about the room as he spoke. "There have been a handful of professed vampires who have acted on their insatiable need for human blood; in fact, the first such case that was of notoriety involved an FBI manhunt for a guy in California who did in fact drain his victims of their blood and drink the stuff. Since then, there've been several others, including the celebrated case of Mad Matthew Matisak—who, by the way, was not on the Vampire List compiled by the FBI, because, in point of fact, there's really no way to track all the wackos out there."

Price took the ball, continuing, "Anyway, that madman Hoover and others in the agency began keeping book on people who, for one reason or another, professed a liking for the vampire lifestyle. Needless to say, most of the list is made up from subscribers to *Vampire Dreams, The Red Knight, The Blood of Lucy Wistera,* and other such publications, along with vampire orders, cults and clubs. There are more than you might expect, and many of the members are playacting at the masquerade, finding something appealing in the whole mythos, you see, but some embrace it as a way of life, a religion even, a kind of devil worship, and these are hard-core believers who sleep in coffins and go about only at night."

"That doesn't fit Judge Mootry or—"

"Perhaps not recently, but he may've become disillusioned with his religion, as anyone might; he may've changed his lifestyle and beliefs as he aged," suggested Price. "Else he hid it well . . ."

"He wasn't sleeping in a coffin," said Lucas.

"Coffins are harder than they look, and no room to stretch," added Bullock with a laugh. "Tell me this: Any graveyard dirt found under the man's bed?"

"I didn't see any, but then, forensics had already come and gone."

"Check it out."

"Did he go about during the day?"

"He was a judge."

"Night court?"

Meredyth bit her lip. "Appellate court."

"Liked the black robes?" Price facetiously asked. "Check into it. You'll find he kept the lights in his courtroom dimmed and kept no mirrors in his chambers or at his home, or so our information has it."

"Eccentricity," suggested Lucas.

"Night person?" asked Bullock. "Did he party late into the night?"

"Yes, he did, but he donated tons of money to charitable causes," she countered.

"He had lots of money to give. Nothing in the book says a vampire can't be a philanthropist, too" suggested Bullock. "Look, we're not saying that we believe he was a practicing, kosher vampire, okay? We're saying some people could and may well have perceived him as such, especially since he was retained on that damned list, and if the list did fall into the wrong hands . . ."

"And perception is everything in this life, isn't it?" Price suddenly added. "By the time of his murder, the old man may well've been in the process of . . . of trying to buy his way back into the good graces of the Lord of Light. Who knows?"

"In fact, one of his last major donations was to some

off-center religious order based in Houston, a very generous sum," agreed Meredyth. "Maybe he was a changed man."

"We all of us do things we later regret; who hasn't lied, cheated, stolen something from someone somewhere in a moment of temptation," suggested Lucas. "And who hasn't championed a cause to later regret it?"

"The FBI first began tracking Mootry when he was a college student," Price said, thoughtfully sipping his coffee now. "He had become fascinated with the dark side of world religions, the black arts, cults, cultism. Even his selection of classes mirrored this interest, and for a time, he planned to be an archaeologist, which would have more readily masked his vampiric tendencies, I think; then something turned him around, and he began to see the beauty of the U.S. legal system, and he believed he could make a difference there. At least that's been our thinking, right, Bullock?"

"Of course, a lot of people at that age are confused and seeking some touchstone of identity," added Bullock. "Hell, I know I was."

"And Palmer?"

"Much the same, only in an Ivy League setting. All it took to get on the list was to dabble and tell others you were a practicing vampire and then make the motions. That early in the game, anyone professing such tendencies, the FBI took seriously and began to watch closely and in many cases to film. It made sense to the behavioral science division to keep some sort of tabs on these . . . freaks."

"You made film?" Lucas should not have been surprised. "Like you did with so many American Indian activists?"

"We did, or rather, they did. It was before Price and I were in the agency."

Meredyth, amazed, asked, "Is this film in your archives?"

"It is, I suppose, unless someone in a position of authority has seen fit to destroy it. Meantime, people on the list are suddenly being killed off, so we were alerted. The keepers of the list and the film have all long since retired, the files pretty well set aside, much like your Cold Room files, except these were electronically set aside."

"And someone, knowing about them, hacked into them?" asked Lucas.

Bullock reluctantly nodded. "Twice, now. Once very recently, in fact."

Lucas and Meredyth exchanged a quick glance, both knowing Bullock referred to Randy Oglesby. "But then, you know that, don't you, Dr. Sanger?" asked Bullock.

"Whatever do you mean?"

"This break-in originated in Houston, Texas."

"Really?"

"From a certain precinct house," continued Bullock. "In fact, from your office, Dr. Sanger."

She knew this to be a lie, that Randy had not used the office computer to obtain the list. "Someone broke into my office some time back," she offered, "Lucas, you remember when it occurred."

Lucas nodded assertedly. "It must be related."

Price added, "When Mad Matisak came into prominence, there was some interest, but no one really wanted to be associated with the Vampire Files, as they were called. Then, as Tim said, people started getting bumped off, and the FBI's main concern was that the victims were on a list created by the FBI. If it got out . . . well, what with Waco, the Ruby Ridge thing, and all the other garbage leveled at the FBI of late . . . well, you can imagine how concerned our superiors are." Price twirled a swizzle stick between his decidedly thick fingers.

The clatter of dishware in the hotel dining room grew with their silent response.

"One more thing we found that almost all, but not quite all, of the people on the list had in common," added Bullock.

"What's that?"

"They were all into computers, modems, using the Net, and as young people they all played computer games."

"Games? Like Doom?"

"Doom, Cutthroat, the darker the better."

"Helsinger's Pit," Meredyth muttered.

"That, too, and don't think for a moment we haven't seen the parallels to these murders. We just didn't know until your input how far back the killings went."

"Then whoever's doing this, they're ostensibly doing it for the same object as the game?" asked Lucas. "To rid the world of devil worshippers?"

"Particularly devil worshippers with money, obviously," added Meredyth.

Bullock gave a shrug, saying, "Root of all evil, right, Dr. Sanger?"

"And the killers have become their own cult," she countered.

"Thanks to the luxury and efficiency of the computer and Internet," added Price.

"Every computer has the potential of becoming a New Age pulpit," finished Lucas. *Isn't that what Randy Oglesby said?* he thought.

"So, what's your next move, Stonecoat, Dr. Sanger?" asked Bullock.

"I'm not sure. Return to Texas, start looking for tracks there, maybe computer tracks?" she offered noncommittally.

"Sounds a logical step, no pun intended." Bullock stood, and the others followed suit.

Price said, "Well, good night and happy hunting. We do hope you two will keep us informed."

"And vice versa," replied Meredyth.

"Of course, of course. . . ."

They all parted at the dinner table, each of them knowing it was a game of who got the answers first. Lucas shook hands with the government men, and Meredyth smiled, and all was congenial. Lucas and Meredyth were stopped, however, when Tim Bullock said, "And by the way, in case you hadn't heard, your friend Covey?"

"Covey?" asked Meredyth.

"John Covey."

"Jack," added Price.

"What about him?" asked Lucas.

"He's dead."

"Dead? How?"

Meredyth's face fell.

"Usual prison whodunit. Still under investigation."

"Damn," muttered Lucas, taking Meredyth by the arm.

"If we're so transparent to the FBI," she whispered to him, "what must we be to the killers?"

Bullock, hearing this, also whispered for their ears, saying, "Have you considered the distinct possibility that the Shirley killings were simply to get you out of Houston?"

Lucas stared at Bullock, incredulous. "What? That's just crazy."

"You two got Covey killed. We never went near him."

Meredyth gritted her teeth. "You can't believe that these people would just randomly select two innocent people for execution for the sole purpose of . . . of . . ."

"Of keeping their dirty operations secret? Yes, we can believe that." Price's voice was sympathetic.

Meredyth was sickened by the thought that the Shirleys had possibly had nothing whatever to do with this.

"Neither of the Shirleys was ever on the Vampire List," added Bullock.

"What are we to conclude from that?" asked Price. "That you'd best watch your backs here, because the murdered couple were setups, dummies, just to lure you two here for a possible ambush?"

Lucas put his arm protectively around Meredyth and walked her out to the valet stand, where they picked up their rental and headed for the Prairie Wind. It was near midnight.

"Pretty damned cooperative for the feds, wouldn't you say?" he asked her as they drove off.

"I wouldn't know. I've never worked with the feds before. Have you?"

"On occasion. They're typically tight-lipped, unless . . . unless they need something from you. Then they're willing to bargain."

"Then I'd say we came away with more than they did. Randy tried to tell us about the killing games on computer, the cyberspace conspiracy, the Vampire List, but we weren't buying it. Now this."

"Don't get any false ideas from those clowns back there, Meredyth. We didn't cause Covey's death or the deaths of the Shirleys."

"But suppose it's true? That we were lured here for a purpose?"

"Then we'd better tread lightly."

She replied coldly, her eyes like broken glass, "We got the order to be here from Captain Lawrence."

"You can't seriously suspect that Lawrence would be a party to such callous murder?"

"Lately . . . I don't know what to believe or who to trust. Do you?"

"Well, darling, that goes double for our FBI friends as well. I'd like to think we had friends in high places, but I'm not so sure about those two chumps."

"I'm beginning to feel that creeping paranoia you always associate with psychosis," she replied.

"Is that feeling anything like being inside a rattle and all the beans are popping and swapping noise, until you don't know which one to listen to?"

She nodded. "That's it. That's the feeling. . . ."

ᴛᴡᴇɴᴛʏ-ꜰɪᴠᴇ

Arrowhead: watchful

"God, I need a shower," Meredyth moaned just outside her door as they stood together in the lodge hallway.

They had let the military jet fly back without them, booking a flight on a commercial airliner for 7:40 A.M.

"How about a nightcap? We can raid your wet bar," he suggested.

"Whenever do you sleep?" she asked. "No, we've got an early flight tomorrow, remember?"

He heaved a heavy sigh, frowned, and nodded, going for his own room. Surprisingly, Lucas found himself very mellow and sleepy-eyed when he pulled back the covers and lay down on the bed. He snatched away his shirt and pants, leaving just his shorts, enjoying the stillness of the night. He had opened a window to the cool South Dakota evening.

He didn't think he'd have trouble sleeping tonight. Something about working as a detective again had helped him in so many ways, he could not begin to thank Meredyth enough. He made a mental note to do so as he drifted off to sleep.

Lucas had been hopeful that he and Meredyth might find a common sexual interest in one another, and to that end, he had changed his room at the front desk. His room had been opposite hers, across the hall, but now it was adjacent, a mere pair of doors between them, which he had toyed with on entering, trying to get up the nerve to knock, but hadn't. Now he heard a rattle, a snake rattle . . . no, the rattle of keys, perhaps, just outside in the hallway, and the second shook him from slumber. At first he thought it might be her, knocking at the adjoining door, but no, this was a set of keys and a turning lock. Other guests, he assumed.

Still, curious, Stonecoat slipped from bed to investigate the noise. He heard muted voices.

"No one there," he heard.

Stonecoat grabbed his gun and the empty ice bucket, tore his door wide while concealing the gun behind the bucket, and saw that it was one of the young Indian sons of the proprietor, snooping in his old room. Their eyes met.

The jet-black eyes quivered, and the boy with the copper skin said, "I knocked, but no answer."

"Were you looking for me?" asked Lucas.

"Yes. They told me to locate you."

"They?"

He looked nervously past Lucas, his eyes darting. "FBI."

"Oh, those clowns." Stonecoat followed the boy's eyes, only to see shadowy figures and some sort of glinting metal in the dark vestibule. He suddenly recognized it as the business end of a crossbow pointed at him—he guessed—from the end of the hall. "Hit the floor!" he shouted and dove at once, springing the gun from the bucket and firing to his left twice, his right once. Two arrows whizzed by, their whirring noise ending with two jarring thuds and an outcry from the boy.

The shadowy assassins had dematerialized with the gunshots. "Meredyth!" he shouted, got to his feet and lunged through her door as she opened it, having been awakened by the noise.

He grabbed her, and using his gun as a ram, knocked over the single lamp she'd turned on, then cushioned her fall as he pushed her down, all in one fluid motion. At the same instant a window was shattered, and over Meredyth's ear, she heard the singing, snakelike hiss of another arrow whipping by.

"Are you all right?" Lucas asked as they lay together in the darkness, their hearts beating a dangerous anthem.

"Why are *these* guys such poor shots?" she asked.

"We had some warning. None of their other victims had the slightest idea they were targets."

Stonecoat made his way to her window, cutting his feet on broken glass but not making a sound, his Browning automatic clutched in his massive hand. He stared out on a moonlit mesa filled with stunted trees, each one looking like an assassin. The South Dakota night did what it was meant to do. There were shadows and deep black holes everywhere he looked, any one of which could conceal assassins with crossbows. He searched for any sign of movement anywhere, but there was only a deafening silence and stillness mocking him. He wanted to climb out the window, go in search of the men who had done this, but he feared leaving Meredyth alone.

"No one out there. Fled like crows in the night," he whispered.

"Bastards," she growled. "Gutless cowards."

They heard groaning and tearful crying from the hallway. The boy, remembered Lucas, rushing to the door, past the steel shaft in the wall. Meredyth quickly followed and lost her breath, seeing the young Indian boy impaled by the neck against the door.

"Damn! Don't move! Stay perfectly still," Lucas was saying to the boy as his family came running out.

There was bedlam and panic from the boy's parents, but Lucas shouted everyone down. "You want the boy to live through this? Do as I say! You, Jake," he said to the big brother, "get on the phone and call 911. Seth," he shouted to the boy's stunned father, "get a pair of metal cutters, no, bolt cutters, you got that, Seth? You got that? Hurry!"

The father ran off after the cutters. Lucas shouted to the mother to be ready with a blanket to keep her son warm, and he told the sister to get a clean sheet to cut and clot the blood with. "And some plastic."

"Plastic?" she asked.

"Like a bag, Baggies. Clean ones."

The arrow had gone clear through, the arrowhead sticking out the other side of the door, the feathers tickling the boy's throat. "Don't struggle against the arrow, son," he now told the boy, whose eyes beseeched him to do something.

"We'll get you to the hospital. You'll be all right. I can see from the amount of blood that no vital blood vessel was hit. You were, believe it or not, very lucky."

He didn't look lucky, Meredyth thought. Rather, he looked as if he had been suddenly turned into one of those helpless butterflies pinned to a box.

The father returned with a pair of large bolt cutters to snip off the arrowhead so the shaft could be pulled through the boy's neck with one quick yank, but rather than turn the cutters over to Lucas, he said, "This is for me to do. Your enemies, whoever they are, are still lurking outside. I heard them. Go."

Lucas nodded and started away. Meredyth shouted, "Wait a minute, Stonecoat. You're not going out there alone."

"Stay with these people. They may need your protection. And wrap the wound in plastic and bandages. It'll stanch the blood flow."

"And who's going to protect you from yourself?" she shouted as he disappeared out the back door.

Lucas had viciously attacked the back door, kicking at the bar lock running across it, throwing it open, and leaping like a pronghorn sheep out into the darkness, going into a tumble, ignoring his limitations, knowing he'd be sore in the morning. He now scrambled to a boulder jammed between two white pines. The darkness painted everything black now, the moon having found refuge behind scudding clouds. In the distance, the howl of a lone wolf tugged achingly at the heart, while a tickling breeze played its fingers over Lucas's perspiring brow.

His heart was beating like a running buffalo's, but he felt alive and strong and at ease with himself.

The door behind him jack-hammered open again, and he saw Meredyth racing toward him. "Get down!" he shouted, as a steel-shafted arrow suddenly twanged into the tree beside his head, inches from his temple.

Lucas had to fire blindly in the direction from which the arrow had come, spitting as it had like a coal from hell, but his true attention was drawn by Meredyth, whom he pulled down beside him. "Damn it, I told you to stay put."

"I'm not leaving you alone to fight these madmen!"

"Then at least be quiet."

"Do you hear something?" she asked.

"Over you, you mean?"

"Sounds like someone moaning."

"A wolf," he suggested.

"No, definitely human."

"Maybe I got dumbshit lucky." He cocked an ear to his left, the direction from which the arrow had come whizzing at him. Someone *was* groaning. "Maybe I hit the bastard," Lucas again suggested.

In the distance, they heard the approach of an ambulance

siren, help coming for the kid. But it also appeared to send the rats scurrying. Shadows were suddenly moving everywhere, two, three, then four, as the moon slowly revealed itself and the purple landscape all around them.

"Fire at will!" shouted Lucas, who raised his weapon and began firing alongside Meredyth, who was also frantically firing, when suddenly Lucas went down with a thud, as if hit.

Meredyth grabbed him up in her arms, certain that he'd been hit, but there was no arrow and there was no blood from a gunshot wound. She called his name several times before he opened his eyes.

Lucas grimaced and jerked awake, not knowing at first where he was but smelling Meredyth's sweet fragrance all around him. He pulled himself up, shook off the blackout.

"What happened, Lucas?"

"I must've gotten hit by a fragment of stone or something."

"I saw no return fire."

"It was a ricochet," he lied.

She remained unconvinced, but glad that he was again conscious. The ambulance screeched its way to a stop around front. "Maybe you'd better go to the hospital, too," she suggested.

"No, no way . . . no more hospitals for Lucas Stonecoat."

"Stubborn."

"It's part of my charm. Did you hit anything? You fired your whole clip."

"No, I don't think so. It was just too dark. Like shooting at phantoms."

"I saw one go down. Think I got him in the leg. They sure ran like jackrabbits. Thought they were going to come back, finish us off." He smiled with abundant pleasure and pride.

"You realize we've become targets of these crazed assassins."

"We're onto them and they know it. And if it was Pardee

and Amelford in Houston who jumped me, and if they were talking about Helsinger's Pit like Randy theorized?"

"Then we're talking a major conspiracy within the department."

"That sounds so . . . so . . . so crazy. . . ."

"People everywhere are sick of the justice system's inability to deal with growing crime," he suggested.

She had to agree. "Juveniles with thirty or forty previous counts of robbery, rape, assault being put into the revolving-door system, only to step back out to murder someone."

"Plenty of angry, frustrated people who might feel it necessary to take the law into their own hands, and cops are people, too, after all . . . myself notwithstanding."

"But a conspiracy within the Houston Police Department to take vigilante justice against men like Mootry, Little . . . It's like . . . like a *Dirty Harry* movie or a really, really bad suspense novel."

"But if it's true . . . if it's only partially true, and we don't have all the pieces by any means . . ."

"Then who? Who's involved? I mean, God knows who such a conspiracy might involve."

"Lawrence?"

"You instinctively disliked him from day one, didn't you? I know I have from the day I met the man."

"Well, yeah . . . but . . . maybe it's just my dislike for authority and white men in control of my life."

"He stood in your way, didn't he?" She hammered her point home. "And he's stood in my way since the first moment I showed concern over the Mootry case. Maybe his thick-headedness has a cause I was never supposed to uncover."

"You're jumping to conclusions," he said, trying to caution Meredyth.

"And who else knew we were coming to South Dakota? We were set up, pure and simple."

"The FBI obviously knew about us, and from what Price and Bullock said, almost anyone could track us cyberneti- cally. Damn . . . damn, but you're right about one thing."

"What's that?"

"Someone set us up for murder, and I should go after them, track them," he told her now.

"No, there's too many of them, and obviously they've planned their escape route, know exactly where they're going. You'll just be wasting your time. Besides, you get out there alone . . . have another blackout, and you could be . . . killed."

"It wasn't a blackout."

"I'll keep your secrets, Lucas, but don't lie to me."

He stood up and marched back to the hotel, leaving her to trail after him.

Inside, Lucas asked one of the paramedics how it looked for the Indian boy. "He's in shock at the moment, but prognosis appears good. He'll survive, thanks to the quick thinking of whoever dressed the wound."

The paramedics were followed by the local police, some of whom recognized Stonecoat and Sanger from earlier. There were questions and reports to be filled out.

They spent some time attempting to change their flight. They were able to do so, taking a flight leaving at 5 A.M. Lucas felt it best if they not stick to their original exit from South Dakota, that a change of plans was in order.

After their travel plans were arranged, Lucas asked Meredyth about how well she knew Randy Oglesby.

"What're you implying? That Randy somehow had some- thing to do with the attack on us tonight? No, no . . . that's nonsense."

"He's capable of learning anything about anything on that computer of his."

"That doesn't make him a moral degenerate."

"He said he played the game, that Helsinger's Pit, as a child."

"Everybody his age played that game."

"All right, but are you sure you can trust him?"

"I . . . I'd trust Randy with my life, yes."

"All right, then you're about to do just that. Telephone him."

"Telephone him now? It's two A.M."

"Call him and ask him to find out who ministered to Judge Mootry's spiritual, medical and legal needs."

"Mootry's minister, his doctor and his lawyer?"

"That's right. He can do it from his PC, according to the FBI."

"All right, and if he supplies us with the names?"

"We go talk to Mootry's closest confidants."

"Disregarding Pardee and Amelford, Captain Lawrence and protocol?"

"When people start threatening my life and the lives of my friends, Doctor, to hell with protocol."

She started to dial the number, but Lucas, taking no chances, suggested they call from the desk. "They might have bugged our phones," he explained.

She shrugged her agreement and they made the call from the lobby.

The ringing on the other end continued four times, waking Randy from a sound sleep. Beside him groaned his newfound love, Ms. Darlene Muentes, who still thought he was a detective named Pardee. When Meredyth announced herself, Randy seemed surprised; it *was* an extremely unusual hour to be calling from South Dakota.

"Dr. Sanger! Great to hear from you. Is everything all right?"

"Fine. I'll explain everything when we get back," she said noncommittally. "Listen, Randy, Stonecoat and I need another favor of you."

"Anything to help."

She was getting as paranoid as Lucas, she thought now, as to her ear he sounded almost too willing, too anxious to help. But then, he always was, always had been. . . . She had always believed him somewhat lovestruck toward her, and while at first it had caused some consternation, the two of them had created a zone in which they could work together. Randy was nothing but a pure gentleman at all times, never suggesting anything but a business relationship, and yet there had remained something of the tension of their first meeting in the air between them ever since.

"What is it, Meredyth? How can I help?"

"We need you to track down the name of Mootry's personal physician, his legal and financial advisor, and his priest."

"He had a priest?"

"Well, no . . . I mean, we don't know, but we want to talk to anyone giving him close advice in these three areas."

"I see."

"Can you do it?" she asked, knowing that he could, and knowing that he loved a challenge, and knowing that he loved to have her ask, so he could bedazzle her with his computerese.

"Sure . . . should be a snap. I have enough records on the man to tap into that, sure. It may be I get an agency or a church instead of a name, though."

"See what you can find out, Randy, and thanks."

"Sure, no sweat, Dr. Sanger. You sure now that everything's okay with you?"

"Just fine. We'll be back in Houston—"

Stonecoat cautioned her with a finger to his lips.

"—soon as we can. Be in touch then."

"You got it, Doctor."

She hung up, feeling badly that she'd suspected Randy in the least. She wondered if Stonecoat trusted anyone, including her.

ᵀWENTY-SIX

Cactus: desert sign

When they arrived at Houston Intercontinental Airport, no one was there to greet them, as no one knew they were arriving so early. They'd gotten some sleep on the plane, but not much, and both Lucas and Meredyth wanted to go home, shower and rest, both knowing that Captain Phillip Lawrence would be wanting a briefing on South Dakota by ten A.M. at the latest.

They took a cab from the airport, dropping her first, their good-bye subdued and matter-of-fact. "See you at the precinct house," he had said.

"Will do," she replied.

"And neither of us talks to Lawrence alone."

She nodded her assent. "And be careful. If they mugged you once, they can do it again."

"They won't get another chance."

He sped off in the cab, leaving her to watch after him, wondering if she'd been wrong to drag him into all this cloak-and-dagger business with her. She admired his grit, his determination, and since firing off his weapon, he seemed somehow different, more soldierly, more confident, if that was possible.

She went in and upstairs to her apartment, kicked off her shoes, and began tearing away clothing, anxious for a shower and a few winks before having to face Lawrence.

After she stepped from the shower, Meredyth noticed that the message light on her answering machine was blinking. She pressed the button. There were two messages from Conrad, anxious about her whereabouts, making her wonder if it was to be like this, or worse, after their marriage. The third message was from a carpet-cleaning company that wanted to do her carpets in the worst way, and the fourth was from Randy Oglesby, who claimed to have hit pay dirt with the priest, the lawyer and the doctor, giving her a list of names. She grabbed a pen and jotted the names down on a list.

> Priest—Father Franklin Aguilar
> Doctor—Sterling Washburn
> Lawyer—Pierce Dalton

She had not heard of any of these men, so why did the list seem so sinister? How had Randy so quickly and efficiently supplied the names? Could cyberinvestigating be that easy? Or was Stonecoat right about Randy? It simply didn't seem possible, but she was beginning to see bogeymen everywhere.

She immediately dialed Lucas's number, wondering if her line might not be bugged here in her apartment. She hung up, but then she rationalized that if her line was bugged, the so-called cult of assassins who had tried the night before to take her life, along with Lucas's, had already heard Randy's message to her. She dialed again and got Lucas on the second ring.

"What is it?" he asked nastily.

"It's me, Meredyth. I've got the list of names."

"Names?"

"The ones we discussed, remember?"

"Oh, oh, yeah, sure. It'll keep till ten, won't it?"

"Yeah, just thought you'd like to know Randy worked all night on our behalf to get this information."

"Sounds like he's motivated."

"He'd do anything for me."

"That doesn't surprise me."

She sensed he was about to hang up. "Wait. In case something should, you know, happen to me? The priest's name is Father Frank Aguilar; the lawyer's name is Pierce Dalton—"

"Pierce? That's appropriate."

"And the doctor's name is Sterling Washburn. Are you writing this down?"

"Speak with you later." He sounded exhausted, she thought. Perhaps he'd get some sleep tonight, despite his chronic insomnia.

"We're in this together, now. Lucas, I don't want to learn of your going to see any of these people without me. You promise?" He assured her and Meredyth hung up, wondering if she could trust him to keep his word on this.

At ten in the morning they got their meeting with Captain Phil Lawrence, but neither of them was anxious to face the man at this point. They were both filled with suspicions, none of which could be proven. Still, the report they gave opened the captain's eyes, wide, then wider still, as he listened to the events they relayed. They told him about the attack at the lodge, but they'd decided to keep the FBI connection to themselves at this point. It was a decision they had made before going into Lawrence's office.

Lawrence immediately wanted to know, "Why didn't you stay downtown at the damned Wagon Wheel where we had the two of you booked in the first place?"

"The Prairie Wind was closer to the crime scene," lied Lucas. "And as it turned out, there was a great deal to do at the scene. It grew late."

"That about sums it up, Captain," she agreed.

"Now we know for certain we're dealing with a fanatical fringe group, but what motive have they?" Lawrence replied.

"We've kicked around a few theories," suggested Lucas. "One's pretty far-fetched, having to do with . . . vampires."

"Vampires?" Lawrence looked genuinely amazed. "What about vampires?"

"More to the point, our killers may be playing out some sick thought they're saving the world from vampires, that they have some sort of genetic link with vampire stalkers of the past," Meredyth suggested in her best psychological mumbo-jumbo voice, but it struck Lucas as quite plausible the way she orchestrated the words.

"That is far-out, Gary Larson far-out," Lawrence replied. "So, what is your next move, Dr. Sanger, Officer Stonecoat?"

"Pardon me, sir?" asked Lucas. "But are you saying we're still on the case?"

"Well, what with Pardee and Amelford dragging their butts . . . I guess I was a bit hasty, premature in my judgments earlier, Dr. Sanger," he lamely apologized as she watched him squirm on the hook.

"Well, sir," countered Lucas, letting him off the prover-bial hook, "we're honestly at a dead end ourselves. We're intending to return to the Cold Room, go back over the files, see what shakes out there, if anything."

"You may's well know that Pardee and Amelford have lodged a formal complaint with the commissioner as to how we're handling things."

"Really?"

"Something about your having cut them off from what you know; something about having had something analyzed at an independent lab and not sharing the results?"

Lucas shook his head as if he simply could not possibly begin to understand the attitude held by the other two detectives.

"This word comes from Commander Andrew Bryce, who's getting an earful of complaints about me lately . . ." His lingering glower told Meredyth he was still smarting from her having done the same earlier.

"They've got a nerve," Meredyth defiantly retaliated. "They haven't got what you cops call jack shit! Nor have they shared a shred of information on the case with Lucas and me, sir."

"Well, it was *their* case. And as for jack shit, Doctor, I'm given to understand you got a certain Jack shit killed up at Hempstead. Knifed through the heart."

Lucas instantly defended her. "Now, hold on, Captain, you can't blame Meredyth for Covey's murder."

"Commander Bryce turned this case over to us," she defended herself.

"He didn't turn it over to you. He told you to work with the officers already assigned."

"We'd be happy to; it's Pardee and Amelford who don't want any part of us, except maybe to bash Lucas over the head."

"What's that?"

"Nothing, sir."

"Then you have had a run-in with those two?"

"Nothing of consequence, sir." Lucas glared at her for

bringing it up, but she was studying Phil Lawrence's every reaction, to gauge the extent or the lack of surprise in his demeanor, so she paid no attention to Lucas's reaction.

"File your written reports with Sergeant Kelton. See that I have them by the end of the business day," he told them. "Keep me informed."

They were dismissed and left the room.

"You were right about the bastard, Lucas."

"Right? About Lawrence?"

"He hardly budged when we told him about the possible vampire connection. He's playing it all just too cool."

"Maybe he's had orders and medication from his doctor to keep cool. . . ."

"I tell you, he knows something, and he's keeping it close to his chest."

"He keeps all his cards there, and I assume he always has."

"Further evidence he can't be trusted."

"Do you think he may be covering for someone else?"

"Don't know . . . I don't know. All I know for sure is that I can't trust him."

Randy Oglesby, rumbling down the stairwell two steps at a time, shouted, "I need to see you, Dr. Sanger!"

She turned, and with Lucas following, they went to Meredyth's office.

"Do you think it's wise talking here?" asked Lucas, signaling the open window they had found earlier.

"Come on," she said, leading them into the ladies' room.

There Randy, gulping on air, said, "About the three names I gave you."

"Yes, what is it?"

"All three went to Texas Christian University."

"Ahh, odd coincidence?" suggested Lucas.

"Just like Mootry, Little, and Palmer at one time or another," Randy shot back.

"You're kidding?"

"The web is woven tight," replied Lucas.

"Damned tight," agreed Randy. "I'm getting so I don't trust anybody, and I do mean anybody. . . . And the deeper I get in, the more paranoid I'm getting. Meanwhile, my personal life is a wreck. You wouldn't believe what I've done to my good name. My life's . . . well, I'm living a lie."

"Living a lie?" she asked.

Lucas looked knowingly across at her.

"I told Darlene that I'm, well, that my name's James Pardee, that I'm a homicide detective with the HPD, and she believed it, and it all started when I went to fetch those crystal goblets you had examined. Darlene works for the lab. Oh, and I had the goblets locked up in a safe deposit box." He surreptitiously handed the key over to Lucas.

Lucas laughed helplessly and Meredyth joined him, all the while apologizing for laughing at Randy's predicament. Stuttering and stumbling for the words, she told Randy, "You have no idea what we were thinking your big, bad secret might be."

He only looked perplexed. "Nothing could be worse than this. . . ."

Again Meredyth and Lucas laughed.

Armed now with additional information supplied by Randy Oglesby, Meredyth and Lucas drove across town. They decided to pay a visit to each of the three people on the list supplied them by Randy's computer hacking. They first went to see Mootry's lawyer, Pierce Dalton. The man seemed to have everything a lawyer could find of value: opulent offices, the most expensive suit money could buy, a bevy of secretaries, each more fashionable and gorgeous than the next. He was the head of his own firm, and he handled trial cases for the defense as well as corporate and personal finances, if you could afford him. Apparently, he was extremely successful, which meant there must be many a man walking the streets in his debt, both financially and otherwise.

Dalton was as straightforward as he was tall, telling them that he had already talked to the cops on several occasions and had opened Judge Mootry's books for them.

"Detectives Pardee and Amelford, you mean?" asked Meredyth.

"Yeah, that's them. Apparently, they're some steps ahead of you two."

"Did you see the judge the night of his death?" asked Lucas.

"As I told the other detectives, I was booked on a flight that night to San Diego. You can check it out if you like."

"Then you didn't have a drink with him that night?"

"No, I hadn't seen the old gentleman for several days." Dalton was cool, unperturbed.

"We learned recently that you and the judge went back a long way, back to college days, actually, Texas Christian," Meredyth said like a well-mannered snake, striking with aplomb.

"That's right. That's why the judge trusted me."

"You're so much younger than he was, yet you were at the university together, same fraternity."

"I was a boy wonder. Graduated from high school at eleven. I was much younger than everyone in my fraternity."

Lucas asked. "Then you're classified a genius?"

"Only by those who need classification and labels."

They said their good-byes. Once outside, Meredyth said, "He didn't give away a thing. I couldn't read him."

"He gave away one thing."

"What's that?"

"He was too damned cool."

"Personally, I find most genius-types that way. I don't know if there's anything there."

"Let's go see Dr. Washburn. See if he's as unflappable as Dalton."

They next ran down Dr. Sterling Washburn at Mercy General Hospital, Houston, half a city away from Dalton's downtown offices. The hospital was in a run-down section of the city, and it appeared to have remained open in order to serve the needy in the dilapidated area in which it was located. Meredyth explained that once it was a very pleasant, upscale neighborhood but gang violence and a series of economic downturns had created a little war zone within the city, and the hospital found itself at the core of the battlefield.

"This Sterling Washburn has to be dedicated to work here," she said in Lucas's ear as they waited. Sterling was being paged, as he was not in his office.

In a moment, a woman in a white coat stepped up to them. "Officer Stonecoat, Dr. Sanger, I presume?" she said.

"We've been waiting twenty minutes to see Dr. Washburn," fumed Lucas. "Is he or is he not in?"

"I am Dr. Sterling Washburn. How can I help you?"

"You?" asked Lucas, surprised, but pleasantly, staring at the lovely green-eyed, raven-haired woman. "I mean, your specialty is?"

Meredyth wanted to both hit him and apologize for him, but she held her tongue instead. She introduced Lucas and herself to the doctor.

"My specialty is heart surgery. I have a private practice,

which is lucrative, and I give as much time as possible to the hospital here," she answered Lucas's question and then some. "How may I be of assistance to you?"

Meredyth jumped in. "We understand you were Judge Charles Mootry's physician?"

"I had that dubious pleasure, yes."

"Dubious, you say?"

"Charles hardly took my advice, but he and I enjoyed a long friendship, and his health was deteriorating along with his mind. Toward the end, he thought he could put his hands all over me. . . . It was, or had become, a distinctly uncomfortable position for me, but I owed him a great deal."

"You owed him? Money, you mean?"

"He supported me through school. He was quite the gentleman about it, until recently, as I've said. It started with cute little old man gestures and remarks but had escalated to, 'You owe me, this, Sterling.' "

"And did you feel obligated to him?"

"I did, of course. . . ."

Lucas asked, "Since Texas Christian days?"

"I wasn't a full-time student there; I was just picking up some credits, still in high school at the time. I went to Tulane in New Orleans. Charles made it possible. I knew I wanted to be a physician, and I wanted a head start. Charles . . . Charles encouraged me, became a big brother to me. He supported me, as I said and as I've told others. There was never any secret about our relationship. I did love Charles, just not what he'd become."

"So, your friendship began with a monetary favor?"

"No, no. . . . We met at a mutual friend's party. It wasn't until years later, when he heard about my situation, that he came to me with the idea of helping me out."

"And you returned the favor over the years by seeing to his medical needs?" asked Lucas.

"Yes, you could say that, although he and I were more like brother and sister than . . . than patient and doctor. He seldom listened to my directions, but he wouldn't pay another doctor, he always said. He was a . . . a funny man, a wonderful man."

"Were you seeing to his pill supply, doctor?" Meredyth asked.

She looked around to be certain no one was listening. "I was. . . . But I only supplied him with what he needed to stay sharp. That's all."

Lucas replied, "You must have been devastated to learn of his death."

"I was. I had just left him hours before," she said. "I feared he might've overdosed when I first heard the news he was dead. Then, as it turns out, he was . . . murdered. I could hardly believe it. But when I spoke to the police, I told them who I suspected and why."

"You saw him the night of his death?"

"Who did you suspect?" Meredyth asked at the same time.

She nodded to Lucas. "I told all this to the detectives investigating the case."

Lucas bit his lower lip and asked, "Did you share drinks or wine with the judge that night before leaving him?"

"Why, yes, I did. He had just returned from a trip to Dallas–Fort Worth where he'd helped to raise a half-million dollars for AIDS research, and he felt like celebrating, or so he said. He was also exhausted. I prescribed a mild sedative and saw to it that he went to bed. He wasn't so old as he appeared, but he had a crippling arthritic condition, and he'd gone prematurely gray, and he had problems remembering things. His days on the bench, he truly missed. He was a lovely man, really. . . ."

"So, who did you immediately suspect and why?" Meredyth asked point-blank.

"Over the past several years, some priest with some weird order was coming around, pretending to be Charles's spiritual advisor."

"Does this priest have a name?"

"Aguilar. Don't ask me where he lives or where his church is. I don't know, but he was some strange person. I only met him a few times, usually leaving Charles's house. I never quite trusted him."

Outside the hospital, Meredyth asked Lucas, "Well? Have you had enough? It appears Mootry's friends were devoted to him."

"Let's go see the priest."

While Lucas drove, she answered his questions.

"What do we know about the three people Randy came up with for us?"

"Not much. The lawyer likes to dive."

"Underwater diving, deep-sea diving?"

"Yeah, right."

"Might mean Dalton's also into spearguns?"

"That sounds like reaching to me, Lucas. But he's also into big-game hunting in Utah, Wyoming, and, get this, South Dakota and North Dakota, as well as Canada."

"Which may well mean he's had some experience with crossbows?"

"It doesn't say so, but yes . . . precisely. He is a collector."

"Collector of what?"

"Weapons."

"Really?"

"As for Dr. Sterling Washburn . . . *she*—how did Randy

miss this?—she's a well-respected surgeon with oodles of hours of community service."

"Naturally," replied Lucas, skepticism infiltrating each syllable.

"You know what you are, Stonecoat?" she asked. "You're a biased snob."

"Me, biased? Me, a snob?"

"Bias, prejudice, call it what you like, but you're a snob toward snobs."

"Oh, that's clever and funny."

"You think because someone's well-to-do, because some-one's successful, and socially successful, at that, then there's something inherently wrong with her."

"Bingo."

"God, you can be irritating."

He ignored her ire. "And the priest?"

"Father Aguilar, according to what Randy's come up with, is, or was, Judge Charles Mootry's best friend and confidant."

"Sounds to me like they all were his best friend and confidant."

"Father Aguilar, however, was given heaping donations by the judge, and a good deal of the estate went to Aguilar's church, a monastic church in an older section of the city, the Third Order of the Sacred Sepulcher of Houston, Texas."

"The Third Order of what?"

"The Sacred Sepulcher."

"Got it, I think. . . ."

"I don't imagine, nor can you, that Mootry was killed for the sake of the church."

"If these assassins are stamping out vampires and evil, and can take the vampire's financial holdings, too, why not?"

"I wonder if the Vatican or the FBI knows about this Sepulcher church," said Lucas.

"Not likely."

"Tell me more about Father Aguilar. Of the three, he does sound the most tempting as a suspect. Don't ask me why, but I've never fully trusted religious leaders, not even among the Cherokee."

"Mootry leaned heavily on the priest for spiritual guidance, and he paid him well for his time."

"Aguilar could have come and gone freely from the house, could have easily gotten close to Mootry."

"If we're playing guessing games, then *maybe* he pulled the same scam on Palmer after the tragic death of Palmer's fiancée. Palmer would need all the spiritual guidance he could *afford* after that, wouldn't you think?"

"I think . . . I think . . . I don't know what to think."

TWENTY-SEVEN

Ceremonial dance area

They had arrived at the ancient spired cathedral that was the centerpiece of the monastery. The structure dwarfed them and their little car. It was like looking up at an ominous, squatting dragon ready to breathe fire. They could smell smoke, and looking down an alleyway, they saw smoke spiraling up from a foundrylike smokestack that rose skyward.

"Whataya suppose they're burning?"

A street person, her face like a baked apple gone bad, cackled witchlike and replied to Lucas's question, "Don't know what they burn but sins; stinks to high heaven some days. Complain to the cops, but they don't do a damn thing, not once. Off limits, I 'spect." Then she cackled more.

"Let's step around to the front, shall we?" suggested Meredyth.

"Oh, don't you be so uppity-pissy, missy," complained the old woman. "Someday, if you live to my age, you'll be as dried-up as I am!" Again the woman erupted in a rooster's cackling as she strode off.

"Grab a cauldron and two more like her, and we can call you Macbeth," Meredyth told Lucas.

Oddly enough, perched on each of the huge front door handles was a book, a candle, and a stark black raven, all lit by the eye of God. Over the door were some Latin letters, inscribed there from the day the church began, which Meredyth translated loosely to read *God brooks no evil here.*

"Well, I guess we can go home," Meredyth joked lightly.

Lucas said nothing, merely rang the bell when he found the doors locked.

"This place is positively medieval." She kept talking as if it might dispel the gloom that descended over her spirit even here, standing in the blinding, burning sun of a Houston morning. "Everything but a moat," she continued.

"They say there were more murders per capita during medieval times than there are today," ventured Lucas on noting a date at the base of the stairs that told them that the place was built at the turn of the century. High overhead, at the pinnacles, gargoyles stared down at them.

A small door, a peephole, opened up in the door and a pair of dark eyes ran over them. "Can we help you?" asked the man behind the door.

"Police officers," declared Lucas, holding up his gold shield to impress the man. "I'm Detective Stonecoat, and this is Dr. Meredyth Sanger. We're with the Houston Police Department. Here to see Father Frank Aguilar."

"Really? Indeed? Does Father Aguilar . . . is he expecting you? Do you have an appointment?"

"No, we're here conducting an investigation into the murder of Judge Charles Mootry, and we have a few questions for him."

"But you have no appointment?"

Lucas sighed heavily. "No, didn't see the need, but if you like, we can return with a warrant." Lucas thought the man behind the door was being testy, and he gave him the same.

"Is Father Aguilar in to see us?" Meredyth said in her most pleasant voice.

The eyes behind the door darted about, a pair of pinballs seeking an answer. "I'll ring him, let him know you're here." He snapped the peephole closed and they heard his footsteps echo off.

After fifteen minutes of standing about the hot stone stairs, they'd located a place in the shade where they might sit. "This place is built like a fortress," she said.

"Yeah, storming it would be a trick. You've got to wonder if the bars on the windows and the locks on the doors are to keep the rats out or in."

"To keep the world and evil out, no doubt."

He nodded. "But evil has a way of seeping through a hairline crack."

"I wonder where they got this magnificent stone?" She didn't expect an answer, and Lucas wasn't providing one, so when they heard an answer, they both looked up to see a man in a cloak and cowl who had inched the heavy door open.

"This magnificent structure was built in 1900 with stones shipped up from Mexico via Veracruz and Galveston." The man's smile was wide, white-toothed, and genuine. "I am Father Aguilar." His hair was white and gray, a beautiful peppered color. He appeared bronzed by the sun, in his fifties, perhaps, but virile, strong and straight beneath the great monastic garb he wore. Meredyth was reminded of the actor Sean Connery. The man had a magnificent presence and grace about him. "I am here to help you with your questions to the best of my humble ability. Brother Leonard tells me it is about the unfortunate business with my friend Charles Mootry. How can I help you?"

"Can we come inside, out of the sun, Father?" asked Meredyth.

"Oh, yes, of course, forgive my ignorance. We can go to my office in the library. This way."

Lucas was reminded of *The Name of the Rose* as they passed along the corridors inside this dark, magnificent place. As they moved along, Father Aguilar pointed out favored pieces of artwork on the walls and in the vestibules. "We nowadays have to keep the church doors locked; so much vandalism and theft, and no way to police it all. Everyone wonders how the world will end one day, by fire, water, ice, you know. I think it will come through moral decay, long before the earth's forces take us all."

"That's a rather cynical view, isn't it, Father?" Lucas asked.

"Working in these streets, like you, Detective . . . ahh—"

"Stonecoat."

"Yes, Stonecoat. Well, you should know of cynicism, and I admit to an occasional indulgence myself. But, of course, I've repented for it."

How often? Lucas wanted to ask, but didn't.

They were ushered into Aguilar's office, a spacious room with a window overlooking the mammoth library. Lucas's eyes played over the bric-a-brac, ancient photos on the walls, and the office machinery here. He nudged Meredyth when his eyes fell on the state-of-the-art computer behind Father Aguilar's desk. Father Aguilar noticed their interest in his PC, and he began extolling the virtues of the miraculous machine. He rattled off the many uses it held for such a place as his, the day-to-day bills, the operation of the place. "And, of course, we can keep an eye on the stock exchange through our monitor," he added. "We are heavily invested these days, but then, what church isn't?"

"I see, and is the Vatican interested in your . . . investments?" asked Meredyth with a glimmer of a smile.

"You mustn't misunderstand the Order of the Sepulcher. We long ago tore away from the Church and their iconoclastic teachings. Look around you." He hesitated, to allow them time to gaze about his office and the templelike library. "Here you will find no icons. My followers have given me full control, and so long as I can pay the rent and keep operations going here, I have no trouble with the Vatican. Have you any idea the number of such churches and monasteries that have closed over the past ten or fifteen years, Dr. Sanger? Most of them adhering to Vatican rule?"

"No, I can't say that I have."

"Appalling, absolutely appalling. Therefore, it has been my duty to brook no such interference here, so long as there is breath in the order."

"So, your computer is used to follow the daily transactions on Wall Street?" Lucas said with a nod. "Maybe if my people were smarter, they'd play the white man's big money game, too."

Aguilar ignored Lucas. "I use the computer primarily to watch the board, yes, but also to monitor the day-to-day here."

"Strange, I should have thought computers, like many other modern devices, would be shunned by an order such as yours, Father," Lucas said.

"We have to adapt with the times."

"Sort of fighting fire with fire?"

"Pardon?"

"You know, turn the devil's own devices against him."

"We have been known to do that over the years, but I don't personally perceive technological advances as belonging to Satan, no. In the right, capable hands, computers,

TVs, movies can and often are uplifting to the moral spirit of man."

When they were all seated in the plush leather chairs here, Lucas studied the priest's eyes, which seemed etched in pain. He had obviously fought back the devil in all his many disguises, Lucas thought.

"So, please, how can I help you?"

"We have reason to believe that you were with Judge Mootry the night he was killed."

"Really? But I told Detectives Pardee and Amelford that I was out of town that evening, gave them the exact location and time, and this was all verified. The detectives questioned me, but they said it was routine to question all of the deceased's closest relatives and friends, and I counted myself among his—"

"You shared a nightcap—wine, you and the judge; we found the glasses—goblets, actually," bluffed Lucas, "and there were prints on them."

The priest smiled, looking amused. "You must be trying to bait me, Detective. Someone's prints, perhaps, but not mine," he insisted, holding his own. "Look, I understand why you're here, but—"

"You do?" asked Meredyth.

"Because my church was awarded a goodly sum from the judge's estate, but that was his wishs—nothing foisted on him. My God, you can't possibly believe I would kill the old gentleman for his inheritance, can you?" He stared at their poker faces and then added, "Perhaps if you had an independent audit of our books here. You're welcome to do so. In fact, we're due for an audit, and if the Houston Police Department would like to pay an auditing firm to come in—"

"That might not be a bad idea," countered Lucas. "We'll run it by our superiors."

"Father Aguilar, we know about your association with at least two other victims of the crossbow killers," said Meredyth.

"Killers? Did you say killers? Are there more than one? Dear God."

"We know you had some dealings with Wesley Palmer and Timothy Kenneth Little. Now that kind of coincidence involving murder doesn't just go away, Father," continued Meredyth. "In fact, we're rather surprised that you yourself didn't report the strange coincidence and connection between these men to authorities."

"But I did."

"You did?"

"Absolutely."

"You told Pardee and Amelford, you mean?"

"Before they found me, I talked to a captain on the force, Captain . . . ahh, Lawrence, yes, Lawrence."

Meredyth and Lucas exchanged a look of biting concern. Father Aguilar dropped his gaze and suddenly threw up his hands, saying, "All right . . . I confess." It was the first sign of any chink in his armor. "I now confess . . ."

Lucas's eyes bored into the man and Meredyth's mouth dropped open. Could it be so easy?

"I have been worried about my own life after these atrocities. All of us, you see, were in school together, college fraternity, actually . . ."

"Texas Christian," added Meredyth. "We know."

"Then you must see that whoever these fiends are, they have some vendetta against us from when we were young people. Something we did; somehow we wronged someone, perhaps unknowingly . . ."

Lucas wasn't sure he could buy into the priest's distraught act, but he withheld judgment.

"Palmer, Little, Mootry, they all contributed grand sums

here to keep the order going; we would have had to shut down years before now if I had not prevailed upon my richer friends for funds, don't you see?"

"What're you saying?" asked Meredyth. "That whoever has killed these men did so because they feel a hatred toward the church?"

"No, a hatred toward the well-to-do, the wealthy; and believing their money tainted, evil, they might easily think the same of me and my church. I have, for a long time now, watched my back."

"Exactly how much did Mootry leave you, your monastery, in his will?" asked Lucas.

"He was a wise man. He left a self-perpetuating legacy."

"I see." *Men have killed for a hell of a lot less,* Lucas thought, his eyes boring into the priest.

"I'm sorry that I am such a disappointment to you," said Father Aguilar, "that I could not be of more help. But I've told you everything."

"Why haven't you requested police protection?" asked Lucas, still skeptical of the man beneath the robe.

Aguilar shook his head and raised both his hands, each hand seemingly independent of the other, fluttering birdlike as if to indicate all that was around them. "No man can protect me if my God calls me to Him."

Meredyth asked if they could see the rest of the order, commenting on how vast it appeared from the outside. "And what is it you use the fires for?"

"I'm sorry, but your presence here has already disrupted the life of the brothers," he replied. "As to the kiln, we make our own pottery, filling orders all the time. It's quite popular, and it's our main source of revenue."

"Aside from legacies, you mean?" asked Lucas.

Meredyth pinched him. "How many in your order?" she asked.

"It varies, given the time of year, but currently there are twenty-nine brothers."

"Really?" asked Lucas. "That many celibates left in Houston?"

"It is a place where men can step away from the rigors, stress, temptation, and ugliness of our modern world to study, reflect, and find their true selves, to get in touch with the one true God." He stood to indicate their time was up.

Lucas remained tenacious, however, asking, "Can we meet some of the brothers?"

"As I said, it would be disruptive for them. This is a holy place of meditation, worship, reflection. You . . . you bring only discord and disharmony. Why, it exudes from your very pores, Mr. Stonecoat."

"Just a few questions, Father."

"They are reclusive for a reason."

"A reason like murder?"

"Such foul thoughts . . ."

"Do you think a court order would make them and you less reclusive?" badgered Lucas as Meredyth tried to get him to settle down and shut up.

Aguilar gritted his teeth, controlling himself, and seething, he added, "I know something of the law myself, Detective. You have no mitigating circumstances to warrant such a disruption in the house of the Lord. Now, if you please."

"Oh, you have friends in high places, in the legal system?"

"Everyone must have friends in the legal profession to get by in today's madhouse, yes."

"Friends such as Judge Mootry?"

"Yes, he was my dearest friend, and as I said, I now fear for my *own* life."

"And what about Pierce Dalton?" Lucas saw the twitch, almost imperceptible in the man's eye.

"Dalton? I only know Dalton as Mootry's attorney."

"He was at Texas Christian about the time you were there."

"It was a large campus."

"What did you talk about with Mootry the night he was killed?"

"Damn you, man! I wasn't there!" He threw open the door and called to Leonard, shouting, "Show these kind people out, Leonard."

TWENTY-EIGHT

Eagle feathers: chief

All the way back to the precinct house, they discussed their separate impressions of Father Frank Aguilar, each unsure as they replayed the meeting in their heads. "If he went to Lawrence with this when Mootry was killed after Palmer, then Lawrence has known all along, and he refused to listen to me anyway. What does that make him?" she asked. "Is he somehow involved?"

"Don't jump to conclusions."

"But—"

"He may just've been respecting the rights of Pardee and Amelford to conduct their investigation without interference."

"Maybe, but I'm not so sure."

"Frankly, I'm more interested in finding out more about Father Frank. Think about it. You see your beautiful fiancée brutally killed, and your wealth, as in Wesley Palmer's big bucks, could do nothing to ease the guilt and pain and horror, so what might you do in your grief-stricken state?"

"Turn to my friends? And maybe the church?"

"Exactly. And Father Aguilar happens to be in the neighborhood when Palmer gets the news, and he's Johnny-on-the-spot."

"God, but you're a cynical cop," she told him.

He winced at the accusation, but replied, "It's kept me alive. Now, stay with me on this," he continued. "You're an aging trial judge and you've seen all of man's inhumanity to man, and maybe you learn you haven't got too many more years left on this planet because your doctor tells you so. Who do you turn to if you're a lonely old man without family?"

"Mootry turns to Aguilar and Aguilar works out a brilliant plan for his legacy to be self-perpetuating, to save his soul?"

"After all, in his early years he was something of a Satanist, enough so that the FBI was keeping tabs on him."

"If this is true, then all the ancient motives apply: vengeance, passion, greed, avarice . . ."

"But avarice in the name of God; a holier-than-thou avarice, which takes us directly back to Father Frank."

Lucas Stonecoat worked his way around to the rear of the monastery of the Jesuit-like brothers, Frank Aguilar's kingdom. He wondered how much like David Koresh Aguilar ran his operation.

It was an overcast night, a threat of rain in the air after a sweltering Houston day that had set new record highs for heat. The sidewalks were cooling down so rapidly, a hazy fog was pushed about by Lucas's feet. The alleyway was relatively clean, making him wonder if the brothers were sent out here periodically to humbly go about picking up trash. There was a soup kitchen operated out back of the church, and a lone bulb shone in the night, indicating this was the place.

Lucas believed it might lead to the bowels of the building, and since Father Aguilar was anxious for them not to see the inner workings of his monastic order, Lucas was doubly anxious to do so. To this end, he wore his worst rags and most dilapidated shoes.

There were a number of homeless people waiting at the door, and as they filed in, Lucas followed. He was inside a dark room filled with the odors of chicken broth and baked · bread. Maybe the pottery kiln was also used to bake bread, he told himself.

He knew he must record every sight and sensation for later, so he could tell Meredyth about his adventure in detail. She'd be upset with him, but he could smooth that over somehow.

His size might draw some attention, so he crouched and hung his head low. He gathered up his soup and bread and was locating a table when one of the brothers began a prayer. Someone nudged him from behind and whispered in a feminine voice, "Sit with me, brother."

He turned to see Meredyth's face hidden in the cowl of a monastic cloak. "What the . . . where did you get the disguise? And what're you doing here?"

"Same as you, only smarter. Now sit before you draw attention to us, and I'll minister to your spiritual needs."

"I thought you were seeing Conrad tonight."

"He, well, we had a difference of opinion."

"A fight?"

"A discussion."

"Spirited one, I imagine."

"I knew you would be trying to get in here, and this time,

I meant to be along. I've got a costume for you on the bench. Come with me."

"Where'd you get the robes?"

"I have a friend in the theater."

They got to the back table she directed him to. There she pointed out the men's room and instructed he change inside. "And then what?" he asked.

"That door through the kitchen takes us into the monastery."

"Are you sure?"

"I've seen it open and close each time one of the brothers comes and goes. It must take them somewhere."

He nodded, waited for an opportune moment and disappeared with the robe into the men's room, where he did a quick transformation, becoming one of them. Outside, he saw that Meredyth was playing her part well, speaking soothingly to the sick and aged and decrepit who came to visit the kitchen. On the surface, it appeared that Father Aguilar was interested far more in souls than in coin, and perhaps he was.

When Lucas returned to Meredyth, she said to him, "I can't imagine these men exchanging their robes for commando gear and black gloves to become assassins. What do we hope to find here, anyway?"

"I don't know," he confessed.

"Then what do we look for?"

"We'll know it when we see it. You didn't happen to bring Randy Oglesby along with you, did you?"

"No, of course not."

"I'd sure like a look into Father Aguilar's computer files."

"That's called breaking and entering nowadays."

"So's what we're about to do. You ready?"

She nodded, and each of them began a circuitous, lazy route toward the door behind the soup kitchen counter. The other brothers were busy dispensing food and advice, not paying them any particular attention as first Meredyth, then Lucas slipped through the door.

They stood in a long, drab corridor which felt for all the world like an underground cavern. It went in two directions, one toward the offices, the library, and the church itself, the other likely to the dormitories and perhaps the classrooms and the kiln area.

"Which way?" she asked.

"Let's see about that computer of his," suggested Lucas.

"All right, but I'm not sure how much luck we're going to have breaking any codes protected by God."

He led the way, despite her skepticism. "Have you considered the possibility that Father Aguilar is exactly what he purports to be?"

"Randy gave us his name. Who do you trust, Meredyth? Aguilar or Randy?"

"All right, lead on."

But in the darkness ahead, they heard heavy footsteps, more than one pair, coming directly toward them. There was no place to hide or divert to, so they were forced to return the way they had come, passing the soup kitchen doorway on their trek. The footsteps continued, thrumming toward them like a locomotive now, and voices, some raised, echoed through the chamber. It was impossible to tell what the men were saying, but the tone was one of anger.

"Sounds like a little disharmony among the brothers," Lucas suggested in a whisper.

She spied a door and pulled it open. "This way."

They found themselves in a totally black room filled with the stench of ancient fires and burning and the smell of trash.

"It's some sort of incinerator room," he told her as they

waited in the dark. Outside, they heard footsteps go by, passing along the corridor.

"Do you have a light?" she asked.

He had come prepared, snatching out a small flashlight, shining the beam around the room. It was a large, dirty, smelly place with a huge incinerator at the center. It probably looked little different from the baking kilns mentioned by Father Aguilar at the time of their meeting. It was a solid, thick brick oven with a huge cast iron door in front. It sat there like a large animal, a pachyderm, against the center back wall, its mammoth face jutting toward them and the door.

"Let's get out of here," she complained. "This place is so damned rank, I can hardly breathe."

"Hold on. . . ." He went toward the kiln door, wondering at the odors that had been created here. Was it more than burning trash that annoyed his olfactory senses? His father had been in the white man's war to end all wars, World War II, and as with many American Indians, he was given shovel and broom duty. When the Allies arrived at Auschwitz, his father had been one of the many unfortunates ordered into the ovens used to exterminate a race, there to comb through the rubble and locate all the bones. His father had described the odor as one of scorched sweet-and-sour pork, a kind of sickly sweet odor that both horrified and fascinated at once, like the smell and sight of putrefaction. Lucas had had first-hand knowledge of the odor of burned flesh when he was trapped in the death car with Wallace Jackson, who had been burned beyond recognition beside him.

For a moment, he felt faint, fearing he would go into another blackout, but he steeled himself instead and determined to face his fear.

The smell of burned flesh and bone here had become part of the stonework.

He felt an overwhelming revulsion wash over him in a wave, and then he went to his knees, unfeeling, going softly into darkness. When he opened his eyes again, he was lying on his back, Meredyth fanning him with her hand and softly calling out his name and cursing him for doing this here, now.

"Oh, damn, sorry . . . I'm sorry," he confessed. "How long've I been out?"

"Thirty, maybe forty seconds, not long, but damn, you gave me a fright. What happened?"

"Involuntary . . . probably triggered by that smell."

"What is that smell?"

"Charred flesh."

She shook her head. "Animal fat leavings from the kitchen scraps, maybe?"

"No, more than that. Much more . . ."

"How can you be sure?"

"You've seen my neck, my face."

There was a moment of silence between them.

"I've got to open that oven door."

She squeezed his hand firmly. "I'm with you. Flash your light inside."

Lucas got to his knees and then slowly to his feet. The odor was bad, causing dizziness. He grabbed on to the furnace handle and yanked down and out, and the heavy door creaked open, revealing a mountain of ash.

The oven needed cleaning badly.

Lucas's flash picked up nothing but gray-blue mounds of ash. He flashed the light about the greasy black room, saw a light switch, and he held the light on the naked, overhead bulb for a moment. Meredyth reached out, about to switch the light on, when noises again came from the hallway. Lucas yanked her hand away and shut off the flash.

The noise of the brothers outside subsided. Lucas again

ran his flash about the room, and he located a long-handled ash shovel hanging alongside the kiln on the wall. He asked Meredyth to hold the flash while he quietly dug, sifted, and turned ash inside the kiln. After several attempts, the shovel twanged metallic, as if it had hit one of the incinerator walls.

"I've struck something," he whispered to her.

She stared as Lucas worked the shovel under the object and lifted a hefty supply of ash, shaking it as he brought the long-handled shovel back toward them. Under the beam, they both saw the ash fall away from the glaring, empty eye sockets of what appeared to be a human skull.

"God bless us," Lucas said, "we've hit pay dirt."

"Oh, my God," she moaned.

"Perhaps what's left of Charles Mootry or Little or—"

"Keep searching. There's got to be more."

"More?"

"Bones, teeth, another skull," she insisted.

"But we can't do a thing about this," he informed her.

"What?"

"We haven't a warrant to search. It's fruit of the forbidden tree, inadmissible in a court of law, unless we can get a warrant to search, but it's a round robin—we can't get a warrant without probable cause, and this is the probable cause."

"What about what Randy's uncovered, about the connections among the deceased and Aguilar?"

"It might be enough, but we have to put everything here back exactly as it was, and we can't ever tell anyone— anyone—about this discovery, you understand?"

"Yes, yes . . . I do. It's got to be the missing parts."

"They dispose of the parts here, ritualistically, so the demons can't rise against them ever again, like Randy said, in the game, Helsinger's Pit, and this . . . this place is the pit, but it's not an Internet pit."

"It's the real thing. So, what do we do now?"

"I sure as hell would like to take that skull to a lab, see what dental records could show us, but it wouldn't be wise."

"Meanwhile, if they discover we've been here, they could dispose of it all," she countered. "We'd have absolutely nothing, no proof to take to Bryce, the FBI, or anyone in a position to help us."

"Can we trust the FBI?" he asked.

"They've been working the case from their side for some time. Least, that's the impression Bullock and Price gave."

"It wasn't long after Bullock and Price saw us that we were nearly skewered, and they were the only ones we told where we were staying, if you recall."

"Jesus, but if that were the case, why'd they give us so much information about how the Net killers work and about the vampire files?"

"They may well have known that we already had that information, that Randy Oglesby hacked it off for us."

"Good God, I don't know who to trust anymore."

"Trust in me, and I'll trust in you."

"And we'll both have to trust in God."

"And our own instincts. Now, let's compromise. We'll take the single skull. Everything else we leave," he suggested. "Who knows, maybe somewhere in this city, we can find a forensic magician who can tell us something about the bone structure, age, and nationality of Yorick here."

"My grandfather," she suggested.

He hefted the skull and cloaked it below his robes.

"Does anyone know you're here?"

"Conrad."

"Great lot of help that'll do."

"Quit picking on him."

"Do you love him?"

"He's a wonderful man."

"You didn't answer my question."

"It's none of your bloody business."

"Ahh, I see. None of my business, huh?"

"That's right."

"Your well-being is my business," he countered.

She looked up into his luminous eyes. "Does that mean you won't let any harm come to me?"

"Never."

She gritted her teeth. "Then get me the hell out of here."

"Consider it done."

$\mathcal{T}$WENTY-$\mathcal{N}$INE

Man: human life

As they stepped out into the silent corridor, someone shouted, "There! There they are!" This was followed by a radio signal voice, saying, "They're at the incinerator!"

"This way," shouted Lucas, tugging at her robes and forcing her along, using his back as a shield for her. He fumbled the now cumbersome skull in his hands, but he held on to it.

They came to a labyrinth of choices, tunnels going off in six directions. Meredyth stopped, stood before the confusing maze, and said, "Which way?"

"Any way, just don't stop!"

They went down the center, located a stairwell that spiraled and coiled about itself. They took this up and up, the noise of their pursuers getting ever nearer. At one point on the stairwell, he grabbed hold of her and stopped Meredyth in her tracks, cautioning silence and no movement.

They could hear the voice of a man speaking into a radio. The killers were in constant contact with one another. He peered over the stairwell and a steel-shafted arrow ruffled his hair, making him leap backwards. They continued their run up the stairs. Their pursuers all wore the heavy robes of the monastery.

Once back on solid ground, they found themselves in back of the altar in the church, where they shrugged off their robes. Lucas threw them across the staging area of the pulpit, hoping their pursuers would see the discarded robes and believe that he and Meredyth had run across the stage toward the opposite side and the exit.

He then pulled Meredyth close and crouched behind some scattered stage props and an ancient piano. They heard the heavy footfalls of the enemy as one, two, three scurried by, one of them calling out, "This way."

Her body was pressed close to his. She smelled wonderful, even spellbound as she was by fear.

"I don't think I can move from this spot ever again," she said, trying to catch her breath.

"Now maybe you understand why I'd have preferred to make this little junket on my own?" he chastised her.

"You couldn't've gotten this far without me," she countered, glaring at him in challenge.

"Then prove your courage. We're getting out of here, now."

"Now?"

He pointed. "Through that exit."

"When?"

"Now," Lucas whispered, getting to his feet, holding on to the skull like a bowling ball, his fingers looped through the eye sockets, holding on to Meredyth with the other hand.

They raced breathlessly for the nearest exit sign, Lucas kicking out at the bar lock on the door, sending it flying open. Behind them, they could hear the shouts of their pursuers, and Lucas felt the biting clutch of one of the arrows as it dug into his shoulder, sending him careening down to the alley floor with the powerful impact, the stolen skull skittering out ahead of him, Meredyth screaming and instinctively diving alongside him to reduce her vulnerability as a target.

Lucas expected to feel the bite of another bone-hard, ice-cold arrow through his back and through the heart at any moment, lying as he was, helpless on the asphalt, but he dared not let them linger here, so he kept pushing onward, getting to his knees, yanking at her with his one good arm, shouting, "Don't stop! Don't look back! Run." But before they could get to their knees, and before the doors they had just burst through could close on their hydraulic hinges, an explosion of gunfire rang out.

Lucas, his back and left shoulder bleeding profusely from the arrow lodged there, instinctively draped himself across Meredyth while the barrage of gunfire continued. Lucas guessed that they were so riddled with bullet wounds they felt nothing now, and he guessed that they were lying in the alleyway opposite the soup kitchen side of the church.

When the gunfire ended, Lucas looked ahead to see the rictus of the skull sourly smiling at him. He felt no pain other than the throbbing and the weight where the steel-shafted arrow wavered in his back. He had felt the impact of the thing with such force because it had slammed into bone, fragments now no doubt spiderwebbing inside the wound. He imagined a hospital stay, if he survived. He felt no bullet wounds.

Then he saw a pair of black leather shoes approach, saw hands reach down and lift the skull, and he heard Phil Lawrence asking, "Now who do you suppose we have here? You got any idea, Stonecoat?"

"Captain Lawrence?"

"Don't worry, Dr. Sanger, Lucas," he replied, crouching now, turning the skull in his hands. "We took out the hit squad. Now we'll turn this place inside out to see just how widespread Father Aguilar's influence was here. That means mass arrests and a hell of a lot of interrogation."

"Let me the hell up," Meredyth complained, and Lucas immediately got off her, sitting Indian fashion now in the middle of the black alleyway. All around them police were shouting for lights, and orders were being bellowed out as uniformed officers raced into the church to begin making arrests.

Staring back over his shoulder, the steel shaft in his back moving back and forth like a pendulum on a metronome, the pain increasing with the sway of the heavy arrow, Lucas saw some five or six cowled brothers, all dead, still bleeding from their wounds, not so much as a moan from any of them, each with a crossbow near his corpse. Among them, his cowl thrown back, his face a mask of horror, was Father Aguilar, a bullet wound through the forehead, blood crisscrossing his face.

"Oh, God, Lucas, you're hurt!" Meredyth shouted in his ear.

"Thanks for letting me in on the secret," he managed a tortured joke, his voice croaking. "How deep is the head buried?"

"Deep," she muttered. "It didn't penetrate to the other side?" she asked.

He felt his chest. "No . . . hit bone. Hurts like hell."

Meredyth and Lucas looked ahead to see the other shadowy gunmen emerge. They first saw big Jim Pardee, followed by the thin, ambling Fred Amelford; then came a stunned Andrew Bryce, Randy Oglesby, and someone Lucas couldn't quite make out until Meredyth said, "It's Conrad." She held on to Lucas's shoulder, sobbing, "Are you going to be all right?" She dared not tell him how close to the heart the arrow had obviously run.

"Go ahead," he said in his most nonchalant voice. "Go to him." He indicated Conrad, her boyfriend.

Randy Oglesby rushed to Lucas, and Lucas, fighting off a fainting spell, heard him explaining that he had gotten a call from Conrad McThuen, and that Oglesby had in turn called Phil Lawrence, who had in turn put together this small squad of commandos familiar with the case.

Phil Lawrence was kneeling over Lucas now, too, saying that the bleeding looked bad. Lucas tried to focus on the moment, to keep control, to not black out. He imagined that Conrad McThuen and Randy Oglesby had hung back beyond the line of fire, and for the first time Lucas got a look at the tall, good-looking boyfriend, who at the moment was utterly shaken, his eyes wide, his mouth agape, trying to do other than ape Meredyth's name as she guided him back to where Lucas remained half up, half down on the asphalt.

Lucas concentrated on his dislike for Conrad. He wore expensive, post-yuppie, L. L. Bean clothes, his glasses alone worth one of Lucas's paychecks. He might be exactly what Meredyth required in a man, Lucas thought but didn't believe.

Beside McThuen now stood a grinning Randy Oglesby, who was praising both Meredyth and Lucas for their courage. He saluted Lucas, as if to say, "Well done!"

Pardee, a heavy man who carried his weight well, rushed past Lucas, as did Fred Amelford, each anxious to have a look at the kill, Pardee repeating the phrase, "We got the bastards . . . we finally got the bastards."

Amelford came back to Lucas, kneeled to be eye-to-eye with the Cherokee sleuth. "I want to shake your hand, Stonecoat, and congratulate you and the doctor here on a job well done. You two were on the right trail all along. We should have been more cooperative. I regret that now. But you know how damned stubborn detectives can be, right? Right?"

He wanted absolution and forgiveness, Lucas thought. Just like a white man. "You made it in time for the kill." Lucas returned the smile and handshake. "Why don't you and Pardee go ahead and claim the collar."

"No, no way. You guys risked your lives inside there. All the glory's yours."

Meredyth was being held tightly by Conrad now, and Lucas wished it was he instead who was receiving her affections. It looked as though she were comforting Conrad instead of the other way around, Lucas thought.

"You think it might be Mootry's?" asked Captain Lawrence, interrupting Lucas's thoughts, speaking of the skull that Lucas had come away with. It had miraculously remained intact.

"Get a call in for an ambulance, now!" shouted Commander Andrew Bryce when he came near, seeing how badly Lucas was hit. "Are you a fool, Lawrence?" Bryce asked. "This man could go into shock at any moment."

"I'm all right, Commander," countered Lucas, putting forth a great effort just to speak, fighting back the stabbing, burning pain of the arrow lodged in his shoulder blade.

Lucas stared up at the skull which Lawrence now held between his hands, soot and ash still coming off the bone. "It may be Mootry's, yes. Definitely male and definitely missing from someone," he continued to joke, but his eyes had returned to Father Frank Aguilar's lifeless body. He saw bloodstains all over Aguilar's robe now, coloring it like so many wine spots. Aguilar, like all his henchmen who'd come through the door, had been riddled with bullets, as if they'd run into a firing squad. Aguilar's arms and legs were splayed apart starfish fashion. He'd taken three bullets to the abdomen and two to the chest area, as well as the single shot through the brain. *Overkill on overdrive.*

Lucas pushed up to a sitting position and remained there momentarily, disobeying Bryce's orders to remain still and in a prone position until medics could get to him. Getting to his feet now, Lucas looked eerily like a dead man walking with the arrow hanging limply from his back.

"Damn it, man!" shouted Bryce, "I'm ordering you to sit down and stop pumping blood through that wound."

"The blood's stopped," Lucas countered. "I don't feel any more blood pumping out. I'm okay." The blood had coagulated around the arrow shaft, adhering to it.

"Just the same," continued Bryce, "you'll open the wound further if you persist."

"Do as the commander says, Stonecoat," cautioned Lawrence. "He's got to know you can follow orders."

But Lucas remained for a moment, standing over Father Aguilar's body and the scene of destruction.

"Are any of them alive?" he asked tonelessly as he stared on the scene of massacre. All eyes were watching him, fascinated and horrified by the sight of the arrow dangling from him.

"Not a chance," replied Lawrence, who'd followed along with him like a man prepared to catch whatever fallout might come. Lawrence now placed a fatherly hand on his uninjured shoulder and said, "You and Sanger did a splendid job of detection, Stonecoat. Good work all around, work you can both be proud of. This kind of thing, it could mean a definite promotion in the ranks."

It sounded like a payoff, Lucas thought. "How did you know we were here?" He wanted to hear Phil's explanation, wanted to study his eyes and body language as he replied.

Lawrence shrugged. "No biggie. Pardee and Amelford had you staked out from the moment you and Meredyth disappeared from the precinct today."

"What?"

"They got wise after you and Dr. Sanger made some connections they missed, so they began tailing you. I got a call from Randy Oglesby saying you were here—"

"But you already knew we were here. . . ." It was said as an accusation. Lucas, feeling another fainting spell washing over him, buckled at the knees and went down. This caused a general wave of murmurs among those standing about.

Lawrence went to his knees beside his injured man. "Well, no . . . not really. Amelford and Pardee were contacted after I learned of your whereabouts from Oglesby," he continued to explain. "I felt they had a right to be in on any sort of raid we might make, and besides, while I was getting the paperwork, a warrant, I wanted someone to watch the church. Coincidentally, they were already watching the place."

"You were able to get a warrant to search here, a church, so easily?"

"No, not so easy. In fact, we couldn't arrange it. Not enough probable cause, and I didn't want to tell a judge you and Sanger were trespassing. That's why we had to wait outside to see what popped, if anything."

He seemed to have an answer for everything, Lucas thought, and it all seemed so damnably pat. Lucas settled into a sitting position, crossing his legs, going into a meditative state to control the pain and the blackness that wanted so much to claim him.

Lawrence seemed in need of repeating himself. "Oglesby called me, but Pardee and Amelford were tailing you for hours. They were already here when I located them. Said they more than half expected you to infiltrate the church tonight when they saw you come out earlier in the day."

"So, everyone knew about the church, that Meredyth and I were here earlier."

"Not everyone, no. Bryce and I just learned about it when Oglesby called saying he got a call from Dr. Sanger's friend over there." He pointed out Conrad McThuen.

"I see. And was it necessary to completely blow Aguilar away?"

"He had you in his sights, Lucas. We were all firing at the crossbows."

"How did you know we were coming through these doors?"

"What is it with you, Stonecoat?" Lawrence was suddenly aware that Lucas suspected him of some duplicity. "We just saved your redskin ass from certain death. Matter of fact, when you went down, you went down hard, and we all thought you *were* dead."

And that's when you opened fire, he thought. "Look, it's all very much appreciated, but call me curious. Again, how did you know we'd be coming through this particular exit?"

But before Lucas could get an answer, he felt the great black wash over him. He did not feel his body as it slumped into Phil Lawrence, who caught him and laid him out on his stomach.

He didn't hear Meredyth's scream or see her tear away from Conrad's arms to race to him. He didn't hear her cry over him.

When Lucas's eyes opened, he found himself on his back, wrapped in a body bandage, the arrow having been extracted by paramedics. He was on a stretcher, still in the alleyway, looking up into Meredyth's tear-stained, glistening eyes, and she was holding firmly to his hands. Her eyes were red and swollen with sobbing.

"You're going to be all right," she promised him.

"I know."

"You think you know everything, don't you?"

"We're a team, like Twain and Kipling," he replied.

She was confused by the reference. "What?"

"Twain once wrote, 'Kipling knows all that there is to know, and I know the rest.'"

This made her laugh, and it was good to see the smile on her tearful face. He said, "Sorry I blacked out on you."

She shook her head. "No apologies, and it's called shock, not blackout, so don't worry about a thing."

He understood, reading between the lines that she would keep his secret.

"You were right about the blood, Stonecoat," said Bryce,

who leaned in, his rugged and grandfatherly features telling Lucas that he'd seen many an officer shot in the line of duty, but seldom, perhaps never, with an arrow. "I have to admire your grit, Lucas Stonecoat. Now, you just take it easy. The medics made you bleed a hell of a lot more while they removed that thing. Had to cut an incision so it wouldn't get hung up from the nasty barbed arrowhead as they brought it out. You're going to be fine, son."

"Thank you, sir."

"And I believe Phil has something he wants to tell you." Bryce pulled Phil Lawrence in closer, and Lawrence was nodding and began exactly where they had left off before Lucas had keeled over.

"Pardee and Amelford had the place bugged, Lucas."

"The church? How and when?"

"They had Father Aguilar under surveillance from early on, never quite sure of his testimony from day one, but unable to pin anything on him. As to bugging the place, they're quite resourceful."

"I've seen evidence of their resourcefulness, yes. So, they knew we were inside the church this morning?"

"All right, I confess," said Phil, his hands up in the air now. "After what occurred in South Dakota, I asked them to be extra watchful of you two fools. By the way, one of the men who attacked you and Dr. Sanger in South Dakota was located."

"Located?"

"Dead, but located."

"Dead? Where?"

"In the trunk of a rental at the airport in Rapid City. He had a hole in his head, execution-style killing, but he was also gut-shot. The bullet taken from his abdomen was from a Browning, most likely your slug."

"No ID, I suppose."

Lawrence shook his head as if the question were foolish. "We think we'll trace him straight back here to the church. As to knowing when and where you and Meredyth would exit, we couldn't know exactly what exit you'd come out of, so we had every exit covered."

"And you guys chose door number three and got lucky?"

"I'd say you and Sanger were the lucky ones. Now, I'm going to hand this over to the coroner when he gets here." Lawrence had held firmly to the skull. "You want to tell me precisely where inside you located it?"

"An incinerator at the lower level."

"Were there signs of more incriminating evidence?"

"A truckload, sir."

"Great, then we'll settle this damned business tonight, and one shitload of Cold Room files will have been cleared in one fell swoop, thanks to you, Lucas. It will look great on your record. The chief of division can't overlook results like that." He indicated Bryce with a flutter of his eyebrows.

Bryce had been asking after Meredyth's condition like a solicitous father. Lawrence followed Lucas's eyes to Meredyth, and Phil added, "Who knows, Stonecoat? Maybe you'll pull detective rank sooner than any of us expected."

It still sounded like a payoff, Lucas thought. "Only one problem, sir."

"Oh, what's that?" Lawrence's eyes flickered in the dim light.

"Discovery, sir."

Bryce, as if wired to them, rankled at the word, homing in to its source, rejoining them. "What about discovery, Lucas?"

"We made the discovery of the skull and bones, sir, while in an unlawful search, Commander."

"Damn, of course." Bryce snatched Phil Lawrence away and the two men discussed this thorny problem between

themselves, and it seemed Lawrence did all the talking.
Lawrence then turned back to Lucas and Meredyth, and
with Bryce looking on and nodding solemnly, said, "You
two actually returned to ask Aguilar over there a few more
questions tonight, didn't you?"

"What?" asked Meredyth.

"You returned to the monastery to put a few unanswered
questions to bed."

Lucas knew from the tone of Lawrence's voice what he
wanted to hear. "Yes, sir, we did."

"But Lucas," she began.

"Dr. Sanger," interrupted Phil Lawrence, "do you want to
stand in the way of justice served?"

"Well, no, Captain, but—"

"Then you two returned to seek answers to a handful
more questions when Aguilar, knowing he was cornered,
threatened you with death," suggested Lawrence.

Meredyth exchanged a look of indecision and incredulity
with Lucas.

Lawrence continued with his scenario. "The both of you
escaped, hid out in the incinerator room where you discovered all those missing parts we've been searching for for
years, and then you made your escape. Pardee and Amelford, knowing your intentions, called for backup."

Lawrence studied their faces. "Is that understood?"

Meredyth looked from Lawrence to Stonecoat.

Commander Andrew Bryce stepped closer and awaited an
answer.

Lucas said, "That's about the size of it, sir."

"Good, then it's settled," replied Bryce. "Now, we have
all the goddamned probable cause anyone can ask for. We
don't need any damned court's permission to search this vile
place. Aguilar has untied our hands. Good work, Dr. Sanger,
Officer Stonecoat."

"Yes, sir. Thank you, sir," Lucas responded, while Meredyth said nothing.

"Dr. Sanger?" asked Bryce. "Can you live with this version of events?"

"I . . . I . . ." Lucas pinched her arm. "All right, I guess I can."

Still, Meredyth continued to stare at Lucas if he had betrayed her. She was wondering if he was simply thinking of promotion, a permanent escape from the Cold Room. She stormed off to rejoin Conrad, who once again enveloped her in his arms.

"Now call for the evidence techs and the coroner, Phil," said Bryce. "I want everything done precisely by the book and no foul-ups. Nobody takes souvenirs and nobody takes evidence home overnight to sit in their coolers or refrigerators, you got that, Phil?"

"Yes, sir, Commander."

"And if that means you're here all night to oversee this thing, then so be it. It's going to hit the papers in a matter of hours. I don't want us looking like fools."

"No, sir. Everything will be taken care of to the letter, boss."

Bryce nodded and started away, mumbling. "Good . . . good . . . good . . ."

Phil Lawrence grinned over the bodies. "Don't worry, Lucas," he said, "we'll clean this bloody church out for good and all. And we won't overlook Aguilar's computer logs."

I'm sure you won't, Lucas thought, still wondering just how deep into the mire Phil Lawrence was. He didn't believe in miraculous coincidence, not in fiction and not in the real world, especially.

"If you're finished with the questions, Captain," offered Lucas. "I think Dr. Sanger ought to be sent home."

Meredyth looked into Lucas's shimmering brown eyes and was pleased that he was thinking of her comfort.

"Yes, yes, of course," Lawrence replied. "The both of you had best get some rest, and Lucas, you'd best get to the hospital. Go along with the paramedics; allow that shoulder to heal properly."

One of the paramedics, hearing this, added, "The doctors are going to want to open up the wound, remove the bone fragments. We saw some damage," he finished.

"I'm all right," Lucas stubbornly countered.

"Do as the captain says, you mule-headed fool," Meredyth almost shouted. "And you stop worrying about me. I'm fine."

"You'll likely be inundated with press tomorrow," warned Lawrence, "so be prepared, the both of you."

Lucas nodded, wishing he could get up and guide Meredyth away from all this horror, but as his eyes turned, he saw that this little chore was being taken care of by the dark-haired, blue-eyed Conrad McThuen. Lucas suddenly felt a failure, a clumsy football player, unintentionally fumbling and passing Meredyth off to the other man, who enveloped her in his arms and led her to his waiting car. As had happened so many times before, Lucas felt a fool for even giving the notion a thought. She was, after all, out of his reach.

"You okay, Lucas?" asked a concerned Randy Oglesby. "Damn, but that was close."

THIRTY

Headdress: ceremonial dance

The case against Father Frank Aguilar was strong. Bones from Mootry, Little, Palmer, and the more recently deceased couple in South Dakota were all found in various incinerators around the monastery. One of the hooded four killed alongside Aguilar was a woman, and endless, tireless questioning and probing and threatening began to show that Aguilar and a small contingent of his most trusted followers had acted alone. The Mad Priest of the Church of the Sacred Sepulcher, as the press was now calling Aguilar, had also kept a room filled with ancient weaponry, a collection of weapons with a bloody history, including several crossbows. Of course the five dead, robed bodies in the alley that night had all had crossbows of modern design on them. Further damning information was unearthed on the Mad Priest's computer in the form of a diary detailing his actions and rambling on about a world that resembled and refracted the computer game, Helsinger's Pit. His diary entries named his coconspirators, Brother Lyle, Brother James, Brother Aaron, and Sister Inez. A fifth assassin was also found, a Brother Paul Timmons, who matched the dead man found in South Dakota, stuffed in the trunk of a rental car. All the other *brothers* were in various stages of indoctrination.

The motives expressed in Aguilar's diary pendulumed between madness and monetary gain. He claimed those selected to die were enemies of his church, vampires who conspired against him. He was obviously a religious fanatic. He described Whitaker, Palmer, Mootry and the others all as various aspects of the anti-Christ, men who worshipped the pleasures of the flesh, wealth, self-aggrandizement, and ultimately Satan. The only way to stop them from reforming and returning to this realm was to behead them, cut off their extremities and genitals and burn the parts, after staking them through the heart by the most modern and efficient method they could find, the crossbow.

Randy Oglesby had been prophetically correct. The cult members had taken as their model of destruction the computer game Helsinger's Pit, and they'd been led to believe, thanks in great part to the FBI Vampire List, that their victims lived lives of extraordinary, supernatural powers from the dark side; by the same token, the vampire stalkers weren't above partaking in a devil's plunder, amassing as much funds as possible from the so-called anti-Christ before dispatching him again and again.

Father Aguilar's diary entries to this end clearly marked him and his followers as religious maniacs. Furthermore, it turned out that there were numerous women among the "brothers" of the Sepulcher, and many of these women were pregnant with Aguilar's offspring.

The good father was simply doing his part to cleanse the earth of the filth and vermin that had proliferated over generations, and he wasn't above taking the ill-gotten demonic wealth in the bargain, to put the ill-gotten money to a pure and holy use. He was also amassing an army of followers who would willingly assassinate the anti-Christ in his name.

From Aguilar's diary came the truth about the assassinations of John Covey behind bars and the Shirleys in South Dakota, who'd been pawns in Aguilar's distorted, aberrant game of who lives and who dies for the greater glory of his fringe religion. He had indeed selected the Shirleys at random, calling them martyrs to his cause.

The *Houston Star* and *Chronicle* ate up the sensational story, and every newscast was full of the sordid details. The Order of the Sacred Sepulcher and its cathedral church, monastery, and soup kitchen were closed, the members, some of whom remained behind bars for further questioning and disposition, disbanded, but not without an outcry from civil rights organizations and the NRA, who likened the situation to Waco and Koresh.

Phil Lawrence came to see Lucas in the bowels of the precinct, in the Cold Room, where he'd continued to report since the mass arrests had been made. He had been involved in the interrogation of prisoners; few men in the precinct hadn't interrogated one or more of Father Aguilar's followers. However, the precinct house was slowly coming back around to a semblance of normalcy, and Lucas had been given his orders by Sergeant Kelton that he was to return to the damp little hole where the dead files awaited his attention. Meanwhile, in the newspapers, he and Sanger were being touted as heroes in this heroless story.

He felt like the successful artist whose work was being admired by people walking through the Guggenheim Museum in New York City while the artist stood in the unemployment line, filling out a form that might allow him a subsistence living. He questioned the neat little package, too, of how Father Aguilar masterminded the series of killings, and how the widespread murders, crossing so many boundaries and state lines, could be carried out by Aguilar's monastic brothers alone. What troubled him most was how easily it had all fallen into place after he and Meredyth had stepped into Frank Aguilar's domain—like a house of cards, like someone had pulled out the one card holding everything together, but that card remained elusive, unreturned.

That was the glum mood three days after his release from the hospital, his arm still in a sling, when Captain Phillip Lawrence joined Lucas in the Cold Room. Lucas offered his captain a seat, wary of the other man.

Lawrence began by asking him how he was doing, how he was adjusting after all the excitement, and how his wounded shoulder was healing. Lucas punched himself in the shoulder harness, saying, "It's a piece of cake, compared to what I've grown accustomed to."

Lawrence laughed lightly. "I'll give you that much, Stonecoat. You're as tough as your name. I'm glad to have you on my team. Wish I had a squad of men as good as you."

"What's all this leading up to, sir?"

"Well, no easy way to say this, Lucas."

"Then say it straight out, Captain."

He gritted his teeth. "They've denied your promotion request to detective status."

Lucas dropped his gaze. "No big surprise, sir."

"It's just a little soon, having just finished basic. They all know how heroically you performed in the Aguilar affair, but this isn't exactly a business here, you know. We are a paramilitary operation, and that, Lucas, that means—"

"Rank comes only with time; I know. I've heard it before, sir. So what will be my duties, Captain?"

"Well, son, you sorta painted yourself into a . . . a hole here." Lawrence looked around the dungeon, self-consciously cleaning his hands on his pants legs.

Lucas stirred the dust on the floor as he shot to his feet, swearing, "Damn, damn it to hell. You mean I'm stuck with the Cold Room duty, don't you?"

"I'm sorry, Lucas. I want you to know I went to bat for you, for all the good it did."

Lucas thought of saying nothing, unsure of Lawrence's sincerity, but seeing the older man squirm where he sat, he replied, "Thanks for your support, Captain."

"Don't give up on us, Stonecoat, and we . . . we won't give up on you. I promise you that."

Phil Lawrence stood, extended his hand, taking Lucas's firmly and shaking it for some moments before leaving the room.

The meeting added to the insufferable gloom of the place he found himself in. He hadn't seen or spoken to Meredyth since the early days of the mass arrests, which were now turning into mass releases. It did appear that Father Aguilar's clique was small and insulated from his larger flock of followers, by all accounts.

And yet there continued the nagging feeling that Father Aguilar and the four killed with him and the one who'd died in South Dakota had not acted alone. But now the investigation was effectively dismantled, all questions put aside.

Lucas kicked about the confining room, about to run out screaming when his phone rang. He lifted the receiver to the melodic voice of Meredyth Sanger. "How's my favorite Native American detective?"

"Cop," he corrected her. "Just another cop, Doctor. There was no promotion in this for me. I'm still Officer Stonecoat, still here in the Cold Room."

He only heard the mutterings, imagining that she'd

cupped her hand over the mouthpiece as she swore. Then she said, "Well, it can only be a matter of time. I gave you an excellent report. Lawrence has to. Your jacket will be stuffed to brimming in no time, and—"

"I think they like me just where I am, Mere, the cold file wrangler. But enough about me. How've you been?" He wanted to say that he'd missed her, but he suppressed the words, instead asking her, "Have you missed me?"

"We made a good team, Lucas, and we'll work together again. I just know it," she countered, sidestepping the issue.

"And how's Conrad?"

"He's gotten a bit more used to things, accepting of them."

"Yeah, he looked pretty shaken the other night."

She laughed lightly at this. "I was holding him up."

"He seems a good man."

"Yeah . . . yeah, he is. . . ."

"Meredyth," he began.

"Yes?"

"Are you satisfied that Aguilar and his little clique acted alone?"

There was a long silence before she said, "No . . ."

He breathed in deeply, feeling some relief that he was not alone in his belief. "Why?"

"I can't quite say why."

"Has Randy Oglesby any qualms about how things turned out?"

"Randy's been . . . well, quiet on the subject."

"Quiet?"

"If I broach the subject, he turns it away. Makes light of my . . . doubts."

Lucas considered this. "It does seem odd that Pardee and Amelford were so closely tailing us. Have you heard anything from Bullock and Price at the FBI?"

"Only a congratulations call. You?"

"I'm sure they likely assumed you'd forward their regards down here to me."

"How are you getting on with Lawrence?"

"Okay, a bit shaky ground between us, but okay."

"Do you still harbor suspicions about him?"

He considered this. "I'm unable not to."

"Me, too."

"Do you want to get together? Talk about it?"

"Strangely enough, I feel like . . . well, that I'm being watched lately, she confessed."

"Join the crowd. Remember me? Mr. Paranoia?"

"And I think someone's got to Randy, someone's frightened him," she added.

"Threatened his life?"

"I can't be sure, but, yes, I think so."

"Who do we trust? Who do we take this to?"

"FBI," she suggested.

"Ring Bullock and Price. See if they'll meet with us. But do it from a secure phone."

"Will do."

They set up a time and a place to secretly meet the following day. Lucas, on hanging up, began to feel some of the old creeping fear coming over him. They could easily let it be; the killers—any remaining—must be smart enough to end their kill spree at this juncture. But if Meredyth and he continued investigating, they ran the risk of being eliminated like Father Aguilar and his henchmen.

There was no waiting until tomorrow to make a move. He must do something tonight.

Lucas found Randy Oglesby extremely wary of him. He didn't much relish the idea of allowing Lucas into his apartment, and for good reason. He had a girl with him, Darlene Muentes, who looked up at Lucas from the sofa, smiling, her teeth shiny, her body slim.

"I'm sorry to burst in on you, Randy."

"Good, then you can go, Detective."

"Oh, Jim, he is your partner?" asked Darlene.

Lucas only stared at the young woman, while Randy gritted his teeth and dropped his gaze to the floor. "Darlene, I . . . I can't go on with the . . . this lie . . . any longer."

"Lie?" she asked.

"I'm not really a detective with the police department, and my name is not Pardee. My name is Randy . . . Randy Oglesby. . . ."

"Oh, shit, Randy, not now!" Lucas fairly groaned his discomfort.

Darlene stared at Randy as if she'd been told the world was square. She was unable to get any words out. He used this to his advantage.

"I was doing a little undercover work for Detective Stonecoat, here."

"Leave me out of this," Stonecoat said, going for the kitchenette in search of a drink.

Darlene's eyes grew wider. "Stonecoat? Lucas Stonecoat? I . . . I can't believe it. I just don't believe it. I've read all the stories in all the papers. You . . . you were wonderful, how you caught those bizarre killers."

Lucas thanked her, and knowing a bit about her from Randy, that he'd met her at the lab, he said, "And it all started with those goblets we asked you to work on, dear, so you're a hero, too."

She beamed. "Oh, Randy," she tested the new name, "why didn't you tell me the truth?"

Randy's face did a waltz through his conflicting emotions

before he selected his words. "It was all undercover. I'm just sorry you had to learn it this way."

She waved it off as if it were nothing. "But if you're not a detective?"

"He's our expert computer man," Lucas quickly filled in. "Without him, we could have gotten nowhere. That's why I'm here tonight, Randy."

Randy looked at Lucas. "Oh?"

"Some missing parts, and we need your help."

"Oh, how exciting," declared Darlene, beaming.

Randy looked from Darlene to Lucas and back to Darlene again.

Lucas asked, "Well?"

Darlene threw her hands up. "Don't let me stand in your way. I'm fascinated."

"Darlene, all this is like classified stuff," Randy began. "You . . . you'll have to go."

"Damn it, no!" she moaned.

"Oh, let her stay," complained Lucas. "He's such a stickler for regulations. It gets in the way sometimes."

Randy glared at Lucas. "I don't want her in harm's way."

"She won't be, and neither are you."

Randy rolled his eyes and whispered, "The hell I'm not. I've been threatened twice with no less than my life."

"I figured as much."

"You're too clever for your own good, Detective."

"You needn't call me that."

"It's for her sake." He pointed with his upturned head.

"I want you to access Captain Phillip Lawrence's computer files, see if he's clear of this mess or not."

"Are you crazy? Hack into the captain's files?"

"Just do it."

"Look, come here . . ." he replied, going to his computer console and handing Lucas a printout. "Read this."

Lucas stared down at a list of some three hundred people whose religious preferences were classified along the lines of hard-core spiritualism, witchcraft, demonology and vampirology. There were more than just names there; there were social security numbers, ages, occupations, as well as the whereabouts of each person appearing on the list. "The Vampire List?"

"That's it, and I've had a visit from the FBI."

"Agents Bullock and Price? They're in the city? When did you have contact with them?"

"They warned me to stay out of it in no uncertain terms."

"But they didn't confiscate your findings?" He hefted the list again.

"That's a copy. They got the original, and they warned me that if I ever accessed FBI files again, they would prosecute hell out of me."

"I see."

Lucas wondered anew about the two agents, pretending friendship and cooperation in South Dakota, now this. Were they to be trusted? Should he call Meredyth, get her over here? Should they brainstorm this thing here and now?

"Take Darlene home. I'm going to contact Meredyth Sanger, get her over here, and we're going to put our heads together."

"Fine, fine, but I'll be damned if I'm going to do any hacking inside the HPD Net for you two. I've already got the damned FBI upset with me, Lucas."

Lucas stared at Randy Oglesby's bright blue eyes and boyish features, doubting that Randy could ever or would ever look old or sinister or capable of anything but honesty and forthrightness, yet he daily indulged in an electronic dishonesty in his work, or at least he had since Lucas had known him, since Dr. Sanger had entrusted her secrets about the case to him. Again, Lucas wondered if Randy could be trusted, if he had been gotten to, not only by the FBI, but by forces closer at hand.

"I'll call Dr. Sanger. You come right back. We have more work to do. It's imperative we take these final steps, Randy."

Randy frowned, nodded and took Darlene by the arm. "I'll be half an hour."

Lucas immediately telephoned Meredyth, telling her to meet him at Randy's apartment.

"What's up?" she asked.

"Not over the phone. Just get here as quickly as you can."

"I have an evening planned, Lucas."

"Tell Conrad it's an emergency, tell him you've got a wigged-out cop on your hands, tell him anything."

"Damn," she muttered. "This better be good, Lucas."

"I can't promise you anything, but I have a direction."

"Well, now, that would be novel." Her sarcasm was more biting than she'd meant it to be. "Sorry, I'm just so frustrated."

"With the case or with Conrad?" he joked.

She fumed at the other end. He could feel it. "I'll see you there as soon as possible."

She hung up, and Lucas stared at the phone a moment before returning it to its cradle. He wondered what direction he was talking about and why he felt so strongly that he must see Meredyth tonight.

THIRTY-ONE

Rattlesnake jaw: strong

"It's not over," Lucas told Meredyth and Randy when they had all assembled. "The priest did not act alone."

Randy exchanged a disturbed look with Meredyth. "You think the same way?"

Meredyth slowly nodded.

Randy swore under his breath and started pacing. "The man was a lunatic."

"Agreed."

"He had a Messiah complex."

"Agreed."

"He thought he could hideously destroy people, whole families, and that his actions would be rewarded by God."

"Agreed."

"In the man's mad rantings, he calls himself Helsinger and Questor 1, doesn't he?"

"Agreed."

"But that's not enough for you two?"

"Agreed."

"Damn . . . damn," muttered Randy as he paced, nervously biting at his nails. "I've got something to show you, something I was afraid to show anyone, still am," he qualified, going for his desk, tearing open a bottom drawer, rummaging there and coming out with a sheet of computer paper.

Meredyth looked over Lucas's shoulder. "What is it?"

Lucas stared at the bulletin board message he held in his hand while Randy explained, saying, "I located that just after you two went off to South Dakota, but I didn't know what to make of it until I heard about your being ambushed there."

With Meredyth looking over his shoulder, Lucas read the veiled threat on their lives.

```
764LT1:\C42119\Category    42 . . . Topic
49LOG . . . Message 440 . . . Sat.
July 30, 1996 . . . 2:10:21
Questor 1 . . . Helsinger's Pit . . .


Q1: There is a further threat. A new
enemy has risen in perdition, this realm.
These are two enforcer demons—male and
female. They must be stopped. Do all
necessary to protect the brothers and
sisters and children of Helsinger. Reply
this board after evil is wiped out. God's
speed to you. Questor 1 . . . END TRANSMIS-
SION, Category  42, Topic  49LOG . . .
2:13:26



Category 42 . . . Topic 49LOG . . . Mes-
sage 441 . . . Sat. July 30, 1996 . . .
3:55:05
Questor 2 . . . from the Pit . . .
```

```
Q2: Understood. Will take care of per-
dition's problem. END TRANSMISSION, Category
42, Topic 49LOG . . . 3:57:01

Category 42 . . . Topic 49LOG . . . Message
442 . . . Sun. July 31, 1996 . . . 8:10
Questor 1 . . .

Time to take out all threats. Set trap and
exterminate the mice. No more fun and
games. Eliminate the leaders of our enemy.
See message drop, new station . . . END
FINAL TRANSMISSION. THIS E-MAIL.
```

"Good Lord," Meredyth said with a gasp. "It's an electronically ordered hit."

Lucas agreed. "And we were—probably still are—the targets." He turned back to Randy and asked, "How did you come by it?"

"Surfing the Net; purely accidentally, I assure you. When Aguilar and his goons were killed, I figured it was over, so I put it aside. I'd planned to talk to Meredyth about it when . . . when things settled a bit."

"How did you come by it?" he repeated.

"Like I said, damn it. I was plugging into any Helsinger Pit activity, not expecting to find anything."

Lucas badgered, repeating his words. "Not expecting to find anything?"

"The Net is jammed full with such trash, but as it happens, nobody's really playing that particular gloom and doom game anymore, except maybe Aguilar and his friends."

"It's not over, kid, just because you want it to be," replied Lucas, staring a hole in Randy. "It doesn't work that way."

Meredyth snatched at Lucas's arm, saying, "Take it easy, Lucas."

Lucas pulled away, while Randy, taking offense, shouted,

"Hey, I'm nobody's fool, Lucas! I know this much: Any damned ranting lunatic nowadays who has access to a computer can and will set up his own vigilante committee, just as Aguilar set up his own little electronic shrine to declare himself the vanguard of a war against Satan—the authority, the one fount of truth, the goddamned cyberspace church, where all his followers and converts either kneel before him or die. And you know who Satan was to this guy, Lucas? You, Redskin, you and Dr. Sanger and me . . . yeah, me. . . ."

Randy fell into an overstuffed chair, throw pillows flying.

"But he didn't act alone," countered Lucas. "I can feel it in my bones."

"Four, no, five died alongside him!" countered Randy, sitting up.

"No, not followers. There was a mastermind behind the whole damned thing. I can't put my finger on it, but I believe Phil Lawrence is somehow involved, him and his pals Pardee and Amelford."

Randy looked for Meredyth's support, his hands going up in the air. "So, you want to rattle some more cages, is that it?"

"Lucas thinks," began Meredyth, "we think . . . Aguilar took the fall for a much bigger operation. The same thought must've crossed your mind, too, Randy."

"It might have . . . it might've, sure, but I was smart enough to run away from it. . . ."

"What about Lawrence, Randy?" she cajoled. "We need to eliminate him. Can you scan his computer for anything like this?" She held out the sheet of paper that represented their death warrants.

"I did it already, once."

Meredyth and Lucas looked from Randy to one another. "And . . ." she finally said.

"That's when I came across this." He walked to the computer console and turned on the monitor; onscreen was the encrypted message, using the same category number and log number as the threat on Meredyth and Lucas. It was the message to kill the Shirleys, although their names were not spelled out.

Randy's state-of-the-art computer was so silent, Lucas had not known it was on. "You say you got this from Lawrence's computer files?"

"I found it while tracing the other message's origin. I followed the computer tracks right into Lawrence's files. He's Helsinger One."

"Damn, then that makes it conclusive proof."

"Proof for whom?" asked Randy. "Who's going to believe us? Before we're all killed, that is. Damn, I wish I'd never met you two. . . ."

Randy was shaken, his face a mask of fear illuminated only by the dim light reflecting off his computer screen. He wheeled so they could not study the fear in him.

Lucas again wondered about Randy. He had told them that he'd played Helsinger's Pit as a child, that it had become an addiction for him for a while. Suppose the baby-faced computer whiz had never actually overcome his addiction? Suppose he was behind the real-time, real-life vampire stalking murders? Suppose he was Father Aguilar's light and salvation? Lucas felt a thousand doubts swirling about his head. "How long have you known about Lawrence's involvement? Why didn't you confide in us before now? Why did we have to drag this from you?" Lucas said, suddenly turning on Randy.

"Damn it, I was trying to keep us all alive. This gets out, that I know this stuff, and . . . and we're all dead, *all of us*. . . ." He looked long and hard into Meredyth's eyes.

Meredyth tugged at Lucas's slinged arm. Lucas relented.

Randy sounded convincing, sincere, and Lucas cursed himself for being unable to trust in anyone anymore.

"We've got to get help, tell someone," Meredyth told the other two. "This just has become to big for us to handle alone."

"Bullock and Price?" he suggested. "The FBI?"

"I tried to get them earlier, but I got a strange response."

"Strange?"

"Just a foul-up, I'm sure—a secretary who didn't know anything, had never heard of Tim Bullock and Stu Price."

His eyes danced with hers in a slow waltz of measured confusion. "Bullock and Price didn't exist?"

"But then why would they warn us?"

"Maybe someone likes sporting events to be sporting. I don't know."

"I'm sure it was just a mistake. I'll call the FBI here, ask them to patch us through to wherever Bullock and Price might be." She got on the phone and attempted to reach the elusive FBI men, but again she was told there were no agents matching the description or the names given.

"They were sent in to find out how much we knew," he offered.

"And to keep a tail on us," she agreed.

"Damn . . . damn," muttered Randy, distraught now, locating beers for them all from his refrigerator, weakly joking, "We may's well empty out the fridge so nothing'll spoil after I'm killed dead."

"Who do we take it to?" Meredyth asked.

"Commander Bryce," replied Lucas, "and we have to do it now, tonight."

The three exchanged glances, agreeing to make their move.

Commander Andrew Bryce could only be reached at his home, a sprawling horse ranch he owned just outside

Houston. There had been a heated controversy when he'd become a chief in the Houston Police Department that he give up living outside the city lines and move his family into the city proper, that a city police chief had to live in the city he swore to serve and protect. It was the kind of nonsense that Lucas had no patience for, and he had heard that the now Commander Bryce had continued to fight the ancient ordinance in court.

Bryce was receptive to the idea that Aguilar could not possibly have been working alone. In fact, he had said over the phone that the more time away from that night when Aguilar was gunned down, the more he had pondered the possibilities, and the more he had felt a definite pat hand had been dealt them all by Captain Phillip Lawrence, Pardee, and Amelford. He didn't need much prodding once Lucas opened up about his misgivings with respect to what he feared were perhaps the dirtiest cops he had ever run across.

"We'll need conclusive proof, though, Stonecoat, you realize, before anything can be moved on. Can you give me anything more than your suppositions?"

"We can, sir. We can."

"You and Meredyth Sanger, you mean?"

"Yes, sir."

"Then why don't the two of you drive out to my place? It's the only private place I know of where we won't be bothered. Then we'll talk this thing through over coffee or a drink, perhaps? If you're certain of your facts, and if you've really got the goods, Stonecoat, we'll bring in the D.A."

Lucas intentionally left Randy Oglesby out of it. "Yes, sir. We'll be there as soon as we can, sir." Lucas took down the address, a map of landmarks, actually, and the name of the ranch: the Rocking B.

Nightfall painted the deserted, dust-laden landscape outside Houston where tall cacti stood sentinel to time and comings and goings of men in machines as cars hurtled along the superhighways. Lucas and Meredyth pulled off the Interstate onto narrow County Road 341, occasional houselights like fallen stars here. Small roads led deeper into the desert area west of the city, which had disappeared in the distance behind them like the setting of the moon. Storm clouds scudded about, harmlessly dispersing, but in the distance, great streaking lightning bolts split the darkness with a laser display, like a scalpel tearing at the dark folds of the sky, the world tonight like so much leftover fabric being incised. In the distance, quietly sloping hills lay like sleeping camels, disturbed only by the intermittent light display. The occasional trailer home in the middle of nowhere rose and fell behind them as they drove on toward the Rocking B.

In a moment, they began to see signs for the ranch, fences leading them now, guiding them to the great, wide, tree-lined drive. It was thirty minutes out of the city, but it may as well have been days, the place was so remote.

Commander Bryce welcomed them from a brightly lit wraparound porch, the front porch quite a showplace in itself. The house was elegantly done up, rivaling any ranch house in the country, Lucas thought, its warm log frame both richly textured and inviting. Noisy cicadas chirped all around them as they exited Lucas's car. The night air was crisp, a breeze playing its fingers over Lucas's brow and playing a lilting tune on a collection of wind chimes all about the expansive porch. Lucas stared appreciatively at the chimes.

"My wife's collection," Bryce noted. "She loves the sounds they make. Me, sometimes it drives me nuts." He gave a full-throated laugh. "Come on inside where we can get comfortable."

On entering the beautifully kept house, nothing aside from books and newspapers out of place, Lucas was struck by the number of photos lining the walls and each mantel and table, pictures of children and grandchildren.

Meredyth noticed, too, asking Bryce how many grandchildren he had. He laughed, his face beaming. "I stopped counting at sixteen!"

"Then you must have had quite a few children of your own," she continued with the small talk.

"Seven, two daughters and five sons, but who's counting? Can I get you two coffee, a drink, anything?"

"We wouldn't want to impose on Mrs. Bryce," replied Meredyth.

"Who said anything 'bout Mrs. Bryce? No, no, she's off to her sister's place for a week, and as you see, all my children have grown and have families of their own now. I gave them each a parcel of land here, kinda as a bribe, to keep them all nearby, you see. Now, what about that drink?"

"I could use a whiskey, scotch if you have it," confessed Lucas, looking about, seeing several mounted hunting trophies on the wall, an enormous elk, a Rocky Mountain longhorn goat, and even a buffalo, which Lucas's eyes lingered over.

"Purchased that one," confessed Bryce, a bit sheepishly. "Against the law to actually kill a buffalo nowadays, you know. Found it at a place that sold all sorts of Indian artifacts and antiques in Carson City, Wyoming. The wife and me, we both thought it would set off the place, give it the kind of rustic look we were looking for."

There were hawks and stuffed eagles in the corners as well, their long-dead eyes as piercing and sharp in death as in life.

"White wine," Meredyth suggested for herself.

"Coming right up. Make yourselves at home."

"Beautiful surroundings," Meredyth said, taking a seat, but feeling a bit uneasy under the gaze of so many dead eyes.

Lucas nodded and pointed at a Remington painting of several trail-weary soldiers circa 1870 on horseback, just returning from what appeared a failed Indian campaign, one of their number slung across a saddle. He then stepped over to admire Bryce's impressive gun case and collection of rifles. "Invested well, wouldn't you say?"

In a moment, Bryce was back with the drinks, asking them to please use the coasters. "Otherwise, I'll catch hell from Della about it when she gets back. Woman can spot a water ring from a hundred yards," he joked, making Lucas flash on the coasters he himself had spotted at Judge Mootry's the night he had gotten past the yellow tape at the old man's mansion. It occurred to Lucas that Bryce may well have traveled in the same circles as Mootry, and most certainly would have known of him and his charitable work.

"How well did you know Judge Mootry?" Lucas found himself asking as he took the drink from his chief.

"Well, of course, our paths crossed many times over the years, both of us being in law enforcement, but we seldom saw each other outside of city business. We weren't on any commissions or committees together, and we didn't share common interests, if that's what you're wondering. I was stunned, of course, to learn he had died in so brutal a manner." He turned to Meredyth, handing her wine to her. "All right, so let's get down to this sorry business you've come to discuss with me. Just what have you got on Lawrence, Dr. Sanger? Lucas?"

Lucas, satisfied with Bryce's response and coolness, nodded to Meredyth, who dug out the papers given them by Randy Oglesby, the ones he'd traced to Phil Lawrence's computer. Lucas explained to Bryce exactly what he was staring at as the older man's eyes traveled over the documents.

"This . . . this is alarming," he said, putting his gin and tonic aside. "My God. I must admit, when you first called, Stonecoat, I thought it just a bit strange, and wondered if you were perhaps lashing out at your captain for slights you may have felt when no promotion had come through for you, but this . . . if it can be believed . . ."

"Believe it, sir."

Meredyth backed Lucas. "We do."

"Well, Meredyth, given the history of bad blood between you and Phil, again, I didn't count on you two having actually dug up anything of this nature, you see. I really need time to digest all this. Damn, damn that Lawrence. I can't say that I've always admired the man, but I never dreamed of anything so sinister as . . . as his controlling a hit squad within the department."

Lucas and Meredyth explained, as best they could, about the computer murder game being played out, Helsinger's Pit, and about the Vampire List. About how Lucas, Meredyth and Randy had all been threatened, of Covey's sudden prison murder, of how they were ambushed outside Rapid City. When they were done, Bryce sat in stunned silence.

Finally, he made a lightweight joke again, obviously his way of dealing with tragic news. "And the public is concerned about my not living within the city limits. . . . Few people, Lucas, Meredyth, understand my passion for open spaces and horses. My stable is my temple, and my horses . . . well, let's say, aside from my children and family, they're my best friends. Thing about a horse, Lucas, as I'm sure you know, is that a horse will never intentionally harm you, not like humans so often do."

It was wonderful sentiment, Meredyth thought, and a sad one.

"What's our next step, Commander?" asked Lucas.

He stared at Lucas, set aside the papers they'd brought and shook his head. "I'll need to make a phone call from my den. Don't keep a phone in any other room in the house, except the one beside my bed. Need to call on Richard Bishop, the D.A. We need to bring him in on this. We need to set the wheels of justice in motion, get a grand jury to act and act fast, for indictments to be handed down."

Meredyth smiled and Lucas grinned at her as Bryce, looking ten years older now than when they'd arrived, ambled off toward his study and the phone. Meredyth got to her feet, paced the room, her nervous energy sending sparks about her, Lucas thought. He went to her, placed his one free hand over her shoulder, and she turned, their eyes meeting.

"You did it," she said to him.

"No, we did it together."

"You know, I've learned there's much to admire about you, Lucas Stonecoat."

He smiled. "And I you . . . And, if it's not too bold of me to say, if I can't be your lover, Meredyth Sanger, then at least allow me to be your best friend."

She blushed, a tear coming to her eye. "I was hoping you'd say something like that."

"How very touching," came a female voice behind Lucas. He turned to see Dr. Sterling Washburn, a gun raised and pointing at them.

"Dr. Washburn," said Lucas.

At a second entryway stood Pierce Dalton, also with a gun, saying, "You two couldn't leave it alone, could you? Damn you both."

Commander Andrew Bryce had long since abandoned the telephone, and now he stood just behind the deadly Dr. Washburn and her gun. Sterling Washburn asked, without taking her eyes off Lucas, "Have they located the other one?"

"They have," replied Bryce. "They're at the gate with him. May as well wait until they're all here, and we'll do them all together."

"Bryce, you bastard," roared Lucas, "it was you all along."

"Save your breath, Redskin. You and the doctor brought this entirely on yourselves."

"And Phil Lawrence?" asked Meredyth. "You planted evidence against him, just in case? Or is he part of your bloody mob?"

"Shut up!" shouted Dalton, his hand nervous on the gun.

"You don't think we came here without a plan, do you, Bryce? We have copies of everything in a safe deposit box," bluffed Lucas, "with instructions should anything happen to us."

"He's bluffing," shouted Sterling Washburn, her evil grimace telling Lucas she wanted nothing more than to destroy him.

"You all had a hand in Mootry's murder, didn't you?" asked Meredyth. "Mootry and Palmer and Whitaker before that . . ."

"Gather any weapons these two have on them," ordered Bryce, "and let's be done with this night's work before any of my children should show up."

"Bury them in the usual place, beneath the horse manure pile?" asked Washburn, a sneer on her face as she plucked Lucas's Browning automatic from him and Meredyth's .38 from her. Just as she did so, there was a commotion at the door as Randy Oglesby was pushed through it by the two goons known to Lucas only as Tim Bullock and Stu Price. He'd been wrong about Lawrence, Amelford, and Pardee, but he didn't have time to think about it. With the distraction at the door, Lucas suddenly cast off his sling and threw it into Washburn's face. He then dove out the nearest window, but Price had him in his sights just outside, asking, "You anxious to die, red man?"

THIRTY-TWO

Butterfly: infinite life

Lucas was led back inside where Randy Oglesby and Meredyth stood shivering together, but he didn't come in quietly, shouting rather that they were all too cowardly and too poor at hunting to give him a fighting chance. He was bolstered only by the fact that Price's quick pat down of him hadn't revealed the Bowie knife couched in the small of his back. "Some great white hunters you are!" Lucas repeatedly said. "Just what kind of sport is it to gun down three unarmed people? One of them a woman, another a boy? Where's the sport in that, Bryce?"

It was a challenge, a tossing down of the gauntlet, and Lucas prayed the white-haired mass murderer would take it as such. But Bryce said nothing; rather, his eyes moved about the room, taking in his cohorts in crime, assessing the timber of each man and woman on his team.

Lucas kept it up, saying, "Give us a five-minute head start."

Meredyth piped in. "At least make it interesting. Give us something to defend ourselves with."

Bryce's grim eyes lit up with a new fire. The old man of the bunch, Helsinger 1, looked from one to the other of his remaining converts. Finally, Sterling Washburn said, "Let's do it. . . . It will be a privilege to hunt this Indian down and put an arrow through his red devil's heart." She looked smugly in Lucas's direction.

Bullock and Price each agreed with gestures of acceptance, while Pierce Dalton suggested they simply kill the intruders here and now and be done with it.

"Four to one against you, Pierce," said Bryce. "I'm not too old for a bit of sport."

"We don't need the others, Bryce," suggested Sterling, her teeth bared. "I want just the two of us to hunt them down, like old times . . . like we did with the last person who got in our way."

And that would be a guy named Gunther, thought Lucas, but all he said was a repeat of his request. "Just give us five minutes lead time, to make it sporting."

"Unarmed?" said Meredyth. "How sporting is that?"

Lucas realized he was in a room full of trophy hunters. "No guns, though," Lucas suggested. "Only your crossbows, like Dr. Washburn says."

Grimly, a smile spread across Bryce's lips. "Be like old times, huh, fellas? All right, Sterling."

"Don't be a fool, Andrew," Dalton said through his teeth.

"You hunted together as kids, during your college years, didn't you?" asked Lucas. "Do you think you have what it takes to go against the most dangerous animal in the woods, an Indian?"

It was a challenge the people in the room could not walk away from. Even Bullock and Price, the obviously younger, newer members of the kill squad, now wanted this opportunity to even the score after their failed attempt in Rapid City.

"Well?" pushed Lucas.

"We'll do it, five minutes. You'll never get beyond the property line," replied Bryce, a hearty laugh for his colleagues in crime. "Turn the three rabbits loose."

"Wait . . . wait," said Randy, his voice quivering. "How did you make it look like Lawrence? How did you snake your communications through his computer?"

"Sorry, kid, but it would take all night to explain it to you, and we're too anxious for the hunt, aren't we, folks?" asked Bryce of his people.

They were ushered out into the night by Bullock and Price, Sterling shouting out, "Run, run, run. Five minutes, red man, and we send you back to the filthy, pagan god from which you came, but not before we cut you into little pieces!" Her bansheelike laughter trailed after them.

Inside the house, the old man, leader of the group, began passing out crossbows and arrows.

Lucas ushered Meredyth and Randy along, Randy stumbling. "Make for the trees along that riverbank!" he told them, pointing.

"What trees? What river?" Meredyth marveled at his quick ability to adjust his sight from the light of the house to the darkness of night.

"Straight ahead."

"You bought us time, but we're helpless without any way to defend ourselves," she complained.

"There are ways, if we can put some distance between us and them. Hurry! Trust me," he pleaded, and they ran on.

Now they were the object of a crazed manhunt; they were the sweated, chased prey. "There are weapons all around us," Lucas informed them. "You just have to know how to

see. There, that branch lying over there, Randy! Pick it up
and hold on to it. You get within a few feet of one of those
goons, you see how he likes wood and bark in his teeth."

Randy grabbed on to the heavy limb as if it were a
Remington rifle. He tried it out with a few swings. It felt
good, comforting in its heavy solidity. Randy clung to it.

"Collect stones, Meredyth, as many as you can carry."

She did so. Lucas knew it was good putting them to work,
although it slowed their progress, and the primitive weapons
were little to no match for Bryce's high-tech arsenal. And
Lucas knew what Bryce had said was true. The size of the
ranch made it unlikely that they would get anywhere near its
boundaries.

"You think they'll come on horseback?" asked Randy on
hearing the whinny of a horse.

"It's quite possible, yes."

"With those sighted crossbows with laser beams on them,
and them on horseback . . . damn, we don't stand a
chance. They'll shoot us down like rabid dogs. What does it
matter if it's with guns or arrows? Damn it, goddamn it to
hell, they're going to murder us and there's not a bloody
blasted thing we can do about it!"

"Shut up and search for a place to hide!" Lucas angrily
shouted.

They ran on into the night, now hearing the pounding of
hooves behind them.

Randy ranted further. "Damn it, they're right on us,
heading straight for us. How do they know?"

The howling of dogs gave them the answer.

"Some sporting chance," muttered Meredyth.

"Take off your clothes," cried Lucas.

"What?"

"Some of your clothes! Take them off! Both of you!"

Randy started to protest but thought better of it, stripping away his shirt.

Meredyth hesitated. "What about you?" she asked Lucas.

"Strip down, Meredyth! Now, no questions!"

She joined Randy, stripping down to her bra and panties Randy down to his boxer shorts. Lucas collected the clothes and said, "I'm going to take the killers off your scent. Keep following the river south. Eventually, it should take you out to the road. Try to flag down help and get to a phone."

"But what about you, Lucas?" Meredyth didn't like this plan. "They'll follow you and kill you."

"Follow me, right . . . that's the idea. Kill me? Not without some doing. Now go! Randy, take her and go!"

Lucas raced off northward along the riverbank, carrying their clothes with him. They watched him disappear into the thick brush and trees until Randy was able to pull her away, saying, "We've got to trust he knows what he's doing, and there's no better game in town, and they're coming, Dr. Sanger. Come on. Come away . . ."

At the river's edge, Meredyth spotted an uprooted tree that might provide them with some cover. Behind them, the thundering hooves and the howling dogs had come nearer and nearer. Randy agreed to the hiding place, slamming down behind the tree with her.

The dogs—three in all—slowed at the spot where they'd split from Lucas, circling the spot for a moment, separating momentarily until the leader yelped and hauled himself off in the direction Lucas had taken. The other two followed, but then one of them circled back and slowly, easily sniffed its way toward the overturned tree.

Riders on horseback came over the rise and tore down toward the river, hearing the yelping dogs that now pursued Lucas. The riders reined in and turned their horses in the new direction, not seeing the lone dog making its way toward the downed tree behind which Randy and Meredyth had stopped breathing. She realized as if for the first time she was holding fast to two heavy stones, but they were useless against a snarling dog, she told herself. Even as she thought this, she was glad to have something firm and solid to hold fast to, and if the dog should get within range, begin tearing at her and Randy, she could, if called on to do so, bring the stones to bear on the animal's skull. Lucas was wise. The stones in her grasp gave her courage, hope.

The horses thundered away, momentarily confusing the hound that made its inexorable approach toward Randy, who was closest to the animal.

"What're we going to do?" Randy whispered.

"*Shhhh*. Use your weapon."

The dog leaped, its teeth bared, straight for Randy, who stuck the pointed and jagged edge of the tree limb straight up and out. The dog's chest and shoulder area came down on the limb, ripping its skin and sending it sideways, snatching the limb free from Randy's hand. The dog was stunned, slowed, but not incapacitated. It had yelped in pain and now growled as it worked its way up, fell, and stumbled to its feet, trying to get to all fours again.

Meredyth dropped one of the stones she had held on to and pushed past Randy, crouched over the snarling beast, and brought the stone down on it, striking the bared teeth and snout, sending it reeling back in shock.

Meredyth dreaded striking a second blow, feeling the animal's pain, but she hadn't a choice. As Randy looked on, she brought the stone down a second time, striking the dog in silence with a blow to the side of the head. Meredyth's hands and the stone came away bloodied.

Randy felt his stomach give a dry heave, the pain excruciating. He had been bitten by the dog somehow in the moments between hitting it with the stick and Meredyth's attack on the little monster. He now doubled over and this time vomited his evening's meal.

"Damn," he tried to joke it off, "now when they find my body and they do the autopsy and try to learn my last meal, they won't find a damned thing. . . ."

"Nobody's going to find your body. Remember? They're going to stuff us all below a manure pile by the stables. We'll never be located. We will have simply *disappeared*."

"You really know how to comfort a guy," he replied, and then began to laugh hysterically.

"What is the matter with you?"

"Darlene. I'm in love with her. She loves me. My screwed-up life was just getting in order. Now this. Now I'm a dead man."

She was in tears. Randy crawled to her, exhausted, frightened, cold with the chill of a cold Texas night breeze sprinkling raindrops like confectioners' sugar on his bare skin. He tried to comfort her, but she pulled away, saying, "We've got no time for tears and self-pitying blubbering damn it! We've got to help Lucas."

Randy looked stricken. "Are you crazy? He told us to get the hell out of here, led them off in his direction so we'd have a fighting chance to get to the road, flag down help. It's what he wants."

"He could be dead by the time we get help."

"If we go after him, we could be dead even sooner."

"I'm not arguing this. I've got to find Lucas and help him. You do whatever you think best, Randy. Go on, get to the road, get help! It's a good plan." *We saw a hell of a lot of traffic out on the road leading in,* she sarcastically thought but did not say. She shoved at him, nodding, telling him it would be smarter.

"No, no, no . . . He said for us to both find the road, get help, remember? He wanted me to take care of you."

She almost stated the cruel and obvious truth, that he could not in his wildest dreams take care of her. "You find the road. I'm going to find Lucas." She pulled away from him.

He chased after her, tackled her, and held on. "You can't! I won't let you!"

She pounded him with her fists. "Randy, I'm not leaving him to the . . . to the dogs."

Randy was over her now, pinning her arms, staring into her eyes, breathing wildly, a human umbrella against the falling raindrops. "Are you just plain crazy, Meredyth?"

In the distance, a lightning bolt streaked across the sky.

"Let me up! Let me go, Randy, now, damn you!" God, but she hated the helplessness of her female weakness against his male strength.

Randy found himself helplessly drawn to her, despite his professed love for Darlene. Meredyth just felt good beneath him, and she was down to her bra, and Randy was getting randy for her. He held her there longer, staring down at her, saying, "God, Meredyth, you . . . you're even prettier when you're mad."

She pushed and shouted. "Goddamn it, Randy, let me go!" She kicked out, her knee catching him in a vulnerable place, sending him reeling in pain.

He relented, rolling to one side, helplessly groaning as she skittered away. In a moment, however, his groans turned to laughter at her.

"What is so bleeding funny?"

"You . . . you and me. What possible good can we do here, Meredyth? We're unarmed, and even if we were armed, neither one of us can shoot straight."

"Lucas gave me some lessons," she said defensively, even knowing he was right.

"Just the same, we have no weapons. A stick and a stone

against a hunting dog is one thing, but against five mad humans? Please, please be reasonable and come away with me."

The silver drizzle began slanting in at them from the south, from the direction where the road must be. Dark clouds overhead swirled as if stirred, a celestial cauldron filled with gray, black, and purple ingredients. She said nothing, mulling over his words, Randy hoped.

"It's suicide, Meredyth, and even if you never knew it or never acknowledged it . . . I . . . I love you . . . and if anything should happen to you . . . I'd never forgive myself. . . ."

She stared at him, realizing for the first time why he had gotten himself so deeply involved in this most deadly of games, why he had never once said *no* to her. "Damn you, Randy Oglesby," she muttered, found her footing and stormed away, running off in the direction the horses had taken.

Randy was left with the blank night and the unconscious dog and his tree limb. He finally decided to follow Meredyth, the rain drenching them but also drenching any odor trail left by Stonecoat for the dogs to follow. Had Lucas Stonecoat somehow conjured up the rain? Randy wondered. Did he know the rain was imminent when he had so heroically made off with their clothes to create a false trail for the dogs to follow?

Randy wasn't so sure that the Indian didn't possess some magic or medicine bag of tricks he kept tucked away. In any case, Randy was now shivering, sloshing through a black forested area in the cold rain in his skivvies, one part of his brain wishing he were a little kid again, at home with his parents yelling up the stairs for him to come away from his computer games and down to dinner, another part of his brain wondering why he was not going in the direction of safety but in the direction of danger in senseless pursuit of a woman whom he could never have, trying to keep up with a woman who often had made him feel weak and foolish, a woman who had saved him from the fanatical fangs of a wounded and angry dog, a woman who was tough and resourceful and beautiful and stubborn as hell.

THIRTY-THREE

Running water: continual life

Lucas knew the dogs were on his heels, and he also knew that he had little chance of surviving this night, but he'd be damned if he would go out alone. He wanted in the worst way to take Bryce out with him, and maybe that bitch doctor and some of the others.

As he ran, he scattered Randy's clothes here, Meredyth's there in a continued attempt to keep the dogs—both animal and human—confused. Confusion now was his best and only ally, that and his native intellect. He hadn't given up his Bowie knife, which had been hidden the entire time in the sheath at the center of his back. It was his one hope, but a knife, however well he might wield it, was no match for sighted, laser-targeting, high-tech crossbows.

He led his pursuers deeper and deeper into the most rugged terrain he was able to find here. The forested area gave way to a dry riverbed, the sort of gulch that filled in an instant during a flash flood. He had little hope of seeing a

flash flood here tonight, although the ancient riverbed was
soggy and gave way beneath his feet as he raced on. Still,
with the rain increasing, he hoped his scent and his tracks
might be obliterated, but the hounds seemed on a scent and
direction from which they could not be dissuaded—slowed
perhaps, but not dissuaded.

Out of the earth, like spirits from another world, a
spectral fog began to rise, the earth being too quickly cooled
by the rain. Lucas blessed the sight. It would provide more
cover, and from the gloom, he might more readily strike
One more ally for him.

He continued into the rocky, pitted foothills, his arms free
of the last vestiges of Meredyth's clothing now. He concentrated on locating a weapon, anything he might arm himself
with, but the boulders here were all too large to handle and
there were no tree limbs lying nearby.

One of the dogs had caught up to him; another was just
behind. The first one attacked, leaping straight for him. He
could hear the horses coming at a gallop, the shouting of
excited hunters who smelled blood.

Lucas brought the Bowie knife up to strike the wild-eyed
dog, but he missed, the speed of the animal too much for
him. He tumbled over, the dog held away from his throat,
yipping, biting out viciously, then Lucas brought the huge
knife up and into the animal's gut, twisting and yanking
upwards as if zipping the animal open. The result was
immediate shock for the animal, and its whimper was
painful to hear. Lucas lifted the dog while lying on his back
and hurled it at the second dog, striking and confusing it.

Lucas got to his knees, the knife held out threateningly
toward the animal, which was obviously trained well to
please its master. The dog hurled itself at Lucas and was
suddenly struck down in midair over Lucas, taking the

arrow meant for Lucas when it jumped into the path of the laser beam.

Lucas felt the weight of this dead animal thud into him and he immediately yanked on the arrow shaft in the dog's back, rolling to his left, dragging the dead carcass with him, over once, twice, and into a small crevice between the rocks here. The dog was hung up overhead now, the arrow pointing straight down into the crevice. Lucas pulled it free, the animal's blood flowing over him, painting his features in wild color.

There was an exit behind Lucas and he crawled for it, taking the steel arrow with him, still holding firmly to his knife as well. Above and around him, he could hear the clatter of horse hooves and the voices of his assassins.

Bryce was shouting, "The red devil's killed my dogs! That son of a bitch is going to suffer for this. Find him, find him and kill the bastard. Fan out!"

Lucas rolled and crawled and pulled himself along, staying low among the rocks. He heard the noise of a babbling creek and went toward it at a run.

Behind him, he heard the woman shout, "There! There he is!"

He felt the pain as an arrow tore across his calf, cutting a swath but veering off, not penetrating. He lunged into the creek, already soaked, hoping the water was deep enough and swollen enough to take him downstream. The hunters behind him had abandoned their horses for the moment, coming straight for him.

The water was deep and the current swift. He allowed himself to be carried along.

A singing arrow bit the water before his eyes. A second one slapped the water harmlessly beyond him. Several other shots were fired, and Lucas wondered how long his pursuers would take before they began using high-powered rifles that could open a hole in him the size of a grapefruit.

Lucas was slammed into a tangled nest of brambles, dead tree limbs, and growth in the stream, and he hung on, trying to catch his breath. The water felt soothing on his wounded leg and his shoulder where he'd torn out his stitches. He felt his blood streaming along with the cool waters now.

He heard Washburn, Dalton and Bryce taunting him now, calling out racial sneers. Besides being murdering assassins, they were also a pack of bigots, he thought.

He pulled himself along the shallows and found a bevy of reeds and cattails. It was shallow enough here to stand, the bottom mushy but holding. He quickly cut a reed at both ends and descended below the surface in the best of Indian traditions.

His hearing was impaired by the water, but not by much. He sensed that two or perhaps three of the deadly hunters now had passed his location. He waited patiently for any others, but he could hear and sense nothing. Finally, he gave up the vigil and surfaced.

He now moved with the stealth of a cat, slowly, making no sound as he found the true shoreline and inched his way from the water. Rain still pelted the world, and darkness and gloom and fog lay over the creek, smearing the woodlands here with grim despair.

From what he could gather, from the number of horses he'd heard and seen thundering up, Bullock and Price had come along on the hunt. Some odds, he mused, five to one. Any betting man would not give him much of a chance.

He gave a moment's thought to how he had become embroiled in this horror, thought of Meredyth, pleased that the hunters had come after him in the mistaken belief they were all still together. Lucas wondered if he'd ever see her again, if she and Randy had made it out to the road, or if they were dead and lying somewhere beneath the cold rain. He had counted three dogs from the yelping and yet there were only two lying back there among the rocks. But he had to keep focused, keep his mind on survival. There were five deadly Questors, five murderous, live Helsingers in these black holes all around him, just waiting for him to step on a dry twig so he could be drilled through the heart by their arrows.

Again he blessed the rain. It had shielded him thus far, saving his life. He wondered if there wasn't some distant ancestor looking out for him.

A blazing eruption suddenly burned an image into Lucas's mind, an image of a man being electrocuted as a tree exploded within fifty feet of Lucas, a lightning bolt having caused the explosion. The lightning filled his nostrils with ozone even as it sent Lucas sprawling several feet and onto his back. It lit up the entire area, the fiery tree sending deadly shards in all directions and sending both a flaming body that looked the size of Stu Price and a burning tree limb cascading around Lucas's prone body. Lucas felt the other man's body whiz by like a twig, and he felt both lucky and vulnerable at once. Had anyone seen him?

The burning tree was lighting up the sky with crazy lights that flickered bright and low, now high and mighty, then dipping into a near-dark death with the wild rush of wind the fire itself had created. The raindrops hissed as they touched the fire.

The light was dangerous for Lucas, and the shock wave from the lightning strike had thrown him down so hard that he could not find either his knife or the arrow now ripped from his grasp. His singed eyes sought out the body near him, but Price, his body sending up a smoke cloud, had no crossbow fused to his hands. Lucas tried to frisk the smoking corpse for a gun, but the body was extremely hot, and it suddenly erupted once again into flames, sending Lucas scurrying back.

Now without weapons, he saw Pierce Dalton, silhouetted against the light from the fire. He came directly toward Lucas. Had he seen or heard Lucas's shout? Lucas couldn't recall if he had shouted, but it seemed likely, given the impact. His ears were still ringing.

Pierce Dalton didn't shout for Bullock or the others, but Lucas could hear the other three at a distance, shouting for Dalton and Price in the wake of the lightning strike. Perhaps they thought their comrades had been struck by the bolt or disoriented by it, and if so they were half-right. Perhaps the others feared that, in the tumult, Lucas had managed to get his hands on one or the other's crossbow.

Lucas thought it not a bad idea, so he worked his way around, slithering snakelike toward the burning tree. The closer he got to the tree, the more lit-up and exposed he felt. Still, if he could locate Price's crossbow, he thought he might have a fighting chance.

And there it was, lying at the base of a rock not far from the inferno. He inched toward it.

So far, Dalton hadn't seen him. Dalton had, however, found Price's body, and he was turning the dead man with his foot, gazing down into the shocked eyes, the still-burning hair. Dalton had been close to the flash as well, and he appeared shaken.

Lucas made a grab for the crossbow, found it blazing hot, burned his hands, and dropped it all at once, knowing the noise alerted Dalton. Dalton wheeled as Lucas rolled into a deep shadow created by a nearby overhang of rock and brush. Everything outside the firelight now was darker than ever, the black shadows multiplied tenfold by the flames.

Counselor Pierce Dalton, who no doubt had given Judge Charles Mootry his last legal advice before killing the man, came ever closer to where Lucas lay in the deepening shadows of this area. A second smoldering limb lay just out of Lucas's reach, but its jagged, pointed edge made for a tantalizing prize. Lucas dared inch toward the limb.

Dalton kept coming as if he had his eyes trained on Lucas, as if he could see into the empty wall of blackness here, but Lucas saw no evidence of the telltale red laser beam rising from his weapon. Closer and closer the malevolent man and the powerful crossbow came at Lucas, who now feared Dalton would see the whites of his eyes.

Dalton turned sharply in a 180-degree turn, hearing another sound directly behind him. He instantly lifted his bow and readied to fire, searching for the source of the noise. Lucas had heard it, too, but could not worry about it. He had only a split second in which to make his move.

He rolled to the burning limb, lifted it and himself toward Dalton's back, and as the man turned, his crossbow ready, Lucas jammed the pointed end of the burning limb into Dalton's gut and rammed it upwards with all his might.

Even as Dalton's scream pierced the air, his cocked arrow twanged into a nearby tree as he keeled over like a felled tree, the limb sticking from him, still afire, its blaze suddenly sparked, it seemed, by the fuel of the man's blood. Lucas instantly tore the crossbow and arrow pouch from Dalton's lifeless, staring body, half expecting to be fired on from the other three killers. But from the darkness came only a terrified deer, suddenly skittering away like a graceful, saving angel.

Lucas raced back up along the creek, placing some distance between himself and his remaining pursuers, entertaining some thought at taking their horses. But with the lightning strike, it was doubtful the horses would have remained, most likely having returned to their stable by now.

Once he located a safe place to catch his breath, Lucas saw that Dalton had only two arrows left in his pouch. In the distance now, he heard Tim Bullock cursing the sky over Dalton's body, shouting, "Stonecoat! Stonecoat! You bastard! I'm coming for you!"

Lucas, his bad shoulder throbbing now, fought with the stringing of the crossbow to ready his first deadly arrow for flight, realizing the math was all wrong—two arrows to fell three assassins who believed vehemently in their cause. The one-handed struggle with the bow was extremely difficult, taking precious time, but finally he managed to get the weapon prepared.

He lay on his back now among some boulders and overhanging trees. He didn't see Sterling Washburn or hear her approach; it was as if she'd been there all along, waiting for him, knowing he'd select this exact spot to nestle down into to hide and regain his strength. It was obvious she had not been with the other two, who had gone south, further along the river, hunting for Lucas in the shallows as he'd hoped they would. And now their eyes met, and his bow was down, lying across his chest, while hers was pointed, the red beam making its way to his heart.

She fired just as he lifted the slate stone beside him to cover his heart, knowing that she and the others always aimed for "the demon's heart." The powerfully strung bow sent the steel shaft into the stone with incredible force, shattering it into two separate pieces and piercing Stonecoat's chest over the heart. It failed to penetrate beyond a centimeter, however.

Dr. Sterling Washburn believed him dead, and this belief made her hesitate a moment before starting to restring.

Lucas quickly brought up his bow and fired without using the laser attachment, sending an arrow in the blink of an eye into Sterling Washburn's own breast, the powerful shaft pinning her to a tree where she writhed in pain, her screams rivaling the banshee winds and the thunder overhead.

She was still flailing like a pinned butterfly against the stunted Texas box elder when Lucas got to his feet and found another location in which to hide. He fully expected Andrew Bryce or Tim Bullock to come running to the horrid sound of pain and anguish sent up to the heavens from Dr. Sterling Washburn's rain-soaked throat.

"White bitch," Lucas said to allay any feelings of sympathy for the mass murderess. He couldn't waste another arrow on her, and he dared not linger to attempt gathering any additional arrows from her.

Lucas climbed to a higher vantage point, awaiting Bullock and Bryce.

Randy looked up to see Meredyth's rain-slicked apparition ahead of him, somewhat shielded by the rising, breathing ground fog which owed its life to the grueling heat that had baked the land all day long. Where the rain soaked the ground in meadows here, large steaming clouds were created to shroud the night's grim work.

They had heard the booming, earthshaking lightning strike followed by the sudden quaking, god-awful cry of a dying man, worse than any lightning or bobcat, Randy thought.

Meredyth ran back to Randy, their eyes meeting, both wondering the same thing. Was Lucas Stonecoat dead?

"We've got to turn around, make for the road," Randy insisted, when suddenly several horses trotted, confused and frightened, into view.

"We've got to get those horses," she told him.

"I've had some experience with horses," he told her. "Approach them carefully, gently, hand out and talk baby talk to them. They'll respond if they're not too frightened."

Each went for a different horse, and Meredyth did as Randy had suggested, but when she got within reach and snatched for the horse's reins, he bolted and ran, a second one following him.

Randy walked back with a horse in tow. She instantly refused to mount up, as he suggested.

"You go, Randy, turn back and get help. Get to the ranch house; find a phone. I'm going on."

"I can't leave you here."

"If you want to help, get to a phone."

Another horse showed itself, pitched its way down an embankment to them as if on cue, and began nuzzling the already captured horse. Meredyth took this one's reins and carefully, easily climbed up into the saddle.

Randy held her hands in his across the gap between them. "Are you coming back with me?"

"No, I'm going on. Look." On the other side of the horse, stashed into a sheath below the saddle, there was a rifle. "I'm going to do what I can for Lucas. Now, go! Get to the house and get a call out to 911, Phil Lawrence, and anyone else you can think of."

"Are you sure, Meredyth?"

"Yes, now go . . . go!"

"All right," he relented, kicking at the sides of the animal he rode, going due east in the direction of the ranch house. In the distance, he could see faint light.

Meredyth pushed on alone, praying against all odds that Lucas had killed one of them rather than that he had been killed. The runaway horse was, she believed, a good sign. She snatched out the rifle and held it up, checking out its balance and sight and determining if it was loaded. She tried to recall all that Lucas had taught her about firing a weapon.

She moved on cautiously but quickly, telling her horse repeatedly to giddap.

She realized how deep her feelings for Lucas had run; she realized that he was, in fact, the best friend she had ever known, and that he had sacrificed everything for her.

Lucas struggled to locate another safe haven in which to await his quarry with the patience of a turtle, knowing that his enemy would come. But he also knew that he had only one arrow left. If Bullock and Andrew Bryce came together, he stood no chance.

He waited. His shoulder throbbed, his leg burned, and he was exhausted, but he tried desperately to remain alert. In a moment, he heard them coming.

They were together. They had seen what devastation Lucas Stonecoat could wreak, and they wisely remained in sight of one another. Lucas heard their whispers as they approached, but could not tell from which direction they came. Overhead? To his right? Left? Front? Back? It was impossible to tell in this rocky area where echoes bounced like stones ricocheting.

Lucas heard no one now, the voices falling silent, but he sensed that his two would-be executioners were extremely close, certainly within range of the deadly weapons they carried.

Lucas saw no one, heard not so much as dust flake from the rocks when an arrow burned through his side, cutting a wide, angry swath through his flesh and pinging on the rock surface he lay against, making him yelp in pain.

"I got the bastard!" It was Bullock's voice.

Lucas fired where he saw the shadowy figure raise a victory sign by lifting his bow over his head. Lucas's arrow was a shock to Bullock, who didn't quite believe it was sticking from his stomach and out his back. He dropped his bow and grabbed on to the arrow shaft in his abdomen, holding on to it as if it were the handle for a ride. This,

moments before he toppled over backwards and some forty
feet into the dry riverbed behind him.

Lucas had no more arrows now, and he was bleeding
badly from the new wound to his side, his shoulder stitches
and his leg. He feared moving and he feared staying. He
didn't know where Bryce was, and he didn't know if an
attempt to move now would be met with another arrow.

There was only silence.

Bryce was the only one left, but Lucas had lost. He was
empty-handed, wounded, unable to defend himself. Lucas
tried to soothe his frustration and anger with the knowledge
that Meredyth and Randy had had time to get free, and that
he had killed the lot of them, save Bryce.

"End of the road, red man!" shouted Bryce, whose eyes
and red laser were directly covering Lucas where he lay in
shadow among the rocks.

Lucas gulped for air, feeling the blackness and weakness
overtaking him, feeling a blackout coming on, grateful that
he would not feel the arrow sting, when suddenly a gunshot
exploded from somewhere in his subconscious—some
wishful thought, he believed—and he blacked out, imagining he'd never wake again in this life.

Overhead, Andrew Bryce let fly with the arrow meant for
Lucas Stonecoat, but it had gone astray, high into the sky,
because he was clawing at his back where the melon-sized
hole in his chest had originated when the hunting bullet
ripped into him. He twirled, knowing he was dead, pirou-
etting on recoil and to face his killer.

"I'll see you to hell, woman!" he cursed Meredyth
Sanger.

"No, I think you'll be quite lonely there, Helsinger One!"
She used the stock of the gun to shove the dead man over
the side and into the rocks below where Lucas had unsuc-
cessfully hidden.

Meredyth wasn't sure if there were others nearby still stalking Lucas and her, so she held fast to the rifle, climbing down to Lucas, praying he was still alive. He looked quite dead.

Panting, listening for any flicker of noise or movement, she made her way to Lucas, finding him still breathing, the arrow in his side looking nasty and menacing. Lucas had stripped away his shirt at some point, likely to throw the dogs off, and his body was painted with streaks of blood.

She feared for his life, grabbed him up in her arms and held him tightly to her, reassuring him, speaking gently and soothingly into his ear, telling him that Randy was getting help, that help was on the way. She cried as she spoke, the huge Remington rifle at her side, but no one came and Lucas's blood began to discolor her skin, bra, and panties.

He could barely speak, but she found Lucas mumbling some gibberish about a creation myth, saying "My forefathers believed that their homeland was in the center of the universe . . . pictured Earth as a floating island suspended by four cords from the heavens, and the sky was made of solid rock."

"*Shhhh*," she tried to get him to rest.

"Before the island was created, all men lived above the rock sky . . ."

She tearfully pleaded, "Don't you die on me, Stonecoat. . . ."

"But it became crowded above the sky, so the water beetle was sent down to explore the water world beneath the floating island. It was the beginning of *this* world. . . ."

"Hold on, Lucas. . . . Damn you, hold on. Don't you go dying on me," she said in a threatening voice, which disintegrated into tears.

ℰPILOGUE

Bird: lighthearted

Dawn woke Meredyth where she had fallen asleep beneath Lucas's weight. Her eyes opened in reaction to the noise of a helicopter, which came slowly over the rocks, first sounding like a chain saw, then a lawn mower, until suddenly it was deafening. She saw it go over so quickly she hadn't time to react. It had the HPD logo on it, and she dared guess that Randy had gotten to Captain Phil Lawrence.

She lifted the rifle so its stock was balanced against the rock and fired a distress shot into the air.

"Damn noise is enough to wake the dead!" Lucas shouted at her as he came to.

"Lucas! You're all right."

"Shot all to hell, if you call that all right. God, I got pain to complain about now. Damn, but this arrow in my side is annoying as hell."

She laughed and kissed him, his face grimy from perspiration and dirt.

"Ouch! Owwww! Easy, easy on me," he complained.

They heard horseback riders, and over the stones now rescuers appeared, followed by Phil Lawrence and Randy Oglesby, alongside of whom stood Fred Amelford and Jim Pardee. They all saw Meredyth, the rifle and Stonecoat. Beyond them, they saw Bryce's dead body. Not far off in another direction, they saw what remained of Bullock.

"Damned dead people strung all along the gulch!" shouted Lawrence down to them. "I can see that Stonecoat's a bloody mess, but are you hurt, Dr. Sanger?"

"No!" she returned. "But Stonecoat is hurt badly, and he's lost a lot of blood. We need to airlift him out of here to the closest trauma center."

"You got it!" Lawrence radioed for the chopper to return to their quadrant.

"So, what happened to the water beetle after he dove into the great ocean world?" she asked.

He only hazily recalled telling her of the creation story. "He dove below the waters and came up with mud, and on that mud the earth's land masses were built, and then he returned to the sky people."

"To tell them there was a land for them?"

"No, he then told the buzzard to fly down to see if the island of the earth was dry enough for the animals and ready for the *Ani-yun-wiya,* the chosen people, to oversee it. And everywhere the buzzard's wings touched the earth, which was still soft and mushy, a valley was created, and whenever the buzzard lifted his wings, there came into being a mountain. This, it is said, is why the Cherokee country is covered in mountains."

"That's beautiful, Lucas," she said.

"You came back . . . like a War Woman of the Wolf clan," he said.

She smiled at the images, and shook her head. "I only did what I had to do."

"You got Bryce," he said. "I wanted Bryce for myself."

"You got all the others. You couldn't have all the fun. Not fair."

"You saved my life," he said again. "And you stayed with me through the night. You renewed my spirit."

The deafening noise of the helicopter swooped up his final words and he could not hear her reply. A basket was lowered down to Meredyth, who helped a stubborn Lucas, who wanted her to take the ride up before him, buckle into the basket.

She leaned in over him where he sat in the basket, his legs dangling now. She pulled him close and shouted, "Behave at the hospital!"

He stared into her bright blue eyes, and still amazed at the depth of her courage, shouted, "You weren't supposed to be within miles of me, yet you were here, and you saved my life."

"I got lucky."

"I'll never be able to repay you."

"The hell you say."

He kissed her and she returned his kiss, unsure of the future or if they had a future together. She yanked on the rope and they took him and his carriage up, the electronic winch doing its work. She watched as Lucas was hauled safely into the chopper and the big black-and-white machine swerved off and away per Phil Lawrence's orders.

Randy and Phil Lawrence were very near her now, having made the difficult climb down to her. With Phil taking charge of the weapon and Andrew Bryce's body, she hugged Randy and began to cry again. Randy held her for a long moment before he draped a coat he'd brought from Mrs.

Bryce's closet around Meredyth's shoulders. She buttoned up and thanked Randy.

"I brought a change of dry clothes for you. They're up in the Jeep." He pointed overhead.

Together, they made their way back up the sloping rocks. From the gulch below, Phil Lawrence began coordinating the effort to recover the additional bodies before wild animals should get any of them.

"Stonecoat did a hell of a number on this bunch of creeps," Randy commented.

"Yeah," she agreed. "You get the sense that God was on his side?"

"God and you," countered Randy.

"And you, Randy . . . and you. . . ."

They'd made the treacherous climb up to flat land. "Captain Lawrence told me to take the Jeep," said Randy, pointing. "He thought you'd want to get over to the hospital as soon as possible."

She nodded, going for it and climbing into the passenger seat, feeling weak and wasted. "I hope he's going to be all right. I got him into this, you know."

"I rather doubt that anyone gets Lucas Stonecoat into anything he doesn't want to get into," Randy countered as they tore off for the main road and the hospital.

Stonecoat survived his injuries, including a broken kneecap, adding scars to his already scarred body. He made life hell for the doctors and staff at nearby Kerney Memorial Hospital, complaining the entire week of his convalescence that it was an awful place and time for him. The staff there was equally anxious to see him go.

In the meantime, Commander Andrew Bryce's computer records were opened by court order and Randy Oglesby was placed in charge of disseminating information. It came as no surprise to Meredyth or Lucas that Bryce had extensive connections to Father Frank Aguilar, and that Bryce had selected Aguilar as a martyr to their mutual cause. . . .

Further investigation into Bryce showed that he had been the son of a fire-and-brimstone Texas evangelist—the worst kind, Lucas had quipped. He had been raised to see Satan's footprints everywhere, his tentacled arms reaching into every avenue, corrupting the fiber of American culture and government and economy. But Bryce also learned at an early age that evangelism and preaching alone could never persuade enough followers to make war on Satan. He learned of other avenues to motivate followers. Andrew Bryce had from young adulthood set himself up in a dual life, that of a forthright, honest, hardworking and peace-making lawman, and that of a secret priest and overseer of a private club that strove to exterminate cult leaders and demonologists with undue influence over many numbers of people.

The financial rewards of his actions engaged in by the cult to destroy cults, according to Bryce's own words, was unexpected pennies raining down. Father Aguilar began to feel that Bryce and the others had become overly greedy, however, and had begun killing more for the money than for the principles set up by Bryce. A growing rift between the "brothers" of Helsinger's Pit had gone unchecked until Aguilar was murdered along with his henchmen.

All of them had begun their religious sect in college at Texas Christian University. The trail led back to the mur-dered lad named Gunther who, as it happened, had been a disgruntled employee on staff with an FBI computer lab. He had gotten close to the group with an eye to playing spy when he smuggled them a computer listing of active vampires, people who professed to live the lifestyle of practicing vampires. Gunther's disappearance went unnoticed, since no one in the FBI had taken him seriously.

Over the years, the sect began to actively deceive and soon murder these so-called vampires. News of the sensational, near unbelievable tale of Internet murder and intrigue involving some of the highest-ranking officials in Houston broke like the lightning that'd turned a tree into tinder before Lucas's eyes the night Bryce was killed. Now, for the second time in the sensational, roller-coaster ride of this case, Lucas and Meredyth had become unwitting celebrities, hounded by the press.

The convolutions of the story, which tentacled to so many parts of the country, led the state legislature and the U.S. Senate and House to reconsider the long-lost concerns over what should and what should not be monitored and outlawed in the land of the microchip.

When the day came for Lucas to walk out of the hospital, Meredyth was there to greet him with a limo at a back entrance, but she had Conrad McThuen in tow as well. Conrad wanted very much to shake Lucas's hand now that he'd become a celebrity, and he wanted Lucas to know that while he had no other friends who were Native Americans, he meant to remedy that situation. Conrad didn't explain how he would do this.

Lucas looked across at Meredyth and realized that she had successfully found a way to keep them—Lucas and her—apart, at least for now.

"They've got to give you your promotion to detective status now, Lucas," she assured him, as if this would ease the pain of realization she saw in his eyes, that, after all they'd been through together, she still wanted him at arm's length, and her Conrad on her arm. "And we're all going out tonight to celebrate."

"We? We are?"

"Oh, I . . . I have a date for you. Her name is Abigail Heston, one of my dearest friends, from a fine family. Says there's some Indian blood in her distant past, too, something to do with a grandmother on her mother's side, oh, and she's mad for you. . . ."

Lucas did nothing to hide his displeasure at the idea of a blind date. He frowned and shook his head and waved his hands, but Meredyth stubbornly said, "Just get in the car!"

Lucas climbed into the waiting limo and found Abigail there, a busty, tall, red-cheeked, red-haired woman with alabaster skin, a striking pair of green eyes, and a tempting pair of smiling lips. She seemed one great invitation, and Lucas sacrilegiously wondered if Meredyth had paid for her. Either way, Lucas decided that Meredyth meant well, even if she was misguided; that one day, perhaps sooner than she realized, she would come to him. In the meantime, she feared falling in love with him, and he could hardly blame her. He had little or nothing to offer, save his feelings for her, and in today's society, in a land called Houston, that wasn't worth a whole hell of a lot. It wasn't like the gift of the water beetle and the buzzard who'd fashioned a world for the Cherokees.

A part of him remained, as always, angry with her; another part of him remained, as always, accepting of her.

"Well, so you must be Abigail," he said to the woman Meredyth had procured for him. "I'm Lucas—"

"I know who you are." She beamed, handing him a goblet of brandy. It was a goblet identical to the one he had lifted from Judge Charles Mootry's home, and Abigail sipped from a second one.

"How fitting," he said, "a girl after my own heart."

She smiled a disarming smile, her curly hair playing coquettishly about her temples. "Beware . . . I'm after more than your heart, Chief. . . ."

Stonecoat settled into the seat as Conrad drove off, Meredyth saying, "I hope you like the opera, Lucas."

"Opera? Well, sure," he lied. He'd never been to an opera in his life.

"Splendid," came Meredith's voice from the front. She seemed not to want to look in the back seat.

Lucas took Abigail in his arms, kissing her passionately, more for Meredyth's sake than anyone else's. But he was surprised by Abigail, finding himself stirred by her return kiss, her searching tongue now deeply exploring his mouth.

Sit back, shut up, and enjoy the ride, he told himself, feeling that he had earned it. If he couldn't have Meredyth, then by the Great One, he'd have this proffered substitute, this police groupie, this Abigail Heston, whose hand now played a flutelike pirouette over his wounded knee. . . .

New in hardcover

BLOWN

DAVID

WILTSE

AWAY

Putnam